The Tube Riders

(The Tube Riders Trilogy #1)

Chris Ward

Novels

The Tube Riders
(The Tube Riders Trilogy #1)
The Tube Riders: Exile
(The Tube Riders Trilogy #2)
The Tube Riders: Revenge
(The Tube Riders Trilogy #3)
The Man Who Built the World
Head of Words

Collections

Ms Ito's Bird & Other Stories
Five Tales of Horror
(Five Tales #1)
Five Tales of Loss
(Five Tales #2)
Five Tales of Fantasy
(Five Tales #3)
Five Tales of Dystopia
(Five Tales #4)

For Isaac,
My first reader

And Matt,
My first fan

You boys rock.

And in loving memory of my Grandfather
Leonard Ward 1921 – 2010
Your little green screen Amstrad
was the first computer I ever wrote on.
R.I.P.

"The Tube Riders"
Copyright © Chris Ward 2012

The right of Chris Ward to be identified as the Author of this Work has been asserted by him in accordance with the Copyright, Designs and Patents Act 1988.

All rights reserved. No part of this publication may be reproduced, stored in a retrieval system, or transmitted, in any form or by any means without the prior written permission of the Author.

This story is a work of fiction and is a product of the Author's imagination. All resemblances to actual locations or to persons living or dead are entirely coincidental.

"Tube riding" is a fictional activity and should be considered highly dangerous. DO NOT attempt to recreate any of the stunts described in this book. The Author holds no responsibility for any injuries that may occur.

Part One
London

Chapter One
Breakfall

THE ROAR IN THE TUNNEL grew louder.

The noise came from far back in the dark, building from a low, distant rumble into a rolling, thundering crescendo like a thousand hurricanes colliding, tearing each other apart. Marta Banks, squatting in a sprinter's crouch, closed her eyes as she always did, concentrating, seeing in her mind something monstrous, untamed. She let out a slow breath, looped her wrists through the leather safety straps and closed her fingers over the cold metal handles of the wooen clawboard.

Bring it on.

She smelt engine oil, heard the hum of the vibrating rails on the track below. She grimaced and shifted her wrists as the straps rubbed against the old marks on her skin.

Seconds, just seconds…

Come on. I'm waiting.

The roar was almost deafening now. Marta's eyes flicked open, her concentration sharp. Muscles tensed in her legs and arms. Her fingers clenched so tight she thought they might break. She glanced up at Paul standing further down the platform, one arm raised into the air.

Marta waited. Three … two … one–

'*Go!*' Paul screamed, as the wind rose to wrap itself around her. His arm dropped, and the fear, the exhilaration, the sheer adrenalin rush struck her like a hammer.

She dashed for the platform edge, while behind her, she heard Simon, Switch and Dan – the new boy – fanning out as they followed. She hoped Dan made it, of course, but in the moment of the ride it was only herself that mattered.

Racing across the cracked, dusty tiles, Marta pressed her wrists against the leather straps and squeezed the metal handles until her fingers ached. The wood creaked, and she prayed today wasn't the day the clawboard failed her.

She held the board up, the metal hooks on the outward surface angled down.

The train exploded out of the tunnel, its glaring headlights blasting through the dust curtain that hung over the station's pallid emergency lighting. The engine roar filled the air. Marta looked up as it came level with her and then rushed ahead, one, two, three carriages clattering past. She saw the thin metal drainage rail that ran along the top edge of the nearest carriage, and she steeled herself for the mount.

'*Now!*' she screamed, a war cry partly for herself, partly for the others behind her. Then she was leaping at the train, the clawboard arcing in towards the rail. Her heart slammed against the back of her ribs, until she thought it might burst out of her chest. Eyes narrowed, teeth gritted, she stared into the blurred, rushing wall of metal and glass, what in these moments was the Reaper, was Death. *Don't fuck up*, her mind reminded her. *You fuck up, you die.*

The metal hooks, two of them, four centimeters wide, dropped towards the outer lip of the drainage rail. Marta's feet brushed the side of the carriage, and for a second she was flying. Then the hooks caught, a massive jolt shuddered through her shoulders and upper arms, and Marta had won. This time.

Her scream rose over the rushing wind: '*Yeeeeeeesssss!*'

With her feet apart, she braced herself against the side of the carriage. Her battered, often-repaired trainers left tread smears in the oily dirt coating the metal. In front of her, from the carriage window, a reflection of her own face stared back, thick dreads of hair fanning out around her like columns of smoke.

Behind her Marta heard two metallic crunches as first Simon and then Switch caught. In a group ride you rode in order of seniority. That was the rule. *I've survived the longest so that makes me the leader.* She listened for Dan, but there was only the roaring of the train, and the rapid clattering of the wheels over the rails.

Something had gone wrong.

She glanced back, terrified of what she might see. Dan should have been exactly one second behind Switch, but he was still running towards the train like a commuter who had overslept, his movement jerky, out of time. *He hesitated! Shit, he lost his nerve and now his timing's all screwed up.*

'Pull out!' she tried to scream, but her lungs, still empty, failed her, and the words trickled out like the last rains of a flood. She stared helplessly as Dan lifted the clawboard, jaw set, eyes hard. His pride was driving him on. When pride was all you had it was difficult to give it up, but down here where the trains roared it could get you killed.

Dan tried to leap. Going far too slow, he was way out of position. His clawboard fell short of the drainage rail, and his body slammed against the side of the train. The motion of the carriage spun him around in the air like a demented ballerina, eyes wide in terror, arms and legs flailing. He ricocheted off, a staccato, barked scream escaping his throat a moment before he landed hard on the platform. Momentum rolled him; the gap between the platform's edge and the rushing train loomed close. *Don't end up like Clive. Please don't. I can't handle that again.*

Dan got lucky. The straps of the blocky clawboard still circled one wrist, and the board arrested his roll, inches away from the edge. He rolled back as the train thundered past, and the clawboard finally spun loose.

'He's hurt!' Simon shouted as the train sped on, carrying the others away.

'Wait!' Marta shouted back as the braided dreads of her hair buffeted her face. 'Wait for the mats! Okay ... three, two, one–'

She kicked off from the side of the train, pushing forward and up as she'd done a thousand times before. The clawboard released its hold on the rail – reluctantly, as always. Marta leaned backwards as she fell, pulling her arms in and ducking her head forward. She grimaced as the pile of old mattresses and blankets at the end of the platform came up to meet her.

The fall knocked the wind out of her. Coughing, she glanced up to see Simon dismount after her, followed by Switch. They landed on the breakfall mats beside her and came to an untidy stop.

As the train roared away into the tunnel and the noise receded, all three climbed to their feet and dusted themselves down. Marta rubbed at her hip where she'd landed on a mattress seam.

'Fuck yeah,' Switch muttered. He shook the straps off his wrists and turned the board over, checking for abrasions. 'Paul, you fat chump, what's my score? *Paul?*'

'Forget your score!' Marta shouted at him. 'Dan failed the mount. He could have died, you idiot. Didn't you see it?'

'Ah, whatever. Live and die by the trains, ain't it just?'

Marta gave him a scowl that said *just sod off,* then looked back up the platform to where Paul was crouching next to Dan. Dan was curled up on the ground, hugging his chest. He tried to stretch his legs out, then grimaced, sweat glistening on his brow. His voice floated back down the platform towards them, echoing off the high rafters. 'Ah fuck, I think I busted my hip. Shit, that hurts.'

Switch cocked his head and gave Marta the kind of smirk a cheeky kid would give a scolding teacher to say he didn't really give a shit. 'Fuck that clown,' he said. Looking back towards the platform edge where chalk lines marked the distance in feet back from the end of the platform, he grinned. His bad eye flickered. 'That must have been sub-twenty feet for sure. Eighteen? What do you reckon, Si?'

'Don't be a cock, Switch,' Simon answered. 'Let's go check he's okay.'

'You pussy. Just because you can't get no distance now you're getting ass, but whatever.' Switch rolled his good eye at Simon and went over to the platform edge.

Simon glanced back at Marta and gave her his best *don't worry* smile. She felt instantly relaxed. Simon was tall and thin with an androgynous face, all angular and smooth. He didn't even seem to shave, his face clear of any stubble shadow. He was beautiful rather than handsome, a pretty boy that seemed more out of place than any of them, but he had a way about him that was calming, peaceful. He was a polar opposite of Switch, who was a ratty little man who'd never win any prizes for charm. Switch was a shameless asshole. He prided himself on it, wore it like a badge around his scrawny neck. But he was loyal. Switch would take your back in a street fight without hesitation, whether you were up against some stumbling drunk with a broken bottle or an armed unit of the DCA.

Marta broke into a jog along the platform. She reached Paul's side as he was helping Dan to his feet. Paul was huffing like an old man trying to start a car, his cheeks red with exertion. For a moment she recalled just how little she knew about any of them. They congregated here whenever they could, but they all had separate lives they rarely talked about. No one knew what Switch did. Simon said he worked in a market, and Paul claimed to be a pickpocket. Overweight since he'd stopped riding, balding and with no obvious muscle, she found it difficult to imagine he had much sleight of hand. She knew what people did around Piccadilly at night, but here you were as anonymous as the trains that roared past every eight minutes, if you chose to be.

Dan had been introduced to them as Paul's friend. He had greasy black hair, and thick brows which pushed his eyes into a permanent frown to make him look nervous, suspicious. He had a deep authoritative voice that suggested he preferred to give orders rather than take them. He'd only hung out with them a few times, and Marta had harboured doubts from the start.

'Are you all right?' she asked him.

Dan looked up and shrugged. He rubbed his hip and winced. 'I don't think anything's broken ... the fall just winded me. Shit, I can't believe I missed the hook. I thought I had it.' He shook his head and squeezed his eyes shut, one hand rubbing his forehead. 'I almost died there, didn't I?'

Marta looked away and said nothing. You didn't tell someone new that if you messed up you could end up unidentifiable, a mangled, bloody chunk of meat which the next twenty trains would wipe away. She closed her eyes, and the image that appeared was of Clive, as always, his eyes desperate, his hands scrabbling uselessly against the broken tiles of the platform as he was dragged down into the gap between the platform edge and the train. There had been others, but that one ... that one was the worst. That they'd been dating at the time too ... it was the closest she'd ever come to turning her back on the trains for good. The nightmares still haunted her.

He's done, she thought. *That's it. No one who cares much about life lasts long.*

Paul patted him on the shoulder, trying to be reassuring. 'Maybe you shouldn't ride the commuters for a while,' he said. 'Get some practice on the late night freights. They're a lot slower.'

Dan shoved his arm away. 'Don't touch me. I'm all right.' He squared up to Paul, who stumbled back out of his range. Dan glowered at them, his eyes flicking back and forth from one to the other. 'I'm no chicken. I just missed it, that's all. I was unlucky.'

'Dan, it's all right,' Marta said, putting herself between them. 'Are you sure you're not hurt?'

He turned away. 'Leave me alone. I'll be fine.'

Switch and Simon reached them. Marta glanced at Switch, the little man swaggering like a gunslinger after a kill. She gave him a little shake of her head, trying to steady his mouth.

He didn't notice, or if he did, he ignored her. 'Unlucky, man,' he said to Dan, flashing a wild grin. 'What did you score? Two hundred and twenty feet?'

Dan's eyes blazed, fists coming up. He had wide shoulders and thick arms, and was at least double Switch's weight. He probably thought he had a chance.

'You want some, you crippled prick—'

'Guys!' Paul shouted, but too late.

Dan threw a sharp punch at Switch, who backed into Simon as he tried to get out of the way. Dan would have missed, but Simon created a human barrier trapping Switch in front of him, and Dan's blow slammed into Switch's cheek, knocking him sideways. As Switch stumbled and tried to recover his balance, Dan nailed him again in the stomach. Switch doubled over, coughing, and Dan closed in to finish him off.

'Help me stop them!' Marta shouted.

Paul was no fighter, and even Marta outweighed Simon. Knowing there was little chance of any help, she tried to push herself between them, but Dan shoved her aside. He threw another punch, but Switch, having recovered his balance, ducked away this time. His thin lips curled back, anger and excitement in his face. His bad eye flickered like an old movie reel.

'So you wanna dance, is it?'

There was a flash of metal in the air.

'Uh ... uh ... no–'

Dan staggered back, a hairline of red cutting a trail down the side of his face from temple to jaw. Blood pooled and bulged, and the knife came to rest against Dan's throat. The blade, barely longer than Switch's index finger, reflected the emergency lighting above them, glimmering like a hospital light.

'You *never* fuck with me,' Switch said, good eye narrowed, face tight. 'You fuck with me, you die. You got that?'

'Easy, Switch,' said Simon, trying almost comically to muscle his thin frame between them.

The knife vanished and Switch stepped back. For a moment his good eye fixed Dan with a dark stare, then he turned and stalked back down the platform towards the breakfall mattresses.

'Don't worry about him, he's just–'

'Fuck off,' Dan said, turning away from Marta. He wiped a hand down his face, smearing away the blood from the shallow cut. He shook his hand and drops fell onto the platform, mingling with the dust.

'Dan!' Paul shouted.

'And you. You come near me again and I'll fuck you up.'

They watched him walk up the platform towards the far stairs. He glanced back just once as he reached the foot of the stairs, and then was gone.

'And then there were four,' Marta muttered under her breath. 'Good work, Switch.' She turned around, but Switch was at the far end of the platform near the breakfall mats, bent down near the platform edge. For Switch, the dismount length – the distance from the end of the platform to where a rider landed – was everything. Now that Dan had gone, the others couldn't care less.

'Do you think he'll come back?' Simon asked.

Marta gave a frustrated laugh. For a moment she felt like crying, but she shrugged it off. 'What do you think? No chance now.' She shook her head and sighed. 'He never really got into it, did he? He just didn't *fit*.'

Paul looked away. It was hurting him the most. Another friendship ruined. They were hard to come by these days, and like cracked glass, so easily shattered.

'Worth a try,' Simon said, and patted Paul on the shoulder. 'But there's still us, right? There are still Tube Riders while there's the four of us.'

'That idiot. If it wasn't for him ... honestly, sometimes I think we'd be better off–' Paul's voice trailed off. He ran a hand through the scant remains of his hair and pushed his glasses further up his nose. His face was flushed. 'Dan wanted to be part of a gang. I didn't want to tell him about us at first, but he seemed ... seemed willing. Now he's pissed off, angry with us, and feels cast out. Where's the first place he's going to go?'

It wasn't a question because they all knew the answer. Simon cocked his head. 'We have to hope he doesn't tell them about this station.'

'I'm sorry, guys. I just wanted him to be one of us.'

'Don't worry,' Marta said. 'St. Cannerwells is off their turf. The Cross Jumpers rarely leave Charing Cross East.'

'What about the rumours?'

Paul and Marta were quiet for a moment. The Cross Jumpers didn't ply their trade in secret like the Tube Riders did. Word got around quickly, and that word was that the Cross Jumpers had a new leader.

'Why would he want to start a turf war?' Paul said. 'It doesn't make sense.'

'They don't like us. They want us finished.'

'What for? There are only five – shit, four – of us left. We're hardly worth the effort.'

Marta gave them a grim smile. 'It's not about how many of us there are. It's about our legend.' She put her hands on her hips and gave them her best rock star pose, the thick dreads of her hair hanging against the sides of her face. 'We're the mighty Tube Riders, baby.'

They'd often talked about it, grinning with amusement. In squats, underground clubs and illegal bars all across London GUA, there were hushed mutterings about the ghosts that appeared at the windows of the Underground trains. There were a thousand rumours about what the newspapers had dubbed "Tube Riders", a name the original gang had gladly adopted. They were only half-jokingly considered wraiths or demons disturbed by all the noise, or the ghosts of generations of kids who had committed suicide down in the dark tunnels by throwing themselves under the trains. Only a month ago, Marta had found an article in an illegal magazine that claimed the entire London Underground network was haunted, and that it should be shut down.

Simon grinned. 'It is kind of cool.'

'The Cross Jumpers don't like it because no one gives a shit about them,' Marta said. 'They're scared to ride like we do and everyone knows it. That's why they want a turf war.'

Simon glanced back down the platform. 'You know Switch will want to fight,' he said. 'Pitched battle and all that? Tally ho, charge of the bloody Light Brigade.'

Marta watched a trickle of sweat meander its way down Paul's face. 'Well, he's on his own,' Paul said. 'How many knives can he hold at once?'

'Come on, let's get out of here,' Simon said. 'I don't feel like riding anymore today.'

Marta looked down the platform. 'Switch! We're going!'

The other man looked up and then jogged over.

'I reckon that was seventeen feet,' he said as he reached them, grinning inanely. His bad eye twitched at them as though he was trying to suggest something. 'I hit that third mat out, near the front edge.

That's about the seventeen feet mark, isn't it?'

'Not bad,' Marta said, feigning interest. 'That beats my best.'

'And mine,' Simon said.

'Ah, we all know you're a pussy.' Switch tried to wink with his other eye, but it just made him look epileptic. He patted Paul on the shoulder. 'Only Paul has better, eh. And that's why you don't ride anymore, isn't it? Don't need to now you've proved your point, eh?'

'Okay, leave it out,' Paul said, looking down at the platform.

'Come on man, don't cry! That ride was awesome! A Tube Rider legend!'

'Switch, *can* it,' Simon said, and although Switch gave Paul a lop-sided grin he shut up and began picking grime off the hooks of his clawboard instead.

Marta remembered the day Paul had made twelve feet. His clawboard had got jammed in the rail, maybe by a small piece of gravel caught in the railing or an accumulation of packed dirt. He'd managed to free his hands just in time, but he'd landed bad and been left with three broken ribs and a fractured collarbone. That wasn't the worst, though. Marta could still remember his screams when he realised the board was stuck. If there were ghosts down here, that had been the sound of one of them possessing his body. That spine-splitting shriek had been no sound a man should make. It made her shiver even now, two years later.

They headed back towards the stairs, their clawboards slung over their shoulders. The escalator had stopped working years ago, and now its metal teeth were rusted and gummed up with litter and dirt. They climbed up into darkness, emerging on to the old ticket corridor. A couple more emergency lights helped them past the old turnstiles, some boarded-up newsstands and an old donut store. Another staircase at the end led them up to the surface. Their feet rustled through piles of leaves blown in by the wind, while all around them the smell of unwashed bodies and the decomposing remains of takeout food hung in the air. They weren't the only people to use the station; at night it was common for tramps to bunk down behind the metal barrier of the entranceway. They rarely went far inside, though. Mega Britain's illegal magazines had seen to it that only the desperate or the very brave went into abandoned London Underground stations.

Marta went out first and waited for the others. It was a cold October day, the sky a leaking grey bucket that spat rain on her leather tunic and ripped jeans. St. Cannerwells backed on to a bleak park, a rusty iron fence separating them from a slope of untended grass, a cracked, root-rippled concrete path and a small pond filled with litter. Supermarket trolleys protruded from the brown water like half-submerged wrecks; paper-cup boats floated amongst the icebergs of old cardboard boxes while around them trees clacked their bare branches together in mocking applause.

'See you tomorrow?' Marta asked.

'I'm working but I'll come over when I'm done,' Simon said.

'I have some stuff to do but yeah, I'll try,' Paul said.

'Switch?'

The little man was tapping the palm of his left hand with the index finger of his right, muttering under his breath.

'I'll take that as a yes.'

As the others said their goodbyes and left, Marta stood for a moment, looking out across the park towards the huge elevated highway overpass that rose above the city to the south. Half finished, it arched up out of the terraces and housing blocks to the east, rising steadily to a height of five hundred feet. There, at the point where it should have begun its gradual decent to the west, it just ended, sawn off, amputated.

Years ago, she remembered her father standing here with her, telling her about the future. Things had been better then. She'd still been going to school, still believed the world was good, still had dreams about getting a good job like a lawyer or an architect, and hadn't started to do the deplorable things that made her wake up shivering, just to get food or the items she needed to survive.

He had taken her hand and given it a little squeeze. She still remembered the warmth of his skin, the strength and assurance in those fingers. He had pointed up at the overpass, in those days busy with scaffolding, cranes and ant-like construction workers, and told her how one day they would take their car and drive right up over it and out of the city. The government was going to open up London Greater Urban Area again, he said. Let the city people out, and the people from the Greater Forest Areas back in. The smoggy, grey skies of London GUA would clear, the sirens would stop wailing all night, and people would be able to take the chains and the deadlocks off their doors. She remembered how happy she'd felt with her father's arms around her, holding her close, protecting her.

But something had happened. She didn't know everything – no one did – but things had changed. The government hadn't done any of those things. The construction stopped, the skies remained grey, and life got even worse. Riots waited around every street corner. People disappeared without warning amid tearful rumours that the Huntsmen were set to return.

Marta sighed, biting her lip. Her parents and her brother were gone. Marta was just twenty-one, but St. Cannerwells Park was the closest she would ever get to seeing the countryside, and the euphoria of tube riding was the closest she would ever get to happiness.

She gripped the fence with both hands and gritted her teeth, trying not to cry. She was tough. She had seen and done things that no one her age should have to experience. She had adjusted to Mega Britain's harshness, was accustomed to looking after herself, but, just sometimes, life became too much to bear.

As the rain began to get heavier, tears pressed from her eyes and rolled lethargically down her cheeks.

Chapter Two
Jessica

'GET OUT OF MY fucking seat!'

Simon lifted his head from the window, but the shout wasn't aimed at him. Further up the bus, a burly man with a tattoo across his face was picking a fight with a man wearing a baseball cap. Simon watched with only a passing interest as Baseball Cap nodded cordially and stood up, moving back into the aisle. Tattoo Face growled something as he went to sit down, but as soon as he looked away Baseball Cap put two big hands on his back and shoved him hard against the window.

Tattoo Face's head slammed against the thick glass with a resounding crack. Baseball Cap shoved him again and this time the window shattered, showering the street below with little diamonds of safety glass. The bus swerved in towards the curb, and Tattoo Face lost his balance and fell out into the street, landing on the bonnet of a car trying to cut up on the bus's inside.

Gripped by a rage drawn from the cloud of misery that seemed to hang over Mega Britain, Baseball Cap jumped out of the window after him, screaming obscenities. The two men grabbled on the car bonnet with Tattoo Face taking some heavy blows until he pulled a long knife from inside his coat and rammed it into Baseball Cap's side. Baseball Cap cried out in pain and fell backwards, blood clouding out around the wound, turning his blue shirt a dirty brown. Tattoo Face saw his chance and shoved Baseball Cap off the car just as the bus began to move again. The driver, hollering something incomprehensible over the top of the screaming people, tried to steer the bus back into traffic, only for it to roll over Baseball Cap's body, the wheels crushing his chest with the sickening crunch of bones.

The bus ground to another stop. The driver jumped up and climbed out, shouting at someone out on the street, arms gesturing frantically. Tattoo Face had fled, no one in the growing crowd making an effort to stop him. Sirens were already wailing in the distance, but what disturbed Simon most was how little people cared. There were a few gapers on the pavement, but there was as much laughter as there were looks of horror. A couple of people further up the bus had got up to watch, but behind him two middle-aged women were continuing a conversation as though nothing had happened.

This country's screwed up, he thought. *No wonder some of us like to hide underground. It's safer and you don't have to deal with the people.*

He stood up, crossed the aisle, and jumped out of the open back door. With the growing number of abandoned cars left along the streets it only took a little trouble to cause a jam, and now the bus was boxed in. Simon had hoped to make it a couple more stops into central Fulham, but he was close enough to walk from here. He headed across the street, away from the commotion, and slipped down an alley. He emerged on to a residential street running parallel to the main road which was so quiet in comparison that it spooked him. He looked around for people, but saw none. It was as though he'd stepped through a portal into a ghost town.

Then a muffled explosion sounded, pulling him back to reality. The bus had gone up. He increased his pace, aware that within minutes there would be a full riot happening. It was always the same. Then, in twenty minutes or so, the police or the Department of Civil Affairs would show up and start killing people.

Hate, anger, and resentment fueled people now. Food was in short supply, and the last oil was almost gone. The streets were becoming clogged by abandoned petrol-powered cars and the few who owned electric vehicles could barely afford the spiraling costs of the recharging stations. At night there were often electrical blackouts; those times were the most dangerous of all as looters took to the streets in large gangs.

Simon's father had set up an illegal internet connection, so Simon knew what other countries were saying about Mega Britain. None of it was good. His father, a wannabe revolutionary who in reality did little more than sit around their flat bitching about the state of society, had fallen victim to his own attempts at understanding.

Simon had been riding when the DCA came a month ago. Treason was the usual charge, punishable by life imprisonment or death. And, like so many people taken away by the government's thugs, there had been no word of his father since. For all Simon knew, his father had been blasted into space aboard one of the government's doomed hulks. Whatever, it seemed unlikely Simon would ever see him again.

The DCA had seized his father's apartment and possessions. To go back there was to walk into a bugged, wired hornet's nest. He had lost what little stuff he had, some of which could be used to trace him. Now, he feared that the DCA would come for him too, but there was nothing he could do except keep his head down.

And there were other things to live for.

He was almost there now. He turned down another residential street and headed uphill, past terraced houses which defied the failing world with their tidiness. Some areas weren't so bad. Groups of heavily-armed residents kept order in a feudal way, working in shifts to protect the streets from the kind of riffraff that looted shops during the blackouts. You couldn't see them, of course; they waited in alleys, behind curtains, inside the dirty windows of abandoned cars. But they were there.

At the top of the hill he turned right on to a road called Denton Avenue. At number fourteen he stopped outside the little red gate and looked up at the windows.

He looked at his watch, an old Lorus that he'd been wearing the day the DCA showed up to take his father. Three fifteen. He'd said three, but she knew what the traffic – or lack of it – was like.

He looked up at the house again, the top window on the left, wondering whether he should shout. Then the curtain flickered, jerked back. Simon felt his heart jump in his chest. A face appeared. It was difficult to make out the features at this distance, but Simon knew them well: the thin, delicate cheekbones, the tight bob of hair curling in around the jaw line, the small lips and the bright blue, defiant eyes.

'Jessica,' he murmured, as always relieved to see she was safe.

The curtain dropped back.

He waited. Thirty seconds later the door opened and the same face peered out. 'Okay, I've deactivated it,' the girl called. 'You can come through now.'

Simon reached out for the gate, still tentative after the first time he'd visited. The red should have been a warning, but he had been thinking about other things. He remembered the paralysis and the intense pain as the electricity had surged through his body, leaving him a writhing, frothy-mouthed wreck on the ground. Jess's father worked for the government and had access to security technology most people didn't. Everyone their family considered a friend knew to call ahead or use the buzzer beside the gate. All other people were regarded as potential enemies, and as such the electrified gate was a suitable deterrent. As he reached the door she pulled it wide and stepped out, almost falling forward into his arms.

'I missed you,' she said. 'More each day.'

'I've missed you too.' Simon pulled her close and breathed in the sweet smell of her hair. He closed his eyes, feeling her heart beat against his chest. There were few reasons to live in London GUA but he had found one.

Jess was eighteen and worked in a used bookstore near the market where Simon sold pirated movies and antiquated music CDs on a stall owned by an old friend of his father. Simon felt a hundred years older than his twenty. The weight of his fear for her safety kept him awake at night. If he could, he would keep her by his side, but neither her parents nor Jess herself would allow it. As she constantly reminded him, having grown up in the same city, she was streetwise too. And with a father who worked for the government, she had to be even more careful.

'Did you ride today?' she asked.

He hesitated. He knew Jess didn't like him to ride the trains, but she understood.

'Just once,' he said. 'The others had stuff to do.' He didn't mention Dan's close call.

She drew away, and looked up at him. For a moment he thought she was going to scold him again. *It's the trains or me, Simon. You can't have both. It's your choice.* When she did speak, her request surprised him. 'I want to come,' she said. 'I want to try it too.'

'I've told you I don't want that. It's too dangerous.'

'So why do you do it then?'

'I ... I–' He shook his head. 'I don't know. It's ... my *thing*, I guess. My identity. It's all I have left.'

She put her hands on his cheeks and pulled his face towards her. 'Not anymore,' she said, and kissed him. 'Not anymore.'

She was right. He should quit tube riding and look after her. He'd met her just six months ago, but in these fractured times that could be half a lifetime. He couldn't imagine giving her up, and he hated every moment they were apart, but the Tube Riders – Marta, Paul, even crazy Switch – they were his family. He couldn't give them up either. Until he had met Jess, riding the trains was the only thing in his life that had mattered. He had found companions there, people like himself.

'Let's go inside,' she said. 'Off the street.'

Her family was out – as always – when he visited. Jess's father was a government official – a position he neither talked about nor entertained questions about – and her mother worked for the MBBC, the Mega Britain Banking Corporation, the country's only bank.

'Did you find out anything about my father?'

Jess closed the door before she answered. 'No, I'm sorry. I tried to ask Dad, but it's difficult to do it without him becoming suspicious. He asks so many questions, without answering any. I tried to make it look like I was interested in the newspaper story about it, but he just spouted some propaganda about heretics earning their rewards.' She shrugged. 'To be honest, he probably doesn't know.'

'You know I had nothing to do with it, don't you?' Simon said, taking off his shoes. 'I wasn't involved with anything my father did, any of those leaflets he used to print out. I just looked at his internet a couple of times. That's all.'

She cupped his face with her hands again. 'I know, Simon. But I wouldn't care anyway. Sometimes I think these so-called heretics...'

'I want to take you away, Jess,' Simon said, kissing her. 'If we could only get out of Mega Britain, get over to France ... it's different there, you know. They have a government who gives a shit, there aren't any of those fucking perimeter walls ... God damn this place.'

They climbed the stairs up to her bedroom. 'There's hope,' she said. 'There's an ambassador over from Europe, Dad told me. He came today for talks between the European Confederation and Mega Britain. Dad said the Confederation wants to open up trade again. End the blockade.'

'Do you think they will?'

Jess sat down on her bed. 'I don't know. They might have to. The country is bankrupt, Dad says, but the government doesn't listen. People are starving, there's hardly any oil, there are riots everywhere...'

Simon put a finger on her lips. 'Okay, stop now.' He leaned forward and kissed her again.

Jess sighed and pulled him backwards onto the bed. Simon closed his eyes and let her take the troubles of the world away.

#

Later, dressed again and lying next to her on the bed, Simon said, 'I'm going down again on Sunday. Around lunchtime, after I finish my morning shift.' He stroked her face. 'You can come if you like. I mean, if you haven't got work and you're not busy.'

'Really? You want me to ride?'

Simon shrugged and gave her a non-committal smile. 'I don't know about that. Maybe just watch at first? New people have to practice on the freight trains, because they're much slower. You can almost walk alongside. The commuter trains slow down when they go through each station, but they're still pretty fast.'

Simon had talked about tube riding before, but Jess seemed endlessly fascinated. Until Simon had revealed his secret to her a couple of months after they had met she had believed the ghost stories too.

'Sounds difficult,' she said, eyes lit up with interest.

'Not so much.' He grinned. 'Not when you know what you're doing.'

'And you use this?' She lifted his clawboard up off the floor and turned it over in her hands. It was a piece of sanded hardwood about two feet long. On one side, bolted to the wood with a series of little screws, was a long piece of curved metal, scratched and dented from use. On the other side were two thick leather straps, again fixed to the wood. The board itself was sprayed black. It looked like there had once been a design on it, but time had worn it away.

'What the hell is this thing?' she said wistfully, only half to him.

'It's called a clawboard,' he said. 'We made them ourselves, although some of them get handed on by people who ... quit.'

'Quit?'

'Um, yeah. Some people get scared, you know? Other people just don't want to do it anymore.' He didn't mention the deaths. There was no need to scare her.

'And you made it?'

'Yeah, this one, I did. The metal hook thing used to be part of the fender of a car. Some of the other guys have two or three smaller ones instead. The leather is horse leather, which is stronger.'

'Where did you get it?' I haven't seen a horse since I was a kid.'

'Junkyard. Told you it was strong. I think it used to be part of a guitar strap, something like that.'

'And you painted it black?'

'Yeah, you know.' He cocked his head and raised an eyebrow at her. 'To personalise it. Switch – that's one of the other guys – got some friend of his to paint a dragon on his board. Kind of suits his personality.'

'But, *black?*' She touched his arm and smiled. 'That's like the opposite of your personality, Simon.'

'Yeah, well,' he grinned. 'I guess I was in a mood or something at the time.'

She wrapped one of the leather straps around her wrist and tugged. 'I bet this hurts.'

Simon pulled something out of his pocket and held it up. 'Sometimes we wear these,' he said. 'It's like a wrist guard.' It looked like a tube of rubber, a thick bracelet. 'It's an insulator for a water pipe. It was Paul's idea, before he stopped riding. You don't *need* them, but if you ride regularly you get burns on your wrists from the straps, particularly if your timing isn't all that great.'

'And you just hang from the train?'

'On most trains there is a rail that runs along the top of the carriage, just above the level of the door. It's for water runoff, I think, so that the windows don't get stained by dirty water.'

'What if there's no rail?'

He smiled. 'We pull out. Otherwise we'd just slide off.'

'Where does the water come from? There's no rain in the Underground.'

'Most of the trains run above and below ground. The network goes right out into the suburbs, and some of those trains run in the open air.'

Jess nodded, grinning. 'Of course it does. I'm such a moron.'

Simon smiled back. 'Anyway, as the train arrives, we start to run. It slows down as it comes into the station, but it's still traveling about fifty miles an hour.'

'Doesn't it pull your arms off?'

'Ah, you see, when the board catches the rail you slide a bit. It jerks, of course, but not as much as if you caught on a solid fixing. Sometimes the rails get rocks or dirt jammed in them, though. That can hurt.' He grinned.

'What happens if you miss?'

'We don't.'

'Never?'

'Not if you know what you're doing.' He hated lying to her. He'd missed once, early on. Like Dan this morning, he'd been lucky. He had suffered some bad bruising, but nothing serious. He remembered Clive, though, caught in the gap between the platform edge and the train. He'd been mangled, mashed up. They had tried to revive him, but just ended up with got blood all over themselves. Marta and Clive had been a couple at the time and Simon couldn't believe she still came back after seeing that. There had been a definite darker look in her eyes after Clive's death, as if whatever innocence she'd had left had been blown out of her. He had stayed away almost two weeks himself, but when he'd finally given in to the urge, he'd found them – Marta, Paul and Switch – down there as if nothing had happened.

Clive had been given a traditional Tube Rider burial, laid across the tracks for the trains to claim. It was pretty gruesome, but that was the Tube Rider code. Clive had been a homeless runaway, he'd had no family, and taking his body to the police would have only created more questions.

'And at the end of the platform you just jump off?'

'Kind of. You brace your feet on the side of the train, push the board in and up, and kick back. We use old mattresses to land on, but if you know how, it's possible to land on the platform and roll without hurting yourself.' *Much*, he didn't add. It hurt like hell, you just didn't break anything if you did it right.

'I'm looking forward to it,' she said.

'If you're careful you'll be fine,' he said. 'Don't worry, I'll look after you.' He glanced at his watch. 'I have to go,' he said. 'It's almost five. Your parents will be home soon.'

'Okay,' she said, standing up and smoothing out her clothes. As she led him out on to the landing and down the stairs, she said, 'I'll meet you in the market after your shift. You can take me then.'

He smiled. 'I don't want to go,' he said. 'I want to stay here with you.'

'Yeah, whatever. Stop being such a sap.' She punched his arm, but he saw a dewy look in her eyes. He swallowed, desperate not to get tearful in front of her. Every time he left her he felt like he would never see her again.

'You know,' she said, pointing at the clawboard, tucked under his arm. 'It's a wonder no one ever gets suspicious of that thing. You carry it around everywhere like an advertisement above your head. "Look at me, I'm a Tube Rider".'

He shrugged. 'People just think it's a kind of skateboard,' he said. *Or a weapon*, he didn't add. Enough people carried those. 'No one really takes any notice of me, because I just look like a girly skater kid.'

She touched his arm. 'Well, you just carry on not being noticed, and keep yourself safe for me.'

'I'll try.'

He kissed her and said goodbye. Jess tapped in a code on a keypad by the door to deactivate the front gate, and Simon headed down the path, glancing back every few feet to make sure she was still there.

'Bye,' he said again as he stepped out on to the road. 'Be safe.'

She stepped forward. 'Wait a second.'

'What?'

She reached into her pocket and pulled out a small silver box. She lifted it and pointed it at him.

Simon frowned. 'Is that a–'

'Digital camera? Yeah. I just want a picture of you to look at while you're not with me.'

'Where did you get it?' He hadn't seen one in years. You needed a license for any electronic product. That included televisions, computers, and mobile phones.

'Dad gave it to me.' She shrugged. 'It's government loot. Go on, smile.'

Simon had barely opened his mouth when Jess pressed a button and a little click sounded. She peered at a small screen on the back. 'There. I'll make you a copy.'

'Thanks,' he said, not really caring either way. 'Anyway, you'd better get inside.'

She smiled and winked at him. As the door closed, Simon felt that familiar despair welling up in his throat. He turned away and gulped it down as he headed off along the street. Light rain still hung in the air beneath the grey sky, and he zipped up his jacket to the point where the zip got stuck on a broken tooth about halfway up. It was a long way back across London to the burnt-out ruin of a bedsit some shark was renting him now.

He wondered if inviting her to meet the other Tube Riders was a good idea. The first ride would get her hooked, and that would be his fault. He felt like a drug pusher – he knew what it would do to her, but he couldn't help himself. He wanted her to share his life, but at the same time he knew it might destroy her.

The wind got up, ruffling his hair. He grimaced at the cold, pulled a beanie hat from his pocket and slipped it over his head. Then, with the clawboard tucked safely up under his arm, he headed off towards the cold little room he now called home.

Chapter Three
Huntsman

AFTER LEAVING THE OTHERS, Switch headed off across the park, cutting past the junk-filled pond and up the hill on the far side. One or two grim-faced couples eyed him warily, and he matched their glances with his own flicking stare until they turned away. Confrontation was his key to survival. Hide from people chasing you and eventually they would track you down. Face them, stand and fight, and you got them off your trail.

A couple of streets away he found a rundown fast food joint and bought a burger, which he ate back out on the street. In a bin he found an old newspaper from two days ago, but there was little of interest. Most of the news concerned crime within the city: murder, robbery, arson. The only mention of the world was from opinion columns that criticised the European Confederation's trade blockades, and there was no mention of America at all. Switch had met a man once who'd been there, but as the man was begging for his life at the time Switch didn't know if it was just a claim to still the knife or a true event. In any case, the promise of a ticket out of Mega Britain had not been enough to safeguard the man's wallet. Switch had granted him his life, though; he wasn't all bad.

He tossed the paper into the next bin he passed. He cared little for news; cared less for thoughts of revolution and rebellion. Once, as a kid, things had been different, but he'd made his peace now, found his ways to survive. Tube riding and enough money to keep him alive were all he needed.

After finishing his burger he headed back across the park, away from the shadow of the huge unfinished highway overpass. He tossed the wrapper into the pond and climbed the hill towards the old station entrance. He looked about for the others, but as he'd expected they'd all gone. *Good.* He smiled and went back inside.

Tube riding was all Switch cared about. He had no memory of his parents, and had lost his uncle William, the man who had brought him up, when government scumfucks had abducted Switch and dozens of other children from the streets of Bristol GUA for transportation to labour camps up north. That had been ten years ago, and his uncle was probably dead now, especially considering the line of work William had been in. Switch would never qualify for a travel permit to leave London GUA, and there was no other way out of the city.

He descended into the depths of St. Cannerwells, feeling the hum of the trains in the walls around him. He shivered and took a deep breath. Tube riding was like a drug. For the others it was identity, comradeship, union and all that other buddy-up shit, but for Switch it was all about the ride. Hanging off the side of the trains as they roared along the platform was like wanking on heroin times ten. He'd done everything, tried every real drug he could find, and nothing compared. Sex, too, was a pale comparison, but with his eye the only sluts he could get were paid for anyway, and money wasn't something he had much of. Tube riding was free oblivion.

Down on the platform he let a couple of trains through before he made his move. There was an express train every hour at eighteen minutes past, and it was his dream to ride it. The commuter trains were fast, but the express *roared*. No one had ever ridden it, and Switch wanted to be the first. There was only one way to get on the express, though: practice.

He heard the building roar back in the tunnel and closed his eyes, tensing every muscle in his body. As the glow of the lights appeared, Switch's eyes flicked open and he started into a sprint, much earlier than the others ever did. When the train shot out of the tunnel he was already in position, and he leapt for it, clawboard swinging high to catch the rail. As always, the yank on his arms as it caught made him grunt, but then he was on, feet braced on the side of the train. He had a second to glance in through the window, and saw a pair of scruffy teenagers opposite him, a boy and a girl, their heads close together.

First one, then the other looked up. Shock registered on their faces. One of them pointed and the other started to stand up, saying something Switch couldn't hear over the roar of the wind.

He smiled, adjusted his grip just enough to give them the middle finger, and then he was off, kicking back and up, the clawboard coming free. The train moved away from him, accelerating even as he slowed, leaning back. The air wrapped around him, the mattresses coming up below him as he landed, feather-light, on his back.

He looked up from the mattresses to see them moving closer to the window, looking for him. He knew, though, that in the dark and amongst the reflections, he was already gone, a wraith vanished into the dim emergency lighting of a station no one knew existed. Later, when they told their friends, they'd struggle to recall exactly where they'd seen the ghostly figure. A few sightings were all that was needed to maintain the legend, but it was important to keep St. Cannerwells a secret, which was why they rarely rode during rush hour. There were too many people watching, too many who might remember.

Once, before those cross-jumping fuckwits had started to appear, they'd used several different stations, but most were too dangerous now. Had there been other Tube Riders, Switch would have welcomed an open turf war. But while Marta, sweet as she appeared, could be useful with pretty much any weapon she had to hand, Simon was just a pretty boy and Paul was a borderline fag. Neither would help in a fight. Switch had liked Dan's attitude for the scrap even if he'd picked on the wrong guy, but he was a blip, over now. Back when there had been ten, fifteen of them, they could have fought, but while Switch could take one or two, there were rumours of people cross-jumping in their dozens.

Switch climbed up from the breakfall mattresses and glanced at the chalk marks on the platform edge. He'd made around twenty-eight feet, a pretty standard length. He always dismounted early the first couple of times, getting his range and timing right. He had gone up to fourteen feet safely. Twelve, still his record, had given him the twitch in his eye. Only one man – Marta's brother, Leo – had dismounted under ten feet and lived.

He jogged back along the platform, eager for the next ride. During the day the trains ran every eight minutes so he didn't have long to wait before he heard the roar back in the tunnel again.

This time he left his dismount length long like before, but when he kicked off, instead of tucking his arms in and falling backwards, he jerked the board around to the right, spinning his body through 180 degrees. The landing knocked a bit of the wind out of him, but he jumped up almost immediately, delighted with his success, and jogged back down the platform again, rubbing his sore stomach.

He did a couple more one-eighties to the right, then one to the left, against the flow of the train. This was more difficult, and he landed awkwardly, twisting his ankle a little.

He rubbed it for a while, watching a couple more trains pass. He didn't care about the pain, only whether or not he could run quickly enough for the mount. The others didn't know about the tricks he did, and one day he hoped to astound them with a stunning display of dismount moves. He wasn't far off, but with an audience he'd have nerves to deal with too. And for his last move, he needed full concentration.

The back flip. He'd done it twice without hurting himself, but didn't trust himself to pull it off in public. Still, it was the last thing he needed to make his repertoire complete.

He sprinted as the train roared out of the tunnel and leapt for it, clawboard stretching for the rail. He caught and braced himself against the side, peering in but without concentrating. Several people had seen him today, but he was thinking of his dismount too much to worry about cultivating their legend further.

He quickly realised this wasn't a normal commuter train, though. A group of men in dark suits stood near the window with their backs to him, and he recognised them as the special police, the Department of Civil Affairs. They were the ones who made people disappear, who rounded up heretics and dissenters and pretty much anyone else they didn't like. He had come across one of the bastards drunk once and had cut the guy up, carved the word "cunt" into his back and left him for dead. Whether the guy had survived or not, Switch didn't know or care.

He was starting to think about an early dismount to avoid them seeing him, but then one moved slightly and through a gap in their bodies he saw a cloaked, hooded figure sitting down, facing him. Leather straps with metal chains threaded around them kept the figure's arms at its sides. They were transporting a fugitive, it looked like, and he leaned closer to the window, trying to see the face under the hood, wondering wryly if he might recognise the man.

Then a roar over the top of the wind seemed to shake the window in front of his face. The cluster of DCA agents separated as though blown apart by the bound figure as it jerked into a standing position, straining against more bonds that held it down. To either side, more agents tried to restrain what was not a man but something else, something alien, something monstrous.

As the wolverine face roared at him again, its sharp teeth bared, Switch recoiled in shock and his feet lost their purchase.

'Oh, fuck–'

For a second he hung loose from the side of the train, feet dangling just above the gaping hole between the train and the platform edge. He glanced forward and saw the end wall of the platform rushing towards him.

He looked back into the carriage and saw the thing trying to reach him, its bound hands shaking, its jaw snapping, a group of men trying to restrain it. He closed his eyes–

And his feet gripped. He kicked up blindly, falling backwards, not caring about his dismount, just wanting to be away from that snarling, menacing thing. He plummeted through the air, hearing the sound of the train cut off early, way too early, and then he landed hard, the mattresses catching him, the clawboard striking his temple as he failed to control its momentum. His forehead ached, but he was safe, he was off the train, he was away from that thing.

As the train vanished into the tunnel he rolled on to his side, dismayed to see blood dripping on to the mattresses. He untangled himself from the clawboard and wiped his face, holding a finger over the gash in his forehead to stem the bleeding. The pain barely registered as he looked up at the empty tunnel as though the beast might still come back for him. Despite the muggy heat in the station, he shivered.

So the rumours were true.

He remembered the furry, dog-like muzzle, the sharp, dripping teeth. He also remembered the metallic shine of wires protruding out of the creature's neck, the sacking hood that covered the top of its head, its eyes. The eyes of a man, the face of a dog, the mind of a machine.

The Huntsmen were abroad.

Switch could only hope it was being transferred from one secure location to another. He knew the stories, everyone did. Into your house at night, stealing you from your bed, letting you live only if its orders said so, and even then only if it chose. Otherwise it was death: slow, fast, torturous or just plain painful, whatever its misfiring mind decided.

The Huntsmen had been gone for fifteen years, since the government last brought them into service to end a rebellion in the Manchester-Liverpool GUA. Switch had heard the horror stories of slaughters after dark, the malfunctioning Huntsmen rampaging, tearing apart whole communities irrespective of their political loyalties. The rebellion ended voluntarily to stop the killing. In return for laying down their arms, the government vowed to take the Huntsmen out of service, shut them down, and never again let them loose on the streets. The Huntsmen were a liability, the remnants of a scientific greatness and knowledge that Mega Britain had let fall into dereliction and decay. The Huntsmen were too dangerous, too unpredictable, and now almost uncontrollable.

There were rumours, of course. There were always rumours, but no confirmed sighting of a Huntsman had been made since the uprising.

Until now.

Switch picked up his clawboard and walked back up the platform. He'd planned to do a few more rides, but his enthusiasm was gone. Seeing that thing, that monster, straining at its bonds, wanting his blood, made him tremble. Switch feared no man, but there was no humanity left in the Huntsmen.

The knife appeared in his hand, and he turned it over, considering it, letting the light reflect off the sharpened blade. It was nothing if one of those things came after him. Nothing at all.

At the top of the old escalator Switch hauled up the shutter of one of the old newsstands. Behind the door, the light revealed a little den: a sleeping bag and a few blankets, a handful of torches, a small table. Switch went inside, switched on a battery lamp and pulled the shutter back down.

This was where he made his home. St. Cannerwells Underground station was the obvious choice: riding the trains was the only time he felt pleasure so it made sense to live close to what he loved. The others didn't know, and he didn't want them to. Part of him felt like a guard, protecting what was theirs, watching over it. Another part just felt at home underground, in the labyrinth of tunnels beneath London.

He pulled a can of cola out of a twenty-four pack he'd stolen off a delivery truck and popped it open. The carbonated water fizzed down his throat, stinging him, and he gulped most of it back before he felt any better.

In a bag on the table he found some tobacco and a small packet of pot. He rolled himself a joint and lay back on the blankets to smoke it. He'd removed one of the metal rungs near the top of the shutter to act as a chimney, and now the smoke drifted up and out into the station. As he reflected on what he'd seen, he realised his hands were shaking, and even the weed wouldn't make them stop.

Chapter Four
Owen

P AUL WAITED OUTSIDE the school gate. Nearby, two burly guards armed with assault rifles watched him impassively. He had tried to start a conversation with one, but the man hadn't seemed interested. Five days a week Paul waited here at this time, and the guards rarely changed, but even so, they shrugged off any attempt at conversation, as though speaking to him would compromise their positions. He had no particular desire to talk to them anyway; he just liked to pass the time.

In the distance he heard a huge lethargic rumble, what might have been a bomb caught in slow motion. He turned towards the sound, guessing correctly that it came from the east. A few seconds later, with the roar decreasing to a low, even growl, he saw it.

The spacecraft rose up into the air at almost a ninety degree angle. Even at this distance he could tell the craft was huge and oval-shaped, slightly thicker at the back end, certainly too large to fly well. It looked like an eraser, a piece of gum, white and featureless. Flickers of fire from a rear thruster darted out like the tongue of a snake. For a while the craft held its upwards trajectory, a perfect straight line up into the smog, until it disappeared from sight, becoming just a flickering orange glow behind the clouds.

Then came a groan from the distant engines. Paul sighed in spite of himself; he didn't care about the government's spaceships but there was an inevitability to the situation that pained him, as if it reflected everything that was wrong with society. *Please make it*, he found himself thinking.

The orange glow grew bright for a moment. The growl of the engines became a drone and then the craft appeared again through the clouds, plummeting towards earth. It flipped end over end, the boosters spraying occasional bursts of fire like a firework that had failed to properly ignite.

He couldn't look. He turned away and saw the guards had done so too. One scratched at some non-existent stain on his shirt, a pained expression on his face, while the other peered at a fingernail as if the secrets of the world were etched there. At the last moment, though, Paul couldn't help himself. He glanced up to see counter thrusters had been activated at the craft's front end, trying to slow it, trying to keep it from a destructive impact. It briefly straightened, wobbled on its axis, and for a second Paul thought its bomb dive might be reversed. Then there was another explosion, the counter thrusters flickered, and the craft returned to its spiraling descent. A moment later it fell behind the line of the houses and was gone. Paul listened, but heard no indication of its fate. Still, obliterated or just damaged, he knew that somewhere across London people were dying now, in a mess of wreckage, fire and rubble.

It was always the way. The government launched their spaceships from Southend, on the east coast outside of London GUA. He had seen six others. All fell. He'd heard that the launchers aimed the craft out over the sea so that the inevitable fall resulted in less destruction, though he knew of one that had fallen in the Thames, destroying part of Tower Bridge and the Tower of London. More than a hundred civilians had died, and there were other reports of whole streets being flattened. News passed by ear often became distorted and exaggerated, but he'd seen enough with his own eyes to know that part of what he heard was truth.

A few weeks would pass while the dust settled. Then the next massive craft would be pulled out of its hanger, and the whole sorry process would begin again.

No one knew what the space program was for, nor who piloted each doomed flight. Speculation said stolen people. Marta's brother Leo had disappeared off the street three years ago, and so the spacecraft were never discussed in her presence. But in reality, the only truth was that the truth could be anything.

Simon claimed it was bitterness, that Mega Britain once had supremacy in space and colonies on the inner planets, but the Americans had shot down all the craft and taken over the settlements. Now, a bankrupt Mega Britain was stealing money and its own people to try to revive past glories.

Behind him a bell rang. A cheer went up from inside a low building behind the gate, and a horde of children rushed out into the playground. Around Paul, parents, wards, foster-carers and one or two other brothers and sisters waited. He watched as the kids poured past the guards and then him, out on to the street like human water trickling away. He looked over the sea of heads, searching for Owen. As always he started to panic until at last he saw his brother ambling across the playground, a school bag slung across his shoulders. Owen's head was lowered, his face sullen, and Paul recognised this as a sign of wellbeing. His twelve-year-old brother loved school. They got on well, but Paul always felt school was the only thing that truly made his brother happy. Inside those walls Owen was safe within his learning. The violence and the struggles of life in Mega Britain didn't figure, and it was as though he was just a normal school kid, working at his studies with the future bright ahead of him.

'Hey,' Paul said, as his brother came up to the gate amidst the last trickle of children. 'You okay?'

'Hi, Paul.' Owen handed Paul the bag. It was Paul's job as big brother to carry the luggage. As always he was surprised how heavy it was, loaded down with the science and math textbooks that his little brother loved so much.

'You just missed one of the spaceships,' Paul said as they turned away from the school and headed for the nearest bus stop.

'Did it make it?'

Paul raised an eyebrow. 'What do you think?'

Owen smiled. 'Don't worry, one day I'll show them what to do. I'll make sure they all stay up, and we can all go and live on Mars.'

'I hear the weather's pretty good there,' Paul said.

'There's a whole industry in dust baths,' Owen quipped.

'Yeah, well, water's overrated, don't you think?'

Owen punched his brother on the arm. 'I want to go to the ocean, someday,' he said. 'I was reading today about tropical reefs and all the fish you can see—'

'Talking of fish, how about we go get fish n' chips for tea?'

'Sounds good.' Owen smiled. 'Do you have enough money for takeaway?'

Paul patted his pocket. 'Yeah, of course.'

It was more of an estimation than a lie. If they had no extras and he only bought a small portion, he could afford for Owen to feast. Paul, twenty-one and thirteen stone, didn't need to grow anymore. He'd gained weight since he'd given up active tube riding, something that was difficult to do with the food shortages London often suffered from.

They headed out of the school grounds and turned up the street. Ahead of them the intersection was clogged, so Paul led them across the street and down a road heading right. Once-stately Victorian buildings loomed over them from either side. Perhaps just one in three of the buildings they passed had windows, while many had been gutted by fire. For a while they would walk on clear, tidy pavement, then a moment later they'd be negotiating their way around a heap of garbage or an abandoned car, holding their noses against the stench of something rotting, or stepping through potholes where the tarmac had been torn up.

'I hate this shithole,' Owen was saying. 'There are so many nice places in the world, Paul. Why are we stuck here?'

Paul shrugged. He didn't know whether Owen should believe what he read in books anyway. For all they knew, the rest of the world was as bad as London GUA.

'Look, Paul! What's going on over there?'

They had just turned a corner and a short distance ahead a group of men were approaching a small mini-mart. They swaggered rather than walked, probably the result of illegal homebrew, and the assurances of the knives and bits of wood they carried. Paul had seen their kind a thousand times before: anarchists, rioters, troublemakers. Wasting away the day in a dark, basement bar somewhere, they'd got drunk and riled each other up, wound themselves tight like a coil. They'd convinced themselves that this was right, that going on a rampage was what the city deserved, what the people needed. In truth it meant most of them would be dead before the end of the day, but probably not before taking a few innocents with them.

'Owen, get behind me,' Paul said, shepherding his brother away from the edge of the pavement. They had come too far out into the open; the mob only had to look up to see them. There was an alleyway across the street, but Paul knew they would have to run. 'Be ready, Owen. When I say...'

Up ahead, he saw one man toss a glass bottle at the mini-mart window. There was a loud crash and then flames burst out through the shattered glass, spitting at the approaching men who flinched back, laughing and shouting. As the flames eased, they started forward again. Several covered their faces and rushed inside. Paul heard shouts and cries, and then some of the men reemerged, arms laden with canned food, bottled drinks, and over-the-counter medical supplies.

A gunshot sounded inside, followed by a cry, then another shot. Moments later two thugs dragged a man who could only be the shopkeeper out into the street. Another man was trying to wrestle something out of the shopkeeper's hand when the gun went off again and the looter went down. He screamed as blood pooled around him.

Frozen to the spot, Paul said, 'Owen, don't look!'

'They're setting fire to him! We have to stop them!'

Paul watched as two looters held the struggling shopkeeper down while another splashed something out of a bottle over the man's clothes. The same man pulled a small box from his pocket and lit a match.

'No!' Owen screamed as the man dropped the match and the shopkeeper's clothes ignited, engulfing him in flames. The shopkeeper screamed. The two looters jumped out of the way as the body writhed, burned. One man laughed as he batted at a spark that had caught on his jeans.

'Hey look!' someone else shouted. 'Gapers!'

The man who had shouted pointed towards them. He shouted something incomprehensible over the screams of the dying man.

'Owen, let's go. Quickly now.' Paul grabbed his brother's arm and together they dashed across the street and into the alley as several of the looters gave chase. With their pursuers drunk and laden with weapons and loot, Paul knew they had a good chance of escape, but there was no telling what they might find around the next corner, or the next.

'Where are we going? Home is the other way!'

'Exactly!'

Owen's school bag was slowing them down. Paul tried to keep it over his shoulder while pulling his brother with the other hand, but it kept slipping off. He wanted to jettison it, but the cost of replacing Owen's books was more than he could afford. If he didn't have the money, Owen couldn't go to school. Paul didn't know what the future held for either of them, but he was convinced Owen had far more chance with a little education.

But he was huffing. What he did at night to keep them fed and clothed was most of the exercise he got, and mostly he just closed his eyes and tried to blank things out. 'Owen, I can't run anymore. We have to hide.'

'Where?'

The alley intersected with another smaller one and Paul dragged Owen down it. 'Down here, we can hide behind those bins.'

'Paul, no, are you stupid?' Owen tried to protest as Paul hauled him along, deeper into the dark concrete crevasse, past upturned dustbins and piles of old furniture.

It was too late. Paul had fallen into the old alley trap. He had hoped to be out of sight before the looters spotted them, but the junk in their way had made progress too slow. They heard a couple of men run past, but another stopped and turned to follow.

It was the one who had set the shopkeeper on fire. His age was difficult to determine, his face scarred and soiled as it was. He might have been fifty or fifteen. 'Well, look what we have here,' he snarled, giving them a sour grin. He swayed drunkenly, a piece of metal pipe in one hand.

'Get behind me, Owen,' Paul said, closing on the looter, not giving the other man time to think, to formulate a plan. He wished he had his clawboard with him to use as a weapon, because even though he didn't ride anymore he usually took it to St. Cannerwells with him as a kind of ceremonial memento, but after riding this morning he had gone home first. The others carried theirs everywhere like a badge, but Paul found the extra weight unnecessary, especially when he met Owen after school.

He reached out for whatever he could find, and his hands closed over the bent wheel of an old bicycle. He pulled it in front of him like a shield, unsure how much use it would be against the looter's pipe.

'You boys got any money?' the looter said, voice slurring a little. He smacked the pipe into his palm. 'That looks like a school bag you've got there. Hand it over and I won't fuck you up too bad.'

Paul heard the sounds of sirens in the distance. 'Back off,' he said. 'The police are coming, and probably the DCA. They'll get you.'

'Those fucking idiots? No chance. Not before you and your gay little brother here bite it.'

Paul's heart was thumping. The bicycle wheel shook in his hands. He wasn't much of a fighter; he had other means he used to get out of most trouble. He had no idea what to do if the man came for him, but so long as Owen got away...

Something grey flew past his face. The triangle of concrete hit the looter's shoulder, throwing him off balance. He grunted and swung the pipe at Paul, who managed to half block it with the bicycle wheel. He stumbled sideways against the alley wall and the bicycle wheel fell out of his hands. He started to raise his hands in a useless gesture of defense, but then Owen was beside him, something metallic in his hands. His brother screamed a war cry and jabbed his weapon at the looter's stomach. There was a meaty squelch. The looter gasped and stumbled, then Owen was stabbing him again. Paul grabbed the man's metal pipe and landed a weak punch on the man's cheek.

The looter went down. His hands clutched at the screwdriver handle that protruded at an odd angle from a wet hole in his t-shirt.

Owen wasn't done. While Paul watched in horror, his brother grabbed the discarded metal pipe and slammed it down on the man's nose. Blood sprayed across Paul's shoes and he jerked back out of the way. 'Jesus Christ, Owen–'

'Come on!' Owen shouted. 'We've got to get out of here! The pigs are coming!' He kicked the looter square in the face, and Paul was dismayed to see a couple of the man's teeth fall loose. 'Fuck you, man!' Owen shouted and aimed to kick the looter again but Paul dragged him backwards.

'Owen, what did you do...?'

'Nothing he didn't deserve. Now let's get out of here.'

Owen tugged on his arm and Paul let himself be dragged away. Behind them, the looter groaned, trying to pull the screwdriver free. Paul was sure that would only cause the flow of more blood, speeding up his fate.

His brother had effectively just killed a man.

They dashed out of the alley, crossed the street and slipped through a small city park, overgrown with weeds and with pulled-up swings lying on their sides across the path. On the other side of the park they slipped down a quieter residential street, then another, and finally the sirens and the shouts of the looters were gone or too distant to fear.

Paul stopped and grabbed his brother's arm. He swung Owen round to face him. While he knew his brother had maybe saved them both, he was angry.

'What did you do back there, Owen? Is that what Mum or Dad would want from you?'

'Someone had to do something,' Owen looked at his shoes, a kid again.

'That man might die because of what you did!'

'No, Paul. He'll *probably* die. I say fuck him. Eye for an eye, Paul,' Owen said, looking up, his eyes defiant.

Paul flicked his ear. 'Don't get cocky with me! I know what he did, but that doesn't excuse you. Look at the mess this country's in. Perhaps if people just stopped hurting each other–'

'The government wouldn't have to worry. They could just continue to fuck with us as much as they want.'

'Where did you get that screwdriver from? We don't even have one in the house!'

'School.'

'You stole it?'

'They gave it to me.' Owen matched his brother's stare. 'Yeah, that's right. The teachers at my school gave me, and everyone else, a screwdriver. Said to use them to protect ourselves if necessary. Said they were sorry they couldn't give us anything better, but that's all they could get.'

'Seriously? What the hell kind of school is that?'

'They're teaching us to survive. They said to twist it as you shove it in because it causes more internal damage and is harder to pull out. We practice in Lifeskills class on old armchairs.'

Paul was flabbergasted. 'Your school is allowed to teach that?'

Owen shook his head. 'Not all of the teachers know. Only one or two. But we trust them, because they look out for us. Like you do for me. Like you *try* to do.'

Paul had a sudden moment of realization. Owen was right. It had been the looter or them, and they had won. He smiled, and the tension was broken. 'You know, I was only two seconds away from sticking that guy myself.'

'Oh, *really*. What with? That bicycle wheel?'

'Yeah, I was going to ram it over his head. Then I was going to pickpocket your screwdriver and stick him with it.'

Owen laughed, a comforting sound. 'You'd never be able to get me like you do all those rich people.'

Paul smiled, forced it to look convincing. Picking pockets was what he said he did down around Piccadilly, Westminster, and Charing Cross at night. That's where he said their money came from. Owen didn't need to know any different, didn't need to know the truth.

'Can we get dinner now?' Owen asked.

'Sure.'

Paul put an arm around his brother's shoulders, surprised at just how tall Owen was getting. Maybe it wasn't so unusual for Owen to protect him anymore. He certainly had better survival skills than Paul had.

As he led his brother away, he hoped that the fish n' chips shop hadn't been looted by a different mob. He was starving.

Chapter Five
Dreggo

Dan pulled the cap off the cola bottle and took a long swig, coughing right after. He retched, spitting bile on the ground. The cola was long gone, and Dan had filled the bottle with rum instead, using the soft drink bottle as cover to keep away any alcoholics or drunks more desperate than he was. Alcohol was difficult to procure, and hard liquor had a high price. Dan, who earned enough to stay alive by selling marijuana and black-market cigarettes in the dark recesses outside major train stations, had taken himself to a new level with the rum. In the aftermath of breaking his association with the Tube Riders, he had needed something to reaffirm himself.

Now, with the black fuel burning inside of him, he was searching for a new association.

He had wanted to be part of a gang. Gangs were everything in London, comradeship and protection. Allowed into the circle of the Tube Riders, Dan had felt whole again, the meandering of his life from one mistake to another forgotten for a while. The gang had given him purpose, and he had wanted to be one of them so much.

Cast out, the only thing he could think of was to destroy them.

Paul ... they were friends but Dan had never trusted him much. They hung around the same regrettable places at night, and while Dan knew what Paul did, he had seemed like a cool guy otherwise. Paul had said he knew some guys who hung out, asked Dan to come along. Said they were straight up, and Dan had taken a chance. Simon, he'd thought was cool. A bit feminine, but cool. And Marta ... with near-black hair that was a mixture of braid and dread framing that cute, pale little face, those bright, smart eyes that saw everything ... and with her body tight from all that tube riding, he had been pretty hopeful they would get it on. God knew he needed something to keep him warm at night, and he could have handled a piece of that no problem. She would have done nicely.

Yeah, Simon was cool, and Marta was hot. And Paul, well, he was okay.

That mutilated bastard Switch, though, him with the swagger and the look-how-fucking-good-I-am attitude, Dan would happily see him go under a train. Would do the pushing himself if chance allowed it.

He knew that by coming here he might get the others hurt. He didn't really want that but they came together, and if they had to fall together, then so be it. Dan wanted the final word; no one would mock him again. No one would laugh at him; no one would ever imply he wasn't good enough, just because he slipped.

'Fuck you, you fucked-eye bastard,' he muttered, swigging on the rum, seeing the entrance to the old London Underground station coming up ahead of him.

Bartholomew Road had been closed for fourteen years, but now he saw the metal gate stood open, a space there wide enough for a man to pass through. With the last of the rum clutched close to his chest, Dan squeezed through and headed down the stairs.

The smell was the same as St. Cannerwells, the scent of decomposing takeout mingling with *eau de* unwashed tramp. There was less litter here, a sign of more frequent passing.

Bartholomew Road was the third station he had tried today. Wapping Road and Coldharbour Avenue had both been quiet and empty with no sign of habitation. There were dozens of abandoned Underground stations across London GUA; he had known his search might only lead him as far as the rum lasted. But here, as he passed through the dusty, broken ticket gates, he heard the sound of voices up ahead.

Had he been more sober he might have taken more care, but with the rum sloshing around inside of him, Dan stumbled down the stairs and out on to the platform as though he were rushing to catch the last train.

A group of people inhabited the shadows at the far end of the platform. He staggered closer to them as a familiar roar built up in the tunnel. He glanced back, and saw those terrifying, demonic eyes rushing towards him.

Drunk, his hands flexed, feeling for the clawboard he'd tossed away, while further down the platform, a row of people crouched down like sprinters at the start of a race.

Dan slipped behind a support pillar and leaned out to watch the Cross Jumpers in action. As the train rushed out of the tunnel they set off, sprinting towards the platform's edge, moving in a staggered line, the nearest to him starting first, with each following jumper starting a fraction later in an unfolding human fan.

At the far end, one or two other people had started off far earlier than the others, their run-ups longer. Dan recognised them for what they were, because he'd been one amongst the Tube Riders: practicing novices, trying to become good enough to gain acceptance from the rest of the group.

The train roared along the platform. Dan winced as the Cross Jumpers disappeared in front of it like flies in the face of a battering ram. He listened for the sound of their impact, expecting a blunt thud as their bodies broke apart against the train's flat nose, but he heard nothing at all until the end. It was barely perceptible, a hard knock, like someone's hand on a wooden door.

As the train vanished into the far tunnel, Dan saw the Cross Jumpers now stood on the opposite platform. One or two lay on the ground, others stood around, brushing themselves off. Near the far end, a group had clustered around the platform edge, looking down. There were curses, gasps of shock, and the sound of a girl crying.

'Garth broke twenty-five feet!' Someone nearby shouted. 'That's a medal there!'

And further away, the voice higher, verging on panic: 'Petey missed! Petey didn't make it!'

Other people not active in the jump jogged towards the far end of the platform.

'Oh God,' someone shouted. 'What do we do with him? Dreggo? *Dreggo!*'

Dan arched his neck, trying to see their leader. Then something struck him hard in the back, and he stumbled out from his hiding place, dropping the bottle on the ground.

'Look what I found here!' someone said behind him. 'I got us a spy!'

Dan looked round to see a muscular, shaven-head man with a black tattoo of a hawk to the side of his left eye. Sober, Dan would have put up a decent fight, but drunk he had no chance. He grunted as a fist slammed into his face and he sprawled forward on to the ground.

'Pick him up, Maul.'

'He just watched Petey die, Dreggo. Want me to throw him under the next one?'

'I said, *pick him up.*'

'Okay, okay.' Strong hands pulled Dan to his feet. His face ached under his right eye, but as he went to rub it he found his arms clamped to his side.

A young woman of no more than eighteen or twenty stepped in front of him. She was slim, with long hair that framed her face, and a hawk tattoo beside both eyes. If they were a sign of authority then Maul was merely a henchman.

She smiled and reached up to cup Dan's face. Her skin was smooth but icy cold.

'You just watched one of our group die,' the girl said, in a soothing, serpentine voice. 'Tell me why I shouldn't have Maul do as he suggested.'

'I didn't–'

Dreggo's other hand came across hard, and Dan recoiled from the shock of the blow, the rum doing little to mask the pain. She hit harder than the goon did.

'Don't waste time lying to me.' The hand holding Dan's chin squeezed tighter. 'Answer my question.'

'I want to join you.'

'Is that so?'

'Yeah. And–'

'And *what?*'

'And I want you to help me.'

With a flick of her hair Dreggo laughed. It was cold, like her hands. 'Um, why? Give me one reason. This really is your last chance. It doesn't bother me if you live or die.'

'I'm a Tube Rider.'

Dan felt Maul's hands tighten on his shoulders and begin to pull him away. In front of him, Dreggo's eyes thinned, her face going hard.

'*Was* a Tube Rider,' Dan corrected.

'Let go of him, Maul.'

The hands dropped. Dan allowed himself to breathe. 'I left them, and –'

'So you've broken their code by coming here. Regardless of what I feel about the Tube Riders, breaking codes is something we don't believe in. Breaking the code of the Cross Jumpers means death under the trains.' Dreggo took a step away from Dan and waved an arm back towards the platform. Her arms too, bore a number of tattoos. He caught a glimpse of her inner elbow, and saw the scars of old needle track marks there.

'They have their code, and we have ours. But one thing links both – community. If you become a Tube Rider or a Cross Jumper you join a family. Our two families might feud, but dishonour is something we both understand.' She gestured behind him. 'Maul, take him to the track.'

'I know where they are,' Dan blurted.

He heard the intake of her breath, sharp, desperate. 'Wait. Maul, leave us a moment.'

'Are you sure?'

'Yes.'

The big man shot a dark look at Dan and lumbered away towards the other Cross Jumpers, most of whom were looking down at Petey's body. Some were openly crying now, others were comforting each other, cursing, punching the concrete pillars in anger. Dan wondered if the other Tube Riders would have acted like this had it been him lying down there on the tracks. He didn't think so.

'So, you know where they ride now,' Dreggo said. 'While I pity your disloyalty, I admit this is information I want.'

'And what do I get in return?'

Dreggo smiled. Despite the coldness of her eyes she was attractive. *Pretty face, nice ass, pert tits*, he thought, *tucked away under that t-shirt of hers*. She wasn't in the same league as Marta, but she would do well enough. The act of being completely asexual and robotic might be something she just kept up around her goon army.

'Aside from keeping your life?' Dreggo said.

'I want to join you,' Dan repeated.

Dreggo gave him a condescending smile. 'Really? Well, it is normal for there to be an initiation.'

'What?'

'Do you understand what we do here, er – what's your name?'

'Dan.'

'*Dan.*' She rolled the name across her tongue like a piece of candy. Her tongue flicked out and ran across her lips, and she gave him a thin smile. *Oh yeah*, Dan thought, staring into her eyes like a hypnotist's victim. *I definitely would.*

'I know what you do,' he said aloud. 'You jump across the tracks as the train comes in.'

She cocked her head. 'In a nutshell. Do you know how we choose a leader?' Dan shook his head. 'We mark the point at which we jump,' she said. 'And the point that the front edge of the train has reached at the moment of the jump. An average length is between thirty and forty feet for a normal train, higher for an express. The holder of the shortest jump ... is leader. And,' she added, 'remains so until that jump is either beaten or the leader dies.'

'What did you jump?'

'Did I say you could question me?' Her hand shot up and her index finger stabbed into Dan's cheek just below the bone. He flinched back. 'But for the record, I jumped twelve feet. No one else has ever jumped under twenty.' She smiled, dropping her hand again. 'And landed with all their limbs.'

Dan knew about the dismount lengths that characterised tube riding. 'How–'

'Did I do it?' Dreggo stepped closer to him and glared into his eyes. He felt a mixture of arousal and fear. She stared at him until he looked away. With his gaze on the ground, she said, 'Because the day I made that jump, I didn't want to make it to the other side.'

He couldn't help but look up at her, his mouth dropping open in shock.

'I wanted to die,' she said, her voice barely a whisper. She leaned close, her breath tickling his ear. It too, was icy cold. Further down the platform Dan caught a glimpse of Maul looking decidedly pissed off.

'I had no fear of it,' she breathed into his ear. 'You know what life is like in London GUA, don't you, Dan? You have your nightmares, I'm sure. Let me tell you mine.' She ran a hand through her hair. 'Do you remember the riots three years ago?'

He did. In the summer of 2072 some spy had got hold of a secret government file and a list of possible informers was pasted up on every lamp post or bus shelter in central London. Mobs had looted and smashed up the city, lynching those people named in the list who hadn't gone to ground quickly enough. He remembered seeing people burned alive, noosed up off street lamps, beaten to death. The DCA had engaged in pitched battles with gangs of rioters and hundreds were killed. It was a wonder the Huntsman hadn't been deployed to make it worse.

He said dourly, 'How could I forget.'

'My father's name was one of those printed,' she said, and he could hear the sadness in her voice. 'He hadn't done anything. He was just a postal worker who worked in the recorded post section, and somehow his name had gotten on that list. Didn't matter. I came home to find my parents dead. My mother had been thrown from the top of the stairs and had broken her neck. My father had been tied to our kitchen table and gutted with a bread knife.'

Dan squeezed his eyes shut. 'That's fucked.'

'Yes, it is. The worst thing, though, was that the looters were still there. In my parents' room, in the basement, searching for anything of value they could find. They were just about done, their hands full of some money my dad had secreted away, and my mother's jewelry. And then I walked through the door. I was fifteen. I'd just come home from school.' She gave a bitter laugh. 'It must have been like Christmas.'

Dan risked a glance at her, and was surprised not to see a single tear in her eyes. Her face was cold, hard like stone.

'There were six of them. By the time the first three or four were done, I was past caring. When they'd all had their fill, they beat the living shit out of me and kicked me out on to the street like a piece of junk. Then they torched my house.'

Tears welled in Dan's eyes. He suddenly regretted coming here. Regretted it very much.

'Things got worse,' she continued. 'The usual downward spiral. I took drugs to blank it out, ended up homeless, whoring myself for money. What I really wanted was to die, I just didn't know how. Then, three months ago, a guy who called himself my boyfriend dragged me down here, promising a new high. When I saw those trains and what people were doing, I saw my chance to escape. I jumped at that train, wanting it to end me. But when I landed on the other side, it was like I had passed through a wall. I had emerged into a new world.'

Dan didn't know what to say. Behind them, a train roared through the station, leaving more screams and tears in its aftermath, as the gradual job of clearing away Petey's remains began.

'I put a knife in my boyfriend's heart as we lay together that night. And since then I have hunted and killed every one of those men who hurt me and slaughtered my family. Cross jumping gave me peace. And in return, I will protect it.' She turned and walked a few steps away from him.

'The Tube Riders play a game,' she continued. 'They hang from the sides of the trains like kids on a climbing frame. The Cross Jumpers joust with death itself. You make it, you live. You miss – like Petey did – you die. Our only game is to see how close to death we can get.'

Dan remembered the way the Tube Riders had talked about the Cross Jumpers, that cross jumping was considered easy, that having no contact with the trains at all was an easy way out, but Dreggo had impressed him. Perhaps coming here hadn't been such a bad idea after all. If nothing else, he wanted to join them just to be near her.

He waited until she turned around, then he looked up. It took him a moment to speak because his heart was beating so hard. 'So? Am I in?'

'Tell me where the Tube Riders are, and I'll let you take the initiation.'

'What–'

She turned back towards him, a knife in her hand. 'This is the knife I used to gut those men,' she said. 'The way they did my father. Only I made sure it took them a lot longer to die.' She rubbed a finger along the blade, and a little trickle of blood appeared on her skin. 'I'll let you take the initiation, *if you tell me where the Tube Riders are.*'

He hesitated only a second. 'St. Cannerwells,' he said, voice shaking.

The knife vanished. The same hand rubbed Dreggo's nose. Her thin brow furrowed. 'I don't know that one,' she said.

'It's on the old Piccadilly Line, two or three stops past West Green. There's only one entrance left, at the top of St. Cannerwells Park, opposite a boarded-up launderette.'

Dreggo stroked her chin, and the seductive tone was back. 'My, my, keen to sell out our friends, aren't we?'

'They're not my friends,' Dan said quickly. 'They didn't want me.'

'Who is their leader?'

'They don't have one.'

'Every gang has a leader.'

Dan felt a sudden pang of disgust with himself, but the words were already on his tongue. 'It guess it would be Marta. Yeah, their leader is called Marta.'

'Hmm.' Dreggo turned back to him. 'Okay, you can have your chance.' She turned. 'Maul! This one is going to take the initiation. Let's see if he has what it takes to become a Cross Jumper.'

Maul jogged over. He pulled something from his pocket and handed it to Dreggo. It looked like a black scarf.

'Come with me,' Dreggo said.

Dan followed Dreggo along the platform with Maul trailing behind them both. The other Cross Jumpers parted at their approach, stepping away from Dreggo as though they held her in reverence. Dan noticed the sorrow on many of the faces, the tears still fresh. The others had told him that tube riding was about fun, the rush, the excitement. What was this, where it was so easy to get killed?'

'Come here.' Dreggo went to stand behind Dan. She covered his eyes with the scarf, tying it tightly around the back of his head.

'What are you doing?'

'This is the initiation, Dan. To see if you have what it takes to jump with us. You are seven good strides from the edge of the platform. When the next train comes, you will jump across in front of it. Blindfolded.'

'You have got to be joking.' Dan suddenly didn't feel drunk anymore. He started to pull the blindfold off his face, but felt her knife press against his throat.

'You have made your decision, Dan. Stick to it. Everyone here has done it, as have many before them whose honour you threaten to undermine.'

'I can't–'

'Yes, you can. Listen for the train. You'll hear it come out of the tunnel. You have about eight seconds before it passes you, but you're not looking for a jump distance here. Just to get across. I suggest you start to run as soon as you hear it.'

'How far is it?'

'About ten feet. The biggest problem with Cross Jumping is that we can only do it with single track lines. Try and jump a double track and you just land on the far set of rails.' She chuckled. 'Ouch.'

'Dreggo, one's coming!'

'Okay, Dan, you get one shot at this. Chicken out, and it's over. Jump, and you're one of us.'

'Holy fuck...'

Dan braced himself as he heard the roar building up in the tunnel. This was his chance, his chance to make it as a Cross Jumper, to be accepted. His one chance. He had no doubt that Dreggo would kill him if he didn't try, so it was jackpot or bust. He steeled himself, praying that the lingering effect of the rum would give him enough courage to make it across.

The train burst out of the tunnel with a roar he knew well. Dan kicked off, counting his steps towards the platform edge aloud.

'One ... two ... three ... four ... five...'

He braced himself to jump–

#

In three quick steps Dreggo reached the platform edge, just to the side of Dan as he started to run. She heard him counting under his breath. Good, he was really trying. A shame he'd never make it.

As Dan came level with her, she stuck out her left foot.

Dan gasped as he overbalanced, his forward momentum sending him over the edge and down on to the tracks. There was a thud as he landed: the breath knocked out of him. He didn't have time to cry out. He groaned, managed to prop himself up on one elbow, then the train was on him. It thundered past in a blur, wheels clacking over the tracks. Dan, as a human being at least, was done.

As the train roared away into the far tunnel, Dreggo looked down at the tracks, at the mess that remained of the former Tube Rider. Within twenty trains or so, there would be little left but blood, and rats would clean that up. She turned back to the other Cross Jumpers, many of whom were staring at her open-mouthed, horrorstruck. Her predecessor as leader, Billy Lees, looked like he was meditating at the back, arms folded, head down. He was right not to look at her; any sign of dissent would line him up as the next to fall. Dreggo had more tricks than just sticking out her foot.

One or two others, Maul included, watched her in a solid show of support. Maul, she knew, would have done it for her, had she asked. He would do anything he thought might get him closer to her bed, but it would never happen. The pleasure Dreggo felt from her body had been taken from her long ago by the looters and worse that she hadn't needed to tell Dan. It was something she used as a tool occasionally for personal gain; she would never again use it for love or pleasure.

Almost twenty, she counted in total, as they stood before her, waiting for her to speak. Not so bad, and there were a few not here today. Far better than the Tube Riders, who numbered — what had he said — four? Just four. It wouldn't take much, she knew, to get rid of them. All she had to do was ensure that their disappearance didn't encourage their legend any further, that they were shown up to be what they were, a group of unenviable misfits with too much time on their hands. Then of course, with the Tube Riders out of their way, the Cross Jumpers could start working on their own legend.

'Listen up,' she said. She waited until all their eyes were on her. 'That man, Dan, claimed to be a Tube Rider. He is not dead now because he was a Tube Rider, though that might be reason enough. He is dead because he betrayed those close to him. Let this be a warning to you. Anyone who does the same to the Cross Jumpers will suffer the same fate, or worse. If you betray the Cross Jumpers, I will find you. Do you understand?'

There were murmurs of assent. Eyes fell to the ground below her gaze.

'Petey died today with honour. Petey wanted to prove himself strong enough to run with the Cross Jumpers. He gave us the greatest honour he could give by risking his life for us, and it saddens me that he is dead. He failed, but he will be remembered. This day should have been Petey's day, but instead it has been stolen from him by this coward whose blood, as we speak, mixes with Petey's pure blood and taints it. We will remember Petey for giving his life as a Cross Jumper, and we will also remember this dissenter who dared wear the name "Tube Rider".' She spread her arms wide. 'The Tube Riders are my enemies, as they are yours. But until this day I respected them. I respected them for what they did, for what they are, for what they have become. But I respect them no longer. I'm embarrassed to think that they soil the same places we use for cross-jumping. It *hurts* me.'

There were more murmurs of assent. Maul punched the air and shouted, 'Yeah!'

'Thankfully, this fool's life was not entirely wasted. Before he died, he told me where we can find them.'

There was a ripple of excitement across the crowd.

'So tomorrow...' Dreggo paused for dramatic effect. 'We hunt.'

The crowd erupted into cheers.

Chapter Six
Training

'EVERYONE, THIS IS JESSICA. My, um, friend.' Simon waved a shy hand at her, looking uncomfortable with their scrutinizing eyes on him. Paul looked just as flustered as Simon, while Marta wore an amused smile. Switch wasn't looking at him at all, but was over by the platform edge, staring down at the tracks and muttering under his breath.

'His *girl*friend,' Jess corrected, giving a smile of her own at Simon's awkwardness. 'And call me Jess.'

'Nice to meet you, Jess,' Marta said, reaching out to shake the other girl's hand. 'Marta. Short for Martina, but God, I hate that. Sounds like a shit type of car.'

Jess laughed. 'I can't decide if "Jessica" sounds more like a doll or a bar of soap.'

'I'm Paul, short for, um, Paul.' He shook her hand too.

'Switch?' Simon said, looking back at the little man as he continued to examine the tracks.

'Is she cool, Simon?' Switch asked without turning around. 'We can't have another bailer on our hands.'

'Huh, what are you, a Cross Jumper?'

Switch turned quickly, eyes firing. 'Don't say that.'

'Well, ease off the inquisition.'

'Hi, I'm Switch,' he said without coming closer.

'Hi.'

Switch nodded then turned away. He started to walk along the platform edge.

'Wow, he's a little—'

'Sharp?' Marta finished. 'Yeah, he is. Sharp as the knife he carries. He's a loyal friend, but he's under no illusions about the world up there.' She cocked her head towards the ceiling. 'Be nice to him, but don't expect him to be nice back, for a while. It takes time to earn his trust. He doesn't hand it out easily.'

Jess shrugged. 'Sounds like he has it right. Trust kills, some people say.'

'Maybe,' Marta said. 'But some of us prefer to maintain a higher level of optimism.'

'Sure. Why do you call him Switch?'

'See that twitch in his eye?'

'Couldn't miss it.'

'Steve's twitch. Over time, *Switch*.'

'Oh. That makes sense, I suppose.' Jess looked around her. 'Are you the leader?'

Marta grinned. 'What? The leader of fat boy, thin boy, and weird boy? Lucky me.' She shrugged. 'My older brother, Leo, was the first Tube Rider, but we're just a group of friends.'

'We don't really have a leader,' Simon said.

'No,' Paul agreed. 'There's nothing much to be decided except when to go home. We do have an order of seniority, though. Kind of like a code. Marta's been here the longest, so she rides first. Simon comes next, then Switch, then me.'

'There are just four of you?' Jess asked.

Marta looked away towards Switch, now standing down by the breakfall mats. 'There used to be more. Things happen, though. Some people drift away, others get scared, or lose interest.'

'What happened to your brother?'

Paul and Simon tensed, and Jess immediately wondered if she'd said the wrong thing. Marta, though, just gave her an easy smile, and Jess found herself warming to the other girl quickly. 'He disappeared,' Marta said. 'I don't know what happened to him, and the speculation kills me. I try not to think about him, and being here, doing this thing he started, strangely enough it helps to put him out of my mind.'

'Hey, I'm sorry.'

'We all have our horror stories. Even you, I suppose.'

'My father works for the government. I don't know what he does, but every day I worry that he won't come home. My mother, too. She works in a bank. My family, inside the protective gates and security locks and bulletproof glass, we live a normal life. Not many people have that, and I fear losing it so much I could just ...' She trailed off, feeling tears she didn't want to show start to come. She gritted her teeth and clenched her fists at her sides, determined not to cry in front of Simon's friends.

Marta patted her shoulder. 'Easy, easy. We know. We understand.' She took a step back and spread her hands. 'Welcome to the Tube Riders.'

'Thanks.'

'So, Simon, are you going to get her started or what?'

'I don't know. I just wanted her to meet you guys.'

'Can I try?'

Marta put an arm around her shoulders. 'Not until you know what you're doing. We don't want you getting hurt. Even then it's entirely your choice to ride. You're welcome to just come and hang out.' She smiled. 'But if you want an idea of what it's like, come this way.'

She led Jess up the platform, beneath the stairs to the blocked second exit, and through an opening in the wall beside the platform edge which led into a maintenance tunnel. The emergency lighting was dimmer here. The sound of dripping water came from back in the dark.

'Why are there lights on?' Jess asked. 'Doesn't the government turn them off?'

Paul said, 'Even though the station is closed now, the trains still follow the same rules as when it was operating. They have to slow down as they enter the station, and the lights are kept on so that the trains can see it as they come in.'

'That's *his* theory,' Simon said. 'I just think the government forgot to turn them off. It's not like they have much control over stuff, is it?'

Marta had her hands on her hips. 'Enough of the history lesson, boys. It's study time.'

She reached up and took hold of a water pipe about a foot above her head. 'This pipe runs straight for about thirty feet. It's about the same height as the rail you have to catch on the trains. So...'

Marta handed Jess her clawboard. 'You can try with mine. It's a bit lighter than the others.'

Jess took the offered board and turned it over in her hands. The wood was thinner than Simon's, and the outside face was painted silver. It looked polished, better maintained than his. It also had two hooks instead of one, with a small space in the middle. 'What do you want me to do?'

Marta pointed. 'Start running from over there. Try to get into a sprint going parallel to the pipe. When you're moving as fast as you can, angle in sharply and jump. Lift up the board and try to hook the pipe. Here, hold the board like this.' She helped Jess hook her arms through the leather straps. 'Okay, go on then. Have a try.'

Jess looked nervously back at Simon. He didn't look too happy but he forced a *good luck* smile. 'Well, here goes…'

She backed up a few steps and then sprinted forward as Marta had instructed. About halfway along the pipe she darted inwards, leapt, hooked, and caught. She pulled her feet up off the ground, slid a few inches and stopped, hanging from the pipe like a bat in an old industrial factory. She looked back. 'Well?'

Simon pouted. 'That was okay. I think you understand the basic concept but you probably need to work on your technique a bit.'

Marta laughed. 'He's just jealous because it took him about ten attempts on his first day.'

'It wasn't ten,' Simon said. 'It was more like, I don't know … six?'

'Maybe you're a natural,' Paul said.

Marta pointed back along the platform. 'Again,' she said. 'Do it again.'

Jess did, again landing safely on the pipe. Then, at Marta's prompt, one more time and one more, until Jess had lost count. By the time Marta called a halt, Jess was out of breath and her arms ached, but she was doing it smoothly, with barely a sound.

'Now, the dismount,' Marta said. 'You're not jumping off a pipe, you're jumping off a train moving at anything up to sixty miles an hour. Get it wrong and you die, it's as simple as that.'

Jess looked shocked. She glared at Simon. 'You didn't say people died.'

He looked away, his cheeks reddening. 'I didn't want to put you off.'

She glared at him a moment and then shrugged. 'Try and stop me doing it, more like.' She grinned. 'I guess you're probably as likely to die crossing the streets these days.'

Marta nodded. 'Like I said, there's no pressure for you to do it for real. You can help Paul keep score if you like.'

Jess glanced at Paul. Simon had told her they were the same age but Paul didn't look like a man barely out of his teens. He could have passed for forty with his receding hair, glasses and middle-age spread. She hadn't like to say so, but she couldn't imagine him running, leaping out and then hanging off the side of a moving train. He wasn't exactly athletic, but she supposed looks could be deceiving, sometimes intentionally so.

'Paul doesn't ride?' she asked.

Paul looked sheepish. 'I hurt myself, and it's difficult to ride now.'

'He hurt his mind,' Simon said. 'The rest healed. It's psychological.'

'Okay, enough,' Marta said, scowling at him. She turned back to Jess. 'You all right? You want to have a break? I didn't mean to turn into a boot camp sergeant or anything—'

'No, I'm good. Let's nail this.'

Jess hated the way a lot of people saw her as some frilly-dress Daddy's girl. The neighbours all felt she was privileged, particularly with the home security system that made them the only family on the street which could sleep in peace. She felt a constant urge to prove herself, and now, in the presence of Simon's friends, she felt the same desire.

While she had been practicing, Switch had been riding alone over on the far platform. She'd seen him clinging to the side of the train like a bug on a tree branch, and it looked exhilarating. She wanted to do it more than anything now, and she wanted to do it better than any of them.

'When you dismount,' Marta said, 'you have to brace your legs on the side of the train, and push your board in and up at the same time as you push upwards with your feet. You can't just pull the board off. It's caught on the rail, and the only way to unhook it is to push it in and flick it off in one motion.'

'Kind of like undoing a bra,' Paul said.

'Didn't realise you wore one,' Simon scoffed.

Paul grinned. Jess noticed how Marta watched them with a wry smile the way a mother might watch her kids. Marta was pretty, but the brief pang of jealousy Jess had felt when they had first met had gone. The Tube Riders were more like a family.

'Try it on this pipe over here. It's a little lower, but it's nearer the wall so you can brace better. On a real train there's only a slight curve on the outside of the carriage, so the rail you hang from is about the same level as your feet. This means you are leaning backwards, making the pressure on the clawboard greater. All of which means it's easy to stay attached, but difficult to get off.'

Jess hooked the pipe and braced her feet on the wall. 'Okay, so up and out. How do I land?'

'Usually on your back, but if there aren't any breakfall mats there, you have to roll.'

Jess stared. 'You're joking, right?'

Marta shook her head. 'I wish. If the train's going slow enough it's not a problem, but on a train going at speed, if you try to land on your feet you're going to break something, or worse, damage your back with the impact. When you dismount, you have to turn your body in the direction the train is going and pull your clawboard into your body like a shield. Duck your head in to protect it. Keep your legs straight. If you do it right, it doesn't hurt so much because your forward momentum is so great you just kind of touch down. Like a plane.'

'It hurts?'

Marta looked pained. 'Always. But do it right and it won't hurt too much.'

'It's the reason we have the big stack of mattresses at the end of the platform,' Simon said, pointing towards them. 'Something nice and soft to land on.'

'I'll catch you the first time,' Marta said, going to stand behind her.

Jess grimaced. 'Okay, well here goes.' She reached up and hooked the board over the second pipe, bracing her feet on the wall. She took a deep breath, then kicked up and pushed the board in and upwards as Marta had instructed. She kicked a little hard though, and fell back into Marta. For a moment Marta had a hold of her – Jess marveled at how strong the other girl's hands felt – then Marta lost her balance and they both landed in a heap on the floor.

'Ow!' Jess muttered. 'I banged my bloody elbow.'

Marta, who appeared to be unhurt, laughed as she stood up. 'Not bad for a first attempt. You don't need to kick quite so hard, but it was good.'

Simon helped Jess up. 'Are you all right?'

Jess brushed herself down and nodded. 'I'll live.'

'Do you want to rest for a bit? Watch us do a few rides?'

Jess smiled. 'Nope. I want to ride with you.'

'Well, I don't know that you're ready yet.'

Jess shrugged. 'Come on, let's go see what–'

She broke off at the sound of a shout and running feet in their direction. Switch was bolting along the platform towards them, his clawboard hung loose in one hand. 'Quick!' he shouted. 'We've got a problem!'

Chapter Seven
Confrontation

'HURRY!' DREGGO SHOUTED, waving an arm towards the entrance to St. Cannerwells Underground station. Spread out across the park like a net ready to close, the Cross Jumpers responded, slinking between the trees and along the cracked tarmac paths, closing on the small brick building at the top of the hill. Her scouts had seen the Tube Riders go inside a couple of hours ago. They had looked around for other entrances but found none. All the Cross Jumpers had arrived, and they had begun to close on the entrance when one of the Tube Riders had emerged at exactly the wrong time.

With her keen eyesight she had spotted him from the other side of the park, stepping out from the station entrance, immediately tensing, his sixth sense alerting him to danger. He had frozen just a second before feigning cool and calmly looking around, noticing several closing Cross Jumpers. He was good, she had to admit, the way he sauntered back inside as though he'd just stepped out for a cigarette and then changed his mind. Brought up on the hardest streets, she had no doubt, but too late. The Tube Riders were still trapped inside.

Moving through her trees to the left was Maul, a big sledgehammer held in both hands. It was his weapon of choice when it came to smashing up people who messed with him, the reason for his name. He glanced at her often, she noticed, and while she found it irritating, she appreciated the gesture. He was looking out for her, as usual, when out of all of them she was the one who needed it least. Muscular and mean though he was, Dreggo could make short work of him or any of the others. In fact, she didn't need their help at all, but she had to involve them in this if she wanted to maintain her control of the gang.

'When you get inside, spread out across the platform,' she growled to several Cross Jumpers as she reached the entrance. 'Make sure they have no escape routes. If they go into the tunnels, that's fine. They'll be mine then.'

Maul grinned inanely as he passed her. Others looked less excited about the prospect of a fight, but they were too scared to argue. They stuck together in twos and threes, and she hoped they would give each other strength.

Billy Lees went last. He gave her a long, cold look as he passed, longer than she felt was respectful. He had led the Cross Jumpers for more than three years before she showed up, and he didn't look happy about being back in the ranks. Her jaw tensed as she followed him inside.

#

Switch, doubled over, hands on his knees, was trying to get his breath back.

'I went outside to go get some drinks,' he said. 'But as I got to the top of the stairs I saw them coming. Lots of them. Armed with clubs and shit.'

'Who?'

'I think it's pretty obvious, don't you?'

Simon glanced at Paul and Marta. 'Are you sure they were coming in here?'

'Of course I'm fucking sure. They were headed straight for the station entrance.'

'How many?' Marta asked.

'I saw at least ten but there could have been more. They had knives, clubs, lengths of pipe, the usual street fight bullshit.'

'You could see their weapons?'

Switch shook his head. 'Didn't need to. I could see from the way they were walking what the fuckers were concealing.'

Jess's lip trembled. 'What do we do now?'

Switch rounded on her. 'Did they follow you here? Spies from Daddy?'

'No!'

Simon put up a hand. 'Switch, give it up.'

'Or what, Simon?'

'Just shut up!' Marta shouted. 'We've got bigger problems to worry about. I think we all know who they are and how they got here.'

Simon shook his head. 'How would Dan know how to find them?'

'I don't know, luck? Now shut up before they hear us, while there's still time to find somewhere to hide–'

'Too late,' Paul said quietly. 'They're here.'

As they peered out from behind the pillars, Marta saw the group descend the far stairs and spread themselves out. With the other exit long ago bulldozed and concreted over, there was no way out.

'We've got to go into the tunnels,' Simon said.

Marta turned to look at him. 'And go where?'

'I don't know, keep going until we reach the next station?'

'It's about three miles. We'd get chased down.'

'Or run down by the next express,' Paul added.

Simon glanced at Jess. The girl was looking down at her waist, fiddling with what looked like a money belt tied around her stomach. 'What are you doing?' he asked.

'You know, if we get in trouble, it's evidence–'

'You've got a digital camera?' Switch said, incredulous, pushing Simon out of the way. 'You were planning to get us on the fucking TV?'

Jess looked upset. 'I just wanted, you know, a memento of the occasion.'

'Dumb bitch,' Switch muttered, turning away.

'Hey!' Simon said, stepping towards him, but Marta silenced them both with a sharp: 'Now is *not* the time! They're coming closer!'

She glanced around the side of the pillar again and counted maybe fifteen people, spread out across the platform.

She turned to Switch. 'How long until the next train comes?'

'Huh, what?'

'The next train!'

He frowned. 'The last one was ... about four minutes, give or take.'

'Okay, that's enough. I have a plan. Jess, do you think you can ride?'

'What, *now?* I don't know.'

Simon put a hand on Marta's shoulder. 'Don't be ridiculous, Jess can't ride, she hasn't practiced enough. And anyway, when we dismount –'

'There's no dismount. Not this time.'

The others looked at her. 'You're joking, right?' Paul said, frowning.

'It's the only way. If Jess doesn't think she can ride, maybe she can hide here and they won't find her. If Dan told them about us, he'll have told them four. They won't know about her.'

'I'm not staying here!'

'She's not staying here.'

'That's settled then. Paul, give her Dan's old clawboard.'

Paul stepped forward. 'We were going to have a little ceremony and stuff, but there isn't time.' He held out a clawboard. 'Here.'

Jess took the board and turned it over in her hands. The wood was dark with varnish but otherwise had no design. It looked like a piece of skirting board that someone had fashioned into a crude Medieval weapon for a kid to play with. The wood was scratched and scored, but the single metal hook was smooth from dozens of rides.

'It's amazing,' she said. 'Was it someone else's?'

'Yeah, but we weren't going to say that.'

Before Jess could reply or the others could say anything else, Marta left them. With her clawboard held in one hand she walked out in plain view of the approaching Cross Jumpers. Switch hurried to catch up, while the others followed more nervously.

'What do you want?' Marta shouted.

A girl, probably younger than her, stepped forward out of the group. Marta raised an eyebrow. A girl? They had just assumed this Dreggo was a guy. The girl's angular features were attractive, if a little thin. Her eyes, though, were hard and unforgiving. Marta grimaced. The new leader of the Cross Jumpers didn't look about to negotiate.

'So, this is it, where the mighty Tube Riders hide.'

Marta's heart was pounding, but she had to stand up for the others. Switch would start a suicidal battle they had no hope of winning, while Paul and Simon would probably run and be cut down. Perhaps she could offer a one on one with the girl ... perhaps make a deal ... her mind raced with ideas but none of them stood out, and she knew she would have to trust her intuition, something she often hated to do.

'What do you want? You have no business here.'

'I'm afraid we do,' the girl said. 'As of now, the Tube Riders are disbanded. I have an ultimatum for you. Throw your ... *catching boards* ... on to the tracks and walk away from the trains and this station for good. Do it and we'll leave.'

Marta felt anger welling up inside her. Her brother had begun this, and his legacy lived in every ride she took. She wasn't about to get forced away from something she loved by some bitch. She held the clawboard tight in both hands. Her board, unlike some of the others, had twin hooks, which she filed daily. They were sharp enough to tear Dreggo's face clean off.

'No,' she shouted. 'This isn't about the trains, or what we do, is it, Dreggo? There are plenty of abandoned stations in this city for both of us. You know that's no reason for us to fight. This is about *you*.' She held her clawboard across her chest, the hooks facing out. 'You want to fight, then come on. You and me. Leave the others out of this.'

A man who looked like he spent half his life in a gym stepped forward, hefting a sledgehammer in his hands like it was a plastic straw. 'Want us to do them now, Dreggo?'

The girl raised a hand and flapped it at him dismissively. 'Maul, back off.' Dreggo looked back at Marta and spread her hands. 'It's very simple. Give up this silly game, and you can live.'

Marta glanced back towards the others. Paul, Simon and Jess still hung back behind her. Switch took a few steps towards Marta's right flank as Maul inched forward. Marta pretended not to notice.

'Why is it so important to you?' she asked.

Dreggo tried to smile disarmingly, but it was forced, fake. 'It's not. There isn't room for both our gangs anymore.' She waved a hand behind her. 'Look! Our numbers have grown far beyond yours. We want other places to practice.'

'You stay in your stations, we stay here. That way no one gets hurt.' Marta hoped it wasn't obvious she was stalling for time. Behind her she heard the low rumble of a train back in the tunnel. *A few more seconds...*

'So it's a no, is it?' Dreggo's smile had vanished.

'You and me,' Marta said, trying to sound a whole lot braver than she felt. 'Come on, Dreggo. What are you, chickenshit?'

Dreggo's eyes blazed. 'I'd cut you open, you Tube Rider slut, but this is about more than the two of us.'

'I don't think it is,' Marta said. 'I think it's about you wanting something you have no right to because what you have sucks more cocks than you do.'

Dreggo tensed, then gave a little shake of the head as if to say *you're making a big mistake*. She lifted an arm and waved the other Cross Jumpers forward. Marta noticed that while the few nearest them looked frenzied, wild, caught up in their own bloodlust, a greater number hung back, reluctant. Just from their body language she could tell they had no taste for the coming violence. Perhaps if they could break through the Cross Jumpers' front line they could get away ... but the odds were still overwhelmingly against them.

Marta glanced behind her. The train noise was still growing, but it was still too far back, probably just exiting the previous station. They had no choice: they would have to fight.

'Hold them off until the train comes,' she muttered to the others. 'Ride the first chance you get.'

She let go of the clawboard with one hand long enough to reach under her shirt, looking for her own weapon, a small can of pepper spray. Her father had given it to her some years ago, before he died. Last summer, after a group of punks had jumped her not far from here, a friend had made some modifications to it. She wasn't sure exactly what was in it now, but he'd assured her the burn would be a lot more permanent than simple pepper water.

To her right, Maul closed on Switch. Switch's good eye shone; he was ready to go down fighting. He looked almost excited. The others were hanging back. Simon would fight to protect Jess, but Marta had never seen Paul lift a hand in anger and wondered if he would now. Perhaps he would just run.

If she could just take out Dreggo, maybe she could end all this–

Dreggo leapt at Marta with impossible, unnatural speed. Marta didn't even have time to gasp. One hand was still caught inside her shirt. Pushed to the floor, she swung the clawboard up with her other hand, trying to knock Dreggo off her. The wooden edge connected hard with the side of the girl's face and one hook scratched a line of red along Dreggo's cheek, but Dreggo shrugged off the blow as though it was nothing. Strong hands closed around Marta's neck. As Marta tried to roll her off, she saw Switch dart at Maul. Maul swung the sledgehammer, but Switch was too fast, ducking like a flyweight boxer and flashing the knife across the big man's throat. Maul wobbled for a second, and then clutched at his neck as blood sprayed across the platform.

Switch was already moving away as Maul crashed to the ground like a falling tree, blood gushing from his throat. Switch tossed the knife from hand to hand as others closed in. 'Come on!' he screamed. 'Come on you Cross Jumper fucks! Let's have some!'

Marta tried to kick Dreggo's legs, but Dreggo was no longer looking at her. Her face had turned towards Maul, filled with a look of sudden, unexpected horror. She pushed away from Marta as though their fight was already done. 'Maul!' she screamed, crawling towards the other man through a puddle of his blood.

Marta rubbed her sore neck as she scrambled to her feet. Looking around, she saw three others had passed her and were closing in on Simon, Paul and Jess. Two more moved towards Switch, while the rest hung back. The blood had scared many, but Dreggo alone might prove strong enough to take them out. There was something wrong about the girl, something unnatural.

And then the train roared out of the tunnel, its engines booming like thunder.

'Now!' she screamed. 'Ride, Tube Riders, ride! Go!'

Switch slashed at one of his new attackers and they backed off out of range. Marta glanced back and saw Paul swing his clawboard in an arc at the nearest of the three that circled them. It connected hard and the man went down, giving them room to move.

'Come on, Jess!' Simon shouted, pulling the girl by the hand. Paul, surprising Marta with courage she had never realised he had, rammed the end of his clawboard into the stomach of the next man and then swung it into the face of the third.

The train was halfway through the station now. They had just seconds left to catch it before it was gone and they were dead. Simon and Jess sprinted towards the platform edge. Jess, crying in terror, leapt and somehow managed to catch a hold, with Simon catching behind her. For just a second Marta marveled at how good the girl was. It had taken Marta weeks to pluck up the courage to make her first ride.

'Dreggo, they're getting away!' someone shouted.

'Kill them!' Dreggo screamed without looking up, her voice hoarse and desperate. 'Kill them all!'

'Paul!' Marta screamed. 'Come on!'

Paul turned toward the train. His face was contorted with fear and he looked more scared of the train than the Cross Jumpers. For a moment Marta thought he would pull out, but then he broke into a lumbering run. He was going far too slow, years without riding ruining his fitness. He squeezed his eyes shut and grit his teeth, summoning the nerve he needed. He reached the platform edge and leapt for the train. For a moment Marta thought he would miss: he was too low, his leap not high enough. The image of Clive's smashed body flashed through her mind, then Paul's clawboard caught with one edge and she gasped with relief. Using a deft skill he probably forgot he had, Paul shifted on the train side, pushed up with one foot and leveled the board out. Then the train was taking him away.

Marta couldn't help but smile. He still had it. Once he had been good – no champion, but respectable – and that skill obviously didn't fade easily. Maybe it was just like riding a bike after all.

It was her turn. She sprinted and caught just as the front of the train entered the far tunnel. From the side of the train Marta looked back towards the platform as the wind whipped her hair around her face. Switch was still back there, on the platform, running for the train. Another second and he would miss it. At the last moment, Marta saw Dreggo look up from Maul's dead body. She bared her teeth in anger and for a moment looked feral, lupine. She screamed something Marta couldn't hear, and her arm whipped through the air.

Switch, incredibly, had a huge grin on his face as he sprinted for the train. He was a hundred feet ahead of Dreggo, but as his board caught, he arched his back, crying out, and his face contorted with pain.

Then the darkness of the tunnel engulfed them.

CHAPTER EIGHT
DISCOVERY

MARTA FELT THE TRAIN begin to slow. As the chilling, buffeting wind eased, she heard the faint sound of crying not far ahead of her.

Jess.

What an introduction to tube riding, she thought. Despite the danger, the deaths, the main reason they did it was for fun. Now, one man lay dead back on the platform, several others were hurt, and they were on the run. She had dealt with struggle and violence all her life, but tube riding was supposed to have been their escape.

'Marta!' Paul's voice came from not far ahead. Just a shadow in the strobe lighting from the emergency lights in the tunnel and the glow through the carriage windows, he was inching back along the carriage towards her, sliding his board carefully along the rail of the jerking, bumping carriage as the train thundered through the darkness.

Paul stopped just short of her. 'We're coming into a station,' he shouted into her face, struggling to be heard over the echoing roar of the engine up ahead and the clattering of the wheels over the rails. 'You want to dismount here?'

She shook her head. 'Not yet. There's another disused station two further stops down the line. Westfern Street. Remember?'

They had used to ride there but a stop light had been installed a short way into the far tunnel so the trains came through too slow. 'We can get off there,' Marta said. 'We should be safe.'

'Sounds good. I'll tell Jess and Simon. They're two carriages ahead of me.'

'Paul, wait. How are *you* doing? First ride in a while, remember?'

The laugh Paul gave her verged on hysteria. 'Piece of cake,' he shouted, and she could tell he was barely holding it together in the nightmarish dark of the tunnel. 'Not looking forward to getting off but it's better than getting battered by a group of thugs.'

He inched away from her along the carriage. As the train decelerated into the station, she looked through the windows at the passengers inside. This carriage only held a handful of kids and a group of old women, hunched over, their hands wrapped tightly around their bags. Marta remembered being young and her father telling her about the old days, before the government changed, before Britain became Mega Britain, before the perimeter walls and the class segregation, as he called it. She remembered him telling her that despite the riots, the violence, the banning of the internet, mobile phones, and unregulated television, that some things never changed. Some things you could just rely on.

He said the London Underground was one. You could ride the tubes, and it could be any time of the last one hundred and fifty years. Looking into that carriage now at the kids and the old women, it was like looking back through a time portal into London's past. She started to smile, but tears welled up in her eyes.

Her father had been hit by a car while crossing the road. It wasn't the car's fault, he told her on his hospital deathbed, just minutes before internal bleeding claimed him. He'd had things on his mind, and had been looking the wrong way as he jogged out across the street. An old-style death for a man who had always believed Mega Britain could be saved.

Her mother died a year after, killed by a terrorist bomb placed in a litter bin outside the foreign consulate. She'd been there trying to get a visa for Marta to study in America, a thinly veiled plan to get her daughter out of the country before things got really bad. She had been in the wrong place at the wrong time. The police said that the device had been poorly made and hadn't exploded properly, but Rachel Banks had been right outside and was the only casualty.

A letter arrived just a day after the funeral declining the application. That was two years ago. Since then, applications themselves had been outlawed.

Unlike her father's, her mother's death had been an old-fashioned one for an entirely new reason. Despite the bombings, the protests, the uprisings,

Mega Britain rolled on.

Paul inched back towards her again as the train came to a complete stop, and the doors opened on the other side. People stood up and got off as others got on.

'Simon said he's cool,' Paul said. 'Jess is in a bad way, though. In shock. Simon's worried she's going to fall off. Not helping that it's so damn cold.'

Marta grimaced. 'Tell him to keep a hold of her. There's been enough death today already.'

Paul looked at her and shook his head. 'I can't believe Switch killed that man. He seemed to enjoy it, like he went blood-crazy.'

'It was them or us. It might still be us, if we don't keep our heads down.' The train doors closed, and it began to move again. 'That girl Dreggo seemed to care for him a lot. It looks like we're on her hit list now.'

Paul sighed. 'Switch didn't need to kill him. He's quick enough with that knife he could have just slashed him up a bit. My brother, Owen, he's just twelve, but I'm worried he'll end up like that. You know, not caring.'

'What Switch does is out of our control,' Marta said, feeling unexpectedly defensive. 'Remember, he was protecting us. I noticed you were pretty quick with that clawboard.'

Paul leaned closer as the train picked up speed momentarily before beginning to slow again. 'Simon wasn't going to leave Jess's side. They were going to get cut off from the train. It was the only way to give them both a chance.' He smiled. 'It's a good job we had Dan's clawboard for Jess. Otherwise we might have been stuck.'

'Well, we made it, but I think Switch is hurt. He's hanging on back there but I think she got him with a throwing knife.'

'Something was odd about her,' Paul said. 'Did you notice how young she was?'

Marta gave a nervous laugh. 'You didn't feel her hands around your neck. They were like iron. I'd be dead now if Switch hadn't got her attention by killing that guy.'

Paul sighed, and it sounded as though he was holding back tears. 'It sucks so bad that it has to be this way. An eye for an eye, always.'

'Dreggo hasn't got hers yet, remember. We're going to have to lay low after this.'

The train rolled into another station. They were on the right side of the train, and again the doors opened on the left. Marta knew that getting off at Westfern Street was their only chance, because the station after was a connecting station, where the train changed lines. The doors opened on the right side there, and they would be discovered.

Paul inched a little closer. 'Look at them in there,' he said, speaking right into her ear. 'Some of them look right through us. Why don't they notice us?'

'They do,' Marta said. 'But what they see is a ghost. They see a person outside the window peering in, mixed with the reflections from the people inside, the flicker of the lights, the emergency signs, and the advertising on the wall behind us ... so many things. Most of the time we don't know what it's like to see one of us from in there. I remember once coming home from school and passing through the abandoned station at Field Park and for a few seconds seeing someone hanging from the train. It scared the living shit out of me, and worse, the figure looked like my brother. It was after I told him about it that night that he told me about tube riding. It *was* my brother.'

'I guess that's why most of the people who acknowledge us are drunk, high or mad. They're more willing to trust what their eyes show them.'

'Exactly.'

The doors closed again and the train pulled away, the engines roaring as it gained speed. 'Okay, next one,' Marta said. She shouted the instruction back to Switch. The little man had used the stops to move forward to the carriage behind them, but he looked groggy and weak as he gave a slight nod of his head.

'I hope he's not hurt too bad,' Paul said. 'Asshole though he is, I'm fond of that bastard.'

Marta smiled. 'Me too.'

She leaned out from the train, looking ahead down the track. In the distance she saw a bright red light, still just a pinprick like an animal's eye far off in the dark. It was the stop light just past the next station. The train should start to slow down, enough that Jess would be able to dismount without hurting herself. She worried about Switch, though. How hurt was he?

Marta heard the squeal of the train's ancient brakes as it slowed, wrinkling her nose as the stench of smoke and oil drifted up from the wheels below her. A moment later they were surrounded by emergency lighting as the train staggered into the station.

Ahead of them, Simon and Jess jumped off. Simon rolled well, while Jess landed with a grunt but seemed to be okay. As the platform appeared below them, first Paul jumped, and then Marta gritted her teeth and jumped after him. She ducked her head and held her arms in as she'd learned, but she still cried out in pain as she landed on the cold, hard platform. It had been years since she'd dismounted short of the breakfall mats, and the pain was refreshingly sharp.

She climbed to her feet as the train rolled past her. It was slowing almost to a full stop, and as the last carriage reached them Switch jumped down, landing on his feet, twisting and falling to the ground. The train rolled away into the tunnel and came to a stop a few hundred feet inside.

'Are you all right?' Marta said, helping him to his feet. Her hand came away sticky, and she smelt the copper scent of blood.

'That bitch stuck me,' he moaned. 'How'd she do that from that distance?'

'You need a doctor,' Paul said.

'Fuck it. I've had worse. Let's just get out of here and then worry about it.'

Simon and Jess walked over. Jess's face shone wet with tears, but otherwise she looked all right. Simon had one hand on her arm as if worried she might faint.

'The way out's up there,' Marta said, pointing towards some stairs behind them. Let's get out of here and reassess ourselves in the light.'

'Is the station open?' Paul said.

'This end used to be. I don't know if it's been closed up since, though.'

They started up the stairs, Marta in the lead with Jess at her shoulder, Simon and Paul helping Switch along behind them. At the top of the stairs the corridor turned to the right, opening out into a wider lobby where Marta remembered the ticket gates were. Beyond that were two more staircases before the station exited on the corner of Hatton Road. There might be a locked gate, but if it was old and rusty they might be able to force it.

The station had been abandoned longer than St. Cannerwells, for at least twenty years. Marta wasn't expecting to hear voices, nor see lights from the lobby area. Dazed, still in shock from the Cross Jumpers' attack, they walked right out into plain view of a group of men standing in a huddle just beyond the old ticket gates.

It took a moment for Marta to recognise the black suits the men wore. When she did, noticing at the same time another man in their midst, on his knees with his hands tied behind his back, his face battered and bloody, she lifted a hand to stifle a scream.

The Department of Civil Affairs.

One of the men lifted what looked like a baton and smashed the kneeling man across the face. The battered man gave a watery grunt and fell sideways, but another man caught him and held him upright. The battered man started talking quickly, his voice high-pitched and faltering. He was crying for his life in a language Marta didn't recognise. The tears though, tears of utter terror, were something she understood. An image of her mother flashed into her mind, her mother with tears streaming down her bloodied cheeks as she lay in the hospital bed an hour after the terrorist attack. 'I don't want to die. I don't want to leave you,' Rachel had wept. Half an hour later, she had done both.

One of the DCA agents looked up. He turned to the others and said something sharp, looked back at them and pointed. Three men pulled guns. Two aimed them at the Tube Riders, but the third held it up to the battered man's temple and pulled the trigger.

The gun went off, impossibly loud in the empty Underground station. Behind Marta, Jess screamed, and she heard Simon retching.

For a second everything seemed to stop. Marta glanced at Jess as the girl said, 'I know that man, oh God, *I know that man...*' As she trailed off her hand fell to something tied around her stomach.

Marta's heart seemed to twist in her chest.

The camera.

'Hey!' shouted the man holding the gun. 'Stop!'

'Run!' Marta screamed.

One of the other men fired. The shot rang out, and a puff of dust and broken tiles exploded out of the wall just inches wide of where Paul stood. Then they were running as though it were Huntsmen and not just men who pursued them, their ears still ringing from the gunshots.

Switch, with a determined grimace on his face, went first down the steps, three at a time. Paul was close behind, while Simon hung back a little, dragging Jess, who looked close to passing out. Marta, at the back, glanced behind her and saw the men closing.

'Come back here!' someone shouted. 'Come back or you're all dead!'

Down on the platform, they heard the rumble of the next train as it approached.

'Ride this one?' Switch shouted.

'No,' Marta replied. 'It stops in the tunnel. They'll catch us.'

'Well, what the fuck do we do then?'

They were relying on her. If they hadn't needed a leader before, they did now. She looked around, thinking quickly. She saw the train's lights approaching the tunnel mouth, looked the other way and saw the glow of the red stop light in the far tunnel. There was another rumble coming from that direction, too.

'We have to get across the tracks,' she said. 'That train stops to let one through the other way. If we can get across, this one will cover us and we can ride the next one back. Hurry!'

'The train's coming!' Paul shouted.

Marta heard the sound of rapid footsteps on the stairs behind them. 'We have to jump across!' she shouted.

'I ain't no fucking Cross Jumper–'

'Just *do* it, Switch!' Marta screamed. 'And the rest of you! Jump or we're dead!'

Jess and Simon didn't need another warning. They sprinted for the platform edge and leapt out, easily landing on the far side. Paul landed just behind them, stumbling and rolling over. Marta glanced back to see the men halfway down the stairs, all now with guns in their hands. She turned and sprinted for the platform edge.

As she leapt out across the track, she looked to her left and saw twin eyes of light rushing towards her. She stared in terror. From this angle the train looked like some giant beast, rushing forward to crush her.

She hit the far platform just as the train broke from the tunnel. As she rolled, she looked back and shouted, 'Switch!'

The little man hung in mid air between the platforms, legs and arms flailing like a bizarre cartoon caricature, his face was caught in a grimace of pain. Time seemed to stand still for a moment, and then there was a crack behind him. A gun muzzle flashed. The train was huge and just feet away; there was no way he could make it–

–yet he did, landing and rolling on the platform beside Marta as the train rumbled past them. He jerked and sat up, one hand reaching for the injury on his back, the other rubbing his left foot, now shoeless.

'I don't believe it,' he muttered, wincing in pain.

Behind them Paul and Simon were already on their feet, Simon dragging Jess along behind him.

'Come on,' Paul said. 'They'll have a clear shot in about five seconds.'

As one train rushed past, another roar built up in the adjacent tunnel, on the opposite side. A moment later it surged along the platform, going far faster, not stopping.

'Go!' Paul shouted, racing for the train, Simon and Jess just behind him.

'Come on, hero,' Marta said to Switch, pulling the little man to his feet.

'It ate my fucking shoe,' he muttered, grabbing his clawboard off the platform and following after her. 'I liked those shoes!'

As Marta jumped and caught, she looked back towards the far platform, revealed now that the other train had vanished into the tunnel. She counted six men there, standing still, watching them. The guns had disappeared, as though they knew they couldn't shoot without risking the lives of the passengers inside the train. One man at the front lifted a hand, pressed two fingers to his temple and then pointed them at her.

I'll remember you, that gesture said.

Switch caught just behind her, and Marta felt the vibration of his landing shake the rail. As the train entered the tunnel and darkness surrounded them, the image of the six dark men fixed itself in her mind together with the image of the dead man whose face was now just a memory.

As they raced out of sight, she couldn't quite get her head around what they had seen or what had happened. She knew, though, that Dreggo and the Cross Jumpers were now the least of their worries.

Chapter Nine
Enemies

AS THE TRAIN'S RUMBLE receded into the tunnel, Dreggo looked up as the other Cross Jumpers crowded around her. Maul lay in front of her, his skin pallid, his body already cooling as the blood thickened and dried around him. Her heart rose and fell in her chest, pushing bile towards her mouth, wanting her to choke.

Maul, her friend. Dead. She didn't love him, but as he lay before her she wondered what she did feel. He would have loved her had she let him, and in his brutish way he would have taken care of her. On the outside he was an animal, but he would have treated her well, respected her.

And he was dead.

She had brought her Cross Jumpers here to start a war with the Tube Riders, and she had found them more cunning than she had anticipated. To ride off into the tunnels like that was a masterstroke. They had time to go to ground now and it would take at least a few days to track them down. She could have handled them escaping, though. It was humiliating, but that was how wars were fought. But to escape mostly unharmed, leaving one of her own dead, one close to her at that …

'Are you sure they aren't back in the tunnel?' she asked the closest Cross Jumpers, her voice cracked and hoarse.

'No,' said one called Spacewell, a skinny weirdo who made his money from petty theft. 'They've gone. There's no sign of any bodies back there either.'

'Okay.' She glanced back at Maul. 'Let's get him over to the tracks.'

Three men came forward to drag Maul's heavy body away. Others just stood around, their knives and clubs at their sides, their eyes on the ground. Dissent was brewing. Dreggo had become leader of the Cross Jumpers through the code, and she had reinforced her leadership with acts of wanton violence. She ruled through fear, and they knew now what she could do with a knife. But dissent was growing nonetheless. She had brought them here, and now Maul was dead, for nothing.

As the three men pushed Maul's body down on to the tracks, Dreggo turned to the other Cross Jumpers.

'Listen up.' Faces turned towards her, but they were angry, mutinous. 'We came here today to give them an ultimatum. You all heard me offer them a chance at freedom. Didn't you?'

There were one or two murmurs of agreement.

'They didn't need to fight. All they had to do was give up what they had, and walk away. Simple. *They* wanted the fight.'

'No. No, they didn't.'

Dreggo's eyes bored into the assembled group.

'Who said that?'

'I did.' A black-haired girl near the back raised her hand. Even at this distance Dreggo could see it was shaking. The hand belonged to Bethany, a former prostitute, now a night worker in a supermarket. 'They didn't want to fight, *you* wanted to fight.' One or two others grunted in agreement.

Dreggo glared at her, and then let her gaze fall on the other stony faces. 'Does what we do mean nothing to you people? Do you not understand what it means to be a Cross Jumper?'

'We have violence above ground,' said Matty, a shoplifter. 'We didn't come here for this.'

Dreggo's mouth fell open. 'Wake up, you idiots! Open your eyes! Maul is dead now because he believed in what we have! The Tube Riders were a legend, but the Cross Jumpers can become an even bigger legend!'

'Whatever,' Matty said. 'Some of us don't care about being a fucking *legend*.'

A knife appeared in Dreggo's hand. 'Is that so? You were happy to watch that Tube Rider die yesterday. Yet when it comes to fighting for your cause, you give up? How about I cut you open and see if you have a spine?'

She only had one knife left. There were more than twenty of them. There were secrets about her past that none of them knew, but that was too many even for her.

'Some of us love what we do,' said another voice. 'But we didn't want this. We didn't want a turf war. Why don't *you* leave? Go make your own legend.'

She looked for the speaker, and found him standing at the back.

Billy Lees, the man she had replaced.

Her anger boiled over, and before she could stop herself, she whipped her hand over, the knife whizzing through the air. It struck Billy in the neck with a soft thud, handle deep. He made a sound like a gurgling drain, his breath cut off, and staggered backwards, hands scrabbling for the knife. As his dying fingers knocked against the handle blood began to spray in little bursts, like a water pipe split by a hot sun. He staggered backwards a few steps and keeled over. His body writhed on the platform, his legs kicking out at the tiles. The others stared in horror, but not one person moved to help him. After a few seconds he fell still.

Behind Dreggo, a train raced out of the tunnel and roared past them, causing a soft popping noise as it struck and dragged away Maul's body. Dreggo felt a well of regret fill her stomach as she remembered they should have had a farewell ceremony in honour of him. His body was gone now, his memory forever tainted.

'Okay, leave,' Dreggo shouted, waving towards the stairs. 'You're not Cross Jumpers, you're cowards. Maul would have spat on you, all of you. Go on. Get on with your lives somewhere else.'

There was a murmur from the group as the backmost members of the crowd began to shuffle away towards the stairs. Few wanted to turn their backs on her, so to hurry the moment she did it for them, turning away and stalking back up the platform towards where Maul's blood stained the ground. She knelt down and dipped her finger in it, feeling the stickiness, still warm.

Dreggo did not cry, but Maul had been her friend. She hadn't loved him but she had respected him, appreciated his kindness. Now, her group, her identity, had been disbanded. There was blood on her conscience, and blood on her hands. And all because of *them*.

She clenched her fists and slammed them against the tiles, once, twice, three times, until tiny cracks appeared. No matter. She would hunt the Tube Riders herself, and one by one they would die. Then, and only then, would she start a new order of Cross Jumpers.

She looked back towards the stairs, and found the platform empty. Billy Lees's body still lay where it had fallen. She took hold of one of his limp arms and dragged him over to the platform edge.

'You were a coward, but at least you stood up to me,' she told his dead eyes. 'That in itself makes you deserving of a Cross Jumper burial.' She put one foot on his chest and shoved him down on to the tracks. Then she turned away, the last living person in St. Cannerwells Underground station.

Dan had told her there were only four Tube Riders, but she had seen five. The punky girl Marta had been their leader. That was without question. The one with the jippy eye who had murdered Maul and the fat guy had ridden pretty well. Then there was the couple, the pretty boy and the cute, homey-looking girl with the neat hair and the nice clothes. It had to be her, she had to be the new one. She had looked more tentative, more uncertain than the others. The others looked like street kids, and might live anywhere, maybe even moving from place to place. But the homey girl, she probably had a proper home. If Dreggo could find her, she would find the others.

She rubbed the side of her head, just above her eye, and for a moment her hair lifted up a fraction, revealing a cluster of wires that disappeared into her skin just above her ear.

Feeling a renewed sense of purpose, she moved across the platform to where she'd first seen the girl standing, looking for a scent.

#

The older of the two men in the DCA uniforms rubbed his chin thoughtfully, his grey eyes narrowed. In front of them, the rails still hummed from the recently departed train.

The taller, younger of the two said, 'Tell me that didn't just happen, Clayton. Tell me we didn't just get interrupted by a bunch of kids with a fucking digital camera. You think they got footage of that?'

Leland Clayton began to massage the bridge of his nose. He glanced back towards the stairs, where the other four men had gone on his orders to start cleaning up the mess that his gun had caused. He lowered his voice, aware that echoes could carry in a place like this. 'Are you aware who those ... *kids* were, Vincent?'

Adam Vincent shook his head. 'Meth heads, runaways, what does it matter? They saw us kill the Ambassador, and they might have got digital footage of it. That's a big problem.'

'They were Tube Riders.'

'What?'

Clayton put a hand inside his coat and pulled out a little pamphlet magazine, sixteen pages in black and white. The single word title identified it as

VOICE. It was an illegal magazine printed and fastened in some filthy squat somewhere and distributed with the main intent of talking shit about the government. Clayton made a point of getting his hands on such things as it made the perpetrators easy to track down. There were always clues in the pages somewhere, and while Clayton was no latter day Sherlock Holmes he had a pretty good reputation for flushing out rebels and revolutionaries.

'Page thirteen or fourteen, I believe. It's just a little article in amongst all the government hate bullshit.'

'The Tube Riders?' Vincent muttered, scanning the poorly copied, unaligned text.

'Come on, Vincent. I'm sure even you've heard of them.' Clayton, who enjoyed a good ghost story, smiled. 'People say they're ghosts, demons, the souls of train suicides.' He shrugged. 'But they're not. As we've just seen, the Tube Riders are just a group of kids.'

'Look, Clayton,' Vincent said, handing the magazine back. 'I don't give a fuck who they were. I want to know what we're going to do about it.'

Clayton turned towards the younger man. Adam Vincent, while not quite fresh off the DCA boat was still a junior officer. With his spiked, mullet hair, know-it-all swagger and disrespectful attitude, Clayton, who considered himself a tolerant person, had taken an instant dislike to the man directly beneath him in order of seniority. His grizzled, pockmarked face was set, his eyes suddenly hard. 'Don't make me remind you of your rank, Vincent,' he said.

For once, Vincent looked sheepish, his cheeks reddening. 'I'm just, you know, saying that this talk isn't doing us any good. We have to find them. Eliminate them.'

'I'm aware of that.'

'So what's the plan of action?'

'Let me speak to the Governor first.'

'Is that wise?' Vincent shook his head. 'Do we even have time? If they have digital footage of that hit they're capable of starting a goddamn war.'

Clayton nodded. 'I know. But while we're on government orders we have a duty to make a report.' For a moment he felt a pang of fear. The thought of an audience with the Governor was something that could keep him awake at night. 'We have to follow procedure, Vincent. Trying to clean up this mess without the Governor knowing could be the death of all of us.' He sighed. 'First though, let's get that body down onto the tracks as planned.'

Chapter Ten
Revelation

CHANGING TRAINS AT THE NEXT STATION, the Tube Riders rode six stops out on the old District Line before dismounting at Kew Gardens, where the Underground still buzzed beneath the derelict national rail line above. No guard was on duty at the ticket gates, and they duly went out into the daylight, happy just to be out of the tunnels. They sat down to rest on the abandoned platform of the national rail line. Above them the rain had given way to a hazy blue sky, and a light wind ruffled their hair.

Marta walked over to the tracks, listening to the sound of traffic on a nearby bridge while on either side of the station abandoned residential buildings watched her silently. She breathed deeply, trying to still her thudding heart, trying to think of a plan, a way to get them all out of this mess. She felt the others looking to her to lead them, but she didn't know that she had the skills to keep them all safe. Now that they were on the run as fugitives, someone had to stand up and take responsibility.

But why her?

She didn't need the answer, because she already knew it. There was no one else suitable. Switch was too unstable, Simon had Jess to look after, and Paul didn't have the mettle for it.

She sighed again, feeling that familiar lump in her throat that threatened to bring tears. Her parents had tried to look after her, and they would want her to be strong. 'For you, Mum, Dad,' she whispered. She reached up and tugged at two braids of her hair, as if the motion would balance out her thoughts.

A few feet away, Paul had taken off his t-shirt and was ripping it up into strips to make a bandage for Switch's knife wound. It wasn't more than skin deep but they would need antibiotics to prevent infection, and antibiotics were hard to find.

Behind her, Simon was comforting Jess. 'You don't understand!' the girl gasped through sobs. 'You don't get it, Simon! They're going to come after us!'

'Just calm down,' Simon told her. 'It's over now, we've got away. No one, not the Cross Jumpers nor those men in the tunnel, is going to find us now.'

'You don't understand! *I know who he was!*'

'Who?'

'The man they killed. The man who they shot. I know who he was ...' Jess buried her face in her sleeve. Simon tried to hug her to him but she pushed him away.

Marta crouched down beside her. 'Who was it, Jess?'

'Don't worry about her, she's just taking it hard—'

'The ambassador. The ambassador from the European Confederation.'

Marta felt a knot in her stomach. 'The ambassador?'

Jess looked up. Her eyes were red and her face was flushed and swollen. 'I know because my dad told me. He works for the government. He showed me the story in the newspaper, and said the ambassador was coming to Mega Britain to discuss the reopening of trade routes. Dad said there was a chance Mega Britain would open up again to Europe, and these talks were the key.' The modicum of control in her voice vanished. 'And now he's dead. They've killed him!'

'Are you sure? Why?'

'I don't know. What I *do* know is that we saw him die. They're going to come after us now.'

Paul had limped over. He was perhaps the only one of them who looked more exhausted than Marta felt. Switch was sitting down by the side of the platform, legs dangling over the edge. He didn't look at them.

'What's she talking about?' Paul said.

'Jess says that we just witnessed the assassination of the European Confederation's ambassador.'

'Are you serious? Just think what might happen if we can get to the press!' He pointed at the camera she held in her hands. 'Did you get any photographs?'

Jess squeezed her eyes shut and turned away. Simon took the camera from her. 'More than that,' he said. 'She had the video function running. She recorded the whole thing. It's a bit difficult to see, but if you enhance the light on a computer you'll be able to identify people.'

Paul looked like he wanted to ask to see it and then changed his mind. 'I'll take your word for it,' he said, looking grim.

'The press won't be any good,' Simon said. 'The government owns all the newspapers.'

'Then we distribute it in the underground.'

'What would be the point? At best we'll start an uprising and then the government will let out the Huntsmen to slaughter everyone.' At mention of the Huntsmen, Switch's head jerked up.

'Or take it to Europe then. If we can get this video over to Europe, maybe the Confederation will intervene.'

Marta gave a bitter laugh. 'And how do we do that?' she said. 'We can't even get over the perimeter wall.'

Jess had managed to swallow down her sobs. She stood up. 'How can we prove it's real?' she said. 'It's easy to doctor footage.'

'A skilled technician could determine what's fake and what's not,' Paul said. 'I heard it's easy if you know what to look for. Finding someone who could do it is the problem, though. Most people with that kind of skill work for the government.'

'We're dangerous to them,' Jess said. 'Which is why they're going to come after us.'

'Your father,' Marta said. 'Can he help us? Would he be on our side?'

Jess looked uncertain. 'I don't know what he does exactly, but he wants peace, I know that. And freedom. If we show him the footage, maybe he can help.'

'Okay,' Marta said. 'We have a plan, then. First, we need to get Switch to a doctor. Afterwards, we'll visit Jess's father.'

'What about the Cross Jumpers?' Jess asked.

Marta gave a half smile. 'I think all we have to do is keep one step ahead of them. They're the least of our worries right now.'

As they picked up their things and headed off towards the station exit, she wondered just how much she believed it.

Chapter Eleven
Hunted

LELAND CLAYTON TOOK THE ELEVATOR up to the Governor's suites on Parliament Tower's 50th Floor. The tallest building in Mega Britain, it stuck up like a blunt pencil out of the Docklands landscape, the area around it cleared some years ago of neighbouring buildings and other geographical features. The old office tower, once known as One Canada Square, no longer housed private companies. Now its sole function was as home to Mega Britain's government. The old political centre in Westminster was now derelict and abandoned, infested with squatters and fought over by gangs.

Clayton stepped out of the elevator and moved to the nearest window. In a ring perhaps half a mile wide around the front of Parliament Tower were the most beautiful landscaped gardens you could hope to see, a manufactured Eden of wide lawns and wooded groves, clear ponds and splashing fountains. He saw movement down there too, the deer that wandered wild, the occasional bird flying from tree to tree.

Then around it was the guard wall with its constant patrols and anti-aircraft gun placements. He could see the gate he had entered by, a huge medieval-styled portcullis, inside which was an x-ray checkpoint and a garrison of security personnel. He had been subjected to far more rigorous checks than usual, a sign of the Governor's growing paranoia.

Clayton sighed. He had his job and his work, but sometimes he wished for the old days too. Beyond the Parliament Tower enclosure London GUA stretched away, a grey, poverty-stricken wilderness where murder, rape, arson and violence were everyday occurrences. Even from here he could see the smoke and flames of numerous fires, and the flickering red lights of the few police cars which still had them working.

To the east, where the edge of the city was closest, he could see the main perimeter wall, rising a hundred and fifty feet into the air. He'd been through it on several occasions, out into the GFAs where there was almost no crime, and little of anything else beside overfed farming communities and holiday homes for those city folk rich enough to afford a permit. The world was the vision of the Governor, a man who had been in power as long as Clayton could remember; too long if he were honest with himself. Once, it had seemed to work: the segregation of communities and regions serving to focus people's energy and creative abilities. The country had briefly prospered, but now things were falling apart as people began to understand just how much the government had stolen from them. There were rumours of rebellion even out in the GFAs, as the people demanded their lost toys: television, internet, magazines, free-speech newspapers. The Governor's iron hand controlled everything and the threat of the Huntsmen was still enough to enforce his laws. But his hold was failing. Even Leland Clayton, who had spilt blood in the Governor's name more times than he cared to remember, sometimes wondered if things wouldn't be better if someone put a knife in the old man's back.

Clayton hadn't wanted to kill the ambassador nor witness the brutality he had allowed his men to dish out before the bullet finished him. The man had come with honourable intentions, and the order to stage his murder as an example of the problems faced by the Mega Britain government had struck Clayton as borderline madness. It had been an order, though, and Clayton always followed orders. Many men who'd started in the DCA alongside him were gone now. Clayton was still alive because he did what was asked of him without question. He might not like the order, but he certainly enjoyed being alive.

He went through into the Governor's Secretarial Office. There were several office staff inside, writing reports, making phone calls. As always when he got this far his hands started to shake, and he felt a lump in his throat.

He went over to the desk nearest to a pair of closed double doors.

'Madeline, is the Governor free to see me now?'

The woman behind the desk was maybe fifty, with grey streaks in her hair and glasses perched on her thin nose. Her eyes looked up over the rims, grey with hard-earned experience. He wondered how she could stand it, how she could work in the presence of such a man on a daily basis. He guessed that with time you could become desensitised to anything.

'He's expecting you, Mr. Clayton. Please go through.'

'Thanks.'

He pushed through the doors. Beyond them was a long corridor with another door at the far end. A thin, grey carpet led him towards it. There were no windows, but on either side were framed photographs or portraits of every British Prime Minister going back to colonial times. As he walked towards the far door he saw many names he recognised: Disraeli, Churchill, Wilson, Thatcher, Blair, Michaels ... the only one missing was the current Governor.

Some had reputations that outlasted them, while others were remembered for their failures. In life they were all different but here they all shared a common, bizarre theme.

Every single picture was hung upside down. As he walked, an army of chins followed him, while upside-down eyes stared up at the ceiling.

The Governor had been making a point: that everything that came before was beneath what stood now. Whether he agreed or not, Clayton wouldn't pass comment to anyone. There were too many ears, always listening.

At the end of the corridor two guards wearing black and green checkered uniforms stood on either side of the door. Their heads were shaven clean and each had a thin pointed beard. Their eyes watched him as he approached; his own searched their clothing for the bumps that gave away hidden weapons. They were elite, he knew; he wouldn't know about their weapons until he was dead. Even a raging Huntsman would have difficulty defeating a pair of the Governor's Personal Guard.

'I'm here to see the Governor,' he said to them as he approached, but it was of no consequence; neither moved nor made any sign of acknowledgement. The Governor had kept some traditions of the old life, then. Before the internet was banned, Clayton had seen a video of Buckingham Palace before it had been burned and razed; he wished he'd had a chance to watch the guards change like so many people once had in the old days.

He paused a moment, then reached out and pushed through the door, half expecting one to reach out suddenly and take hold of his wrist. But nothing happened. They stayed in their positions, as still as the dead.

The door opened on to a darkened lobby. A dim standing lamp on a table in the corner was all that lit the room. Clayton could smell the soft aroma of jasmine incense, while through a door standing ajar into another room floated the delicate piano sound of lounge jazz.

'Sir?' Clayton took a few steps towards the inner room. Around him, framed art classics hung from the black walls, Cezanne, Monet, Picasso, each illuminated by their own individual spotlight.

'In here,' rumbled a voice as dark as chocolate. Clayton went through the door into a plush room, part office, part lounge. Thick black leather sofas made a circle around a lacquered coffee table, while along the sides of the room deep bookshelves held a huge personal library. The entire south side of the room was a single enormous tinted window, revealing the world outside in a shade of sepia.

Maxim Cale, the Governor of Mega Britain, was standing by the window. He wore a black suit, and was gazing out of the window towards the crumbling remains of London city centre.

The man didn't turn. 'Thank you for coming,' he said.

Clayton moved a few tentative steps closer.

'I understand there was … a problem.'

Clayton's hands were shaking. He held them in front of him, the left holding on to the right, trying to steady himself.

'We did as was ordered, sir. The ambassador has been … martyred, and his death … *rearranged* as an act of revolutionary terrorism.'

'You were ordered to do it with utmost secrecy.'

Clayton had gutted children in front of their parents without breaking a sweat, but now his lower lip trembled. 'What happened could not have been anticipated, sir. To be disturbed by those … kids, was something that—'

'—has put us under threat of war, of invasion. Is that what you want for our country, Mr. Clayton?'

The Governor turned from the window, and Clayton swallowed the fear he always felt when looking on that terrible face.

The Governor was of African origin: thick lips, strong skin, big eyes and tightly curled hair cropped short. What set him apart was his albinism, so extreme as to leave his skin as white as sun-dried bone. Whether natural or engineered, Clayton didn't know, but in the centre of that face, eyes the deep crimson of fresh wounds stared out.

The day he had first met the Governor, while still a junior official, he had been sick in a washroom afterwards, and woke up that night with his face caked with the salt of dried tears, his bed soaked with sweat. And it hadn't improved as time went on; he still had nightmares about this man, even though he'd been among the highest ranks of the Department of Civil Affairs for more than a decade. The Governor, the man who controlled everything from behind a façade of democracy, was a fearsome man. You didn't disappoint him, and you didn't cross him.

'No ... of course not,' Clayton stammered in response to the Governor's question. 'It was due to unforeseen circumstances. But I assure you, our best people are on the streets now.'

'Your first officer – Mr. Vincent – called my office earlier. He said these kids are famous. That they were part of some gang?'

Clayton groaned inwardly. It was typical of Vincent to step in ahead of him with the Governor. Vincent ranked below him and was constantly fishing for promotion; if Clayton had his way, people would be fishing for *him* – in the Thames.

'Well, it appears so,' Clayton muttered. 'We saw how they escaped. They hung from the side of the train as it went into the tunnel. We believe that these kids or others of their kind are behind the rumours of the, um, Tube Riders.'

The Governor smiled. 'Ah, yes. Even I have heard the stories. So, you were discovered by chance by this *gang*, and they witnessed your martyring of the ambassador?'

'Unfortunately–'

'Yes or no?'

'Yes, sir. And–' Clayton could barely bring himself to say the next words. 'We suspect they may have been in possession of a recording device. A digital camera.'

The Governor's face tensed so slightly as to be almost unnoticeable, but in that moment Clayton felt a flash of white heat cross his face and felt that same sudden incomparable terror he had once felt when a fugitive had pulled a gun on him. Clayton had fired first on that occasion, but he could still remember seeing the darkness inside the barrel like a tunnel into Hell. This time, he knew he would get no chance to fire first.

'Well. That is ... unfortunate. You say your best agents are now looking for these Tube Riders?'

'That's correct, sir.'

'And what is the likelihood of these Tube Riders being caught and ... *silenced* ... before they can get this information into dangerous hands?'

'I would say very high, sir.' Though he wasn't sure he believed it.

'Mr. Clayton, you live in London, I believe.'

'Yes, sir.'

'So you know what it is like to live here?'

'Sir...?'

'You know about the violence and the riots. You know about the problems we have in London, while in other parts of the country things are working like, how to say? Clockwork.' The Governor lifted a pearl white hand and ran it through his hair, the milky curls bouncing back into shape as it passed. 'To be honest with you, Mr. Clayton, London GUA is close to becoming a lost cause. Our electrical generation is performed near entirely in the Scottish wind farms, our gas is still produced in the North Sea ... most major manufacturing has been moved to the Bristol and Birmingham GUAs. London isn't policed with the quality and efficiency with which it should be, and the funds don't exist to improve it. London is waiting to implode on itself, and unfortunately the people feel it too. The city is a mess, a turgid swamp of human detritus, churned up, mixing in on itself and ...' The Governor paused, appearing to get caught on his words. He coughed slightly, and then continued. 'So, within that chaos, you think your agents can find these people quickly enough to prevent outsiders hearing about this or seeing this potential footage? The terrorism funding aid we could have pushed for from the EC is in jeopardy.' He flapped his hands. 'If they find out we killed their man, they could mobilise themselves for war, and our space program, our military ... we can crush a revolution from within, but we don't have nearly the strength to stand against the entire European Confederation.'

'Don't worry sir—'

'There are a million places out there a mouse can hide. And a homeless mouse, always on the move...' The Governor smiled, almost sadistically. 'You have no chance.'

'I assure you—'

'*Never assure me!*' the Governor roared, slamming both hands against the window with a resounding plastic thud. 'Never, *ever* assure me of anything you can not prove!'

Clayton took a step back. The whole room vibrated around him. Paintings tapped against the walls, and expensive vases shuddered on their glass shelves. Clayton wiped the sweat from his hands onto his trousers. This could end badly, he knew. But, he promised himself, if the Governor called for the Personal Guard, or worse, closed the door to leave them both alone ... he would go down fighting. He would die with blood on his clenched fists.

The Governor was breathing hard, hands still pressed against the window. Little rings of condensation had formed around them.

Clayton, who'd survived similar outbursts before, knew the only course of action was to relent, admit his failings, and allow the Governor the authority to suggest a better answer.

'What do you suggest, sir?'

'I think we both know there is only one way to catch these people before they have time to cause harm. We must deploy the Huntsmen.'

Clayton gasped despite himself. The idea was madness. The Huntsmen were near uncontrollable and the Governor knew it.

'Sir ... if I may suggest, that might be a little unwise...'

'And why is that?'

'The Huntsmen have been out of service a long time–'

'There are newer models. Our laboratories are always improving their capabilities. Dr. Karmski has assured me that the newest Huntsmen are the best yet.'

'They're untested.'

The Governor's face tilted sideways, and Clayton saw the back of a smile. 'Then now is the perfect time.'

'Sir, the Huntsmen, are ... unpredictable. Innocent people could die.'

The Governor scoffed. 'Out in that slum of a city there are very few innocents left, as I'm sure you're aware.'

'Sir–'

The Governor turned from the window. In the dim light those glowing eyes were dark, like coals. Clayton felt his back tense, his toes curl.

'You have served me a long time, haven't you, Mr. Clayton?'

'Yes, sir.'

The Governor nodded. His rumbling, thunderous voice dropped. 'You have a good record. I would hate for your memory to be soiled, Mr. Clayton.'

Clayton's jaw tightened. 'Of course not.'

'Then don't jeopardise your life by disobeying me. You will send the Huntsmen to clear up this matter.'

Clayton nodded. 'Yes, sir.'

'Good.' The Governor turned back to the window. 'Now get out of my office and do not return until these Tube Riders are dead.'

Chapter Twelve
Help

THE TUBE RIDERS MADE their way out of the old Kew Gardens station. Simon and Paul helped Switch to walk while Marta and Jess carried the clawboards. The roads were quiet, but from time to time they passed other people, young and old alike who gave them barely a second glance. They were faceless unless they had worth, and signs of fighting, like Switch's injury, made people avoid them even more.

'It hurts,' Switch muttered.

'How far is it to where this friend of yours lives?' Marta asked Paul.

'Out past Richmond, so we need to catch a bus. It's too far to walk.'

They found a stop not far from the station on Sandycombe Road, but the street was quiet and they were waiting almost quarter of an hour before the next bus came. By that time they were edgy and uncertain, glancing over their shoulders as though the Cross Jumpers or the DCA would appear at any moment.

'It's a damn good job it isn't serious,' Switch muttered as they finally climbed on board, going up the stairs to the top where they sat near the front, looking out through cracked, dirty windows at the city as they passed. The bus had the road pretty much to itself because the traffic out in the suburbs was nowhere near as busy as Marta remembered from her childhood. There were still cars, of course, but their numbers had dwindled over the years. Both petrol and bio-fuel were expensive and rare, these days used almost exclusively by the rich or for government-run buses and trains. As the bus rumbled along the street, abandoned, stripped-down cars lined both sides, long ago dragged out of the middle of the road and dumped on the pavement by the government's clearing crews.

Marta remembered the time years back when horses had been a common sight, bred, apparently, in huge farms north-east of the capital, another madcap plan to solve the growing transport crisis. To a ten-year-old, the city had started to remind her of the Medieval Britain of picture books, and sometimes she'd imagined she was a princess as she looked out from her bedroom window, waiting for a prince to rescue her. Only years later, after the GFAs had been totally closed off and the supply had fallen away, did Marta learn that for many years horsemeat had been a savored delicacy amongst the lowest classes.

'I can't believe we had to cross jump,' Switch said with a smirk. 'I need a shower now. I feel dirty.'

Simon smiled. 'Me too.'

'It's not so difficult,' Paul said. 'Doesn't have much fun to it, though, don't you think?'

'You make it or you don't,' Simon said. 'That's it.'

'You know, they choose their leader by whoever makes the shortest jump,' Switch said.

Marta frowned. 'How do you know that? Is there something you aren't telling us? You're a turncoat as well as an asshole?'

He shrugged. 'Oh, you know. I keep my ear to the ground. I overheard a group of guys once. I think one of them was a Cross Jumper, but I didn't hear his name. It was probably "cocksucker", or something like that. Whatever, I doubt anyone's ever come close enough to have their shoe taken off. Makes me their new leader. That's kind of cool. First thing I'd do is tell the bastards to fuck off and get a decent hobby, but I think I'd rather have my shoe back.'

'You were lucky,' Marta agreed. 'Do you have others?'

'Paul can steal me some.'

'Yeah, I'll just pop out while you're in the doctor's.'

'Thanks, knew I could count on you. I'm size eight.'

'*Eight?* That's a girl's size, isn't it?'

Marta punched Simon's arm. 'I'm not size eight! And I bet Jess isn't either!' She turned to the other girl, who was sitting by the window, her head leaning against it, eyes on the road outside. 'Jess?'

Jess sighed and looked up. She had tears in her eyes and her cheeks were red. 'Is everything such a joke?' She sat up and twisted around to face them.

'We just watched two men die. If that wasn't bad enough, we're now fugitives. This may be fun for you guys, but it really isn't much fun at all for me.' She looked away again.

Marta opened her mouth to speak but Switch got in first. 'Look here, Polly Pocket, you didn't just get a knife in your back. If I hadn't done what I did you might be lying face down right now.'

'That's enough, Switch.'

'No, it's *not*, Simon. I ain't the fucking villain here. I was happily going about my business when someone decides they want to bash me up. It's a dog eat dog world, Daddy's girl.'

'Shut up, you pig!' Jess shouted. She aimed a punch at Switch but Marta got in the way and held her back.

'Okay, that's enough.'

Switch's hand came up and the blade appeared in his fingers. 'You wanna know what it feels like to get a knife stuck in you, ask me any time.'

'Shut up now—'

Switch rolled his eyes. 'Sit your ass down, Simon. Paul would have a better chance than you.'

'What's that supposed to mean?'

'Take a guess.'

Jess was crying again, Marta trying to comfort her. She glared at the three of them as they faced off.

Paul stared at Switch for a few seconds. Then, his mouth creasing into a barely perceptible smile, he muttered, 'Cock-eyed asshole.'

For a moment Switch tensed, then the knife hand fell away and a small smile broke his face. 'I see better with one than you do with two, specster,' he said.

'Sod off.' Paul pushed the glasses up his nose. Simon had a smile on his face.

'When exactly do we have to get off, Paul?' Marta broke in.

'Shit, now!' Paul said, standing up. 'Quick, next stop!'

They crowded down the stairs. Simon tried to take Jess's hand but she pushed him away. 'Just leave me alone a while,' she said.

Marta paid their fares and they jumped out on to the street in front of a boarded-up coffee shop with *Rebecca Hilton's Star-fucks!* followed by a phone number written across the metal shutter in pink graffiti and encircled with a left-leaning heart symbol. Across the street, an altercation had broken out between a group of tramps, with knives being waved about amidst shouting and pushing. Marta watched them warily as she ushered the others up the street.

'Okay,' Paul said. 'It's not too far. A couple more streets on we have to turn left.'

Just at that moment a huge bang sounded in the distance, like a car misfiring but loud and powerful enough to cause the ground below their feet to tremble. A moment later there was another smaller bang.

'What was that?' Paul said. 'A bomb?'

'Sounded like it,' Marta replied.

'Terrorists?'

'Could just have been a car blowing up,' Simon said. 'I guess we'll have to wait and find out.'

They started on. Within a few minutes they heard sirens in the distance but none heading their way.

'If nothing else,' it might draw a little attention away from us,' Marta said. 'Assuming we're being searched for.'

'We are,' Jess said sullenly. 'Of course we are.'

'This way,' Paul said.

He led them up some steps to a Georgian terraced house with a blue door, now scratched and chipped. More graffiti adorned the walls and the gate at the front. Paul knocked on the door.

'Are you sure this guy can help us?' Simon said. 'I feel a little exposed up here.' He turned and looked down at the road below.

'If he's in,' Paul said. 'I haven't been here in years, but my father used to bring me here when I got sick as a child. Don't worry. Frank operates under the law. We have no worries there.'

Behind the door, they heard the sound of someone descending a flight of stairs. Then a little grate opened about halfway up the door. They saw movement behind it. A thin, reedy voice said: 'Who is it? What the hell you want?'

'It's the mailman,' Paul said, grinning.

'I don't want any mail. Sod off.' The little grate slammed shut.

Paul pounded the door. 'Frank, wait! It's Paul. I was joking!'

The little grate opened again. 'Ha, I know. So was I.'

The door swung open, revealing a tiny man of advanced years, no more than four feet high. Even from a couple of steps down they towered over him.

His wrinkled face broke into a wide smile. 'It's good to see you again, Paul,' he said. 'You've grown. Outwards, particularly.'

Paul smiled. 'You haven't.'

Frank glanced at each of them in turn before his gaze returned to the blood on Switch's hands and shirt.

'You're in need of a doctor, I take it.'

'He got knifed,' Paul said.

'It was a fucking throwing knife. I practically got impaled on a train.'

'You got money?'

Paul raised an eyebrow at the others. 'Yes, of course,' he said.

'Well come on in then.' Frank stepped back and they filed into a thin hallway. The old man closed the door and pulled across several deadbolts. He pointed towards a door at the end of the hall. 'That way to the surgery.'

'Frank is a doctor,' Paul explained to the others as they went through. He worked for a private health company, but when the company got dissolved the government wouldn't pay him the same salary, so he went black market.'

'Glad to hear it,' Marta said. They couldn't afford a real doctor, assuming they even got to the front of the queue before Switch bled to death. She hoped this friend of Paul's was joking about money too. She doubted they had more than a handful of change left between them.

'Still collecting, I see,' Paul said.

Frank grinned, revealing chipped and blackened teeth. 'Always,' he said. 'You never know when something in one of these shit heaps might come in handy.'

In the hallway, junk filled every available space. Books and stacks of newspapers balanced precariously on top of half-complete bicycles, shadeless lamps, dismantled tables, numerous kitchen appliances and at least half a dozen old stereo players. Frank was stockpiling for something, but Marta couldn't imagine that this junkyard was worth much. Her eyes widened in surprise at the sight of piles of old teddy bears, cups and saucers spilling out of the open doors of old microwaves. Simon also looked amazed. Only Jess, who knew more about wealth than the others, and Switch, who was injured, seemed unconcerned by Frank's thrift shop storeroom of a home.

But in the back room, the 'surgery' was a stark contrast. Clinically white and scrubbed clean with an examination table in the centre of the room, it was like going into another world.

The others stood around while Frank examined Switch. With his bloody t-shirt off and the wound wiped down, Marta was relieved the blood had made it look worse than it was. A thin cut about two inches long clung to the side of his hip, a little wider at the top than the bottom.

'I fucking twisted on it and pushed it in deeper,' Switch said, as way of explanation.

'You were lucky,' Frank said, prodding it with a surgical instrument. 'It went in through the fat on your lower back and got stuck in the muscle here,' he said, prodding Switch's side and making him wince. 'It was a small knife, I take it?'

'Yeah.'

'You pulled it out yourself?'

'Yeah.'

'You still got it?'

'In my one remaining shoe.' He kicked it off and held it up.

Marta smiled in spite of herself. Typical Switch.

Frank plucked it out and held it up to the light. 'Nice,' he said. 'Thrower. Proper one, too.'

'You wanna buy it?'

Frank smiled. He looked around at the others. 'Well, I'm guessing Paul said you had money just to get you in the door. I'll trade it for stitching you up.'

'Done.'

Frank got to work cleaning the wound. Switch yelped in pain as he dabbed at the exposed flesh with antiseptic, but the only thing he could offer to numb the pain was a shot of some cheap homebrewed whiskey.

'I don't know what's worse, the pain or this piss,' Switch growled, gulping it down. Simon, who took an experimental swig after him, couldn't testify to the pain but had to agree the taste was pretty bad.

'I could put you under, but I don't think you've got enough of those knives to pay me for it,' Frank said. 'And plus, by the look of you kids, I'd say you want this chump on his feet pretty soon.'

Their silence was affirmation.

Frank sewed Switch up, dressed the injury and gave him some antibiotics to keep it free of infection. 'Do *not* lose these,' he said. 'Take one a day, and do not forget. If it starts to itch, or pus starts to come out of the wound, double up for a day. It should seal itself over in a week, and then you're safe. Until then, take care. If it gets infected and you can't get to a doctor, well, you're fucked.' Frank cackled. Marta couldn't tell how serious he was.

Switch climbed down from the table. 'Thanks old man, I owe you one.'

Frank raised an eyebrow. 'Many people say that, few deliver.'

'Well, one day I might.'

'I hope so. Take it easy, kid.'

'And you.'

Switch followed Simon and Jess out into the hall. Frank turned to Paul. 'How's your brother?'

Paul shrugged. 'Still there. Starting to raise hell.'

Frank nodded. 'Good, good. Keep him alive, he'll be leading the revolution one day.' He patted Paul's shoulder and started to laugh again.

'Thank you for your help,' Marta said to Frank in the doorway.

'No problem, young lady,' he said. 'I just suggest that whatever you were doing for that to happen you try to avoid it in the future.'

'We'll try,' Marta said. 'If only it was that easy.'

Frank gazed off into the distance. His eyes grew suddenly wistful. 'Don't give up on this country just yet,' he said. 'Keep your heads down, one day them dark clouds are gonna clear.'

'We hope so,' Marta said.

Frank nodded. He looked at Switch. 'You. Come here.'

Switch sauntered closer. 'Yeah, what?'

Before Marta could blink, Frank's hand had gone to Switch's throat, the throwing knife held there, hard against the skin. Switch's good eye went wide. There was a collective intake of breath, and then Frank gave a gap-toothed smile and cackled a laugh. He dropped his hand. 'You'll need this metal more than I will, I think,' he said, holding out the knife, handle first. 'A present from an *old* man.'

Switch took the offered knife and tucked it under his shirt, his composure once more unruffled. 'Thanks. I don't suppose you have any spare shoes around?'

Frank pouted. 'I doubt we're the same size, kid.' He looked around at the others. 'Now, if I can give you kids some advice, stay on your guard. Don't trust anyone.' He cocked his head and flashed a smile. 'Except me.'

With that he nodded goodbye and went back inside. The door slammed behind them without sentiment, and several latches thudded back across.

'On our own again,' Paul said. 'Right, let's go.'

As they headed down the steps back to the street, Marta heard Switch muttering in front of her, 'Damn, must be getting slow...'

Chapter Thirteen
Lab

THE DCA CAR STOPPED outside the warehouse and Clayton got out. He barked a quick order at the driver who turned the car around and sped away, leaving Clayton standing in the street. Around him the air had chilled. The wind maintained a wintry howl that it lacked in other, busier parts of London. Across from him a stand of trees swayed, their branches pressing against a chain-link fence, causing it to creak and groan.

The road was empty. A drink can lay by the curb, half the red label scratched off. The old warehouse rose behind him, a grey box, unmarked, unnamed. Clayton watched it warily and was pretty sure that somewhere hidden up on that plain grey building a camera or two watched him back.

Inside, he knew, was where nightmares began. He'd been free of them a while, but now his turn had come again.

He walked down an overgrown driveway to the building's entrance, a small metal door which showed signs of attempted forced entry: scratches near the hinges, grazes on the large, reinforced steel chain padlock that held it shut.

If only they knew what was inside, Clayton felt those prospective burglars would not have come within a mile of the place.

He stopped within a few feet of the door. He made no attempt to open it, nor knock on it. Instead, he looked up at a tiny spyhole in the corrugated wall a few feet above the door.

'It's Clayton,' he said. 'Code 3715J. You're expecting me. Let me in.'

A sudden rumbling sound made Clayton step back a few feet. The whole building shook, then an entire section of the wall detached itself from the building and swung up to reveal a white-tiled corridor about ten feet wide, gradually descending into darkness. The padlocked door was just a decoy; nothing but concrete lay behind it, part of another door eight inches thick. Inside this unmarked, unnamed building was what remained of Mega Britain's high technology. No one on the outside knew everything that it housed, certainly not Clayton, and he doubted that even the Governor knew all its despicable secrets. The place was quite literally a production line of misery masquerading as science.

He went inside and the door swung shut behind him. Inside the air was cool, fresh, air-conditioned. Artificial strip-lighting flicked on to illuminate his way and behind the smooth walls he could hear the hum of generators. He shivered and moved on downwards, towards an elevator that waited at the end.

He took the elevator down to floor 15B. The entire research complex was underground. Down here were numerous government agencies, everything from medical research to torture chambers. Clayton had been to the former a number of times, the latter only once, and as an observer. Even now, some years later and after everything he'd done, the memory still made him sick.

As the elevator opened, a sign welcomed him to the *Mega Britain Security Research Program*.

He sighed under his breath. The MBSRP was yet another over-funded department of an under-funded country.

He walked through into a reception area. A few grim men and women in lab coats strode back and forth, on errands he could only guess at. Most ignored him, but one man was watching him intently, waiting.

'Mr. Clayton.'

'Dr. Karmski.' *You nasty little bastard.* Clayton nodded a reluctant greeting to the blond man. Karmski was in his middle forties, but his pallid skin showed few signs of aging. Clayton considered it both a result of Karmski's mole-like existence and from self-experimenting with his own research projects.

'I trust you found your way without difficulty? It's been a while since I've seen you.'

'Not nearly long enough,' Clayton replied, to which Karmski smiled. 'This way,' he said.

As Karmski led Clayton deeper into the facility, Clayton said: 'You know why I'm here, of course.'

Karmski nodded. 'What you have ordered is ... *unwise*.'

'It is a matter of national security.'

Karmski held up his hands. 'Oh, don't think for a minute I plan to disobey you.' He raised one eyebrow and tapped his nose in a way that made Clayton want to lay him out cold. 'No skin off my pecker,' Karmski said, and uttered a bird chatter laugh. 'After all, down here *I'm* quite safe.'

'The orders are from the top.'

'Of course they are. No one else is insane enough to let out the Huntsmen.'

Clayton's breath caught. Were Karmski's words to be reported, he'd be killed. 'That's treason,' Clayton said.

Karmski smiled. 'Like I say, I fully intend to comply with the order. But off the record, *fuck you*, Leland Clayton.' His beady little eyes were dark and soulless. 'With my brain I'm more immune than you are.' Karmski rubbed his hands together. 'Hmmm. I'm quite looking forward to the results, actually.'

Clayton promised himself he'd put a bullet in the man's back one day. He said, 'Are they prepared?'

Karmski laughed. 'As well as they can be, I suppose. Come this way.'

They went down a flight of stairs and through a heavy metal door reminiscent of an airlock. Behind the door, plain stone tunnels replaced the manicured corridors of the facility's upper levels. Armed guards patrolled beneath thin strip-lighting wedged into cracks in the walls. Clayton felt like he'd stepped into the middle of an archaeological excavation.

'Are we near?'

Karmski just smiled. 'Nervous?'

'Aren't you?'

Karmski cocked his head. 'Like any man who handles an exotic pet ... familiarity eventually overcomes fear.' He stopped. 'Through this door.' He pulled it open and stepped back. 'After you, Mr. Clayton.'

Clayton glared at Karmski and went through. On the other side the door, he found himself on a circular balcony overlooking what looked like a small gladiatorial arena, complete with straw-covered floor and metal rings in the walls to hold chains. From inside the pit, high stone walls allowed no escape, and only shadows cast by the poor lighting allowed cover.

Karmski put a hand on Clayton's shoulder, making the other man jump. 'Jesus Christ, don't do that.'

'Behold, my children.' Karmski waved an expansive hand towards the pit.

'Where—?' Clayton began, but he'd seen them. Each of them standing nose-close to the perimeter wall, cowled heads bent forward, snouts just showing as pointed lumps of shadow. From fifteen feet above them it was difficult to see how big they were, but Clayton estimated they were closer to seven than six feet tall. They were lithely built, but he knew their strength and agility, altered both by genetic and biotechnological means too advanced for him to begin to comprehend, made him weaker than a small child in comparison.

The greatest and the worst achievement of the last surge of technological advancement were now barely sustainable in this staling age. What had begun as the development of the ultimate war machine had ended up as this: a handful of barely controllable, psychotic super-tracking monsters, their fragile internal setups corroding more as each day passed. But for now they were still fearsome.

Infused with the mind of a man, the tracking ability of a bloodhound, and the physical strength of a cyborg, here they were. Mega Britain's ultimate invention: the Huntsmen.

Clayton leaned over the pit, terrified but as ever fascinated by them. He counted twelve in all, but he knew there were more, locked away in cells further underground. This was what Karmski called the exercise yard, but no matter how long they stayed on the dirty sand and straw of the pit, they didn't move from the walls; dark, twisted wraiths wanting only to get out.

A drop of sweat beaded on his forehead and dropped into the pit.

'*Daaaaaaaaaaayaaaaaaaa!*'

The nearest Huntsman howled like a dying animal and leapt at him, jumping higher than any man should, frothing, rabid jaws snapping towards his face. Even as it dropped back to the floor, having got no closer than five or six feet, Clayton staggered backwards into the wall, mouth dropping open, hands unable to support him. He slipped and tumbled to the ground, a low moan coming from his throat. His eyes rolled and he felt an uncomfortable warmth in his groin area. He would have lost consciousness if Karmski hadn't slapped him hard across the face.

Recovering his composure, Clayton pushed himself up against the wall, eyes darting about.

'Aren't they beautiful?' The scientist grinned into his face. 'Oh dear!' Karmski wrinkled his nose. 'Had a little accident, did you, Mr. Clayton?'

'Get me out of here,' Clayton growled.

Karmski called forward a couple of guards and they helped Clayton to his feet. Back in the pit he heard the snarling of one of the Huntsmen, the hideous scrape of its clawed hands scratching at the pit walls.

Clayton excused himself and a guard showed him to a crude bathroom. After he'd cleaned himself up under a single hanging bulb, he stared at himself in the mirror above a dirty sink. He was dismayed at how different sanitary standards were down in these lower levels, but they were the least of his worries. It was madness to let those beasts out on to the streets. If one of them got loose the slaughter could be unimaginable, but within hours they would be in his charge.

Back out in the corridor, Karmski said, 'I apologise for Craul's behavior. I'm afraid you upset him.'

'Fuck, Karmski, you have names for those monsters?'

The doctor rubbed his hands together. 'Well, you don't leave a litter of kittens unnamed, do you? And they are at least partly human.'

Clayton just shook his head in disbelief.

'We have handlers for them, you know,' Karmski said. 'The Huntsman can be restrained using various means, until of course they have the scent. Then, in order to get the job done, we release them.' He smiled. 'They are capable of following orders, but how closely they stick to them is uncertain. They tend to become ... how would you say? *Incensed* ... by certain situations.'

'How many of those vile things do you have?'

'Currently, in an operational condition, almost one hundred. We have countless others in various states of, um, repair, as well as a number of other prototypes in various stages of development. Some, my dear Mr. Clayton, would astound you.'

Clayton sighed. 'We have five targets. They may or may not be closely related and they may or may not try to run. We have a starting point for their scent, an abandoned Underground station. As we speak I have DCA agents moving back along the rail line to find out which station they came from. That should give us all the scent we need. Now, tell me, can we make it clear to those monsters who we want dead and who we don't?'

Karmski grinned, and Clayton's blood chilled. 'Not at all,' he said. 'We can instruct them which scents to chase, but once we set them free they will eliminate anyone they feel is a threat. Anyone harboring the quarry, anyone assisting them in any way...'

'Good God, Karmski, what is it you've created down here?'

'The Huntsmen were designed as ground infantry. To be dropped behind enemy lines with the orders to wreak destruction on all the enemy they encountered. They were designed to hunt and kill until death.'

'They have weapons?'

'Of course. Physical and mechanical.'

'Guns?'

'We prefer something a little more ... *classical*. We give them crossbows.'

Clayton raised an eyebrow. 'Why the fuck do you give them crossbows?'

'Let's just say that if you give them automatic weapons the death toll could match a small war.'

Clayton shook his head. 'This is madness.'

Karmski flashed his eyes. 'When do you want them released?'

Clayton took a deep breath. 'Immediately.'

Karmski smiled. 'As you wish.' He pulled a radio from his belt and barked an order into it with a sharpness of tone that surprised Clayton. A moment after he put the radio back on his belt there was a cacophony of noise from behind the door. Clayton flinched.

'Don't worry, they're just being brought in from the exercise yard. They'll be briefly sedated, then implanted with newer tracking chips and given their orders.'

'Can you imagine what would happen if one of those things escaped?'

Karmski shrugged. 'Oh, sometimes they do. We usually recapture or eliminate them pretty quickly. They don't get far when they leave such a wide trail.'

'Good God.'

'That's what happens when the government cuts security spending.' He grinned. 'Still, none have got out for a couple of years.'

'That recently?'

Karmski cocked his head. 'The one that escaped was safe, though. Not fully integrated, still mostly human.'

'Should I be relieved to hear that?'

'It won't matter to you, Mr. Clayton. For the next few days at least, you're going to be much closer to the Huntsmen than me.' Karmski grinned. His teeth gleamed. 'Enjoy.'

'I swear, Karmski, that one day I'll gut you like a stray dog,' Clayton said through gritted teeth.

Karmski gave a shrill laugh. 'Oh Mr. Clayton, you're going to have such fun with my babies. Make sure you send a postcard, won't you?'

Chapter Fourteen
Trail

THE SCENT OF THE GIRL and her boyfriend were easy to pick up, once Dreggo had differentiated them from the others. Her heightened sense of smell was good enough to follow a trail as fresh as a couple of days old. The girl was easy to distinguish because she had been wearing a light perfume, but it was necessary for Dreggo to head up the stairs to work out which of the men's scents was her pretty boy boyfriend.

At first they were all mixed together, but once they reached the station entrance, the couple's trails separated off from the others, and Dreggo could easily pick them up.

It was a slow, arduous business. The area wasn't busy, but every person who had passed in the last hour or more had left a fresh scent trail. Some were stronger than others; cheap perfume, thick sweat, dirty water, feces, or blood. Following by body smell alone was difficult, but at least she was tracking two people, not one.

She followed for a mile or so, crossing a couple of streets, when abruptly the trail went dead. She knelt down and leaned close to the ground, trying to pick it up. A few feet in either direction offered nothing. Then, she saw it: tagged to a nearby lamp post was a rusty metal sign advertising a bus stop.

'Damn it.' She kicked at the ground. If they'd taken a bus, there was no way she could track them; she'd have to find another way. She looked up at the sign, looking for the bus numbers that stopped here, wondering if she could guess from their destinations where they might have gone. The sign was empty, useful only to someone who already knew the routes the buses took.

It was futile. They could be anywhere.

Dreggo cursed again, turning around on her heels in despair. She'd have to go back to her original plan, which was to track them down the traditional way: find out who they were, where they hung out, who they were friends with. But that could take days, and she wanted revenge now. What little life she'd had as leader of the Cross Jumpers was gone, and her hatred for the Tube Riders was growing like a cancer fused into her soul.

They wouldn't be back, she knew, the Cross Jumpers. They might form again in small gangs from time to time to practice their dangerous hobby, but their unity had been undermined, and that was her fault. She had thought they wanted the same as she did, the urban legend, the infamy, but with the exception of Maul and a handful of others they were just cowardly street kids looking for a way to pass the time. It had been fun until too much blood was shed.

I should have known better.

Dreggo wanted to blame herself but that was mental suicide, and she had blamed too much on herself already. The abuse, the suffering, the violence, the rapes; for years she had shouldered the blame.

Not this time. The Tube Riders had caused this. And the only way to restore her pride and build the infamy for herself that she wanted was to track them down and kill them, one after another.

'*...orders...*'

Dreggo jumped. She looked around, searching for the source of the word, faint, almost indistinct. There was no one behind her, no one anywhere near. Then she heard another sound, a buzzing sensation like a radio stuck between stations, the crackling of static.

The sound was inside her head. She felt suddenly uncomfortable, as though plumes of blood were pressing against the inside of her skull, and she pushed her hands against her forehead as though to stop her brain from bursting out.

The buzzing paused for a moment and then began again, louder. She heard more words, faint and indistinct. At first she thought she was going mad, and then memories of another horrible chapter in her life began to resurface, a time she had been held captive underground, a prisoner of the government, used as a test dummy for experiments. From those dark days she remembered little other than fear, pain, and suffering, but her skills had come from that time, too: her strength, her tracking ability, her ability to jump higher or run faster than any normal human, her ability to sense fear or danger just from breathing in the air.

She sat down by the side of the road as the buzzing got louder. She had no choice but to listen as the words became clearer, but she squeezed her eyes shut anyway, trying to push them out, waiting for them to end.

'...orders ... five people ... two women ... three ... all die ... known as ... *Tube Riders*...'

Her eyes flicked open. Dreggo began to listen. *I know you. Huntsmen...*

So, they were loose again. And they were hunting the *Tube Riders?* It hardly seemed possible. What could those fools have done to have the Huntsmen set loose on them?

Dreggo didn't know and didn't care to know. What it did mean was that her dead end had suddenly opened up again and she had another trail to follow. Maybe the nightmares from her past could help her settle her own score.

Despite the growing nausea she felt, Dreggo smiled.

Chapter Fifteen
Scent

CLAYTON HUNG BACK AT THE REAR as the group of handlers led the muzzled Huntsmen down into what had once been St. Cannerwells London Underground station. One hand rested on the butt of his gun, in a holster at his right hip. The creatures were surprisingly sedate as the men led them along, walking upright like respectful prisoners with their heads bowed, their faces invisible beneath their cowls. Unseen metal collars encircled the Huntsmen's necks beneath their robes, with a thin chain that reminded Clayton of an overlong watch strap leading back to a loop that each handler held as they walked about ten feet in front of their respective charges. The five handlers, one for each of the creatures, wore metal face protectors, thick bulletproof jackets and padded leg wear. It wasn't bullets that they feared, though, Clayton knew. It was ripping, tearing claws.

So far, everything had gone to plan, even though sitting in the back of the DCA's van with them had been perhaps the most terrifying experience of Clayton's life.

'They won't move,' the head handler, a man called Jakob, had told him. He had indicated a button on the loop of the leash he held. 'See this? The dog moves and I shock him. These give electric shocks strong enough to render an elephant a gibbering wreck. They won't move because they've all been given a demonstration of what it feels like. The part of the brain that still contains human thoughts and cognitive processes understands how much it'll hurt if they try anything. But–' and here Jakob gave a devilish grin, '–if I let go of this leash for just *one second*, that dog'll tear us all apart before you can even think about getting your gun.'

Vincent, sitting beside Clayton, had scoffed. Lifting his hand, he had put two fingers together in a gun shape, pointed it at the Huntsman opposite and made a quiet popping sound.

'And even if you did,' Jakob had continued, with a dismissive smirk at Vincent, 'You wouldn't get off enough iron in time. You black coats have any idea what it takes to bring down a Huntsman? Get it square in the face and you're doing good, but those bodies can take some beating. Next to these dogs, killing revolutionaries is like blowing away bits of paper.'

Jakob had sounded almost proud. Clayton had plucked up the courage to look through the metal grill of the face mask-cum-muzzle the creature opposite him wore, beneath the low cowl and into the unblinking human eyes that watched him from above the dog-like snout. There was intelligence there, he saw. Intelligence and hunger; hunger to be free.

'This way,' Vincent said up ahead of them. 'This is where we found evidence of the kids.'

'You found this place on a map?' Clayton said, glancing nervously back at the Huntsmen. Vincent had one hand under his jacket, on the handle of his own gun, no doubt. *That insolent bastard would as soon as put a bullet in* my *back as in one of those monsters*, he thought.

'We just backtracked along the line, checking in anywhere those kids could have come from, once it was apparent that they used those bits of wood to hang off the trains. The abandoned station wasn't on the most up-to-date map, but we got suspicious at the large gap between the two stations either side and so we checked the archives. And there it was, St. Cannerwells, forgotten for more than a decade. The perfect place for those kids to hang out.'

'And what did you find?'

'Not much. A pile of old mattresses at one end, and some chalk lines along the side of the platform. At the other end a dried puddle of blood, and some pretty nasty leftovers on the tracks.'

'Leftovers?'

Vincent sighed. 'Come on, Clayton. The remains of a kid. Maybe more than one. It's hard to tell after they've been diced up by a bunch of train wheels.'

'You think they had a bust up?'

'From the evidence I'd say they didn't plan to be leaving the station. I think they were running away from something when they came across us, and our … *business*. Knowing this town, probably trouble with a rival gang.'

It was Clayton's turn to sigh. 'Fuck. It sucks, this city, doesn't it?'

Vincent didn't look at him. 'Not our problem. They dig their own graves, we just deliver them.'

Clayton felt a sudden surge of hatred for the younger man. He had an unsettled score with Vincent for going to the Governor behind his back. Being in the presence of the Huntsmen had put it to the back of his mind, but it wasn't forgotten, and Vincent was adding credits all the time.

'Over here,' Vincent said, pointing.

'They've been exposed to the scents of the kids from the other station,' Clayton said. 'If they can pick them up here, we should be away.'

Behind them they heard a canine whining from one of the Huntsmen. If the creature hadn't been so fearsome, it would have reminded Clayton of a dog getting a cuff around the head. Coming from a seven-foot-tall half-human killing machine, it made Clayton shiver.

'There are many different scents here,' Jakob called over his shoulder. 'The dogs are getting confused.'

'Why?'

'I'd guess from the agitation, that there's a whole lot of interaction going on. They're getting secondary smells, intermingled smells … it's going to be difficult to make sure they target the right people.'

'They're all vagrants,' Vincent said. 'A few extra deaths won't matter.'

'Shut up, Vincent,' Clayton growled. 'We're here to protect the State, not instigate a goddamn massacre.'

Vincent smiled. 'Fuck them. The deaths of a few, for the lives of many. I don't see why you give so much of a shit, not like you haven't hastened a few deaths yourself.'

'Show respect to a senior officer!' Clayton hissed. 'I'm your superior! Staple your damn mouth shut or I'll have you reported!'

'My apologies, *sir*,' Vincent said, stalking off along the platform, his expression unreadable in the gloom.

'Okay,' Jakob called. 'The Huntsmen are ready to go. Question is, are *you* ready?'

Clayton felt another shudder. He wondered how long he could last before his mind and his body just fell apart, leaving him like an unfinished jigsaw by the trackside.

'You're sure their orders are programmed correctly?'

Jakob nodded. 'They have their scents, and they have the physical descriptions your men gave them of the targets. And they have their orders. Once the targets have been eliminated, they will return to the lockup facility.'

'Okay. Let's get this over with. Release them.' He noticed how Adam Vincent ambled around to stand behind him like some frightened puppy, and his dislike for the junior officer rose yet another notch.

Two of the five Huntsmen were standing almost motionless by the edge of the track, looking into the dark tunnel. With their long robes and the hoods that covered their faces, from behind they had the tall stateliness of priests, bishops. From behind you would never know they weren't men; only the leashes that hung down from their necks and trailed back to their handlers said different.

The other three, though, were a different matter. One was crouched close to the ground, muzzled face almost touching the platform. The two others were pulling and jerking on their leashes like the bloodhounds part of their genetic make-up had come from. Froth dribbled from their canine mouths, dripping through the grills of their muzzles and down the front of their robes.

One of them began to howl. Clayton winced, for the first time feeling irritated with them rather than just terrified. He dealt in men, not animals. This was so far out of his comfort zone it had come full circle and poked him in the backside. The howl was an oddly human sound, and sent a fresh shiver running down his back.

The creature suddenly jerked upwards and screamed, a sound like two pieces of thin metal being scraped together. Its back arched, then it fell backwards to the platform. It quivered for a few seconds, and then started to climb back to its feet, sniveling like a dog with a cold.

'What happened?' Clayton asked.

'Bill just gave him a little shock to calm him down,' Jakob replied.

'Can you hurry the fuck up and just get them out of here?'

'Sure thing.'

The handlers, faces obscured by their protective masks, moved closer to their Huntsmen charges. Clayton noticed how they held the end of the leashes up where the Huntsmen could see them.

'Come on now, come quietly,' Clayton heard Jakob say.

The handlers went behind each Huntsman and undid a clasp on the muzzles. Each dropped to the floor, and the Huntsmen's faces became more clearly visible. One of them turned towards Clayton, a dark red tongue flicking at the canine teeth that hung over its furry jaw line. Clayton had to look away.

'Now, you have your radios,' Jakob was saying to his Huntsman. The creature gave a slow nod. A low growl came from its throat. 'Okay. When you locate a target, you are to contact Mr. Clayton over there, do you understand?'

'Yesssss...'

Clayton exchanged a look of surprise with Vincent. Neither had realised the Huntsmen could speak.

'*Before* you carry out your orders. Do you understand?'

'Clayton.'

The sound was what Clayton imagined a snake with the flu would sound like; a hissing, sibilant noise like a piece of metal being dragged across sand. He felt the urge to vomit.

'Good,' Jakob said. 'Ready? Okay, let them free!'

He took a few rapid steps backwards and then pressed a different button on his leash control. There was a click and then the chain fell away from the Huntsman's neck collar to clatter on the ground. Clayton watched one Huntsman as it looked around for a moment, then turned and bounded off, one jump taking it down on to the tracks, and a handful more taking it away towards the dark of the tunnel. The hood hung low over its face, and the robes flapped out behind it as it dashed into the darkness, moving low in a half crouch, a two-legged hyena-like gait. In a moment it was gone, the other three close behind it.

Three...?

Clayton's eyes widened, and he swung to look back across the platform, where the last Huntsman still stood, towering over its handler. It was the one that had been shocked, he knew, simply from the way its lips had curled back over its teeth. As he watched in horror, its arms rose slowly up out of the folds of its robe.

'Guns, Clayton!' Vincent shouted, but it was too late. Even as Clayton drew his gun, the creature's arm slashed down at the handler. Clayton glimpsed a furred, muscular forearm, and then blood sprayed out from Bill's neck and chest. The creature turned towards them and its violent, tormented gaze took them all in. Its lips curled back in a snarl, then it howled once and leapt down on to the tracks, loping off after the others.

Clayton, Vincent, Jakob and the other handlers rushed over to Bill's aid, but it was too late. His chest had been ripped open, and dark blood pumped out on to the tiles of the platform.

'Jesus Christ,' Vincent muttered.

'One too many times,' Jakob said. 'They have good memories, those creatures. Fuck, that's awful. But it comes with the territory.' He turned to Clayton. 'Well, it's over to you, now,' he said. 'Good luck.'

Clayton stared at the black tunnel opening where the Huntsmen had gone. He wished that he'd seen the last of them, but something told him that was far, far from the truth.

Chapter Sixteen
Attack

Frank lowered the metal shutters down over the downstairs window. The veins stood out on his thin, sinewy arms as they worked the handle of the old shutter, one that had once covered a shop storefront and which he had bought from a scrap dealer some years ago, when the crime in the city first began to escalate. He had cut the shutters to fit and used them to cover all his windows, both downstairs and up. Many long-term residents in rougher areas preferred just to brick the windows over, but Frank still remembered the days before the anarchy and was damned if he was giving up his daylight and the views from his upper floor windows because groups of wiseass punks liked to throw more rocks about than they used to.

Out on the street he heard a crash, several shouts and the sound of running feet. For a moment he wished he hadn't given the knife back to Paul's friend, although he had several of his own, and other weapons besides. Whoever was out there was unlikely to bother him, though; his reputation and worth as a former medical doctor lent him some respect. No, whoever might be out there would most likely pass him by and go on to fuck over some other place.

He frowned as the mechanism jammed, the old cogs catching on each other as they often did these days. He strained his muscles, seventy-four years young, but still wiry enough to have kept that kid on his toes earlier. Frank gave a little chuckle, remembering the way that twitchy-eyed punk had jumped.

Yeah, diminutive and old he might be, but there was still a little juice in the tank. He wasn't done yet.

He grunted and jigged the lever back and forth. The shutter, halfway down, began to descend again.

As the shutter closed it off, Frank glanced out of the window, night now fallen over London as the evenings drew in towards winter. Looking down from his window he could see the row of houses opposite, and towering over them from behind, the empty hulk of an abandoned office building, seven floors of smashed windows and paint-peeling walls. He gave a wry smile as the shutter began to erase it, and his eyes glazed as his mind drifted back to a time when you could walk the streets at night without fear, when you could take a train out into the country and go fishing or ride a goddamn horse if you so chose.

Floating among his memories, he almost didn't see the low, stooped creature as it advanced up the steps towards his door, its covered head low to the ground like a dog following a scent.

Self-preservation stopped Frank from crying out in terror. He clamped a hand over his mouth as his strength drained away, his other hand dropping from the shutter lever to hang useless at his side. In the silence he heard only his heart beating, and then, slightly out of time, the *tap tap tap* of the knocker on the outside of his front door.

Frank took one, two, then a third step back from the window, dimly aware that it would take a few moments for even a battering ram to break through his oversized, barricaded front door. The door to the hall was behind him and the front door beyond. There was only one staircase to the upper floor, past the junk in his hallway to the right of the front door. There was safety that way, if the door stayed closed.

His hands shook as he stared out at the blackness of the night. The uncommon sight of a car rolled past on the road below, its horn blaring for some unseen reason.

Then the road vanished as a dark shape blocked his view, pressing close against the glass, hands that looked only vaguely human cupping around a face hidden in shadow.

Frank's nerve failed him and he screamed as a dog-like snout pressed forward out of the shadows under the hood. He staggered back across the room at the same time as the creature roared and the glass shattered inwards, the demon out of his nightmares climbing into the room, its savage teeth bared, maw snapping towards him as its clawed hands brushed away shards of glass like bits of paper.

Frank felt the edge of the open door press against his back and he rolled sideways, pulling it shut at the same time as the creature leapt forward. Years ago, out of precaution and paranoia he had replaced all the old doors of his house with stronger, fire-resistant ones. He had also installed deadbolts on all of them, for what event he'd never been quite sure. Now, he reached up and pulled the bolt on the living room door across, just as the creature thudded against the other side. Frank saw the handle rattle wildly, heard it creak and groan beneath the strength of hands no longer human. He backed away through the junk in his hallway, eyes searching for a knife, knowing it would be useless in a few seconds when the door broke.

A loud thud announced the creature's first attempt, and Frank turned and ran, darting through the piles of junk and up the stairs. He gritted his teeth as his old heart pounded in his chest, his body long past its prime for such exertion. Exhausted, he had to pause a few steps from the upper landing, just long enough to see his living room door burst open amidst splintering wood and the creature lurch forward into the hallway.

Frank froze as it stood there, the hood fallen away from its face, and he stared down at the monstrous face swinging back and forth. Human eyes looked out over a bestial, canine snout, while wires and scar tissue crisscrossed its bald scalp. Around its neck, as it breathed he saw the sharp angular shapes of metal implants under the skin, shifting and writhing like sinews beneath a metal, dog-like collar.

The Huntsman didn't look up at him. Instead, it turned right towards the front door, its nose twitching as saliva dripped from its teeth. It growled once and then turned away, taking a couple of steps back towards the surgery. Frank heard a low moan and then the rasp of what sounded like words. Then it leapt forward, disappearing from view as it barged through the surgery door. He listened for a moment, hearing the jangle and crash of his operating table and a desk being turned over, their contents emptying across the floor. Then his legs found their strength again and he stumbled up the remaining stairs to the upper landing.

He hurried into a room he used as a study, slammed the door and pulled across several more deadbolts. There was a desk in the middle of the room, piled high with papers, various ornaments and antiques he had collected over the decades. He stumbled around it and went to a cupboard in the corner.

There, on a shelf above several hanging jackets, was a small handgun. He took it down, cocked it, and checked the chambers for rounds. He had just two bullets left. Years ago, he'd used it to scare off a couple of kids who'd tried to break in through the back, and he'd never replaced the rounds he'd used. Still, two would be enough. If the creature came up, he would use the first on it. If he missed, he would use the second on himself.

Frank took the gun and crouched down behind the desk, squeezing into the space for the chair, his back against the cold wood. At his size there were several cubbyholes Frank could make use of, but he knew that if the Huntsmen came upstairs there were none small enough to save him.

He waited that way for a long time, listening to the creature rampaging through his house. Then, after what seemed an eternity, he heard a louder sound than any of the others, a crunching noise like a door breaking off its hinges. After that, there was just quiet, but even so, Frank didn't move. He just sat right where he was, legs crossed over, the gun on his lap with both hands around it, two wrinkled old fingers on the trigger.

He was dimly aware that he had pissed himself, the warm dampness soaking through his trousers and making a little pool on the floor between his legs. But still he didn't move, holding his position as he listened for sounds that the Huntsman was still downstairs, too terrified to even shift his body as his limbs started to seize up, barely daring to even breathe. In his mind he saw its grotesque face, its human eyes, its snapping, canine jaws, and heard its growl, the rasp of its voice. The words he remembered clearly, two of them, and he wondered just what those kids had got themselves into to have Huntsmen on their trail.

'*Tube Riders*,' he whispered aloud, rolling the Huntsman's words across his tongue.

Chapter Seventeen
Loss

THE FEW STREET LIGHTS that still worked were blinking on as the Tube Riders made their way through London towards Jessica's house. They stayed off the main streets where possible, the general chaos creating a rumbling background noise around them. Sirens mixed with squealing tires, shouts and cries with thuds and crashes. Even the occasional gunshot split through the evening as if afraid of being left out.

The Tube Riders walked quickly but in near silence, the journey across the failing city sobering them up to the reality of their situation. Things looked bleak. By now they were probably being tracked through the streets by the government while Dreggo and her Cross Jumpers hunted them through the London Underground. Only if Jess's father proved honest – and indeed brave enough – to help them, was there hope.

'It's not far,' Jess said, as she led them left down a smaller residential street. A complete absence of cars made it look deserted. 'Maybe another ten minutes.'

'Okay.' Marta trailed at the back. She had tied her matted hair back out of her eyes, but all she wanted was to take a shower and then sleep. The likelihood of either was remote. Ahead of her, Simon tried from time to time to take Jess's hand, only for the girl to pull it away, and Marta could only imagine what he must be feeling. Behind them, Switch and Paul walked side by side, the smaller man limping a little with just the one shoe. He winced with each step, and Marta hoped what Frank had told them was right, that the knife wound wasn't as bad as it looked.

'It's at the top of this street,' Jess said, pointing up the hill towards a row of tall Edwardian houses curving out of sight. It could be any time of the last two hundred years, Marta thought, if it wasn't for the lack of cars, the occasional boarded up window, and a couple of collapsed street-front walls, soil and overgrown sods of grass spilling down into the road.

Marta felt a sudden bloom of sadness. Her own family was long gone, the last being her brother, Leo, the first Tube Rider. Her parents were fading into memory, her images of them brushed aside by her unwavering focus on survival. When she wasn't tube riding she was finding money however she could, struggling to pay her contribution to the rent for the apartment she shared with a revolving door of other street roamers, rent paid to a gang who didn't even own the building she squatted in. Sometimes she found a few days of work, other times she did what she had to do. The handful of creased and torn notes they offered every week kept the roof over their heads, a dirty water mains attached and an illegal electricity connection switched on. On those weeks when the money didn't add up, the women and even some of the men would draw lots on who would pay the rent with other means.

In another time, she might have lived in a house like this with her family. They could have been happy, could have done family things, like visit Big Ben, eat picnics in Regent's Park, walk around London Zoo. In another time, another world...

'You all right?' Paul asked, as Marta choked back a sob, her hand covering her mouth and forcing it out as a half-cough.

She cleared her throat, kept her eyes averted. 'Yeah, yeah ... no problem, just ... dust.'

Paul nodded. 'Cool, that's ... cool.'

'There,' Jess said, stopping up ahead. 'That's my house.'

She was pointing at an Edwardian terrace house across the road at a small intersection ahead of them. The house looked quiet, unoccupied, but otherwise safe. Just a normal terraced house for a normal family.

'Something's wrong,' Jess said suddenly, her voice rising. 'Oh my God, something's wrong!'

'What?' Simon turned to her. 'What do you mean?'

'The gate's open! The gate's *never* open!'

'Jess, there could be danger, wait—'

Too late, Jess was sprinting up the road towards the house. Simon paused just a second before giving chase. Marta looked at the others. 'Live together, die together,' she said, breaking into a run.

'Let's go,' Paul said, and set off after them.

'Easy for you to say,' Marta heard Switch mutter behind her as he limped in pursuit. 'Neither of you got stuck with that whore's knife.'

They saw Jess pause by the gate, saw her reach out a tentative hand. A moment later she cried out again. 'The security's down!'

'Keep your voice down, for Christ's sake!' Switch growled, but Jess was already at the front door, pushing it inwards, broken locks giving no resistance.

Marta had a terrible sinking feeling in her stomach. Jess was inside the house, Simon close by the door. Paul, just ahead of Marta and Switch, was on the path when Jess cried out again, a wail of despair.

'Noooooo...'

'Oh my fuck—'

Simon was inside too. The others were close behind.

Marta went through the living room door behind Paul, with Switch following. She took one glance and turned away, a hand over her mouth.

From the scene Marta could tell Jess's parents were middle-aged, smartly dressed, not overweight, of average height. To give any more description she would need to look at photographs. Both were dead, but quite how they had initially died was difficult to say. The blood covering their bodies and hanging in thick red swathes across the walls made it impossible to tell. Much as it repulsed her, Marta had to look again.

Simon was consoling Jess in a corner. The girl was hysterical, screaming and struggling against his arms as he held her. Marta understood her pain; most of them did. Families were rare and their worth was increased by the sheer number of people around you who had no one. Marta had been there, of course, but that took nothing away from Jess's pain. Marta's parents hadn't been murdered like this.

'*Get away from me! All of you leave me alone! You did this! You caused this!*' Jess shrieked, and Marta looked up to see Jess sprint past her, out into the hall and up the stairs. A few seconds later a door slammed shut and the sound of hysterical screams cut down through the ceiling.

Marta took a deep breath and glanced around at the bodies of Jess's parents. She'd seen plenty of death before, of course, but nothing this brutal. This was even worse than Clive, perhaps. Jess's mother lay backwards over the end of a sofa, her head touching the ground. In the centre of her forehead a thin metal pole protruded out of a bloody gash. Her neck had been torn open and her face ripped up. The smart office suit she had been wearing was ripped and stained with blood.

Jess's father lay across the floor. One arm had been torn off his body and lay underneath a television in the corner. A scattering of books lay across him, from where he'd pulled a shelf off the wall as he fell. Several were open, the pages swollen with blood.

Marta didn't want to look at his face but she did anyway. What she saw there made her eyes water with terror. His right cheek and part of his jaw had been torn off. The flesh that hung off his face contained bite marks, like those of a dog.

Simon rushed past her and out into the hall, making her jump. She'd been so transfixed by the bodies that she hadn't even seen him coming. She heard him run up the stairs and knock on Jess's door. The girl's sobbing grew louder for a moment then quieter again as he went inside.

Switch was sitting on a sofa by the window, looking out. Paul had gone outside.

'The blood's not even dry,' Switch said quietly. 'Whatever did this might still be around. Holy shit, this is nasty.'

'*Who*ever did this.'

Switch raised an eyebrow. 'Come on, Marta. You know what was here, same as me.'

Marta closed her eyes. 'I can't think about that. I just don't want to think about it.'

'Her parents are dead because of us. Because of what *we* saw. If she's right about that murdered guy being an ambassador, then we're wanted right now. We call the police, they'll fucking take us in. If we don't call the police, we'll get tracked down and ripped up into dog meat like this.'

Marta sat down next to Switch. She leaned close to him, and felt his hand go over hers. She looked at him but his eyes were on the bodies. In his other hand he held Dreggo's throwing knife, his only comfort. She noticed a slight sheen in his eyes that on any other occasion would have surprised her, but as her own choking despair welled up again she realised that some situations went to a new level, sucking even the hardest of people into the darkness.

'I don't want to die, Switch,' she said, in a soft voice. 'I don't want to end up like that.'

He nodded. 'Shit, no. We have to run. All of us. You know this was a Huntsman, yeah? You can see what those motherfuckers can do. They can track like bastards, too. It will find us unless we haul ass the fuck out of here right now.'

Marta closed her eyes. 'And I thought the Cross Jumpers were bad.'

'We need to wise up. In some ways we're lucky it was a Huntsman. Those DCA chumps would have left a guard behind in case we came back. The Huntsmen don't work like that. They're tracking, killing machines. It followed her scent back here, found her parents. The scent was obviously similar enough to make it kill them, or else the Huntsman got pissed off about something.'

'How did it get here, Switch? How did it do it?'

He looked at her, and she saw something there that surprised her: an unflinching graveness. When he spoke the sudden maturity in his voice was unnerving, as though the Switch she knew was gone forever, his body possessed by some long-dead military commander. 'Huntsmen can follow a scent anywhere,' he said. 'Even one that's weeks old or left by someone moving at speed. They have an enhanced sense of smell, partly animal, and partly computerised. They hunt day and night until they find what they want. Then they kill it.'

'How do you know this?'

'I asked people, anyone I ever met who knew anything. I always figured the day would come when I might get into more trouble than petty crime. I killed a man today, and that wasn't the first time. I always figured there might be a time when I'd have one of those hybrid pieces of shit come after me.' He shrugged. 'The only way to beat your enemies is to know them better than they know you.'

'Where can we go? Where can we hide?'

'We have to leave London.'

Marta stared at him. 'That's impossible. How?'

'We'll go down to St. Cannerwells, wait for one of the freight trains and ride it right out of London. I have an uncle in Bristol GUA who might help us. If he's still alive. But we can't waste time. We have to go tonight.'

'Is it wise to go back to St. Cannerwells?'

'They'll have found it by now, if they've sent a Huntsman. It's the last place they'll expect us to go. After all, it's just an abandoned London Underground station. The DCA will assume we'll head for the perimeter walls, try to find a way through the gates, but Huntsmen don't work like normal police because they're partly animal. They follow a trail and run down their prey. If we can keep ahead of them we'll have a chance. St. Cannerwells, back at the start of our trail, could be the safest place for us.' Then, as though to remind her of the man she knew so well, he added, 'Fuck, this sucks *ass*.'

Marta sighed. Tears clung to her cheeks. 'How can we escape from a Huntsman?'

'From what I've heard of them, they're kind of junk. They don't work properly, keep fucking up and going haywire. We have to keep our eyes open, watch for them coming. Stay out in the open.'

'What if it's still here?'

Despite everything, Switch actually laughed. 'The Huntsmen don't do stealth, Marta, at least not that I heard. If one was here we would be fucking mincemeat by now.'

Paul stepped into the room, and Marta knew he'd been listening. His face was grey, his glasses steamed up. He'd been crying too, and there was a dried crust of saliva around his chin from where he'd been vomiting.

'I have to find my brother,' he said, voice hollow. If a Huntsman really is after us like you say, I have to get to Owen before they follow my trail back to him. He might already be dead for all I know.'

Marta nodded. 'We should split up, spread the trails and just hope they've only sent one. Go home, grab what you can and hope it's not too late. We'll meet in St. Cannerwells at midnight, and do what Switch says. Take the first train we can out of this shit fucking city.'

'Jess won't leave.' Simon stood in the doorway.

'She has to,' Marta said.

Simon's face was drawn, his words heavy on his tongue. 'She says ... she wants nothing to do with us. She blames us, she says she wants us all to leave, me included. I don't know ... don't know what ...' He trailed off. As the others watched, he ran one hand through his hair and rubbed his face. Then he slid to the ground as though someone was sucking the air out of him from the bottom up.

Crouched in the doorway, he said, 'If I hadn't taken her there ... if I hadn't made her come...'

Paul said, 'What about the camera?'

Simon opened his hand. On his palm was a tiny memory card. 'She threw it at me. Told me ... *fuck*, I don't know.' He looked down, shaking his head.

Marta stood up. 'She *wanted* to go, don't forget that. She told you she wanted to do it, so stop blaming yourself.' She looked around, hands clenched into fists. 'This isn't our fault, we didn't want any of this to happen. Jess's parents are dead because this country is screwed up. We're the *victims*, not the criminals, and we owe it to Jess's parents, and, and … to this whole damn country to get that evidence into the hands of people who can do something about it.' She flapped her hands, her face flushed.

Switch stood up beside her. 'Well, it wasn't quite Che fucking Guevara but it wasn't bad.'

Marta took a deep breath, readying herself to continue. 'Let's get this straight,' she said. 'We have some very, very dangerous people after us. We run, or we die. It's that simple. Now, Simon, get up there and get her moving. We have no idea how many of those things are after us. Maybe one, maybe more. If we split up we can spread the trail, confuse them. Move quickly and don't stay anywhere too long. Keep away from enclosed places and don't travel unarmed.'

'What good is a knife or a club against something that does that?' Paul said, nodding towards the bodies.

'It's better than no knife or no club.'

Simon climbed to his feet. 'Okay,' he said. 'I'll do what I can.'

Marta glanced at a clock on the wall. 'It's nearly six o'clock,' she said. 'We leave at midnight. Simon, you have to convince her. You have to. Otherwise she's going to end up like them.' She didn't need to point.

They went to the front door and peered out on to the street. Street-lighting made a broken line back the way they'd come, while above them the sky was dark purple, wisps of orange and red hanging above the rooftops that stretched away towards the spires and office towers of central London. Marta thought it looked pretty, but she couldn't shake a sinking feeling in her chest that night had never been so bleak, had never before contained so many demons.

Chapter Eighteen
Danger

NUMB.

Like dead hands gripping every inch of her body and squeezing until her skin turned blue and cold. Hands manipulating her, molding her, kneading her flesh into one single amorphous ball, devoid of all sensation and feeling. And from it her eyes looked out, staring but not seeing the walls, the prints and the posters that hung there, the photographs of friends, of her family. The shelf in the corner, the books. Stephen King, Charles Dickens, Zadie Smith, Kurt Vonnegut; tatty paperbacks bought at staff discount price from the store she worked at, as many as she could afford, most read more than once, many three or four times. She loved books, stories and adventures. Her own life, in the relatively calm neighbourhood of Fulham, where things still went wrong, where houses still got burned and cars still got wrecked, but less frequently than across the rest of London GUA, wasn't so much an adventure as a struggle; worry and concern overriding any sense of excitement she might get walking the dangerous streets. Then, only this afternoon, she'd been given an opportunity to take a real adventure, to be part of an urban myth, do something *special* that nearly no one had ever done before.

Except it hadn't ended up that way. Her life had been turned on its head in the space of a few hours. And now, numb, unfeeling, she wondered what would happen next. What *should* happen next.

Numb.

She wanted to stay curled up in a ball, her own body a barricade to shut out the world. She wanted nothing more to do with it, wanted only for it to leave her alone.

He had come again. Simon was sitting on the edge of her bed, one hand on her knee, gently rubbing it. 'You have to pack some things,' he was saying. 'We have to go. They're going to come back sooner or later.'

Jessica didn't care. She didn't care what happened next. She just wanted everything to end, all the hurt and the pain and the sorrow, all of it to be extinguished, stamped out like the embers of an old camp fire.

'You have to be strong,' she heard Simon saying, his voice soothing. A voice she loved, but a voice that she wanted to hate now. She wanted to blame him, and she'd told him so, but Jessica was sensible, educated, and despite her grief she knew this wasn't his doing. He was as much a victim of unfortunate circumstance as she was. Just, with her parents dead, it felt right to blame someone close. It felt necessary.

'Come on Jess, please,' he murmured, talking slowly to her, leaning close. Still she didn't look at him, her gaze holding steady on the wall in front of her. The images of her dead parents flashed up in her mind, torn up and bloody, her parents who'd never done anything but love her and try to do the right thing, try to maintain normality in the face of growing chaos. They didn't deserve to die, but who did? Deserving anything didn't make it more likely to happen. She was no more deserving of life than they were of death, but here she was, still breathing, still trying to debate what she should do if and when she chose to unlock her arms, release her legs and ease her feet to the floor. What to do when she decided something should be done.

Simon was trying to hold her hand. At last she turned to him, looking up into his face, grey with worry, eyes moist with sorrow.

'I love you,' she said, not smiling. 'I loved my parents too, but something got to them. I won't let it get to you too.'

Simon smiled; for a moment he looked like a drug addict who had just taken a hit, overcome with a sudden euphoria. Tears streamed down his cheeks. 'Oh fucking hell, Jess. I love you so much.' Then, 'No one wanted this to happen. It's no one's fault but theirs. The fucking, screwed up, bullshit *government*.' Suddenly remembering where her father worked, he opened his mouth to apologise, but Jess spoke first. 'We'll get them,' she said. 'Somehow, someday ... we'll get them.'

Something had changed inside. A curtain had been drawn over her past, over what innocence she had enjoyed in the years leading up to today. A new mark had been set, a new starting point, and it was one altogether darker. She felt different, felt her heart beating stronger, her hands clenching harder, the focus in her mind sharper than ever before. The girl who had gone down those steps at St. Cannerwells earlier this afternoon had vanished forever.

A siren rose in the distance. 'We have to go, Jess,' Simon told her. 'We have to go now and give ourselves a chance or stay here and die.'

She didn't look at him, but she climbed up from the bed and brushed the hair out of her eyes. She walked past him, down the stairs and pushed through into the living room while Simon trailed helplessly behind her.

The sight of her parents' bodies made her sway, her vision momentarily blurring, and she thought she might faint. A sob rose up in her throat so quickly she bent double and began to cough, thinking it might choke her.

Simon tried to put a reassuring hand on her back but she pushed him away. 'Don't touch me,' she said, though part of her wanted him to. It was just too soon, too early. For now she needed to be alone with her grief.

She couldn't leave them, but she had no choice. The wailing siren was closer now. She had no idea if it was coming here or if there was some other disaster elsewhere it was driving to attend to, but the end result was the same. Simon was right. They had to leave, or their bodies would join her parents' on the canvas of blood and gore that her living room had become, and that wouldn't solve anything.

It hurt to turn away, it hurt more than anything. But she did, glancing at Simon who stood behind her, his mouth hung open, one hand shifting in his jeans pocket, fingers moving over the tiny camera memory chip that had started all this.

In that moment her mind was made up.

She rushed through into the quaint little kitchen her mother kept as neat as a showroom, went to the cooker and turned on the gas hobs. She didn't know if it would work or not, but it was worth a try. Behind her, Simon said, 'You have *gas?*', but Jess ignored him. In a cupboard by the back door her father had an eighteen-litre container of paraffin – another government perk – that he used to fuel a stove heater they had on the upstairs landing. She hauled it towards Simon.

'Douse them,' she said. 'Spread it everywhere you can.'

'Are you sure–'

'Do it!' she snapped. 'I'm not having the government taking them away to experiment on. They were my parents!'

She rooted around in a kitchen drawer for a box of matches while Simon took the paraffin into the living room, grabbing as she did so a handful of small notes and change her mother kept for housekeeping money. At the back of the drawer she found a matchbox, still half-full, with a picture of a Beefeater on the front. Hate for the government boiled in her, and it was all she could do to suppress a scream. She stuffed the matches in her pocket and went to find Simon.

He had taken down two curtains and draped one over each body. For a moment she felt a surge of love for him at this sign of sensitivity, then the siren wailed much closer this time, and she shook it off. Simon had splashed paraffin all over the floor, the walls and the covered bodies of her parents.

'Okay, let's go,' she said. On her way out she grabbed a sofa cushion. She stopped at the door and handed it to Simon while she pulled the matches from her pocket. 'Get ready to run,' she said, striking a match and holding it to the cushion until the frilly cover began first to smoke and then to flame. She waited until the fire had taken hold then grabbed it back off Simon and tossed it through the door of the living room.

'Run!'

They dashed out of the house as a *whump* of igniting paraffin followed them. It might be a few minutes before the gas exploded, and she wanted to be well away before then. 'When we get a chance, Simon,' she shouted as they ran, 'we hunt *them*.'

#

Paul tried not to run as he headed back through Fulham. The streets were alive with the activity of changeover: stores by day barring their doors and pulling down their shutters, while on the pavements and in the market places street vendors took their place, selling everything from skewered snack food to bootlegged DVDs and homebrewed beer and spirits. Many of them worked an under-the-counter service as well, dealing in narcotics, medical drugs, knives and other weapons. By the end of the night, Paul knew, some of these vendors would be dead, others rich, some moved on, and others newly respected. Versions of warfare existed everywhere, and trade was no longer fair.

People called out to him as he passed, offering sausages on sticks, plastic cups of soup, old toys and shabby secondhand clothing. He ignored them all, pushing away one or two of the more persistent.

I have to get to Owen before they do.

There was no way for them to know how many Huntsmen were on their trail. There could be just one, or there could be dozens. His only hope was that because he lived further away than Jess, and he hadn't come straight from home to St. Cannerwells this afternoon. Having had a couple of errands to run, he had a longer trail to follow.

Hope. Like love, so easy to destroy.

He hurried into Fulham Broadway London Underground station, thinking it would be more difficult for the Huntsmen to track him if he moved by train. He bought a single journey ticket and made his way down to the platform, crowded with commuters as it approached six o'clock. The digital display told him it was seven minutes to the next train, though the destination section was cracked and difficult to read. He only had to go four stops, though, and he didn't need to change.

The seconds ticked past endlessly. He shifted from foot to foot, biting his lip hard enough to draw blood, wincing at the pain. Further up the platform, he heard a fight break out, the thud of thrown punches, the shouts and grunts of those involved, the restraining cries of the onlookers.

A minute until the next northbound train. Paul pushed closer to the front of the platform, hugging his clawboard against his chest.

Someone screamed, just as a familiar roar announced the train's arrival. He glanced in the direction of the commotion but could see nothing through the crowd. Then the train had stopped and everyone was pushing forwards towards the opening doors. Just as Paul got inside and turned around, he heard more shouting, a louder disturbance than before. He heard a woman scream: 'Oh, God! He's dead! That thing killed him!'

Paul swallowed. Beads of sweat broke out on his forehead. He stepped forward and shoved a couple of punks back out on to the platform to give the doors room to close.

'You fucking cocksuck–' one of the punks shouted, but the doors bumped shut, cutting off the man's words. The train began to move along the platform towards where the commotion had been. Paul leaned forward to look out, and saw that a space had parted around a robed, hooded man who stood near the edge of the platform, towering over those around him. Paul hadn't seen a monk in years and couldn't believe that such a level of respect still existed.

Then he saw the bloody corpse at the man's feet, a security uniform soaked in blood. As the train passed, the cowled man's head lifted and Paul saw a furry, wolf-like face with dark, human eyes that looked in through the window at the passengers inside. As his carriage passed by, its eyes locked on to his own. The train picked up speed and the creature slipped behind, but its eyes never left him.

Paul's legs shook as the train thundered into the tunnel and the outside became darkness. He looked for somewhere to sit down but all the seats were taken, so instead he just slumped to the floor, clutching the clawboard to his chest like a frightened child might clutch a rag doll. Like the others, he had seen plenty of bad things in his life, but always it had been focused on someone else.

He had seen his own death in those eyes. Death, and worse.

Chapter Nineteen
Preparations

WHILE SWITCH AND PAUL both headed south, Marta headed north. Feeling reluctant to go back to the train station, instead she jumped on the first bus that came past, feeling safer off the street.

It took her on a long, circuitous route around the outer city centre towards Camden Town, near where she lived now. Instead of getting off, though, she rode for a couple more stops and then changed buses on to another route. Fifteen minutes later, she alighted on a quiet street in East Finchley and walked up a narrow residential street leading off the high street until she came to a small churchyard.

It was overgrown and untended now; the few remaining graves rising up out of the tall grass. Most of the granite and basalt stones were gone, pulled up by looters, lugged away and sold. Some less-valuable slate stones remained, along with a few varnished wooden crosses, many of them leaning bent and broken like a mouthful of crooked teeth.

Marta followed the remains of a gravel path around the side of the old church. She noticed another of the old stained glass windows had been destroyed in the months since her last visit, leaving just one intact, near the back corner. Like the others, it had been boarded up from the inside and now just a few jagged shards of coloured glass remained sticking out of the wall.

The church still functioned with a resident minister and a regular congregation, although guns were their religion now. She knew she was being watched, either from a tower or a spy-hole somewhere, maybe with a rifle or a handgun trained on her, depending on what weapons they had.

At the back of the church she followed the path through the stones to a section at the rear of the churchyard which was home to the freshest graves. There, near a low stone wall that backed onto a fenced-off alleyway, she came to a small rectangle of ground where the grass was not as long as the surrounding area. At the top end was a flat, rounded rock that had long ago been borrowed from a riverbed. Marta could just make out the words written on it in faded white paint:

John Richard Banks.
September 18th 2022 to August 9th, 2072.
Forever in our hearts.

Rachel Mary Banks, beloved wife of John.
March 15th 2026 to July 17th 2073.
Rest in Peace.

'Hey Mum, Dad,' Marta said, brushing tears out of her eyes. 'Sorry I've not been up here for a while, but you know how it is ... busy and all that. Huh. Working hard, you know.'

The stone her brother had painted watched her in eternal silence. She hadn't added his name to it; she refused to believe he was dead.

'I just came to tell you that I have to go away for a while.' She squatted down, but didn't sit. She felt vulnerable enough already, and the memory of Jess's parents was still fresh in her mind. 'I don't know for how long,' she continued. 'But I'm in a little trouble, I think. Some bad people are after me and my friends. I didn't do anything wrong, it's just ... I don't know ... wrong place, wrong time.' She sighed. 'I just wanted you to know, that if it all works out – which is unlikely, of course – things are going to change. We know things that could hurt the government, and ... and, we're going to tell the right people, who can fix it all, so that no one else needs to die.'

She sat down, her legs falling out from under her. 'So, Mum, Dad, I just wanted to tell you before I go, and I hope that, whether it works out or not, I hope you're proud of me. Because, I'm proud of you. What you tried to do for me, you know. For ... for *everything*.'

She stopped talking. She ran her fingers through the grass as a cold wind ruffled her hair. Looking up at the sky, she saw dark, spongy clouds drifting in the direction of the falling sun. To the east, the sky was almost completely dark, lit only by the glow of street lights and office buildings.

She stayed that way for quite some time, as darkness fell around her. She didn't have a watch but she guessed from the sky that it was close to eight o'clock when she climbed to her feet. She needed to get back to her flat and grab some belongings. Every second she stayed here was a second closer that the Huntsmen got to her, but for a while she had been locked into the moment by her memories. She didn't know if she would ever be able to come back, and she needed to say goodbye, not just to her parents' memory, but to her entire past.

'Hey you! Stop or you're dead!'

Marta jumped at the voice, spinning around. After all, she'd been here a while, and most of the higher members of the congregation knew her. She heard the click of a gun being cocked, saw a slight movement in the grass not far from her. She was about to say something when a familiar voice shouted: 'Don't fucking shoot! I'm with her!'

'Switch?' She saw him now, in the shadows cast by the church. How did you...?'

'He cool, Marta?' A muscular blonde man carrying a rifle stood up out of the grass just yards from her. It was Craig, one of the ministers. He'd been in the grass the whole time, watching over her. How much had he overheard?

'It's okay, Brother Craig,' she said, using the church's "family" title. 'He's a friend. He's cool.'

The man shouldered his rifle. 'Long as you say so, Marta. If you have any problems, just shout.' He walked off back towards the church, giving them some privacy. She was happy he had kept his distance; she didn't want her scent around him, not after what she had seen today.

Switch stood a few feet away, looking a little embarrassed.

'How did you find me? Did you follow me?'

'I figured you might need some protection since I knew you'd come here. I had to do some, um, shopping first.'

'Really? She raised an eyebrow. 'What did you buy?'

He grinned, and shook his coat. It gave a metallic rustle. 'Man toys. Oh, and a new pair of shoes. You know, since Paul didn't keep his end of the bargain.' He lifted a foot to show her. The sneaker looked pretty old, but it was a definite improvement on the sock.

Marta smiled. 'Where did you get your money from? I thought you were broke.'

'I traded.'

She raised an eyebrow. '*Really*. What with?'

'Promises, mostly. You know how it is. Rules of the street.'

She thought it probably best not to ask. 'Did you get anything good?'

'Not good enough. There's no current market for flame throwers or hand grenades. At least not ones I can afford.' He grinned. 'But I got some cool shit that might help us out. Take out one or two of those canine mutant fuckers if we have to.'

Marta smiled back. 'Switch, how do you stay so cheerful through this? We're being hunted. We could be dead in hours.'

He shrugged. 'I don't know. I guess … hmm.' He shook his head, searching for the right words. 'I guess it's just that inside, I've felt dead for a long time.' He shrugged again. 'Fuck. Not literally *dead*, you know, just … you know how it is. Idling. Like I'm just treading water, waiting for something to happen.' She nodded in agreement. 'And now, suddenly, we're alive. We have something to battle for. We get to open up a can of whoop-ass in the name of revolution. If we can escape those government monsters, of course.'

'I guess you're right. I just wished I shared your confidence.'

He nodded towards her parents' grave. 'You need more time?'

She shook her head. 'No. It's time to go, I think.'

Back around the front of the church Brother Craig materialised out of the shadowed porch. 'Wherever you kids are going, take care,' he said, and then added: 'Godspeed.'

'So you were listening to me!'

He cocked his head. 'Yeah, sorry about that. I didn't mean to, but you looked like you wanted your own time, and I didn't want to blow my cover in case whatever it is that's after you came along.'

'It's okay.' Before she could stop herself, she hugged the older man. Suddenly realizing what she'd done, she stepped back and said: 'Brother Craig, after we're gone, go inside the church and bolt all the doors. Don't open them for any reason. Bad things are after us.'

'I figured that. Don't worry, we've been protecting this place a long time. What are you going to do?'

She grinned. 'Bring down the government.'

Craig laughed. 'Well, good luck to you! It couldn't come soon enough.'

She thanked him and they headed back out on to the street.

'Thanks for thinking of me,' Marta said to Switch when they were alone.

His bad eye fluttered and his cheeks darkened. Embarrassment wasn't one of his common attributes, and it quite amused her to see it.

'No problem,' he said, regaining his composure. 'I figured that being a chick and all you might get a little emotional and leave yourself open to attack.'

'Yeah, maybe,' she agreed with a smirk. 'Being a chick and all. Don't you need to grab some stuff? I have to get back to my flat to get my handbag and my makeup, but we don't have much time.'

Switch smiled. 'There's something I never told you about where I live,' he said. 'It's St. Cannerwells. I kind of live there.'

'*Live* there?'

'In one of the old shops. I can just grab anything I need on the way back, though as a general rule I carry everything important with me.'

Marta shook her head. 'You're crazy, Switch. I suppose at least it's warm down there–'

Switch put a hand on her arm to cut her off. The strength of his grip surprised her, his fingers digging into her skin.

'What are you doing...?'

'Marta, we've got a problem.' He pointed down the street, past the scatterings of vendors setting up street stalls outside shops and wholesale markets, to where a dirty London Underground sign identified West Finchley. A man in a robe had just emerged from the stairs and was looking up and down the street. His face was covered by a hood, and his head was moving in an arc around his chin, swinging from side to side like a pendulum on a clock, almost as if he was smelling the air.

'Please God tell me that's not –' Marta began.

'Um, yeah, I think it is. I saw one on a train a couple of days ago. They were transporting it, I think. I was having a practice.'

The figure turned and began to walk in their direction, quickly picking up pace. It moved like a man, but with its head stooped forward as though straining to see something on the ground.

'Oh shit,' Switch said. 'It's following my trail. I came by tube. I rode. It's tracking me.'

'Come on,' Marta said, her heart hammering. 'We can hide from it, maybe double back around into the station.'

'I say we stay and fight it,' Switch said, turning around. 'I got some stuff that might work.'

Marta looked back down the street. The Huntsman had started into a slow jog. It was heading right for them.

'Uh, no, if it was you alone I'd say go for it, but since I'm here I say we run.' She grabbed his arm, pulling him back up the street. He didn't need much encouragement; pretty soon he was outpacing her despite his injury.

'Is it gaining on us?' he gasped.

'I don't know ... this way!'

They took a turn towards Finchley town centre, large abandoned office buildings looming up on either side of them. Marta glanced back. The Huntsman was just three hundred feet behind and closing fast, running at a full sprint.

'Quick! In here!' Switch said, grabbing her arm and pulling her sharply into the foyer of an abandoned building. 'Back there, get up the stairs! I have a plan.'

Marta didn't hesitate. She pushed through a fire-door and sprinted up a metal staircase. Below her, Switch was trying to jam the door shut. From the second floor landing she watched him stick a knife into the lock and turn it, then jam an old chair under the long handle of the fire-door. Suddenly something slammed into the door from the other side, rocking it on its hinges.

Marta yelped with fear. Switch shouted something at the door then rushed after her up the stairs. 'Go on, run!' he shouted. 'It won't hold for long, but we just have to stall it.'

'Where are we going?'

'All the way up. The roof.'

'Oh, God. Why?'

'Just go!'

Marta dashed up the fire escape, feeling the burn in her thighs as she turned each corner and rushed up each new flight of stairs. She'd judged the building to be six or eight floors tall, but passing a door into the ninth floor, and with a couple more turns above her, she wondered if she'd make it. Far below, she heard a splintering sound, followed by a crash, and then a growl as the Huntsman burst through the fire-door.

She couldn't help but look back. As she did so, she heard a rough scream, a noise that sounded like a word fed through a salt grinder:

'*Stop!*'

She shivered, the word cutting right through her. She stared down towards the floor far below, saw something rushing up the stairs towards them, moving so fast it was a blur.

Then Switch was jerking her arm, pulling her away through a door on to the building's roof. A cold wind struck her face and she recoiled, shutting her eyes. Rough hands pushed her hard from behind.

Switch's voice was filled with frustration. '*Quickly*, Marta!' He was doing another job on the door. The handle was round, and he kicked it hard, once, twice, knocking it out of shape so that it wouldn't open easily. There were few objects on the roof but he managed to find what looked like a rusty metal clothes-horse and jam its stubby legs into the thin gap between the bottom of the door and the floor.

Marta spun around in a circle, seeing the high rooftops of London rising like dark concrete islands out of a sea of twinkling lights. She could only admit that it was beautiful, but as she turned to see the adjacent building rising up some fifty feet to the right, it only helped to press home the desperate enormity of their predicament.

'Switch, we're trapped up here!'

He appeared at her shoulder, breathing hard. 'Get over to the edge, on the main road side. Quickly, go! The door won't hold for long.'

'Is there another fire exit or something?' she asked, leaning over the edge of the roof.

'Look there.' He pointed over the top of her shoulder. She did, but all she saw was the road. There was no way down except to jump, and that was suicide.

'What are you looking at?' she shouted, frustration getting the better of her. Behind her something slammed against the stuck door, making it rattle.

'About ten feet down, you see it?'

She squinted. 'I see a wire of some kind.'

'That's it!'

'What good's that going to do us?'

He pointed across the street. 'We ride it. It attaches to that building over there, the lower one. To an antenna mast on its roof. We get off there, it breaks the scent. The Huntsman can't follow us. It'll take ages for it to find our scent again, by which time we'll be well ahead.'

Marta tugged on a loose braid of hair at her neck. 'We can't ride–'

'If you can jump on to a moving fucking train you can jump on to a stationary fucking wire!' he shouted. Marta stared, shocked, but as the creature slammed against the door again behind them, she knew he was right. 'Now get your ass on that damn wire!' he yelled, shoving her towards the roof edge.

She wrapped her hands through the leather straps on her clawboard and felt a sudden energy pulsing through her arms and legs, that fire that she so loved. It was the board that did it. Always.

She turned back to Switch, flashing a wild grin. 'If this goes wrong, I'll see you wherever.' Then, with the clawboard held out in front of her, she jumped over the edge.

For a moment she was in freefall, with the ground racing up towards her, then the hooks caught on the wire that connected the two buildings, her shoulders jerked and she was hanging there, her feet dangling high above the road.

She had worried that the wire would be too weak to hold her, or otherwise too elastic and would bounce her right back off, but it was thick and it felt strong. It had a little flex but not enough to throw her off, but as she hung there, a hundred and fifty feet off the ground, she realised they had another problem.

'Switch, I'm not moving!' she shouted. 'It's thick rubber casing. It's got too much grip!'

'Shit,' he muttered, leaning over the edge above her. Then: 'The downward slant should be enough. Swing your legs back and forth, get some momentum.'

Marta kicked her legs out and felt herself move forward a few inches. 'It's working!'

'Hang on. I'll try to help you.' After one last glance back towards the blocked door, he climbed over the edge, hanging on by one hand, his clawboard in the other. He jumped, hooked the wire behind her with his board and held on to a metal fixture that held the wire to the wall with his other hand. He leaned his back against the wall then pushed her with his feet. She slid forward a few inches, and then slowly began to gain speed. 'You have a bit more weight than me, so you should have more momentum,' he shouted.

'You're an asshole,' she told him. 'But thanks.'

Switch grinned and kicked her again, just as she swung forward. She felt the rubber casing losing its resistance and she began to slide. Switch shouted something, but she was too far away now to hear clearly. The building in front rose towards her as she slid down, and she started to plan her dismount. It would be slower than from a train, at least.

'Watch out, Marta!'

She heard him this time, and she twisted herself around to see Switch hanging maybe fifty feet behind her, moving much more slowly. His slight frame wasn't helping him gain much speed, and he was jerking back and forth trying to move himself forward. And there, above him on the building's roof, stood the Huntsman.

Marta couldn't see it any more clearly than they had before. It was just a dark silhouette against the night sky, but zhe could see something in its hand, something metallic, something reflecting the glow of the streetlights below.

Thang!

'Whoah!' Switch shouted, and Marta saw him twisting wildly again. 'It's shooting at me!'

Marta remembered the metal bolt she had seen in Jess's house. It seemed ridiculous, but it looked and sounded like a *crossbow*.

She heard another *thang* followed by a thud across the street where the bolt hit, then a whizzing, winding sound as the creature loaded the next.

Marta was still looking back when she crashed into the antenna of the opposite building. With a cry of pain she twisted her clawboard off the wire and dropped to the ground. Rolling over, she managed to regain her footing and make it to the building's edge in time to see Switch still crossing over, some way behind. He was putting on a show of mid-air acrobatics, jerking forwards and back, swinging his legs up and down.

'Get *down*, Marta!'

She had been so transfixed by Switch's skills that she had almost forgotten the Huntsman. A metal bolt thudded into the antenna housing just a foot wide of her, and, aware of her fortune, she dropped to the ground just as Switch bundled over the edge.

'It can't get across,' he said, breathing hard as he crouched beside her. 'It's not stupid. It knows if it tries I'll just cut the wire. Our biggest problem though is getting out without meeting it on the way up.'

'How do we do that?'

She sensed rather than saw him grin in the dark. 'We run like rabbits with fire crackers up our asses. And then some.'

He was on his feet before she started to laugh, moving away from her to look for a way down into the building. As she heard him kick a door in and call for her to follow, she wondered if this was what madness felt like.

She glanced back across the street at the other building. The Huntsman still stood there, a darker shadow against the night, watching her. Perhaps confused by their escape, perhaps amused by its prey's wiliness, perhaps merely considering what to do next, it was observing her calmly, the crossbow that hung idly by its side glinting in the light of the street below.

There was no way to tell what was going through its mind, but going through her own was the realization that she had just cheated death, and that she was probably going to have to do it again in the days to come.

She turned away and hurried after Switch.

CHAPTER TWENTY
ESCAPE

PAUL WAS OFF THE TRAIN almost before it had stopped, pushing through the crowds and up the stairs to the ticket gates. Out on the street he found a bus had just pulled in, and he jumped aboard even though it was barely half a mile to his house. He was so tired he could barely move anymore, but it was also another chance to throw them off the scent.

He jumped off again five minutes later outside the building in which he lived with his brother. Once, 14 Monument Square had been their family home, and Paul could still remember having good times here before the air darkened, the perimeter wall gates shut permanently and the guns appeared on the streets.

The day after the Governor passed the law prohibiting anyone to leave the city without a permit, Paul had watched from his bedroom window as tanks rolled into Monument Square, dispersing hordes of protesters. Eight years old that day, still a year and a half before Owen came into the world, Paul saw his first death, a young man with dark hair and glasses, wearing a student-friendly anti-war t-shirt and an old pair of jeans. Even through the glass Paul had heard the crunch as the body went under the tank.

The boy had been his older brother, Gareth. Just sixteen, he was killed outside their front door. He wasn't the only one, but he was the only one that mattered that day to Paul's family, and their lives, until then peaceful, were shattered.

Owen fulfilled some of their mother's desire for a replacement, as his birth was the only thing that ameliorated her sorrow. That she saw her dead son in the eyes of her newborn was probably one of the reasons why, when Paul was just thirteen and Owen four, she chose suicide as a way out.

Their father too, was dead by the time Paul was fifteen. Weighed down by loss and sorrow, he was unable to cope with two young boys. Paul came home from school one day to find his father had gone. A suitcase was missing from the cupboard in his parents' bedroom, as were some of his father's clothes. There was no note.

Paul had let Owen believe their father might still be alive, but he knew otherwise. There was nowhere to go and their father had been weak; he hadn't had the strength for adventure.

The first few weeks afterwards had been a struggle. That day had proved Paul's last at school, and his next had been part begging, part petty theft. He had lacked the skills for it, getting beaten up, chased by the police and by his intended targets. Then one day he had been caught trying to lift someone's wallet, and the man pressing a knife to his throat had offered him two ways out. One was death. Paul chose the other. He found there was a demand for this kind of work, and he quickly got good. With his face pressed against a concrete floor in an abandoned building or on his knees in a dark alley with rough hands gripping the back of his head, the money came. And the money meant food and clothes for him and Owen. Sometimes, you did what you had to do.

He pushed in through the door and hurried up the stairs to the third floor landing. The whole building had once belonged to their family, but his mother's death had prompted his father to downsize, splitting the house up into three, making some renovations and subletting out the two lower sections as self-containing flats. It was the last genuinely useful thing his father did, and despite a succession of short-lived tenants on the middle floor, a long-term tenant in the bottom floor flat who paid rent on time was a godsend.

'Owen?' he shouted. 'You home?'

His brother didn't respond. As he reached their door Paul prayed he wasn't too late. The flat was unlocked. He dropped his clawboard by the front door and burst in.

'Owen? Owen! Where are you? *Owen!*'

He crashed through into the kitchen, the door thudding back against the wall. On the table in the centre of the room were a half-eaten sandwich and quarter of a glass of orange cordial. There was no sign of a struggle.

He heard a sound behind him and spun on his heels.

'What's with the door slamming and the shouting?' Owen stood in the doorway, wearing a t-shirt and shorts. His arms were folded. 'I was just watching a movie, all right?'

At the relief of seeing his brother alive, unharmed, and as cocky as ever, Paul's legs sagged. He gripped the edge of the table for support. 'Thank God you're okay,' he said.

Owen just gave a nonchalant shrug. 'Of course,' he grunted.

'Listen. You have to get some stuff together. Spare clothes, money if you have any, and anything essential or that you can't bear to part with. Keep it small, keep it light. Just one rucksack.'

'But I'm watching a movie! It's only halfway through!'

Paul slammed a hand down on the table. 'This is important, Owen. We're in danger. We have to go away for a while.'

Owen raised an eyebrow. 'Who's after you?'

'Trust me, you don't want to know. But if you don't hurry up, you might find out.'

Owen grinned. 'Are we going on an adventure?'

'Yeah, I guess you could call it that.'

'Cool.' Owen turned and rushed off to his room. Paul did the same, picking through the cupboards first for some lightweight packets of dried food: fruit, noodles, soup, as much as he thought he could carry while running. He had no idea when they might eat again. Then, with the food and some basic toiletries stuffed into a small bag, he rushed through into his bedroom and filled the rest of the bag with spare underwear and another sweatshirt. From under his bed he grabbed an old clawboard Owen might need, and jammed it into the bag behind his clothes. Rummaging through the drawers of the bedside tables, he found what little money they had left, enough to buy them food for a few days. Then, hauling the bag up over his shoulder, heavier than he'd hoped, he turned back to the door.

An object on the desk to the right caught his attention. He moved closer, his heart caught in his throat. He reached out and picked the object up.

Out of the photo frame his parents smiled at him, his father with his arm around his mother, who was holding an infant Owen in her arms. Paul, age twelve, stood to his father's left, a big grin on his face, a mop of light brown hair sprouting out of his head, blue eyes still unobstructed by the glasses he had started wearing at seventeen.

Above their heads, big white capital letters read, LONDON ZOO.

Thinking back, it must have been less than a year before the zoo closed, and it was the last happy time Paul could remember, before his mother slipped into depression. Had Gareth been there it would have been perfect.

He opened up the picture frame, took out the photograph, and stuffed it into his bag.

In the kitchen he found Owen waiting. 'I'm ready!' his brother announced with a huge smile, as if had been waiting for this chance all his life.

'Christ, Owen, don't you have a coat or something?'

'It's by the door.'

Paul nodded. 'Right, let's go.' He led the way to the front door. As he picked up his clawboard and pulled open the door, he looked back at his brother. 'Owen, I said one bag.'

His brother had one bag over his shoulder and was dragging another one along the ground. 'Ah, come on. It's just some comic books and a few movies. I don't want some bastard looting the flat and getting all my black market stuff.'

'Owen, we have to travel light.'

His brother looked about to argue back, then his expression changed. His eyes had drifted past Paul, out into the stairway. 'Er, Paul, there's some guy down there. How the hell did he get in? Did you forget to lock the bottom door?'

Paul felt a chill pass through him as he looked down the stairs to see the Huntsman standing outside the door of the middle flat, facing up the stairs towards them. Under its hood its eyes were shadowed, but its dog-like mouth seemed to grin.

'Tube Rider...'

Paul reached back, grabbed the bag of Owen's loot and flung it as hard as he could down the stairs. The Huntsman lifted its arms to fight off a hail of books, DVDs, Blu-Rays and ancient VHS tapes. One heavy volume that Owen loved, something about a boy wizard, struck it square in the forehead. The Huntsman howled and slumped to its knees.

As Owen was gasping, 'What the *fuck* is that?', Paul was slamming the door, pulling the deadbolts and a larger anti-theft bar across to buy them some time.

'You got weapons? Is there another way out of here?' Paul shouted.

'What? Just a screwdriver, couple of kitchen knives. I'm just the kid, you're the hero!'

'Let's hope so.' Paul tried to think quickly. 'Okay. Back into Mum and Dad's room, we can get out the window.'

'We're fifty feet off the ground!'

'I know, but I've seen what that thing can do! I'd rather jump than stay here. Now go!'

They rushed through into the bedroom. Paul heard the Huntsman pound on the front door a couple of times, heard the handle rattle, then silence, followed a moment later by a loud crack. The handle shook. The Huntsman had shot it with something and broken the lock, but the deadbolts still held it shut.

'Come on, Paul!'

Paul realised he'd been transfixed, while in the meantime Owen had pulled the window open and thrown his bag down on to the street.

'How am I supposed to get down?'

'The drainpipe,' Paul said. 'Climbed a tree before, haven't you?'

'Trees have a bit more grip, though!'

A splintering sound came from behind them. Paul tossed his bag out of the window, watched it fall a frightening distance and then land with a loud crunch.

'Hurry!'

Owen was already out on the pipe, trying to twist himself around and get a decent grip before starting his descent. He looked irritated rather than scared, which was how Paul felt.

'Hurry *up*, Owen–'

The front door burst open and something stumbled in, too fast for Paul to see clearly. It was off-balance and limping.

'...Rider...'

It veered towards them, one furred, wiry arm loose of the robe, wires beneath its skin clearly visible. The other hand was clutching at something at its waist, something that gleamed metallic under the kitchen light.

It reached the bedroom doorway then jerked sideways as it collided with the doorframe. It staggered across the room and the hood fell back from its face. Paul's mouth fell open as he saw the jumble of wires snaking back and forth across the creature's scalp, above one blind eye and another that oozed blood. He had got lucky. The Huntsman had an old war wound, and Owen's book had hit its remaining good eye. It pursued them now by sense of smell alone.

Owen was still struggling with the drainpipe. Paul watched as the Huntsman dropped into a crouch, the claws on one hand scraping at the carpet, the other still fumbling blindly at a weapon beneath its robe. Its bloody eye flicked back and forth. Its teeth were bared and its nose wrinkled as it sniffed the air.

Paul couldn't breathe. His whole body tingled as though his heart had stopped and he was caught in the moment between life and death. He stared at the Huntsman as it crouched by the door less than ten feet away.

As Owen shouted, 'Paul!', the Huntsman leapt at him.

He reacted instinctively. One hand was curled around the leather strap of the clawboard at his side. As the Huntsman flew at him he jerked it up, swinging it round as though he were trying to swat a fly.

The clawboard struck the Huntsman square in the face. Its momentum carried it forward on to him and his nostrils filled with a pungent mix of blood, animal, and machinery. Then it fell past him, rolling across the floor into the corner.

'Is it dead? Shit, is it dead?'

It took Paul a moment to collect himself and realise *he* wasn't dead. 'I don't know. Get down the fucking pipe!'

'I'm going!'

Paul backed away towards the window as Owen started down. The Huntsman had fallen in a heap, and at first didn't seem to be alive. To kill one of the legendary abominations so easily didn't seem possible, and as he hooked one foot over the window ledge it shuddered and began to turn back towards him, body low to the ground, arms caught underneath it. As he watched, one arm freed itself and rose towards him. Gripped in its clawed fingers was a small metal crossbow.

Paul ducked as a quarrel slammed into the window frame less than five inches from his face. The Huntsman growled, then began to fumble with another bolt in the mechanism. Paul glanced down, saw his brother standing below him holding both rucksacks, then quickly shimmied down, his clawboard still attached to him by one leather strap, tapping against the plastic pipe as he went.

'You okay?' Owen asked, as Paul jumped off the drainpipe and staggered over to him.

Paul tried to smile. 'I'm still alive, that's good enough.' He pointed up at the window. 'I'd say we have about a minute before that thing is back on its feet and after us. Let's make it count.'

'Where to?'

'The station.'

They started off in a run, rucksacks slung over their shoulders. Paul held his clawboard under one arm.

On the way, he said: 'There's something I'd better tell you. Something you're going to need to know about if we're going to avoid those things in future.'

Owen nodded towards the clawboard. 'It's about that skateboard thing of yours, isn't it?'

Paul nodded. 'Yeah, that's right. But it's not a skateboard.'

'Of course not, it doesn't have any wheels.' In the dark, Paul sensed Owen raising one eyebrow at him. His little brother said, 'Hence the expression, "skateboard *thing*"...'

Chapter Twenty-One
Gathering

THE HUGE PORTABLE TELEVISION SCREEN was set up on the back of a stationary truck parked on St. Cannerwells High Street. A large crowd had gathered around it, a line of police in front of them. Switch and Marta stood near the back, in the dark recesses of a cubbyhole stairway up to a tall town house.

The screen showed a press conference. A middle-aged man had just taken the stage. A voiceover announced, 'The Foreign Secretary, Mr. Douglas Lewitt, will read the following statement, made earlier today by our Great Leader, Maxim Cale, Lord Governor of Mega Britain.'

Marta glanced at Switch. He was staring at the screen with undisguised hatred. 'Fucking typical to send his minions,' he spat. 'Too scared to show his ugly ass face even on television.'

'Shhh!' she cautioned. 'He does have some supporters, you know. And most of them are carrying guns.'

On the screen, Lewitt cleared his throat. '"Dear Patrons of Mega Britain,"' he read. '"Many of you will be aware of the explosion that rocked our streets earlier today. This was due to an explosive device that detonated inside Westminster Underground station. An as yet unconfirmed number of civilians have died, as has, tragically, the honourable ambassador from the European Confederation, Mr. Alberto Sucro."'

There were a few *ums* and *ahs* from the crowd. He paused to let the news sink in before continuing. '"Finding those responsible and bringing them to justice is currently the government's highest priority. However, it pleases me to inform you that, due to the unrivaled ability of our own Department of Civil Affairs, the identities of those responsible are already known, and an operation has been set in motion to see these criminals brought into custody. As I speak, our best DCA agents are on their trail and we expect their apprehension within hours. In the meantime, I can only request that the general public be on their guard and stay inside where possible. There may be more insurgents acting with these terrorists, and we are yet to rule out further attacks.

"Sadness springs to our collective hearts as I say these words, and though it brings pain to me to say that death may be worthwhile, in this situation that might prove true. Mega Britain has long been troubled by insurgents and terrorist attacks from within our own borders, trying to undermine Mega Britain's rise towards economic greatness. With the tragic death of one of their own, we can only hope to bring our cause to the hearts of the European Confederation's wise leaders, and seek their moral and financial aid in repairing the cracks in our state caused by those who do not believe, those who do not share our vision...'"

'That's us, Switch,' Marta whispered. 'They're trying to pin this mess on us.'

'It's a conspiracy,' he replied. 'They murdered the ambassador and staged his death to create sympathy in the EC. That fucking deformed bastard...'

Lewitt prattled on for a couple more minutes, his speech descending into general propaganda. Marta listened with disgust. As Lewitt finished off the Governor's statement and left the stage with a barrage of questions leaping in his wake, Marta closed her eyes, remembering the carnage they'd found in her apartment.

They'd not encountered the Huntsman again, but it or another had got to her apartment before them. Two of her flatmates were dead, torn apart, their blood splashed over the carpet and across the bare walls of the squat. Another, Rob, a drifter who'd been staying with them the last few weeks, was still alive, but his eyes were wild with terror. A bloody chest injury had not been bad enough to kill him, so Marta had placed an anonymous emergency call from a payphone store a couple of streets away. Switch had made him comfortable while she grabbed a few clothes and belongings. She had whispered sorry as they left.

'We have to go, Switch,' Marta said, tugging on his arm. 'The others should be waiting for us.'

He nodded, and they hurried off down the High Street. Behind them they heard people shutting down the television screen amidst a growing unease from the crowd, most of which had refused to disperse. Marta heard someone barking an order to leave the street. There were one or two shouts of defiance from the crowd, so she quickened her pace, aware that a full scale riot could break out at any moment.

The road bent away to the right, and soon the crowd was out of sight. Drunken shouts came frequently now, though, and she heard the sound of something made of glass shattering on the road, followed by a gunshot.

'Here it goes,' Switch muttered from in front of her.

St. Cannerwells Park came up on their right. Through the fence they could see a couple of trashcan fires, hear the sound of people laughing, making merry. For once Marta actually envied the drunks and tramps down there in the park. Their existence seemed so carefree.

Switch moved further ahead of her, jogging towards the station entrance, a dark building a hundred yards further on. She smiled a little at his self-assumed role as her protector. They had always been a unit, the Tube Riders, looking out for each other, but Switch seemed to have singled Marta out for preferential treatment. *Perhaps he likes me*, she thought, flashing a wry smile.

A hand fell on her shoulder. Marta jerked away, almost falling into the street. As she looked back she let out a small cry of surprise.

Simon stood behind her with Jess at his shoulder. Both looked grim.

'Sorry,' he said. 'I didn't mean to startle you.'

She rubbed her chest just below her neck, as though compelling her heart to slow. It was a few seconds before she could make words come out. 'I'm so happy to see you both,' she said at last. 'Really, you have no idea. Did you have any trouble making it back here?'

Simon shook his head. 'No, we saw nothing. Maybe there's only one. You?'

Marta nodded grimly. 'Yeah, we ran into one. Thank God Switch was with me.' She briefly recounted what had happened.

'That's terrifying. Are you sure you're all right?'

Marta nodded. 'Still alive is good enough right now. We haven't seen Paul yet.'

'He'll be fine.'

'I hope so.'

They headed after Switch, who was standing in the shadows of the Underground station entrance. Marta glanced at Jess as they walked; under the streetlights the other girl's face was difficult to read. Jess hadn't said a word yet, and her eyes were eerily distant. Her parents' violent deaths would be near impossible to deal with, but Marta felt uneasy seeing the way Jess's eyes had steeled. This afternoon she had been as bright and carefree as London allowed. Now, though it scared Marta to admit it, she looked almost as dangerous as the thing that had attacked them in the office building.

'No sign of Paul,' Switch said by way of greeting. 'But there's no sign of any Huntsmen either. Looks like doubling back was a good call.'

'What time is it?' Simon asked.

'Just after eleven,' Switch said. 'The first freight trains are running about now. We can give Paul a little time. We said midnight.'

'We're not leaving him!' Marta almost shouted.

Simon put a hand on her shoulder. 'After what you told us, he might be dead. We'll have no way of knowing.'

Marta felt tears spring to her eyes. 'We're not ... *leaving him*.'

'If the Huntsmen come before he does, we won't have a choice,' Switch said. 'We run or we die. Don't worry about Paul. He might look like a fat, balding fag, but he can look after himself. He'll catch up.'

'Maybe there's just one,' Simon said. 'Five of us against it...'

'When it's running straight at you I'll let you say that again,' Switch replied. 'I picked up some shit on the street, but ... fuck, man, seeing that thing up close, I don't know.' He shook his head. 'Come on, let's get inside. At least by the tracks we have an escape route.'

Down in the station, Marta and Simon sat down against the wall near the breakfall mats. Jess stood nearby, a few feet apart. Switch was restless, patrolling up and down the platform, knives occasionally appearing in his hands only to vanish again.

The minutes ticked past. The trains were becoming less and less frequent as services wound down for the night. In the minutes between trains the station had a peaceful warmth to it, an echoing, thought-provoking calm.

With her head resting on the wall, Marta realised they had no plan after this. Ride the freight trains away from here, get out of London. Was it even that simple? Were there no checkpoints, no guards?

Her thoughts were interrupted by the sound of running feet. She jumped up and turned towards the stairs as Switch jogged over from the platform edge, a serrated knife in each hand. Jess had turned too, lips curled back in a snarl of anger. Simon had been dozing and had yet to climb to his feet.

Two shadows appeared on the stairs, followed moments later by Paul and a much younger boy whom Marta assumed was Owen, Paul's brother. They'd never met him before, though Paul had often talked of bringing him when he was older. Without his parents around, Paul was a father to Owen, and Paul had said no sane father would let a twelve-year-old kid hang off the side of a train. Now, though, Owen was carrying a clawboard Marta recognised as one of Paul's old ones. It pained her to realise he'd get even less practice at it than Jess had, and she broke out into a hot sweat as she realised just how many holes there were in their plan.

'Paul,' she said with relief, and started to move towards him.

Paul put up a hand. 'No time for greetings, guys. We've got company.'

'What?'

'They were waiting for us. Outside!'

'*They?*'

'In the park, waiting to trap us. They broke cover just as Owen and me reached the entrance. Quick, into the tunnels. It's our only chance!'

Marta's heart filled with dread. Above them came the sound of more running feet. It didn't sound like the Huntsmen, though; the footfalls were too heavy.

Again she realised how stupid they'd been. The Huntsmen might be erratic tracking machines, but they were working for the Department of Civil Affairs. It should have been obvious that the DCA might watch St. Cannerwells in case they came back, but in their blind fear they hadn't realised. Of course they'd not seen them before; the DCA wanted to catch them all together.

'Not so fast,' a man's voice said from behind them. They turned to see a DCA agent descending from the other stairway, the one which led up to the blocked entrance. Back the way they'd come in, two other men jogged down the stairs. All three had guns.

'He was there,' Jess hissed. 'When they killed the ambassador. He was one of them. Those bastards started this.' She started to walk towards him, but Marta put a hand on her shoulder. 'What?' Jess growled.

'That's suicide.'

One of the agents held his gun in the air. 'That's all of them,' Mr. Vincent. We appear to have collected an extra one too. Want us to kill them now?'

Vincent, the leader, held up a hand. 'Wait! Are you sure the Huntsmen have been called off? The last thing we want is those fucking monsters spoiling the party.'

'Four are captive, but one has gone AWOL,' the man shouted back. 'We've lost the frequency on the fifth.'

'We're that important that they sent *five* Huntsmen after us?' Marta whispered to Paul. 'Holy shit.'

The one called Vincent laughed. 'Well, you kids are cleverer than I thought. How did you manage to kill one of them?'

No one answered. They had backed away towards the centre of the platform, where a large supporting pillar offered cover in the space where a confectionary stand and some vending machines had once stood. As Marta shouted, 'Get to cover!' they darted towards it, dodging out of sight just as a gun went off and a bullet cracked into the platform not far from them, causing tile shards to shower their feet.

Don't shoot, damn it!' Vincent shouted. 'I want them alive!'

Beside Marta, Paul whispered, 'Where's Switch?'

Marta realised the little man wasn't among them, and risked a glance out towards Vincent. There she saw him, standing alone on the platform, fifty feet from the DCA leader. Switch held a knife in one hand. The other had vanished, back into his jacket, she assumed. He advanced slowly like a true street fighter, swaying from side to side, ready to drop and roll at any moment.

'Switch, for God's sake, get back!' Marta hissed, remembering his earlier words: *we have something to battle for*. He wanted to go down fighting, but against trained, armed, DCA men, Switch had little chance.

'Well, I guess killing one won't matter,' Vincent said, cocking his gun. 'I'd hoped we could use you, maybe, but it's no skin off my –'

As fast as Marta had ever seen, Switch drew something from under his coat then dropped and rolled just as a bullet passed through the space he'd been standing in. As the gunshot died away a sharp hammering sound rang out across the empty station and into the tunnels. Vincent screamed and fell to the ground, clutching at his leg.

'Wow, that was fucking cool,' Owen said, just before Paul pulled him back out of sight.

'Where the hell did he get a nail gun?' Simon asked, holding on to Jess, who was trying to rush out and join the fight.

'Get off me, Simon!'

Vincent's gun went off again, impossibly loud, the bullet ricocheting off the ground just inches from Switch, who was still rolling across the platform. Vincent was hurt but not dead; Switch had just bought them a little time.

'Fuck this ... *ahhhh* ... just *kill them!*'

Gunshots cracked from the other direction. Paul and Simon moved to the other side of the alcove, crouched low, clawboards held like clubs. Jess had pulled a huge bread knife out of her bag and passed another to an insanely grinning Owen. Marta reached under her shirt and grabbed her pepper spray can.

Switch rolled over the platform's edge and down on to the track. Vincent was moaning in pain while trying to reload his gun. A train suddenly roared past and Marta gasped as it passed through where Switch had fallen.

'Let's rush them,' Jess said behind her. 'They're scared. We have to take them before they call in the things again.'

As if in response, a gunshot cracked, and a small explosion of broken tiles and mortar from the roof showered them from above.

'See?' Jess said. 'They can't even aim.'

Marta stole another glance, this time back towards the front entrance. The two DCA agents were crouching at the bottom of the stairs, blocking the only way out.

She frowned as a shadow fell on the steps behind the two men. Huntsmen? She glanced out again. In the moment before she pulled her face out of sight of their guns, she saw what looked like a woman, being pulled along by something on a leash–

#

Dreggo had caught the Huntsman outside in St. Cannerwells Park. Blind, it had been stumbling about like a drunk down near the old pond, not far from a group of tramps drinking homebrewed spirits around a pile of burning benches and old chairs. Using the metal lid of a trashcan until she was close enough to use her knives, she'd battered the creature, finally sending it into some form of unconsciousness by smashing its head against the low wall that edged the pond. A piece of old rope made a suitable leash.

The buzzing in her head had told her all she needed to know, and she'd slipped back to St. Cannerwells and staked out the DCA units, themselves laying siege. She knew from the transmissions that the other Huntsmen had been called in and restrained. The signal had been faint, but she'd realised the fifth was still alive and getting closer, its receivers damaged but still following the mission. She didn't know what had happened to it, but captured, it was a weapon unlike any other.

She'd failed to track the Tube Riders; their scent had been too faint. The Huntsman, however, had a stronger smell, one she knew well. She'd taken it by surprise; it hadn't been hunting for her.

Its face was caked with blood and both its eyes were useless, but its sense of smell was as good as ever. Among her personal armoury was a police-issued stun-shocker, and with it tied to a piece of old railing she was able to keep the newly conscious Huntsman squirming at the end of the rope. It was damaged goods, but it was still far more dangerous than a gun.

The two men at the foot of the stairs didn't even see it coming. They were focused on keeping the Tube Riders trapped, and the Huntsman had slashed the throat of one and torn the arm off the other almost before they knew it was there. One of them got a shot off, puncturing the Huntsman's shoulder. The creature screamed in rage as its claws and teeth finished the man off.

'Come out, Tube Riders,' Dreggo shouted. She jabbed the Huntsman with her makeshift stun weapon. 'Come out, it's safe. I'm on your side now.'

#

Marta saw Dreggo descend the stairs, saw the captured Huntsman maul the two DCA agents and leave their bodies on the ground. She also heard what Dreggo said and realised they might have no choice but to trust her.

'There's another one!' she shouted, and glanced back towards Vincent. The leader of the DCA was crawling towards them, gasping in pain as he dragged his injured leg. A trail of blood followed him, a dark shadow under the emergency lights.

'What the bloody hell is going on here?' Paul muttered.

'Just keep down and wait for a chance,' Simon answered.

'This is like a computer game,' was Owen's contribution, while Jess stayed silent.

'Hey, you! Drop your gun, or I loose this thing on you!' Dreggo shouted at Vincent.

Marta glanced out to see Vincent lifting his gun. He aimed in Dreggo's general direction and pulled the trigger, but instead of a gunshot there was just an empty click.

'Ah, fuck,' he muttered, and tossed the gun away.

'Come out, Tube Riders,' Dreggo repeated.

'She doesn't have a gun by the look of things,' Paul said.

'She has a whole lot worse,' Jess said.

'Let's go.' Marta stepped out into view. 'What's this about, Dreggo?'

The leader of the Cross Jumpers approached them with the Huntsman still ahead of her, crouched low to the ground. It looked more feral than the one that had chased Marta and Switch.

'I think we can help each other,' Dreggo said. 'I want a way out of this city, and in exchange I can protect you.'

The others came up beside Marta. 'Who says we need protection?' Paul said.

'You'd be dead if it wasn't for me,' Dreggo replied. 'Or you would have been as soon as you tried to run.' She came closer, prodding the Huntsman along in front of her.

'That's the one Paul got,' Owen said, eyes filled with awe. 'Man, you smashed it up bad.'

Dreggo moved past the Tube Riders, who backed off away from the Huntsman. Ten feet from Vincent, she stopped.

'Looks like your plan didn't quite work out,' she said.

'Who the fuck are you?'

Dreggo smiled. 'Don't you remember me? I'm the one that got away. Give my regards to your witchdoctor friends. We'll be seeing you.'

'Fuck you. Release that thing and get it over with.'

'You really want me to?' She let out a little slack and the Huntsman jerked forwards, jaws snapping, making Vincent flinch. Dreggo turned away. To the others she said, 'Together we'll be safer. I have a ... history with these people. I can use it to help–'

Marta gasped as a hand snaked up from below the platform edge and gripped Dreggo's ankle, pulling hard. She cried out in surprise and fell backwards to the ground, the leash and the pole slipping out of her hands. For a moment everything seemed to freeze: Vincent, lying on the ground, wide-eyed; the Huntsman, crouched at Dreggo's feet; Switch, climbing up off the tracks; Marta and the others, caught in the middle.

Everyone was staring at the Huntsman.

It hesitated just a second, as if deciding where the pain it remembered clearest had come from. Then it leapt at Dreggo, its claws and maw ripping and tearing. Dreggo screamed and tried to throw it off her. They rolled away across the platform. Dreggo, despite her strength, was no match for the incensed Huntsman.

'Quick,' Switch shouted. 'We have to move *now*.'

'What about him?' Marta said.

'Fuck him.'

'We'll catch you!' Vincent shouted. 'We'll hunt you down–'

Owen stepped forward and kicked Vincent in the face. The DCA agent slumped back against the ground. 'Just shut up, man...'

Switch grinned. 'Nice footwork, little bro!'

'Guys, this isn't over!'

Marta pointed. The Huntsman had won the fight. Dreggo's bloody, mutilated body lay limply on the dusty tiles. The beast pulled something out of the ruins of her clothes and turned back towards them, clawed hands gripping a silver crossbow. Switch said, 'Its mission!'

The Huntsman's blind head swung back and forth, nose twitching at the air. Then it stopped still, frozen. Slowly, its lips curled back in a snarl

'I have an idea!' Simon shouted. 'Get across the tracks now!'

Paul pushed Owen in front of him. Simon grabbed Jess's hand and pulled her behind him, though at first the girl seemed to want to stand and fight.

'What about the DCA guy?' Marta shouted to Switch, who was already across. She pointed at Vincent's still body.

'Forget him,' Switch replied. 'If it wants dessert, too bad.'

Marta was the last to jump. As she crossed over the tracks and landed heavily on the other side, she heard a whirring sound behind her, and looked back to see the Huntsman loading the crossbow.

'There's a train coming,' Simon shouted, pointing at the tunnel where the faint glow of headlights had come on amid the growing roar of an engine. 'Come on, you bastard, jump!' He picked up a loose tile and threw it at the Huntsman. The tile struck the creature in the chest, and it jerked in Simon's direction, teeth bared, the crossbow lifting. Simon took another step forward.

'Come on!' he shouted again. 'It's fucking Pancake Day, you bastard!'

'Watch out!' Marta said. 'Don't make it jump too soon!'

Jess and Switch had joined him in goading the Huntsman. It snarled again then bounded forward, the crossbow going off with a zipping sound as it leapt out over the tracks.

Simon's body jerked. He screamed and staggered a few steps, then dropped to his knees. The Huntsman, more agile than they had expected, landed easily on their side of the platform with the train still back in the tunnel. Its free hand swiped at Jess, claws raking the air, the other still holding the crossbow. Simon now lay on the ground, clutching at his shoulder. Paul, nearest, swung his clawboard at it, only for the Huntsman to swat it away. Switch darted forward with a knife raised, but it was Owen, slipping behind the Huntsman and clubbing the back of its legs with Paul's old clawboard which caused it to lose balance. As Switch's knife flashed again, the Huntsman jerked backwards and fell out over the tracks, into the path of the train.

For a second the train's warning horn sounded low and hollow. Then the Huntsman was gone as the train thundered past.

As the train rushed away, the others crowded around Simon. The crossbow bolt protruded from his right shoulder and his shirt was soaked with blood.

'I'm okay, I'm fine,' he whined, gritting his teeth.

'Help him up,' Marta said. 'Can you still ride, Simon?'

'I'll try.'

'We have to leave now.'

'I know.'

Marta glanced at the others. Paul's face was ashen, while Switch was busy picking bits of cloth out of the teeth of his knife. Owen was reliving the strike which led to the Huntsman's death, while Jess was stone-faced, staring at Simon as though he were already dead. Marta felt cold inside looking at Jess; the girl she'd met earlier was gone, perhaps forever. But then, she reflected, perhaps there was a part of all of them that was gone now.

Behind them, across the track, Vincent had regained consciousness and was barking orders into a mobile phone. 'They're *here*. Quickly, free the rest of them!'

Jess turned away from Simon and picked the Huntsman's crossbow up off the platform. She turned it over in her hands as though she were inspecting a piece of fruit. Then, with a brief shrug, she pulled a metal quarrel out of a pocket on the side, fed it into the crossbow's mechanism and pressed a button. Marta heard a whirring sound and saw a metal spring drawing back. Jess looked up at the others, face blank. Without a word she turned and walked across to the trackside.

Marta followed her. 'Don't kill him,' she said, meaning Vincent. 'That makes us no better than them.'

'Do you think I care? I *will* kill him, but he has to wait his turn.'

Marta followed Jess's gaze down on to the tracks. What was left of the Huntsman lay there, across the rails. One arm was completely gone, and one leg from the knee down lay between the tracks about twenty feet in front of it. The other arm was mangled and half its torso hung open. Blood pumped out of a long chest wound. Marta saw wires and what looked like metal plating inside, alongside the tissues of a body that had once been human.

And yet it was still alive, its head trying to rise, a low groan coming from its throat.

'Good God, what does it take to kill those things?'

Jess didn't answer. Slowly, she lifted the crossbow. 'For my mother and my father, for everyone else ... die, you fucking ... *prick*.'

She pulled the trigger. The bolt slammed into the Huntsman's face just below the blinded eye. There was a popping sound followed by a crackle of electricity and then the monster was finally still.

Jess pulled out another bolt. Behind them came the sound of another approaching train.

'This is our ride,' Switch said.

'I don't leave until he's dead,' Jess replied, waving the crossbow at Vincent, who was cursing and grunting in pain as he tried to pull a nail out of his leg.

'We don't have time!' Switch shouted. 'Stay with him and die together if you fucking like, girl, but we have to go *now!*' As Switch spoke, four dark shadows poured down the station steps, rushing across the platform towards them. Marta's jaw dropped; it was like facing the door to Hell itself seeing the snapping, nightmarish horde come on, some moving like men, others bounding like dogs.

'We're going to die unless we're on that train!' Paul shouted.

Marta looked at Switch. He had his nail gun in one hand, but his face was pale, hopeless. Even he knew they had no chance against so many.

'Remember what I told you,' Paul said to Owen. 'Don't let me down, brother.'

Owen, endlessly cheerful, nodded. 'I'm a Tube Rider now,' he said, hefting the clawboard Paul had given him.

'Please don't get hurt,' Paul said.

'Run, jump, hook,' Owen recalled.

'You got it, now go! I love you, kid.'

Owen grimaced. 'Man, shut *up*. Christ.'

The train rushed in. Marta heard Jess screaming at Simon to 'Run, one last time, just *run!*', and then she was running after Paul and Owen herself. In these moments, she reflected, it was everyone for him or herself; if someone fell they were on their own. No one could go back.

Two of the Huntsmen had crossed in front of the train. As Marta caught, she saw them stumble as they tried to turn too quickly. In front of her, Paul and Owen were safely caught, Owen whooping his delight as his board hooked on to the metal rail. Just behind her, Switch caught the rail, and she leaned forward to see beyond him to where Simon, his face contorted with pain, had just jumped. His board caught the edge then slipped safely inside the rail. He howled in pain as the train jerked his injured shoulder, his eyes squeezing shut, veins protruding from the backs of his hands as he struggled to hold on. Jess, at the back, caught the rail then quickly freed one hand and pulled the crossbow from her belt. As the nearest Huntsman leapt forward, its claws reaching, she aimed and fired. The bolt hit the Huntsman in the shoulder, enough to knock it back into the one coming behind. They tumbled to the ground as the train roared into the tunnel.

'Hang on!' she screamed as the cold wind and the dark enveloped them. She could only hope the others had enough strength left to listen.

Chapter Twenty-Two
Aftermath

VINCENT COULD THINK of no other plan than to play dead as the Huntsmen, freed on his command, rushed into the station. The Tube Riders were out of sight behind the moving train, and a moment later it was gone, taking them with it. Two Huntsmen were on his side of the tracks, two on the other. Vincent thought for a moment he was the next victim, but then, howling like a pack of rabid wolves, the Huntsmen leapt down on to the tracks and bounded away into the tunnel.

As silence descended, Vincent climbed to his feet. Three nails had hit him in the thigh. One had fallen loose while the other two were imbedded deep and wouldn't move. Every time he touched them bolts of pain lanced up his side.

Still, moving slowly, he could walk. He found himself marveling at the resourcefulness of the Tube Riders; the skinny, odd-looking one in particular. He hoped to put a bullet in that one personally.

A few feet away lay the body of the girl who had captured the blind Huntsman. Vincent hobbled over and looked down.

It had mauled her bad enough that she would never need to worry about boyfriends again, he thought darkly, but underneath the blood he could see the slow rise and fall of her chest. A small moan when he nudged her with his foot confirmed that she still lived.

I'm the one who got away. He knew what she meant, of course. There was no way a normal human could have survived such a mauling. And if what she claimed was true, Vincent thought, maybe she could be of some use to them.

#

Leland Clayton was pissed. Climbing from the car outside the abandoned station, it was all he could do not to draw his gun and flick off the safety. Vincent had gone above his authority, ordering the Huntsmen called off in an attempt to ambush the Tube Riders. Clayton, whose idea it had been to stake out the station in case one or more might return, had expected to view their bodies only after the Huntsmen had finished. Just minutes ago, though, Vincent had called him and muttered some lame excuse that an "altered" plan had failed, and that the Tube Riders had escaped, but not to worry because the Huntsmen were once again on their trail.

Vincent, vying for commendation from the Governor, had gone behind Clayton's back again. Maybe, Clayton reflected, this was one time too many.

Inside the station, he found Vincent leaning against the wall, a couple of aides tending to a wound in the younger agent's leg.

'Okay, so what the fuck just happened here?' Clayton's fingers had gone to the gun again, and he purposefully pulled his hand away and stuck it in his trouser pocket.

Vincent yelped in pain as one of the aides dabbed his leg with antiseptic. 'I'm sorry, Clayton. It was my fault–'

'You're damn right it was. We're under orders from the Governor *himself* to take those kids out. *He* ordered the Huntsmen, and *you* ordered them off. I know you want my job, Vincent, you damn fool, but surely you value your fucking *life?*'

Vincent looked at the ground. 'I'm sorry, I thought they might be more useful alive.'

'Which is why you had them pinned down by two gunmen, both of whom are now dead?'

'They were just to help ... negotiations. I was fully expecting the fugitives to give themselves up.'

'And instead you got taken out with what? A nail gun? You, a DCA agent, gets taken out by a kid with a fucking *power tool?*' Clayton was too angry to laugh. 'You're a fucking disgrace, Vincent. I'd demote you to sorting mail if it wouldn't embarrass me to explain why.'

'I was surprised. And that thing over there, she took out my men.'

Clayton looked over his shoulder. 'The dead girl? One: who the fuck is she, and two: please explain to me, Vincent, how did she manage to kill two agents?'

Vincent raised a hand. His look had taken on a familiar smugness that Clayton always wanted to punch off his face. 'Firstly, she's not dead. And she took out my men by setting a Huntsman on them. A Huntsman she somehow managed to capture. Tell *me*, how the fuck did she do that?'

Clayton rolled his eyes. 'It gets better. Who is she?'

Vincent smiled. 'She's the one that got away.'

'God help you Vincent, if you smile at me again you're going under the next fucking train –'

'She's half Huntsman.'

'What?'

'Go look at her. She's been modified.' For a moment Vincent grimaced and clutched at his leg. 'And for some reason she was chasing them too,' he continued through gritted teeth. 'I thought she might be of some use.'

Clayton narrowed his eyes. His anger still boiled but he was remembering something Dr. Karmski had said about an escapee. That, though, he would deal with in time. 'So, Vincent, you're telling me you managed to lose everyone we're after in order to bring me someone who "might be of some use"? Jesus Christ. Get yourself to the hospital and get out of my fucking sight.'

Clayton walked away from Vincent towards the bloody body on the ground. Vincent was right; wires protruding from her forehead and the glimmer of metal beneath the skin where she'd be mauled told him she'd been modified all right. Clayton felt a funny tickle go down his neck. He knew the government's so-called "researchers" took kids off the streets for this. She might have been a perfectly normal girl, walking home from a café, cinema, whatever, when a bag was pulled over her head and the next thing she knew she was strapped to a chair in a room full of scientific equipment. Now she'd ended up like this, almost more metal than human. And he considered her one of the lucky ones. He didn't know everything about what happened in those evil underground laboratories, but he knew that a vast number of mistakes were made before the "lucky" few ended up as Huntsmen.

He felt like putting a foot on her neck and saving her from more pain, but his curiosity got the better of him. And like Vincent had said, maybe she would be of some use.

'Hey!' he shouted back to one of his agents. 'Get a couple of men over here with a stretcher. We need help for this one. Make sure you secure her arms though. She might be dangerous.'

As the man ran off, Clayton walked to the edge of the track and stared down the tunnel in the direction Vincent said the Tube Riders had gone. The

Huntsmen were out there somewhere, running hard, nearly inexhaustible. His professional mind hoped they ran the quarry down by morning, saving him a lot of trouble and hard work. The part of him that had once had morals, though, wished the Tube Riders luck.

Part Two
Bristol

Chapter Twenty-Three
Lost Boy

MONDAY WAS LOOKING like another quiet day for Carl Weston. The new school term was still a week away and with a little sly help from their housekeeper, Jeanette, his homework was all done and sitting in a folder back at the house. He'd been careful this time to have her write the answers on a piece of paper for him to copy up, rather than directly onto the work itself. A teacher had caught him out last time and he could still remember the sting of the cane. The back of his father's hand had hurt a lot more, though.

Down in the woods, among the ruins of the old town, he'd set up a shooting range where he regularly practiced with his air rifle and catapult. Most of the houses were gone now, the roads torn up, but in some places the skeleton walls of old terraces and shops still rose up over his head.

Transplanted trees and undergrowth obscured most of the buildings. Many of the trees tilted at ridiculous angles because, his father said, when the government began a project to reseed the countryside some years before he was born, many of the newly transplanted trees were not supported properly and had since suffered from the effects of subsidence and wind battering. The natural trees were easy to spot because they rose straight, but as a young child Carl had loved playing among the exposed root systems of many of the capsized trees, prevented from total collapse by the helpful remains of an old shop or house. Brambles, bracken and ivy smothered everything now, but Carl regularly cleared away the entrances to some of the better root-caves to maintain a series of dens where he could while away his days in blissful idleness.

Now, with the morning sun casting long shadows all around him, he crept through the silent ruins with his catapult held ready. As he approached a sycamore tree growing at a forty-five degree angle, he crouched low. With a sudden cry of attack he leaned forward and executed a karate roll, coming up into a squat and loosing the rock ammunition. It clanged off a rusted old construction sign Carl had jammed into a crack in a half collapsed wall.

'Got ya!' Carl shouted, holding the catapult aloft. The old sign, a half-corroded silhouette of a construction worker holding a hand up in a "stop" pose, didn't reply.

Carl stood up and leaned against the thick tree trunk. He listened for a moment, cocking his head, looking up into the foliage. Not far away came the sound of a bird's call, followed by the flutter of wings. He was used to the birds, of course, but there was something else, a low rumbling, somewhere distant. He looked up at the sky, though he hadn't seen a plane in ten years or more. Then he remembered.

'Train!'

With a big grin on his face, Carl dashed off through the trees, quick feet skillful over the treacherous ground from an entire childhood of playing in the forest. The train line was several hundred yards away, slightly upslope, cut along the side of a hill. Twisting sharply back and forth he raced through the trees, following a trail he'd cut along what had once been a main road but now looked like something out of a fairy story, chunks of concrete and the occasional flash of white line hidden by huge drapes of hanging brambles caught up in tree branches, creating a natural tunnel.

Scrambling over the remains of a bungalow, he reached the fence that cordoned off the tracks just moments before the huge train lumbered through. His fingers gripped the fence and he gasped with excitement. He was just in time to count the trucks as they rolled past. Fifteen, sixteen … he counted nineteen in total. Just two short of his record, but it had been a long one nonetheless. No wonder it was moving so slowly. All of the trucks were brown freight carriers. The cab had windows but he'd been too late to get a look inside at the driver. One of the older house servants had told him that the trains had once carried passengers from one town to another. Carl would have found it difficult to believe – after all, everyone knew the cities had been closed up to keep the unsavory types locked away – had he not discovered an old station among the ruins, not far from here. It was confirmation enough that the trains had once stopped, and nowadays, while playing in the forest, he dreamed of a time when the world had been different, when life hadn't all been farming, ginger ale at summer fetes, and algebra.

As the train rolled on into the trees, Carl turned and walked a little way along the fence. It was lower here where the slope was steeper. It was to keep people off the tracks, that much was obvious, but here, with only his family's house within a couple of miles, Carl thought it a little unnecessary. The trains were infrequent, just a handful each day and less at night, rumbling on towards Bristol GUA and back again towards London.

He had borrowed a pair of his father's wire clippers and cut a hole once. He had pushed his bicycle through and ridden along the tracks, all ten miles back to the perimeter wall. Movement over the gravel and sleepers had been sluggish but the weather had been fine and the ride enjoyable, until the hulking grey perimeter wall had risen up in front of him like the end of the world. Above it the sunshine had been sucked away; grey clouds rolled and toiled, trying, he had thought, to get out.

Beneath it all, a dark tunnel had sloped down into the beast itself, breathing out cold, damp air that had made Carl shiver and put his discarded sweater back on. And there, from deep down in the dark, twin eyes had appeared, catching Carl in their stare. Rushing towards him with a roar like a rising storm, Carl had been able to leap out of the way only at the last second before the train rushed like a dragon out of the tunnel.

Looking back from the side of the track where he had fallen, he had seen the mangled remains of his bicycle lying in the train's wake. Unfixable, he had left it on the opposite tracks for the next metallic beast to drag down into the earth.

His parents hadn't fallen for the story that his bike had been stolen. Crime was rare, and even a small thing such as that was treated seriously. His father had taken the belt to him in a bid to discover the truth, and Carl had almost given in and told him, his father quitting the assault perhaps two welts short of a confession. Still, rather than risk embarrassment in the local community his parents had glossed over it. Scapegoating one of the lower house servants or farm hands would have been possible, but they would still have struggled to find a motive. After all, most roads were gravel these days and the bike had hardly been new.

So now Carl just walked everywhere.

Glancing up, he saw the sky was beginning to lighten, the sun to come up. He loved the mornings best, often hunting in the forest before school, but Mother would go mad if he was late for breakfast. He put the catapult into a belt bag and turned to head off. Just as he did, he heard a low moan coming from further along the tracks.

He paused, hand reaching for the catapult, afraid it might be some boys from school come to ambush him, administer a beating. It had happened once before, so he never traveled unarmed now. Although the catapult, like his air rifle, was little more than a way of distracting them long enough to give him a decent head start, he felt safer carrying it. He shuffled forwards, trying to see.

The moaning came again. Carl felt sure it was a person this time, and whoever it was sounded hurt. It could be a trap but doubted the boys from school would bother, especially at this time of the day. Most people just left him alone.

'Hello? Is anyone there?' Carl moved forward a few more steps. There he saw, lying on the other side of the fence, leaning against it as though he'd been thrown there, a man.

Carl sensed the man was badly hurt and hurried forward, leaning down. 'Are you all right?' he said through the fence. He couldn't see the man's face very well but he didn't look that old after all, maybe in his early twenties, maybe the same age as some of the farm hands. Carl was sixteen but often felt younger; over twenty still made the injured person a man.

'Jeh ... Jes ... *Jess*,' he moaned. There was blood on his shirt around his shoulder, a large patch that stained the light blue fabric dark. Carl might have mistaken it for sweat except that it had dried hard, and had that distinctive smell he knew well from helping his father prepare meat for market.

Carl tried again to talk to the man, but he appeared lost in delirium. Carl had no idea how long he'd been lying here, but if he was badly hurt there was a chance he could die.

'I'll be back soon,' Carl said, then turned and sprinted off into the trees.

#

Back at the house he found his father in the upstairs study, reading a book while the television flickered with the sound down in the corner behind him. A bowl with the milky dregs of cereal in its bottom stood on a table nearby.

'Father, can you come with me please? I found a man in the forest. He's hurt.'

Roy Weston slammed the book shut and looked up. The grey shadow of stubble matched the colour of his cold eyes. He stared at Carl for a moment and then put the book aside in a slow, laboured movement. Carl knew it as the first sign of trouble, and stepped back out of range in case his father's hands darted forward.

'Please, I'm not playing games,' he said, grasping for courage for the injured man's sake. 'He might die if we don't get help for him soon.'

'Heaven help you if you're messing with me, boy,' Weston growled, standing up, still a head taller than Carl, who had his mother's lighter build and height. A thick chest looked ready to throw bombs, and Carl backed away across the room, fearing a storm. He had the door behind him, though, and would run if necessary. In the past, his father's anger had often been diffused by time, though Carl had scars on his back as a reminder of the times it hadn't.

'I think he fell off the train. He's inside the fence.'

'Okay,' his father said slowly. 'We'll go and see what you've found.'

Downstairs, his father called a hand from the stables and instructed the man to bring some wood to fashion a makeshift stretcher if required, and some wire clippers to get through the fence. With Carl leading, the three men headed back down into the forest.

'Carl, if this is some prank of yours there'll be trouble,' his father growled, stumbling over a root as they made their way through the ruined village and the irregularly angled trees.

'It's not! He's just up here, not much further at all.'

The man was still there, curled up by the fence. He wasn't making any noise now, and Carl at first thought he had died. Leaning closer, though, he saw the low rise and fall of the man's chest.

'Bloody hell,' his father exclaimed. 'Where did he come from, then?' Directing the stable hand, he said, 'Okay, let's get that fence open and get him up to the house.'

The stable hand cut through the fence and they carefully lifted the man's body on to it. The hand then took the front of the stretcher, Carl and his father the back. It was nearly a mile back to the house and they had to stop to rest several times. When they finally got back they waited in the kitchen while Carl's mother and Jeanette, clucking loudly, as Weston would have put it, prepared a room on the third floor.

Carl's mother insisted on old sheets being put on the bed before they laid him down, despite Jeanette's protests to the contrary. Carl believed his father would have agreed with the housekeeper, but despite his temper and liberal use of corporal punishment, in the house Carl's mother ruled, and so the unconscious man was laid on the floor while the bedclothes were replaced. Meanwhile, Weston dispatched the stable hand downstairs to call for a doctor.

Jeanette, with no children of her own, quickly took charge of tending to the man's wounds. With Carl's father's help she stripped him down and began to mop away the dried blood that stained his torso. Carl's mother held a hand over her mouth at the sight of the wound itself.

'Goodness, what is *that?*' she exclaimed, and they all peered closer to make some sense of the object imbedded into the man's right shoulder.

'Some kind of knife?' Carl ventured.

'Looks more like a thick tent peg,' said his father. Then, in a poor attempt to make a joke, he added, 'He have a bloody camping accident or something?' No one laughed.

Jeanette, who had spent most of her life in a kitchen, said: 'It's like a metal chopstick, but it's too thick. I'd say it's a bolt of some kind.'

'Well, don't touch it until the doctor comes,' Carl's father said, and went to the door. Leaning out, he shouted down to the stable hand to tell the doctor to bring his surgical equipment.

A while later, with the stable hand dispatched back to his duties in the yard and Carl's mother gone to an engagement with friends, Carl, Roy Weston, and Jeanette stood and watched while the doctor, Rhodes, did his work.

'Weston, on my advice, this lad should go to hospital for care,' Dr. Rhodes, a gruff, bearded fellow in his late fifties, told Carl's father. 'He's lucky, that's for sure. The injury is bad, but not life-threatening unless it gets infected. He's also sprained his ankle, but I've splinted it and he should be able to limp about in a few days.' He turned and pointed to a drip bag suspended from a metal frame which the doctor had rigged up to the bed. A plastic tube disappeared into the man's arm just below the elbow, the insert covered with a plaster. 'Refill this with the solution I gave you every two hours. He's been out there for ten or twelve hours, I'd think, got a touch of dehydration. And give him those tablets, two after each meal for two weeks. I still think he should go to hospital, though.'

'The nearest hospital's fifty miles, Rhodes,' Weston said, dismissing it as though it were a stupid idea. 'Over these goddamn roads that's a three-hour bloody journey in the car. At least.'

His father was right, but Carl thought that the real reason was so his father could keep an eye on the man. After all, no one came out of the cities, and if he had been thrown from the train as was how it looked, he surely wasn't a very savory character. Other people might want him as far away as possible, but Weston, who had made his fortune in his youth as a cruiser-weight boxer, had an unusual fascination with the folly and misfortune of others. And if it turned out the man was a fugitive, Weston would be certain to want his reward.

'Don't worry,' Weston said. 'I'll see to it that Jeanette gives the boy the correct doses as and when necessary.'

Rhodes held up the metal bolt and grunted. 'Where the hell did he get that, I wonder? Where did you say you found him?'

'In the woods,' Weston said. He made no mention of the train tracks. 'I don't know him, so maybe he's not from round here.'

'I should say so,' Rhodes grunted. 'From a neighbouring farm, perhaps? You positive you don't want the police involved, Weston? Boy could be a fugitive.'

'Newspapers have nothing,' Carl's father replied. 'We'd know if someone was on the run. Most likely a bunch of boys were playing bow and arrow.'

Rhodes shook his head, a wry grin on his grizzled old face. He put the metal bolt, cleaned of blood now, down on a bedside table. 'Where those boys got a goddamn crossbow from is anyone's guess.'

After Dr. Rhodes had left, Weston took Carl down into the kitchen. 'What have I told you?' he said, pushing Carl's shoulder. 'Keep away from the damn train lines! You have no idea who that kid could be! He could be, I don't know, a bloody spy?'

'Who from? Who would spy on us?'

Too late to take back his insolence, his father cracked him around the side of the head with the inside of his clenched fist, making Carl's ears ring and his vision momentarily blur. 'Don't talk back to me, boy,' he growled, and Carl shrunk away. A couple more years of filling out and he might be capable of fighting back, but his father was still too lean and the memories of a strict childhood were still too close.

'Sorry,' he muttered, looking at the floor.

'I don't want you playing near the tracks again, do you understand me?' Carl's father poked a finger into Carl's chest as though to ram home the point.

'Yes, Father.'

'Good.'

Weston stalked off. Carl was left to wonder about the man upstairs. Who was he? Had he fallen from the train, or had he been pushed? Carl had watched the trains many times, from outside the fence, from the branches of nearby trees, from the platform of the old station itself. They didn't have windows, of that he was sure. They were cargo trains; they didn't carry passengers. And the man upstairs certainly wasn't dressed in anything that could be considered a worker's uniform. So who was he? Where had he come from?

Carl could guess some of the answers at least. He'd come from inside London GUA. But London was closed up, people didn't go in without a permit and people certainly never came out, not dressed like the man was and covered in blood. He was running from something, but from what Carl couldn't even guess. All he knew was that the metal thing that Rhodes had taken from the man's side had come from the weapon of someone who had got very, very close to their target.

Despite everything, Carl found himself smiling. The intrusion of the man into his life was a spark of excitement in a world of boredom barely sustained by his imagination and his adventures amongst the ruins in the forest. The man was a stranger, and a mysterious one at that. Carl could only guess at the stories the man had to tell, but he sure as hell planned to find out as many of them as he could.

CHAPTER TWENTY-FOUR
NEWBORN

WHAT REMAINED OF DREGGO lay upon the cold metal operating table in the middle of the science laboratory. A group of technicians and doctors fussed around her, working hard to repair the damage, both physiological and mechanical. As Leland Clayton entered, his nostrils filled with the scents of formaldehyde, ferrous steel and blood, while the low hum of generators, the clack of needles, and the buzz of drills hung in the air around him.

A poor night's sleep had followed several hours of cleaning up the mess he had found in St. Cannerwells. Adam Vincent had been treated at a government hospital, and the families of the dead men had been notified. Not for the first time, Clayton cursed the decay that had set in over the land; getting the simplest of tasks done often proved a major headache. The Department of Civil Affairs, while brutal and unflinching in the face of duty, was a failing organization, fallen into stagnation after too many years of personnel and budget reductions. Even the men were suffering; below the higher levels of the organization the training was inefficient, and many of his men were less than useful in a firefight. Vincent was a prime example of how worthless, back-stabbing idiots could now rise up into the higher echelons of the department when fifteen years ago they would not have been allowed in. The future was bleak too; new recruit numbers were falling, with many of the agents he needed to put trust in little more than thugs dressed up in silks.

As Clayton grimaced at the smell and took in the sight of the girl's ruined body, he couldn't help pulling the phone from his pocket and glancing quickly at the display. He was waiting for a call from Bristol GUA regarding the arrival of the Tube Riders. He had fully expected them to jump the train at the earliest opportunity and try to hide among London's slums, and had wasted valuable hours having his men check stations further down the line. The Huntsmen, though, had come back with the information that the Tube Riders had ridden right out of the city, hanging from the train as it exited under the perimeter wall from one of the sewer-like tunnels. Where they were now was anyone's guess, and while he would have liked to have followed them immediately he dared not go above the Governor. They had a meeting later today, but the Governor was holed up in meetings all morning regarding the staged assassination of the EC ambassador by so-called terrorists. Clayton couldn't help but think that a noose was tightening around Mega Britain's diseased neck.

At the head of the operating table stood Dr. Karmski, rubbing his chin with one gloved hand while he watched his team work. Clayton noticed an unnatural level of concern on the face of the usually sadistic doctor. He looked like a father overseeing an operation on his own child.

Clayton looked down at Dreggo's body. Half her face had been torn away and there were deep lacerations all down the front of her torso, but he could still see she had once been a woman. Not a normal one, though; metal inserts were evident in her arms and legs, as well as what looked like some kind of plastic body-frame, now scored with deep claw marks. Clayton wondered whether, had it been absent, there would be much of her left.

'So,' he began, trying to sound authoritative. 'Where exactly did it come from?'

'*Her*, Mr. Clayton. Not "it", if you please.'

Clayton scowled. '*Her*, whatever. It's a Huntsman, I presume?'

Karmski smiled. When he spoke, his voice was almost wistful, as though he were speaking to no one but himself. 'She was the first of a *new breed*.'

Clayton opened his mouth to reply, but Karmski continued, 'She's been gone over a year. At the expense of her tracking skills we left her more human. With it she kept her beauty.'

'Okay, Karmski, enough of your crackpot perversity. Can you fix her or not, and if so, what good is she to us?'

Karmski smiled. 'Fixing her is easy. We can make her stronger, we can make her better. Mr. Vincent claimed she knew those others, the ones you hunt. As requested we are readying more Huntsmen for release, but these others ... some of them are ... flawed. Barely controllable. Yet, she ... my Dreggo, she is one of them and also one of us. She can lead them.'

Clayton rubbed the bridge of his nose, considering. 'We have recalled the Huntsmen. I will talk to the Governor later today. It is my expectation that tomorrow we will move out as a unit. Can she be ready by then?'

Karmski laughed. 'Mr. Clayton, you amuse me. You've seen what we are down here, you've seen the wonders we create. *Of course* she can be ready by tomorrow.'

Clayton rolled his eyes at the word 'wonders'. He'd been to Stonehenge and Dover, he'd seen wonders both natural and manmade. In comparison, the creations of this modern day Dr. Frankenstein were *monstrosities*. He said, 'How can it be possible for a body to heal so fast?'

'We replace what is broken, Mr. Clayton. Skin, bones, nothing is beyond our skills. And the tissues themselves, we simply order them to regenerate.'

Clayton seriously doubted the boldness of Karmski's statement, and as he glanced at Dreggo he felt a momentary pang of sadness for the girl, losing the last shreds of her humanity before his eyes. But he nodded, his face grim. 'Good. Report to me when she's walking about again.' He turned and walked out.

Just as he closed the door, he glanced back across the room, at the racks of expensive computer machinery and medical equipment, and shook his head. 'While everything around us rots,' he muttered wryly.

#

Back inside the laboratory, Karmski watched as the technicians fixed in place a black metal plate to hide the ruined part of Dreggo's face. The Huntsman had left just one eye and her nose undamaged. Half of her mouth was gone, replaced by synthetic skin tissue, its vulnerability now protected by the partial mask. Much of her former human beauty was gone, but there was still enough of the old Dreggo left to excite him.

Karmski still remembered the day they'd brought her in, a fifteen-year-old runaway, drugged and bound. Later, strapped to an examination table, still numb with drugs, he'd used her for the first time in the solitude of his private lab. He remembered the soft, suppleness of her skin, the warmth of her body, her taste, her smell. He shivered at the memory.

As his scientists had experimented on her and found new ways to enhance her strength and abilities, Karmski's love for her had grown. The girl once known as Deborah Jones, nicknamed Dreggo, was never left alone out of her shackles. With an endless supply of tranquilisers and memory-erasing drugs to hand, Karmski's love for her had manifested itself often. The day she had slipped her bonds while being transported up to the research labs and escaped, killing three scientists and more than ten guards in the process, was the proudest and also the darkest of his life.

'After all this time, you've come back to me,' Karmski murmured, while all around him the scientists, technicians and doctors worked without pause.

#

Out in the corridor, Clayton pulled his cell phone from his pocket and answered a call from Vincent.

'Vincent? What news do you have?'

'The Huntsmen have returned and been secured as you ordered,' the younger man's voice came through. 'It's as we thought. The kids have definitely gone. There are no fresh scent trails inside the perimeter walls. They're outside. We're ready to move anytime. Your orders?'

Clayton scowled. He hadn't yet cooled on Vincent, still blaming him for the Tube Riders' escape. After sending him to the hospital to have his leg fixed up, Clayton had demanded he return to supervise the search operations and oversee the return of the Huntsmen, a duty which had ensured Vincent got no sleep last night. Still, hearing the weariness in Vincent's voice was scant reward for the wrath of the Governor Clayton might yet have to face.

'We need the Governor's permission to send the Huntsmen out into the GFAs,' Clayton said. 'I have a meeting with him later.'

'If we send them now, they can run down the Tube Riders by early afternoon.'

You've changed your fucking tune, Clayton wanted to say. Instead, he just said, 'No. We wait for authorization. If I have to set those monsters loose in the countryside I'm not being responsible for whatever damage they might do.'

Clayton heard a slow intake of breath that could have been tiredness, could have been insolence. Then Vincent said, 'Whatever you say.'

The train that the Tube Riders had taken was on a direct trunk line to Bristol. The DCA branch there had been notified, and enhanced station security requested. He had demanded armed guards, cover on every exit. In reality, though, he doubted he'd get it. Bristol had almost as many problems as London and the Governor's announcement yesterday evening had caused pockets of rioting in cities all across the country. The police were over-stretched, and the DCA were trying to plug the gaps. He just hoped that the Tube Riders wouldn't slip away before the net was in place.

He knew they wouldn't be stupid twice. They'd taught themselves how to get on and off a moving train, a skill he genuinely admired, and he suspected they'd look for a safe place to jump, either out in the countryside or inside the perimeter wall of the industrial mess that was Bristol GUA. His hunch was that they'd head for the city, feeling safer in what they knew than the relative unknown of Reading Greater Forest Area.

Whatever they did, their free days were short. The DCA needed to organise itself to continue pursuit outside London GUA, but within a day, maybe two, there would be twenty Huntsmen on their trail. Huntsmen could follow a trail weeks old, and, if everything went according to plan, and Dr. Karmski knew what he was talking about, there would be another, better, stronger, Huntsman leading them, one who knew the Tube Riders well enough to anticipate their movements and to bring them in.

Clayton shut off his phone and headed for the exit. He felt a cold sweat bead on his forehead and in his armpits. He wanted to blame the clammy air of the lower levels of the facility, but he knew that was just an excuse. The truth was that the easy part of the day was over. The hard part – facing the Governor with the news that the fugitive Tube Riders, carrying information that, in the right hands could bring war to Mega Britain, had managed to escape not only the Department of Civil Affairs but the Huntsmen as well, and were now somewhere outside the city – was about to begin.

#

While the first sunlight of morning was still struggling to break through the grey smog that shrouded London, inside the facility the light came from the same clinical shadow-killing strip-lighting as ever. Inside a holding cell that doubled as a recuperation room, Dreggo lay sleeping, her one remaining eye closed, her chest rising and falling beneath a mound of bandages that left little clue as to the extent of her torso's damage.

The last technicians had left. Several hours of surgery had repaired most of the damage to her circuitry and closed up the flesh wounds. The latter would take time to heal; although the gene-manipulation she had undergone during her initial development caused her tissues to regenerate at accelerated rates, Dr. Karmski's men couldn't work miracles and she would still be vulnerable for a few days.

The damage she had suffered could never be completely repaired. Her skin tissue could be replaced, but her human sight could not. In its place, the technicians had installed a computerised motion sensor and infra-red night vision "eye", but she would only see clearly and in full colour from her right.

Karmski walked around the table. One hand reached up and touched the skin of her leg underneath the sheet that covered her. He glanced back towards the door. He'd locked it, but was nervous nevertheless. Dreggo had been gone over a year and he'd not had a chance to be alone with her since the DCA van had brought her in.

He sucked in a sharp breath as his hand slid further up the inside of her thigh. He glanced up at her face and saw her eyelids flutter, but otherwise she was still. He'd given her an extra dose of sleeping pills, just to make sure. With the right friends, the street could make you tolerant towards even the strongest medication.

Confident no one could see him and that she wouldn't wake, Karmski let his other hand move inside his own trousers. His excitement was building, and he didn't know how much longer he could hold himself back. He pulled his hand free and began to unbuckle his belt.

His other hand had found her sticky wetness now. He slid his finger inside, delighted to see the way her body shuddered. Awake, she'd kill him in an instant, but in her drugged sleep she felt the same pleasure as any other woman touched by a man as it manifested in her dreams.

'My beautiful Dreggo,' he moaned as he climbed up on to her, his trousers slipping down around his knees. Almost unable to control himself, he eased her legs open and pushed the covering sheet up over her body.

Losing himself in the pleasure of his greatest creation as he eased himself into her, Dr. Karmski felt like he'd come home.

Chapter Twenty-Five
Landing Party

T HE FIRST GREY LIGHT of morning was breaking through the dark as the perimeter wall of Bristol GUA rose up out of the forest a mile ahead.

'The train's finally slowing down,' Switch shouted to Marta. 'At fucking last. Are we going in?'

Marta struggled to lift her head. It had been a long, long journey from London, on the clock maybe less than three hours, but on the heart and the hands an eternity. She remembered Jess's scream as Simon fell, then the girl's desperate assertion that she would find him, and they'd all meet again in Bristol. Marta had screamed at her to wait, but Jess had ignored her, blindly pitching herself off into the dark. Marta still hoped, but the chances of seeing either alive again were slim. She remembered something she had said, *live together, die together*, and her mind toiled with indecision and guilt, for hadn't they thrown that away? Shouting back and forth to each other up and down the train, they had agreed that following Jess and Simon into the dark was near suicide. For Simon and Jess, their fate was their own, but guilt now tore at her like a Huntsman's claws.

She looked around at the others. Everyone was quiet, even Owen, who at first had whooped and screamed like a kid on a rollercoaster. After Simon fell and Jess jumped – two people who weren't faceless *bad guys* – the reality of the situation had set in, as had the cold. Hugging the side of the train, the chill night wind had battered them relentlessly, and Marta had felt the temptation to just close her eyes and fall backwards into the dark.

'We're going in,' Marta responded at last. 'A city has better cover and more ways to throw the Huntsmen off our scent. And if we got out of one we can get out of another.'

'I've never seen the countryside,' Paul shouted back to them. 'Only on TV.'

'Don't worry, you'll get your chance,' Marta replied, hair whipping her face. 'We're not stopping long, just until we work out what the hell to do next.'

Ahead of them the perimeter wall loomed, a huge grey concrete sentinel rising up into the sky.

'It's fucking patroled!' Switch shouted. 'Lean in close, they might see us!'

Marta looked, and saw he was right. On top of the wall she could see soldiers moving around. They were just shadows at this distance, and she couldn't be sure if they had weapons or not, but judging by the security alert they'd set off, there was every chance the guards were watching for them.

'We've had tree cover the whole damn way,' Paul said. 'Now when we need it we get bloody fields.'

'It's a killing ground,' Owen shouted.

'A what?'

'Open space around the walls where they can see people either escaping or attacking. Easier to shoot them that way.'

'How did you know that?'

'Video games.'

Marta cut them off. 'We're coming up to the tunnel,' she said. 'Wait for the train to slow. There's bound to be a station; hopefully it'll be for freight only and we can jump off and hide while they unload the train. We'll have to look for a way out.'

'Here we go!' Paul shouted, as the tunnel rushed around them, cold wind wrapping around their already freezing bodies like iced blankets. 'Hang on!'

The tunnel sloped downwards in impenetrable darkness. Somewhere far ahead the train's headlights had winked on, but from where they hung the glow was barely perceptible.

'Can't see,' Owen mumbled.

'Get your head in!' Paul shouted, and from Owen's pained shout Marta knew Paul had given him a gentle shove. Losing two for the night was enough already.

'We're slowing,' Switch said as the train began to angle upwards again. 'I think this could be the station.'

They saw a glow up ahead. Marta was hoping for a secretive underground unloading bay, one with dim lights and few people, where they might be able to slip away unnoticed, but then the glow bloomed all about them as the train rushed out of the tunnel into an immense, cavernous station, an ornate, glass domed roof above them illuminated by huge spotlights. Looking over her shoulder Marta saw a dozen or more empty platforms alongside theirs before you came to the far wall. Her heart sunk. So much for sneaking away, they had about as much cover here as a fugitive did in the middle of a football field.

The train slowed. Switch jumped first, rolling and landing effortlessly. Owen jumped after him, but the train had almost stopped and he just jogged a couple of steps. Paul waited until the train had completely stopped before climbing down like an arthritic old man. Marta flexed her arms, and a moment later a tingle began to filter through them as pins and needles attacked all the long motionless parts of her body.

Then a door at the front of the train swung open with the grinding of rusty hinges, and she saw a bulky figure climbing down on to the platform.

'Over the edge, now!' Switch hissed, slipping down into the thin gap between the train and the platform edge. Paul and Owen followed quickly. Marta shuffled after them, her body wracked with cramps, and managed to get out of sight just as the driver appeared on the platform. Lying there in the semi-darkness beneath the train carriage, the hot smell of oil and grease all around her, Marta looked up towards the platform as spasms tugged her body back and forth. She gritted her teeth to stop herself from crying out.

Footsteps approached as the train driver walked along the platform towards another man coming over to meet him.

'Good day to you, Barry,' the driver said in a voice as rough and pockmarked as his face. Well met on this fine overcast morning.'

'Hello, Phil,' Barry, presumably the station master, said in a Westcountry accent Marta hadn't heard in years. 'You got the early run I see.'

'Well, one hellhole is as good as another,' Phil the driver said. 'Doesn't matter what time of day it is. Right, let's open them up.'

'What have we got?'

Phil huffed. 'Lose your checklist again? One through six is newspapers. They have to be at the distributors by seven so tell your men to get a shift on. Seven and eight are fresh fruit, boxed. Nine to eleven are furniture, twelve to fourteen are foodstuffs. Fifteen is goldfish.'

'Goldfish?'

'Yes, goldfish. You deaf?'

'Just, who—'

'People buy them, someone has to carry them. Now get them shipped off, we're scheduled to roll out in an hour and it would be nice to actually be on time for once.'

Peering through the gap between the train and the platform, Marta could see the driver was tall and grizzled, wearing a grimy baseball cap that might once have been red. A beer belly hung over the waist of his grey slacks.

She didn't dare move. At any moment his eyes might drop and they would be staring into her own.

'One more thing,' the driver said. 'You get the message from London? There's a chance there are stowaways on this train. I got the radio call about half an hour ago. It's likely they jumped off somewhere in the GFA, but they might be hiding out in one of the carriages. Get your security men over here before you check. You have permission to blow their fucking heads off on sight.' He grunted. 'Especially if you find them in with the fucking goldfish.'

The other man laughed. 'Yeah, we got the message too. We have a couple of DCA men outside, but there were riots last night over in Easton and Knowle West. An office building got firebombed, so they didn't have many personnel to spare. Personally I think the terrorists jumped off out in the GFA. I wouldn't come into this shithole by choice.'

Phil the driver nodded. 'You can get keg beer out in the GFAs. *Legal* keg beer. You hear that? I mean, what the fuck?'

'Yeah, the government has a lot to answer for. Terrorists can blow whatever the fuck up they want for all I care, so long as they stay out of my train station.'

Phil grunted and spat down towards the platform, but his aim was off and the globule exploded off the platform edge down on to the tracks. Marta saw Owen wince as a drop of spittle landed on his cheek but to his credit the boy stayed silent.

'You're sounding more like a rebel every day, Barry,' Phil said. 'I should ship you in and claim my reward. I wonder what that would be, a glass of flat beer and a couple of tins of tuna?'

'The government and the rebels can get in a circle and fuck each other in the ass as far as I'm concerned,' the station master said. 'As long as they do it outside my train station. They're as worthless as each other.'

'Amen, ain't that the truth.'

Both men laughed. Then the driver said, 'DCA'll most likely send men from London. That right?'

'I think so. If they ever get past the red tape. Even the fucking DCA need a permit to travel these days.'

'Huh. Crazy, ain't it? Right, let's get this shit unloaded. The café got bacon this morning?'

'Only if you brought it.'

'Ah, shit.'

The two men started to walk away as others came forward to open up the freight truck doors. Wooden slats slammed down, cutting off Marta's view. The open doors vibrated and wooden boards clattered as men ran up them to unload the cargo inside.

Marta's eyes caught Switch's, then Paul's. So, as they thought. They were hunted.

'What do we do now?' Paul whispered to Marta.

'I have no idea. Switch?'

They looked for the little man, and saw him moving away from them along the side of the platform towards the front of the train, crouched low beneath the metal pipes and supports of the carriage frame. He glanced back towards them. 'Wait here,' he hissed. 'And stay in tight against the wall!'

'Where's he going?' Owen asked.

Paul and Marta both looked at each other. 'You don't think he's going to—' Marta began.

Paul shook his head. 'He's not that crazy. *Is* he?'

#

Switch glanced up from time to time as he moved along beneath the train. He saw workers unloading the freight, men in dirty overalls with thick forearms, scarred faces with bitter stares. So, life in Bristol sucked as much as it did in London, then.

While that was not his concern, protecting his friends was, and Switch had an idea. In a wide open space with no cover, the best way to escape was to have your enemies looking the other way, and he had just the way to make them do that.

He reached the front of the train and ducked beneath the wheels to the other side. Peering up over the platform edge, he saw another train standing a couple of platforms away, providing him with cover. Pushing the clawboard up on to the platform ahead of him, he wormed his way up through the space beneath the cab's step. He crouched in the cab's shadow for a moment, checking again. Then, with one hand he reached up, searching for the handle behind him, eyes never leaving the platform.

He found it and tugged. The handle turned, but the door didn't move.

Switch cursed under his breath. He knew that a common precaution dating back hundreds of years to the days of regular train hijacking was to keep the spare door locked. Most trains were operated by one man, and since most people were right-handed the right-side door was the usual choice for access.

Still, no matter. He gripped his clawboard tightly then jabbed it backwards above his head, ramming the thin end into the passenger side window with all his strength.

Trains had thicker glass windows than a car, and while he felt the window crack it didn't shatter. Wincing from the searing pain in his side and the jarring in his wrists, he hit the window again.

This time he felt a crunch, and he twisted up and around, using the clawboard to break away the shards of broken glass. He slipped his hand in through the broken window and pulled up the door release from the inside.

Inside the cab he put the clawboard down on the seat and looked around at the controls. He'd never been inside a train before, but it didn't look dissimilar to the cab of a bus. There were dials, handles, buttons …

He was choosing which handle to try when the driver's side door opened and the driver, Phil, climbed up beside him.

Phil had been looking down, otherwise he would have seen Switch and had a chance to get away. But, not expecting to find someone else inside the cab, he climbed right up into range before he looked up.

Switch pressed a knife to Phil's throat. 'I've got not quarrel with you,' he said, eyes hard. 'Tell me what I want and you live.'

The driver was overweight, but his arms were heavily muscled. Dark eyes and a mashed nose that was bent a little to the left suggested he'd been involved in many a fist fight. He towered over Switch, and Switch knew that without the knife he'd be in trouble.

'You little fuck.' Phil started to lift a hand, but Switch's other hand came up, holding another knife, a thin flick blade. The man paused, words cut off.

Switch grinned, showing his teeth. Right in front of the driver's face he jerked the knife back and made a thin incision down the side of his own face.

Switch felt a warm trickle of blood dribble over his skin and down his neck. He grinned again, and moved the bloody knife back and forth so that the metal gleamed in the cab lights.

Phil's mouth dropped open, his eyes widened. Growing up on the street had taught Switch many things, and one of them was that while cutting someone else was hard, cutting yourself was far harder. An adversary willing to cut him or herself was one to be feared.

The ruse worked. 'What do you want?' the driver said. 'I have a wife, kids...'

'The handbrake.'

Phil moved his hand slowly, pointing to a red handle. Switch felt a certain satisfaction in that it was the one he had guessed on.

'Release it.'

The man did so.

'The engine.'

'Here.'

'Start it.'

The driver hesitated just a moment, and Switch pushed the blade a little tighter. Phil turned the ignition and the roar of engines filled the cab.

Switch smiled. 'Thank you for your cooperation.' Before the driver could reply, he made a dummy feint with the second knife. Phil jerked backwards, and Switch kicked out, causing the man to overbalance. Phil stumbled backwards down the steps on to the platform.

Switch pulled the door shut. As the train started to move, he heard shouting from outside. Back along the platform came the terrible grinding sound of wooden doors scraping on the tiles, the crash of overturning freight crates mixing with angry shouts. He only hoped the diversion would work long enough for the others to get away.

He glanced out through the driver's window. People were running along the platform towards the front of the train. He saw the driver back there too. Now the knife was gone from his throat, the man had recovered some of his courage and was leading several other workers and security guards in a pursuit of the runaway train.

Switch was pleased. He was drawing them off; perhaps they thought he was alone. He hoped the others were safe.

He moved across the cab and looked out through the passenger side window. He saw more men running towards him from this side too. The train was barely moving at ten miles an hour and without any knowledge of its operation playing with the buttons and levers might cause it to stop rather than speed up. He was keeping in front of them, but only just, and if he tried to get out he risked being caught, or worse, shot.

'Bugger it...'

He grabbed his clawboard, kicked open the door and swung himself up on to the metal roof of the cab. He walked in a crouch for a few feet then dropped flat on his belly, out of sight of the men on the platform. The metal felt warm to the touch and the heat made the wound in his side ache.

He lifted his head to look back, long enough to see several men still in full pursuit of the train as it rolled towards the end of the station. Behind them all, though, he saw the other Tube Riders running across the station, jumping over the tracks like a group of leaping deer.

He'd given them the chance they needed, and as he watched, one by one they vanished down a stairway near to a set of rusting ticket gates that had once fed passengers into the station. Marta was the last, and as she reached the stairs she looked back across the station towards him, lifted her hand and waved. He knew he had to find a way to follow.

He looked back towards the front of the train and found he had another problem. The line came to an end a few hundred yards further on, but blocking the way was another stationary locomotive. He was heading for a collision.

Switch looked up. Where the station building ended, an electricity wire hung from the highest eaves, stretching inwards towards a small building in the centre of the station that had antennae and aerials on its roof. If he could catch it with his clawboard, he could swing right over the chasing men, drop down and have a head start on them heading for the stairway. The only problem was that it was fifteen feet over his head.

Switch smiled. He reached inside his coat and pulled out a coil of climbing rope: thin, strong nylon. He had armed himself well before leaving London, not just with knives and other weapons, but with several other small objects that he thought might come in handy.

He tied it to one strap of his clawboard and then stood up in full view of his pursuers. One or two men had reached the cab and were trying to get a handhold to climb up. The train was still moving steadily, and they were running out of platform.

'Oi, you!'

'There's the bastard!'

Switch threw the clawboard up into the air, above and over the electricity wire. As he caught it on its way back down and pulled the rope taut, he could only hope the wire would hold his weight. The wire across the street where Marta and he had escaped from the Huntsman had held both of them, but this one looked a lot thinner.

He wrapped the rope around his wrists and sprinted back along the top of the train. At the end of the locomotive the wire began to angle away from the platform, so Switch jumped, the rope sliding along the wire and taking him above the heads of the men. One or two turned to give chase, but he was gaining speed, the wire holding firm and beginning to angle more steeply downwards.

Behind him he heard a thundering crash and turned back to see the cab collide with the stationary locomotive. It toppled over on to its side, the next few carriages hanging at decreasing angles until the weight of the train load took over. People were running in all directions, shouting for security, for firemen, and for someone to catch Switch.

Twenty feet before he reached the small building at the end of the wire, he unhooked the rope from his wrists and dropped to the ground, pulling the rope down and wrapping it into a quick bundle around his clawboard. His heart was racing with exhilaration and sweat was beading on his forehead.

He glanced back and saw three men rushing towards him, still a hundred feet away but closing. In front of him was the stairway, across one more set of tracks. As he watched, Marta's head appeared from the shadows. 'Switch!' she shouted. 'Look out!'

He guessed she meant the men, but as he took a couple of steps towards the set of tracks separating him from her, he saw another cargo train rushing into the station.

It was moving too fast to stop; it had to be a through-train, heading on to another station further into the city.

Looking far up the platform, he couldn't see the far end as the trucks continued to flow into the station.

It had cut him off. There was no way to get to Marta, and he couldn't outrun three men, not with his injury.

One hand fell to his knife. He glanced back. They were big, burly men who probably knew how to brawl, maybe even work a blade. One, maybe two, he'd have a chance, but three–

He looked back towards the train and gripped his clawboard, his decision made. Riding the trains was his life, he would let the train claim him rather than the men.

As the train roared past he sprinted towards it.

Cargo trucks didn't always have a drainage rail, but he saw one coming that did. He timed his run and leapt just as the truck came level with him, his clawboard out.

A second later and he would have missed it, hitting the truck behind which had no rail, but his timing was perfect. His clawboard caught the truck's rail, just a couple of feet short of the end. He slid a few inches but used his feet to brace himself. Shouts came from the men behind him as he slipped his left hand free from the clawboard and gripped the rail with his fingers. Shouts of anger and surprise rose from behind him as he kicked off at the same time as he pulled, flicking his body over on to the roof of the train.

He rolled, started to stop, and then pushed himself onwards, rolling across the top of the train and off the other side.

He heard Marta screaming for him as he fell through the air, twisted and landed hard on the concrete. He gasped for breath and struggled to get up as the train rushed by, his wound sending daggers of pain up through his chest.

Then hands grabbed his shoulders and back, and he looked up to see Paul and Marta hauling him up.

'Excellent job,' Paul said, wrapping Switch's arm around his shoulders and dragging him towards the stairway. Marta grabbed his clawboard and hurried after them.

Air slowly filtered back into his lungs as they descended the steps into a dusty pedestrian underpass. From the bottom of the stairs, Owen shouted encouragement.

'We've found a way out,' Marta said. 'There's a door into an old underground parking garage. We can get out into the city through there.'

'Quick, this way,' Owen said. The door beside him opened on to darkness.

'Look!' Paul said. 'Those men found another way down!' He pointed. The three men who had been chasing Switch were running towards them from the far end of the pedestrian underpass.

Marta pushed Switch through the opening. As Owen and Paul went through she dragged the door shut behind them.

It took a moment for her eyes to adjust to the darkness. The parking garage was vast, stretching away beneath the station. One or two rusty, long-abandoned hulks stood wheel-less in the dark.

She squinted. There, far across the parking garage, was the bright glimmer of an exit.

Owen was fiddling with the lock. 'There, that should hold them until they get something to break it with. I've jammed it.'

Marta took a second to breathe. 'Okay, we've made it this far. So far, so good. Now, Tube Riders, run!'

They sprinted off across the empty parking garage together.

Chapter Twenty-Six
White Rage

Clayton felt that familiar sense of foreboding as he walked down the corridor to the Governor's chambers. The eyes of the upturned past political leaders seemed to be staring at him, the reversed mouths downturned in distaste.

The Governor was standing by the window as usual, his back to Clayton. One arm rested on the tinted glass. Clayton quietly closed the door behind him and stood there, looking at the floor, unsure whether it was wise to break the Governor out of his reverie.

After a few moments the Governor shifted slightly. One finger tapped against the glass, causing a dull thud. 'Look at it, Mr. Clayton,' the Governor said, not turning around. His voice took on a musing, wistful air. 'The mess we made...'

'Sir–'

'Agricultural production in the southern GFAs is up six percent on last year, four percent in the north,' the Governor said. 'And in Scotland and Wales, the fisheries are working at closer to ten. Our great wind farms are producing more electricity than ever. We have problems in one or two of the GUAs, but production is still good in the south, industry good in the north. Most people are...' He paused, choosing his word carefully. 'Content.'

'I–'

'But here, in London, in our once glorious capital, crouching shamefully in the shadow of our pioneering space program, anarchy rules.'

Clayton said nothing. He had sensed a tightening of the Governor's voice, and thought that to interrupt again might mean death.

'There are many ways to improve a failing situation, Mr. Clayton. The use of force, for example, crushing the opposition with tanks and bombs. But equally powerful can be persuasion, or manipulation. All can achieve similar results. None, however, work as well as one extremely simple, often overlooked action. Do you know what that is?'

Clayton opened his mouth to answer, but the Governor cut him off. '*Generosity*. Give, and people respond. Give them what they want, and they will give what you require in return without question. Yourself, for example. When the government doubled your salary, Mr. Clayton, did it not make you happy? We gave you what you wanted, and in return you gave us what we wanted. You followed our orders without question, regardless of what you might consider *moral*, and you achieved the results we required...'

Clayton's mouth was dry, but he managed to mutter, 'Yes, sir.'

'Hmm. Until now, don't you think?' The Governor turned. Clayton took a step back as those red eyes bored through his own. The Governor continued, 'With the Huntsmen in range, you called them off. Didn't you?'

Clayton, of course, had done no such thing. Vincent was responsible for the order to halt the Huntsmen as the Tube Riders headed back to St. Cannerwells, slipping behind Clayton's back to further his own ambitions, and then hiding behind his senior officer when things hadn't gone to plan. Clayton wanted to expose Vincent and see him rot in the torture chambers beneath Dr. Karmski's research facility, but he knew that protesting his own innocence would achieve nothing. As senior officer, he was responsible for the acts of his men. If he left this room with his life he promised himself that his score with Vincent would be settled privately.

'Yes, sir,' he said, hanging his head, unable to meet that gaze. 'I thought–'

'You are paid to *do* as ordered, Mr. Clayton, not to *think*.'

'Yes, sir.'

The Governor reached out for a standing lamp just in front of him and in one astonishing show of strength flung it hard across the room. It struck a shelf unit and smashed, the glass shattering, the wooden shelves cracking and collapsing, unloading their books and ornaments on to the floor. Clayton shrank back as the Governor advanced across the room.

'Sir, I – it won't happen again–'

Ten feet from Clayton the Governor's face jerked upwards towards the ceiling, the fiery red eyes revealing white undersides. Clayton felt his feet slip out from under him and suddenly he was lying on his back, his head not far from the door, his feet scrabbling at the carpet as the Governor advanced. Clayton was disorientated, but one thing was certain above everything else:

The Governor hadn't touched him.

He looked up at the Governor standing over him, red eyes like two cherries in a churning bowl of milk. The thick lips and high cheekbones of his face were blankly emotionless, the eyes alone carrying the threat of pain and suffering. Clayton gasped as one hand reached down, ice cold fingers closing about his neck.

For a second he couldn't breathe, and then he was upright again, pressed back against the door. The Governor let go of him, and Clayton stumbled, unaware his feet had been off the ground. He stared at the Governor's chest, too terrified to look the man in the eyes.

'Negotiations have opened with the European Confederation,' the Governor said in that dark chocolate voice, like an old cassette tape playing on weak batteries. 'We have filed a report concerning the ambassador's unfortunate death. We have made a case for certain trade routes to reopen, and in the meanwhile the provision of financial aid to allow us to reduce the poverty in London GUA. Negotiations are going well.' He paused, his eyes falling to the ground. His mouth shifted as though he were chewing on something, and he frowned, thick white eyebrows descending like snow drifts on his eyes. 'We created the mess, Mr. Clayton, and we have created the means by which to solve it. One man's death for an entire city? The ambassador died for a noble cause, Mr. Clayton. If we receive the financial aid we requested from the European Confederation, his death will not have been in vain. His death would have been one of valour, honour, resulting in the saving of hundreds of lives. Do you want your stupidity to jeopardise that?'

'I'm sorry, sir—'

The Governor ignored him. 'Neither do I. If it happens again, Mr. Clayton, I will not be so generous with you as I have been this time. Now, I know you came here to request my authorization for the Huntsmen to be released outside of London GUA in the continued search for these street kids you call the Tube Riders. And my answer is this, Mr. Clayton: you do what you have to do to safeguard the future of our nation. Those kids have knowledge that could bring our nation to its knees. And I will not jeopardise that. I understand the danger of the Huntsmen, but understand this: the needs of the many outweigh the needs of the few. Do what must be done, Mr. Clayton, to stop the Tube Riders.'

Clayton managed a weak nod. 'Yes, sir.'

'Now, get out.'

Clayton didn't wait to be asked twice, bowing and stealing a quick glance at the smashed lamp before pulling the door shut and hurrying down the corridor past the immobile guards and the dozens of upturned photograph portraits. He ignored the questions of the reception staff and headed straight for the elevator.

Downstairs in the lobby, a security guard announced that a car was waiting for him, but Clayton walked past him without acknowledgement. He headed through the reception area and down a small corridor at the back, into the men's restrooms. Spotlessly clean and smelling of peaches, he walked to the end stall and went inside. He locked the door, dropped the seat and sat down.

For a long time he just sat there with his forehead pressed against the back of the door, going over his confrontation with the Governor again and again. He couldn't find the words, couldn't make sense of what had happened, couldn't comprehend the scale of the danger he had faced. Guns, bombs, even the Huntsmen, they were man-made, they were comprehendible. But the Governor ... the albino monster possessed something else.

A lot of rumours circulated in the cesspit illegal bars and gambling dens of London GUA. But, like the legend of the Tube Riders, most were simple speculation, something small built up over a lengthening string of drunken conversations into something grand.

The rumours about the Governor, however, that he had some kind of unexplainable strength, that he had abilities and powers that no other human had, were beginning to manifest themselves in Clayton's mind as truth.

He squeezed his eyes shut, but there, in the darkness where he'd hidden so many times, all he could see was that menacing milk-white face and those glowing red eyes.

CHAPTER TWENTY-SEVEN
SLEEPING PLACE

IT QUICKLY BECAME apparent to Marta that Bristol GUA shared many of the same anarchistic problems as London. As the Tube Riders wandered through the streets, directionless, numb from lack of rest, hurting from their wounds and the sudden loss of Jess and Simon, they found themselves in a similar world of decay as that which they had taken for granted in London.

Long abandoned cars blocked many side streets. Groups of filthy tramps huddled in the open doorways, their eyes fixed on the Tube Riders as they passed, their faces stony, bitter. In the distance came the familiar wail of sirens, skidding car tires, screams, the sound of shattering glass.

They rested for a while in a small park behind a church a couple of miles from the train station. There they ate some of the food they'd brought with them, a few packets of cookies, some apples, half a loaf of bread. Only Paul had remembered to bring any drink, so Switch went off in search of some. Marta and Paul sat side by side with their backs against a low stone wall. Owen sat beside Paul, his head on his brother's shoulder, snoring quietly. Marta envied him, but despite feeling weary beyond words, her eyes wouldn't stay closed.

'How long do you think it would take for a Huntsman to run to Bristol?' Paul said, more voicing his fears than expecting any serious answer.

Marta forced a smile. 'Surely even they have to rest sometime.'

'Do you think the DCA called them off when we got out of the city?'

She shrugged. 'I don't know. I hope so.'

He nodded. One arm slipped around the shoulders of his brother. Owen moaned and shifted slightly, but didn't wake.

'At least one of us can sleep,' Marta said. 'I hate to think what he's dreaming about.'

'The ocean, maybe. He's always said he wants to see it. Or video games.' He cocked his head. 'I don't think the Huntsmen scared him at all.'

Marta smiled. For a moment they were silent, listening to the quiet rustle of the trees in the park. Except for a tramp sleeping on a bench the park was empty. The sun had risen up over a cluster of housing blocks to the east, its pale glow pressing through a thin veil of cloud. The air around them was cool, and the wind brushed against their arms with the chill touch of icy cobwebs.

Marta turned to Paul. 'What do we do now?' she asked.

Paul tried to smile. 'We wait for Switch. After that, I don't know. He said he had an uncle in Bristol. Maybe we can find him.'

Marta grimaced. 'In the unlikely event that Switch remembers where his uncle lives, and the man is even still alive, what do we do then? Sit and wait for the Huntsmen? And what about Jess and Simon?'

Paul looked pained. 'I don't know. I really don't.'

They had avoided talking about it much until now. Nothing needed to be said; they all knew how desperate the situation was. Simon was most likely dead, and Jess too, unless by some miracle she'd survived the jump in the dark. Even Marta wouldn't have chanced it blind, and she'd jumped from moving trains hundreds of times.

For a moment she marveled at what it must feel like to love someone so much you would risk dying for them. The jump had been near suicidal, and the girl's devotion to Simon struck her as quite truly wonderful. There were days she'd lain awake at night, wishing someone would feel like that for her.

She'd had boyfriends, of course, some better than others. She found trust too difficult, and the last time she'd ever let herself feel love had been for a roguish guy called Jamie, whom she had known in her last year of school. They'd been a couple for a while, and she'd loved him far more than he deserved, for just a month after they had started going out he had gone out drunk and got himself shot by the police while trying to hold up a fuel station. She had mourned him for a while, but over time she'd come to see him for what he was: a bum, a freeloader, using her for a place to stay, borrowing her money, lying to her friends. Now, almost four years later, she felt nothing for him other than an odd, detached curiosity.

She sometimes wondered why she had never got together with Paul, or Simon before he found Jess. Simon, while a little too androgynous for her liking, had a smile that would have melted hearts in a happier world, and even Paul was attractive in a dad-like, homey kind of way. Marta, with hair she rarely cut that was matted from lack of care rather than dreaded, and a body that was hard from tube riding, knew she was attractive in a goth-punk kind of way, because enough guys had told her. Yet the kinship she shared with Paul and Simon was more like a family bond. She had never really seen them as anything else.

Until yesterday, she had felt that Switch was different. He didn't let anyone close to him and had issues with trust, she knew. Before the Tube Riders, everyone in his life had let him down, and while Marta felt he looked out for them, she often felt it was only temporary. If the Tube Riders fell apart, he would most likely move on.

Ever since he had assumed the role of her protector though, she had seen him looking at her differently. As though, perhaps, the demons on their tail had scared his own inner demons away, and allowed him to move closer to her, maybe to the others too. Perhaps he had taken their union as Tube Riders for granted, and now he had come close to losing it he was considering things in a new light.

Paul shifted beside her. 'He's back,' he said, as Switch came running over.

Squatting in front of them, he handed out bottles of water. Paul nudged Owen awake, and his brother looked up, eyes bleary.

'What's going on?'

'Went back to the station,' Switch said. 'People about but no sign of the DCA or the fucking Huntsmen either. If they can track as well as they claim, they should be here by now.'

'Was that a good idea?' Marta asked. 'Going back there?'

'Don't worry. I was as quiet as a dead fucking mouse. Whatever, it looks like they've either lost us or got caught up with red tape back in London. Who knows, maybe they got sidetracked looking for Simon and his woman.'

'Jess,' Paul said.

'Yeah, I know her name.'

'She didn't cause this.'

Switch looked away. 'Fucking government caused this. Ain't that who her old man works for?'

Paul glared at him. 'Yeah, before he was slaughtered by the Huntsmen, along with her mother. Obviously not very selective are they?'

'I guess not.' Switch rolled his good eye. His bad eye made it halfway around, then gave up and just twitched. 'Anyway, I think we have to assume the others are dead. If not, perhaps the – *Jess* might get away. Her scent won't have been all over St. Cannerwells like ours was. In the meantime, I think we need to worry about ourselves first, and get to ground.'

'Your uncle?' Paul asked.

'Give me time, we only just arrived. Not been here in a while, you know. A lot of shit's been blown up since then, it looks a little different. If it wasn't for certain familiar landmarks I'd be as lost as you are.'

Paul nodded. 'I guess that first we need to worry about what we're going to do with the information we have before it kills us.'

'Simon had the memory card, in case you forgot. We have no proof of anything now,' Marta said, struggling to keep the hollowness out of her voice. Until now she hadn't really had a chance to think about it, but what she had promised her parents ... it was over. They no longer had proof of what they'd seen. Now they were just a bunch of young people on the run, trying to stay as far ahead of the Huntsmen as possible.

'We have what's in our heads,' Switch interrupted. 'We have enough to start rumours, talk.' He grinned. 'Who knows, maybe they'll even believe us.'

'It's something,' Paul said. 'Otherwise we just run until they catch us.'

'You guys wanna stop talking and start moving?' Owen said. 'I'm getting cold.'

Switch grinned at him. 'You got it right, kid. Let's roll.'

Switch led them out of the park. There was still little traffic on the streets even as midday approached. Buses rumbled along among a handful of cars and motorbikes, some of their windows broken, swathes of dirt and dust along their sides. Glum people in factory uniforms stared out at nothing.

'Wouldn't wanna vacation here,' Switch muttered as they ran. 'Reckon I'd probably kill myself.'

They came out of a side street onto a wider road alongside a river, identified by a rusty sign as Temple Way. A bridge led over the muddy, lethargic water, and beyond it was another litter-strewn park. They could see the remains of park benches, a bandstand, even what looked like a small Ferris Wheel lying on its side. There were groups of people there too, sitting around under black or blue tarpaulin sheets, near fires that burned in old metal buckets and among piles of bricks. The faint echoes of laughter floated towards them from across the river.

They crossed the bridge and followed a sign that indicated the city centre, the road angling up from the river along a row of older buildings that wore the fading logos of old high street banks. There were no people here, and the road was empty of traffic.

'Which way?' Marta asked.

'Trust me,' Switch said. 'I know a safe place.'

'I'm hungry,' Owen muttered, just as Paul said, 'Look!'

Behind them, on the other side of the bridge, they saw a truck moving slowly along the road. Erected on its flat back was a huge television screen like the one they'd seen back in London. They could see the face of a man, hear snatches of what he said.

'It's the same broadcast as in London,' Marta said. 'About us. That crap about terrorists.'

'I think we'd better get undercover quickly,' Paul said.

'Look at those people,' Owen said, pointing.

In the park, people were stirring. A great cry went up as the truck moved slowly along the road outside. People stood up, shouting, waving sticks at the truck, throwing stones. A police officer standing guard lifted a speakerphone to his mouth and demanded calm, which only riled the people further.

As they watched, a mob began to grow out of crowd, moving through the park in the direction of the bridge. They carried sticks, rocks, metal poles, anything it seemed they could get their hands on.

'They're rioting,' Marta said. 'Those police are going to have a problem in a minute or two.'

They watched as the first police officer said something to the driver of the truck. The driver leaned out of his window, and over the distance between them they couldn't make out his expression, but they saw the speed with which he ducked back inside, reaching for the gears.

Too late, another mob had taken a second bridge further down the park, and the truck was surrounded. The driver jumped out and together with the police officer turned and sprinted away down a side street.

'What are they going to do?' Paul asked.

The two mobs descended on the abandoned truck. Within moments several men had climbed up on to the back and had set upon the giant television screen with their weapons, smashing it up even as the Foreign Secretary, Douglas Lewitt, still read the Governor's statement in a voice that boomed out across the park. Someone else had climbed up into the cab and was trying to clear people away in order to reverse it back.

'They're gonna bomb it,' Switch said, grinning. 'They're sick of the government's constant crap.'

'What do you mean?' Owen asked.

'Into the river,' he replied. 'Divebomb it.'

'Wow!' Owen's eyes were wide and he had a big grin on his face as though he were watching an action movie. 'That'll show them!'

'It'll make this area into a hive of police once those guys return with back up,' Paul said. 'We'd better get moving.'

'Just let me watch this!' Owen said, resisting Paul's tug on his arm. Marta and Switch also turned to watch.

A low stone wall marked the edge of the river, but as one person moved the truck into reverse dozens of others kicked and struck the wall with their weapons. A couple of rocks came loose and fell in, then a couple more.

'Clear!' someone shouted, and the truck revved and jerked forward, slamming into the wall. A few more stones fell away, but the wall still held. The truck backed up again and the mob moved in to do some more damage. On the back of the truck, the battered television still played, indistinct flickers of colour darting across the damaged surface like tropical fish in a pond during the rain.

'Clear out!' someone shouted again, and the truck revved. This time, the man inside pushed open the door before the truck started to move. As it rumbled towards what remained of the wall, he jumped out into the arms of several people waiting alongside.

The truck struck the wall with a loud metallic bang and jerked upwards. Then the wheels must have caught again because it suddenly moved up and out, hanging precariously over the river for a moment before plummeting into the water below.

The truck struck the shallow riverbed with a huge crunch and rolled over on to its back. Water rushed up to drown out the colours of the television and with it the last remaining fragments of the Foreign Secretary's face.

A huge cheer went up from the mob at the same time as a wail of sirens began in the distance.

'Run!' someone shouted, and like a stampede of deer fleeing from a predator, the mob split into two, both groups heading for the bridges leading over to the park. The few people who'd stayed behind by the tarpaulins gave a triumphant cheer.

'Round one to the revolution,' Marta said.

'And on that note ... don't you think it's time we made ourselves scarce?'

Paul said.

Switch grinned. 'Follow me.'

He led them down the street between the rows of old banks, away from the park, towards the city centre. The street was eerily quiet after the ruckus behind them, almost empty of people. Even a dog sitting beside a sleeping tramp only gave them a brief look, before dropping its head to its paws and closing its eyes.

The road opened out on to a wide plaza, a central area surrounded by a large roundabout, office buildings, old hotels and theatres rising up all around. To their left, the plaza opened out on to a harbour waterfront, while opposite them the road wound uphill past a towering Gothic cathedral.

'I take it this is the city centre,' Paul said. 'It's rather pretty, but where are all the people?'

'Perhaps they're at work,' Switch said. 'They keep this country running somehow,' he said. 'Who's to say they don't have whole armies of slaves chained up in underground factories?'

The others were silent for a moment.

'Because the police are so pathetic?' Owen said at last.

'Yeah, the ones back there were, but I'm not so sure about those.' Switch pointed towards the road that led up past the cathedral. A little closer now, they saw it was blocked by a tall chain-link fence that ran across the length of the road. Behind it stood two men in dark uniforms, their faces covered by helmets with visors. Each had a rifle slung over his shoulder.

'We had best keep out of sight,' Marta said.

Switch looked around as though getting his bearings. Familiarity flashed across his face, and he pointed. 'See that old theatre over there? We're going in there.'

Paul coughed. 'You mean the one right near the fence over there? Er, pardon me for sounding crazy, but wouldn't it be better to go back the *other* way?'

Switch grinned, good eye wide with a hint of insanity. 'The last place your enemy will look for you is under their own fucking doormat,' he said. 'Trust me, I have plenty of enemies. And have I ever been caught?'

Without waiting for a reply, he headed off to the right, skirting around the central plaza, close to the buildings around it which cast long shadows in the dawn sun.

'That's unless your enemies hunt purely by smell,' Paul muttered.

Marta shrugged. 'He's got us this far, and we don't have any better options.'

Switch skirted around out of sight of the guards by the fence and then headed back in their direction on the same side of the plaza. On this side the buildings all had a second floor overhang, giving them cover. A scattering of homeless people lay asleep in the sheltered doorways, but the buildings looked dark and abandoned.

The front entrance of the old theatre was shut up, huge barred wooden doors offering no way through. Switch, though, ducked into a thin alley that ran alongside. The others followed, having to turn sideways to squeeze through.

'Where's he going?' Paul asked, stumbling on a mess of garbage, old drink cans and plastic bags, a couple of smashed chairs and the charred remains of an old bookcase.

'Voila,' Switch said from the shadows ahead of them. Marta, going ahead of Owen with Paul coming last, stumbled out into a small courtyard at the theatre's rear. A thin lane wound up out of sight behind a derelict pub towards the fenced off area, and in the other direction towards a distant junction.

Switch was standing by a service entrance, a small door in the wall alongside a larger opening blocked by a metal shutter, a drop off point for equipment or stage sets.

'You want to get inside?' Marta said. 'I think between us we should be able to pick the lock.'

Switch shook his head and grinned again. He twisted the handle and the door opened silently. 'It's unlocked.'

Before they could say anything, he slipped through the opening.

'Uh, Switch,' Marta started, then shrugged her shoulders and followed him in. Paul started to tell Owen to wait outside, but his brother was already close behind Marta, his clawboard held up like a weapon.

Inside, Switch pulled the door shut behind them and took a small torch out of his pocket. 'I don't want them to know we're here,' he said.

'Who?' Marta asked him.

'Whoever lives in here.'

'Is this not likely to get us killed?'

He shrugged. 'Oh, I don't know. A lot of things could get us killed right now.' He flashed the torch around and headed across towards a door in the far wall. When he opened it a thin light slipped through. 'Electricity's on then,' he said.

A square emergency light coloured the corridor beyond orange. Switch flicked a switch on the wall near to him and for a moment the loading bay was basked in a clinical brightness before he quickly turned it off again.

'Why did you turn it off?' Paul said, still squinting from the sudden brightness. 'I preferred this place with light.'

'I don't think we're in any danger,' Switch said, 'But I'd prefer it if we got to see whoever lives here before they see us. You know, just in case.'

'You scared, Paul?' Owen quipped. 'The really bad stuff's behind us, remember?'

Paul gave him a mock slap around the ears. 'Shut up, kid.'

Switch headed up the corridor, the others following. He moved cautiously, checking around the corners before he moved on, always light on his feet.

'Could be they're sleeping too,' he said.

'Let's hope so.'

Finally, Switch pulled open a door into what looked like a storage room. He glanced around inside, then flicked on a light. At the back of the room several large chests were stacked against the wall. Switch shut the door behind them, then went over to the chests and started to pull one down.

'We'll help,' Paul said, motioning Owen over.

'It's heavy,' Owen said, as they dropped it down on the floor. 'What's in it?'

'Old costumes, I'm assuming,' Switch said. 'This is a theatre, isn't it?'

'What do you want with those?' Marta asked.

Again came that grin. 'Well, I don't know about you, but after a long night of traveling, not to mention jumping over trains, hanging from buildings, getting stabbed, attacked, shot at...' He spread his arms. 'I fancied a few hours sleep.'

'You've got that right,' Owen said.

'And you, kid, after getting a little shut-eye earlier, have nominated yourself for first watch.'

'Switch, you're one hell of a guy,' Paul said, as Owen scowled.

'Anyway, enough of the deserved praise. Let's get this bastard thing open, see if we can't find something that'll work as a blanket.' He tugged on the catch, but it was locked. 'Okay, that's fucking strange.'

'Perhaps the costumes are valuable,' Marta said.

'Maybe, who knows?'

'Let me try,' Paul said. 'I've dealt with worse locks than that. You got something thin?'

Switch pulled what looked like a metal pencil out of his coat and handed it to Paul.

'What the hell is this?'

'I got it on the black market. It's an old ninja weapon. You throw it.'

'Well, let's see if it'll pick locks too.'

Paul knelt in front of the case and pushed the metal pencil into the lock. The mechanism was big, not made for high security, and after a few seconds of jostling the tool back and forth Paul grunted, 'Okay,' and the clasp snapped up. Switch pulled up the lid and stood back for the others to see the chest's contents.

'Oh my,' Marta said, eyes wide.

'Well, I'll be fucked if that's not quite what I was expecting to find.'

Paul and Owen leaned forward to look. Both gasped with surprise and Paul even took a step back.

The chest was full of guns.

'Well,' Switch said. 'Looks like we've found ourselves a way out of this. There are enough guns here to storm London.'

From the doorway behind them, someone said, 'That's pretty much the plan.'

Switch and Marta spun, Switch with a knife in his hand, already coming up to throw. Paul stepped back, dragging Owen with him.

Three men stood by the door they had not heard open, casually dressed but each with a semi-automatic weapon trained on the Tube Riders.

'Okay,' the man in the centre said. He was around thirty, lean and tight with wiry muscle, and, Marta thought, very handsome. She felt colour fill her cheeks and silently scolded herself for getting all girly at the most inappropriate moment. *What the hell is wrong with me? They're going to shoot us!*

The leader's eyes flicked to Marta, and for a moment he looked amused. Then he glanced across at the others, gave a wry smile and flicked long, dark hair away from his face. 'Well, there'll be time later for introductions, but first of all would you mind telling us how you ended up in our armoury?'

Chapter Twenty-Eight
Lost Girl

It was twilight when Jess woke. She sat up and rubbed her head, then brushed some leaves and twigs off her body. She wrapped her arms around herself, shaking out some of the stiffness. She had fallen badly and lost consciousness, but she was still a novice after all so really she had to be thankful she hadn't broken anything at best.

At first she had thought it was dawn, but then realised the sun was on the wrong side of the sky. It had been dark when she'd jumped from the train, and it appeared she had been unconscious right through the day. Perhaps her body just needed to shut down for a while, work some of the trauma out of her system, or perhaps she'd hit the ground harder than she'd intended and should consider herself lucky to still be alive.

Idiot, she scolded herself. *What good are you to Simon if you're dead?*

She climbed to her feet and saw the crossbow and her knife lying further back up the railway line. Before jumping after Simon, she had thrown her weapons down first. Her clawboard, too, lay in the grass near her feet, seemingly undamaged.

Everything flooded back quickly: the ambush by the Cross Jumpers, her parents' brutal murders, fleeing London with the DCA and the Huntsmen on their tail. She wanted it all to be a bad dream, but the sight of her parents' mutilated bodies was like a knife in her stomach. Almost as bad had been that never-ending race through the pitch black of the railway tunnels, as they clung like lichen to the side of the freight train.

It seemed like they were speeding through the wet darkness forever, the freight train taking a different route to the commuter tubes, following a thin, cold tunnel that sometimes seemed so close that their bodies brushed the walls. Ghosts screamed out of the darkness and rare flickers of light burst from nowhere to dazzle them. Jess felt her hands shaking, her fingers seizing up from the cold as she fought to hold on.

The train roared on endlessly, the wheels thudding a rapid *dakka ta dakka ta dakka ta* over the rails below. Jess screamed her own panic out at the dark as her clawboard jumped and shook, its tenuous grip on the metal rail forever near to failing. Her legs ached from the vibrations, and her neck was stiff from the buffeting of the wind. For a second she leaned her head back into the dark, stretching her neck, only to feel something catch and tear away a clump of her hair. She jerked her head back in, acutely aware just how close they were to the tunnel walls.

Another inch...

The tunnel continued roughly straight as far as she could tell, the train jerking back and forth in a meandering line, tugging her shoulders, making her hips hurt. After what felt like an eternity the tunnel began to rise, and then suddenly they were outside, rolling below the clear night sky, the looming perimeter wall of London GUA receding behind them like a chasing mountain that couldn't keep pace. And as Jess looked out past a thin chain-link fence at the dark shadows of forest behind, lit only by the light of the moon, she felt as though for the first time since escaping the Huntsmen that she could breathe.

Suddenly the train didn't seem so fast. Suddenly her aches and pains seemed to leave her, and suddenly she understood how this could be not just dangerous and terrifying, but exhilarating. Defying the danger she had faced in the tunnel, she leaned her head back into the cold air and let the wind take her hair.

As her eyes adjusted to the night she made out the others on the train ahead of her. Paul, at the front, was suffering worst from the wind; he had a coat but was also trying to shield Owen from the full blast of the cold. Marta and Switch too, had managed to crowd together now the threat of the tunnel wall was gone, but it barely made a difference.

Now that she could see him, Jess shuffled her way forward to Simon, and from his agonised moans she realised his wound was worse than they had thought. His head lolled as he struggled to stay conscious, even the constant buffeting of the wind failing to help.

'I can't hold on!' he gasped, eyes squeezed shut with pain.

And then, suddenly, before she even had a chance to reply, the train bucked, hitting a loose or ill-fitting rail. Simon was there one moment, gone the next, his already tenuous hold unhooked by the train's movement, pitching him off into the dark. The train rushed on so fast she didn't even hear the sound of him striking the ground.

Jess screamed, her mind snapping alert. 'Marta!' she screamed forward into the wind. 'Simon's gone!'

Marta looked back at her, and in the dark her expression was unreadable. Whether Marta had heard or not, Jess couldn't tell.

'I have to find him!' she screamed. Then, 'We'll meet you there!' although she wasn't really sure where *there* was. She heard Marta shout her name, but Jess was no longer listening. She threw her weapons away, then closed her eyes, tensed her hands on the clawboard, and kicked up and off.

She trusted entirely to luck. Life owed her a break, and she took it now. Landing on a slope, the wind was crushed out of her as she rolled, bouncing down through thick grass and brambles that tried to hold on to her clothes. Her head spun, the clawboard falling loose from her grip, and the last thing she remembered was something hard as it collided with her head.

#

As she looked around now under the last remnants of sunlight, she realised the claws of the brambles that had raked her skin through her clothing had slowed her progress just enough. Otherwise the rock she had hit might have killed her.

After finding her weapons, she crept back along the railway line, looking for signs of where Simon had fallen. In the dark, it had been difficult to judge how far the train had gone while she'd been dumbstruck, but she guessed it could be anything up to three miles. It had taken time to alert the others and then throw down her weapons, and also – it shamed her to admit – time to decide if she should follow Simon or not. She had been frightened, of course, but part of her wondered if there was any point. He had been badly injured already, and the fall would surely have killed him. Only the image of her dead parents had spurred her on. Simon was all she had left now, and if there was a chance he was still alive and she could save him, she was prepared to take it.

After half an hour of walking she had still found no sign of him, and had come to a small bridge, under which a fast flowing river made its rocky way down into the valley. While she couldn't be certain, she had no recollection of them passing over a river after Simon had fallen, and she was sure she had gone too far. Frustrated, she began to backtrack.

Just as she was beginning to wonder whether they might have passed over the bridge after all, she saw something wooden poking up out of the undergrowth by the fence.

Simon's clawboard.

Of Simon, though, there was no sign.

Jess looked around her, wondering if he'd crawled a few feet and was lying nearby. There was no sign of him on the upslope side of the tracks, nor in the trees in the immediate vicinity. There was a hole in the fence that he could have climbed through, but there was no blood, no sign of torn clothing. The sky was darkening, but Jess could still see that on the other side of the fence the undergrowth had been trampled down.

As she ducked through the hole she touched a piece of the cut metal with her finger and found it still sharp. In the twilight she'd thought the hole caused by rust, but someone had done this recently with wire cutters. Simon, she knew, had no such equipment, which meant someone had been here and taken Simon with them. Whether he was living or dead, though, was another matter.

She looked back towards the railway line. The overhanging trees already made it difficult to see, and with no torch or way of making light she could easily get lost. Still, Simon was out there somewhere, maybe in danger. And there was no telling how much of a head start they had on the Huntsmen. It could be days, it could be hours.

She turned with her back to the railway line, and started forward into the forest. The undergrowth was sparse beneath the trees, many of which tilted at bizarre angles. For a while she was able to follow the trail left by whoever had taken Simon: the undergrowth was trampled and hacked down in places. Whoever had taken him – almost certainly more than one person – had not feared pursuit, making her more and more certain that it wasn't the Huntsmen or the DCA.

In places, the foundations of old buildings rose up out of the undergrowth. Pretty soon Jess realised she was walking through an overgrown, abandoned town. Wide sections between buildings marked old roads, with occasional patches of tarmac appearing underfoot. She remembered a fairytale from her childhood, *Sleeping Beauty*, where everyone in the castle fell into a deep sleep for a hundred years and everything became overgrown. She felt a little nervous, but in another way it was almost beautiful. Nature, something she'd seen so little of, was untamed here, rapidly reclaiming its stolen land.

If she hadn't been so troubled by the events of the last few hours, she would have marveled at it all.

Few people in the cities knew much about what went on out in the Greater Forested Areas, but because her father worked within the government she had a little more information than most. The official line was that the government had chosen to segregate forms of industry, and the social status that went with it. It had been intended as a commune system, where energy could be concentrated on one or a handful of related tasks, with free movement between the GUAs and GFAs. As dissatisfaction with the system had grown, especially in the cities, which still suffered from a lower standard of living, the perimeter walls became taller and more fortified, with movement requiring first written notification of business, then a local council permit, and finally an official government-stamped document of authorization.

The final closing up of travel between the major conurbation areas of London, Bristol, Manchester-Liverpool, Birmingham and Newcastle-Sunderland to all but officially sanctioned individuals, coincided with the banning of several major forms of communication: the internet, mobile phones and also several major independent television networks. The BBC was shut down and reemerged as the Mega Britain Television Company, broadcasting mostly inoffensive game shows, cooking programs and old movies.

Massive rioting had ensued in all the cities. The people outside in the GFAs, though, with their comfortable standard of living and stress-free lifestyle, barely stirred. There were a handful of meetings, mainly concerned by the demolition of hundreds of minor population areas and the moving of large numbers of underemployed people into the cities, but as the cleanup operation gained pace many of the more powerful dissenters were ameliorated by unexpected financial incentives, or offers of land. Many of those who still didn't sway simply disappeared.

Within the GUAs, though, the rioting lasted for weeks. Armed militias laid siege to government buildings and in some areas held open pitched battles with government soldiers. The uprising was always going to fail, though, and the government brought it to a close with the release of dozens of prototype Huntsmen. The creatures, some uncontrollable once released, cut a bloody swathe through the ranks of the dissenters, until finally the riots were subdued and a relative calm fell.

Then, of course, the government began to close up all the other major urban centres. Ports were shut down, airports dismantled, trade with foreign countries reduced, some cut completely. The food producers – the GFAs –

were pampered and lavished with financial rewards, while all the time the distance from technology and urbanization was slowly lengthening. In the cities, unrest began to grow as the government squandered its financial resources on the GFAs and the increasingly crackpot space program, something that even many of those on the inside of the government failed to understand. The rich who had stayed in the cities lived in better areas, in houses wired top to bottom with security devices, while the poor, the under-classes, got by the best they could.

She began to stumble as the night closed in, hindering her progress. Having spent her entire life in a street-lit twilight zone, an uneasy sense of claustrophobia descended upon her. So used to seeing violence on the streets, flashing sirens, uncontrolled fires, suddenly the sharp call of a bird carried double the menace; the crackle and creak of something moving nearby could be more than just a fox or rabbit. She found her knife in her hand, her breath quick in her throat.

Something rustled in the trees behind her, and the tension that had been building in Jess suddenly broke. With a horrified squeal she bolted, knife gripped tightly in one hand, the other hand held out in front of her to ward off the branches that battered at her face.

For a couple of minutes she ran hard, dodging instinctively between the trees, ducking low under heavy branches. And then her luck ran out.

Dashing through a thicker stand of trees in near total darkness, her foot snagged a root and she tumbled forward into a thicket of nettles and brambles. Crying out as something grunted and bolted away, she rolled over and over, slashing her knife towards unseen enemies in the darkness around her. Finally, almost in submission, she rolled on to her back, and realised she was staring up at the clear night sky. The trees were a dark shadow away to her right. Underneath her was grass.

She was out.

She brushed herself down as she stood up and looked around. The moon glowed brightly in a cloudless sky, a black sheet scattered with glimmering stars, stretching away to meet a slightly lighter blue pushing up from the gentle curve of distant rolling hills. Far away, in a hollow several miles distant, she saw the scattering of lights that indicated a small town. Nearer, though, perhaps just a few feet away, across a flat open pasture dotted with large round humps (which she knew from a childhood book to be hay bales) she saw other lights, four, five maybe, moving about.

People.

Jess smiled with relief, both at being out of the forest and to find there were other people out here after all.

The first natives of this foreign land.

She looked around for the nearest hedgerow, but the field seemed to stretch for miles in either direction. The huge bales would have to be cover, then.

Crouching low, she darted from one bale to the next until she was just fifty feet from the moving lights. Cautiously, she leaned out.

The light was coming from a couple of paraffin lanterns set down in the grass around a large truck trailer and from the torches several men were carrying. She counted six men in all, the glow from the torches revealing them as young, maybe just a couple of years older than her. All of them wore shabby overalls which looked black or brown. Working together, they were rolling the bales up a ramp on to the trailer.

At first, the performing of such an arduous task without the help of any kind of machinery made Jess think they were stealing them, but the snatches of conversation that she caught told her different.

'Six more, boys. Then we'll call it a night.'

'Six? We'll be here til midnight and I wanted to grab a pint!'

'We can be done by ten-thirty if we move quick. And anyway, if you boys want to come by mine when we're done, I got a few cold ones in the fridge and a hot pack of cards just waiting to take your money.'

'Sounds like a challenge!'

'Got an early start though, eh, lads.'

'That old sod Weston booked the cab to come by at seven tomorrow, take the first load. Weather's gonna turn, so forecast says. Got to get these boys undercover 'fore then.'

'Curse on Weston for flogging off his forklift. We'd have done the lot in half an hour.'

'Well, what I heard was that the council took it. Government rechartered it, gave him a payoff. Like they been doing with the cars.'

'Cities are running out, seems.'

'Huh. Seems like everything is, 'cept beer.'

'Don't complain 'bout that! Dumb government want to throw beer at us like water who are we to complain?'

Jess frowned. In London beer was illegal. You could get it on the black-market, of course, so readily that many people thought the government was actually supplying it. Here, though, it seemed people were drinking it unrestricted. She wondered what else they had.

A light suddenly flashed in her eyes.

'Hey! You boys see that? Someone out there!'

'No—'

'I did, looked like a lass! Hey, you!'

Footsteps in her direction. Jess gripped the knife and looked about her. She had weapons, but six guys in the dark would be impossible to fight against. And they were a long way from any help.

She glanced left, right, then picked an area ahead where the bales were numerous. She glanced back to see what head start she had, then sprinted across the field, the sharp stalks of the cut hay scratching her ankles.

'There she is!'

'Hey you, maid, wait up!'

'You from the village? Shouldn't be out here after dark!'

'Come here, we won't hurt you!'

Jess didn't give them the opportunity to prove their word. She ducked behind the nearest bale and dropped to the ground, shuffling deep into the recess left by the curved edge. A moment later the men jogged past, torches flashing back and forth. She knew they wouldn't maintain the chase for long, so she quickly scrambled back out, rounded the bale and jogged back to the trailer where they'd left their lamps burning.

Behind the trailer, a gate opened on to a lane. Jess glanced back, hearing a few more shouts out across the field as the men continued their search. On the edge of the trailer she found a small plastic lunchbox next to one of the lamps. She grabbed it then quickly extinguished the lamp and took that too.

As the men's shouts came nearer as they returned to the trailer, Jess took her treasure and ran for the road.

Chapter Twenty-Nine
Freedom Fighters

THE HANDSOME MAN called himself Ishael. Now, as he sat facing the Tube Riders, the four of them sitting in a row on an old, musty-smelling sofa, he rubbed his chin, picking at a piece of stubble. 'So, let me get this straight. Those damn broadcasts are about *you?*'

Marta, holding a steaming cup of delicious tea in her hands, nodded. 'It seems so. And now we have the DCA, Huntsmen, and God knows what else on our trail. We've not had a great last twenty-four hours, let's put it that way.'

'That's a fucking understatement and a half,' Switch muttered.

'Well.' Ishael leaned back in the chair. His gun was back in a holster on his belt, but one of the other men was guarding the door to the small meeting room where they had brought the Tube Riders, a gun held loosely in his hand.

'That's a pretty good reason not to kill us, don't you think?' Owen said.

'Be quiet,' Paul scolded.

Ishael smiled. 'On the contrary. You realise that by being here at all you compromise our own safety? If you're right about Huntsmen being after you, they'll follow you right here. Perhaps we should just kill you and throw you out for them.'

'You have weapons, you can fight them,' Switch said. 'Give us a bunch of guns and we'll stand out there and wait for the fuckers. All we have is knives and other lame shit. *Mostly* other lame shit.'

Marta couldn't help but smile at his crude attempt at modesty. They had been searched by Ishael and his men, and while herself, Paul and Owen only had their clawboards, Marta's pepper spray and a couple of knives, Switch had yielded up a veritable armoury of his own. The men had looked quite impressed by the array of knives, throwing stars and other weapons. He'd told them with a proud smirk how he'd lost his nail gun in St. Cannerwells, but not before taking out a DCA agent.

'You've survived so far,' Ishael said, raising an eyebrow at Switch. 'Anyway, say they come here and we somehow kill them? Two days later they'll send more. If we manage to kill those, they'll roll out the entire army. We can't win. Do you have any idea how many prototypes they have? Handing you over might be the best way to keep ourselves alive.'

'But you'll expose yourselves,' Marta said.

Ishael shrugged. 'We're just a smalltime gang, of no consequence to anyone.'

Switch scoffed. 'No "smalltime gang" has that many guns, man. We might have stumbled in here by luck, but we know what you are. You might as well admit it.'

Switch was right, but as Marta watched his face as he spoke, she couldn't help but think that luck had nothing to do with it. Switch had known exactly who he'd find when he led them here.

Ishael looked at each of them in turn. 'I don't think you're in a position to ask us to admit to anything. We have the guns, remember.'

Switch grinned. 'Come on, man, if you were going to kill us, you'd have done it already. And if you *are* freedom fighters as I'm pretty certain you are, you're fighting against the very people who enjoy doing that sort of thing.'

Ishael raised an eyebrow. 'You'd better hope you're right then.'

Marta was getting tired of the banter. She shifted forward on her seat. 'Can you help us get over to France?' she asked.

Switch, sitting beside Marta on the sofa, glanced at her. For once he looked taken off guard. His bad eye twitched like crazy. 'France?' he muttered. After all, they'd not really talked what would happen after they got to Bristol in any realistic terms.

Ishael smiled. 'What exactly did you do so wrong that you need to get to France?'

Marta had thought about it a lot over the last few hours, during which they'd been allowed to rest by Ishael's men. While Paul, Owen, and Switch had slept a while, Marta had lain awake, considering their options. Getting out of the country seemed like the only sensible thing to do. Quite *how* to do it was another matter.

'We watched the Department of Civil Affairs murder the European Confederation's ambassador,' Marta said. 'They then set his death up as an act of terrorism, and we were shouldered with the blame to give them a reason to hunt us. We had proof, but … our friends didn't make it. It's left to us now to pass the information on and I'd say that setting the Huntsmen on us proves how important we are.'

Ishael's tone went suddenly serious. 'You said you had proof?'

'A friend of ours recorded the Ambassador's murder on a digital camera. But … the memory card got lost.'

'Then who's going to believe you?'

Marta spread her hands. 'Well, who in Mega Britain has actually *seen* the Ambassador? He hasn't made any broadcast appearances, yet all of us saw him with our own eyes. We can describe him, even what he was wearing.'

Ishael's face changed. Suddenly his doubts had been replaced by hope. 'You think anyone's going to believe you?' he repeated.

Switch nodded towards the door. 'Where did you get those guns? They don't exactly grow them on trees over in Wales, you know.'

Ishael smiled. 'Quite right. Maybe we can help you after all. What happened to the others? The ones with the memory card?'

Marta exchanged glances with Switch and Paul. 'We don't know for sure,' she said. 'We got separated. Out in the GFA.'

Ishael grimaced. He paused for a moment and rubbed his chin. 'That's unfortunate.'

'But now we've found you…'

Ishael stared at her, his eyes narrowing. 'You said you found us by chance? That's a hell of a coincidence, don't you think? That of all the people in Bristol that you could run into it just happens to be us?'

Marta and Paul both glared at Switch. Owen chuckled. 'Sometimes you two are as blind as that Huntsman we ran into. He runs circles round you.'

Switch grinned again. He looked at Ishael. 'Okay, you got me. It was all a bit vague until I saw that fence. Then I remembered. Figured you guys might still be camped out right under their noses, being the last place an enemy looks, and all.'

Ishael looked at him. 'If I thought you were a government spy you'd be dead by now. So how did you–?'

'I've been here before.' He paused, leaning forward on the sofa to fix Ishael with a stare. 'I used to be one of you.'

Everyone was staring at him now.

Ishael's hand dropped to his gun. 'I think someone might remember you. Perhaps I was wrong–'

'Calm down, man.' Switch held up a hand. 'I wanted to ask before, but I guess I was hoping to surprise him, and I haven't seen him about. Is William Worth still with you people by any chance? It's been a few years, but...'

'William? Yeah, William's still here. But how the hell do you know...' the words failed on Ishael's tongue and he stared openmouthed.

Switch spread his arms. 'I'm Steve Worth, man. The long lost son.'

Ishael's hand fell away from his gun. He turned to the guard by the door. 'Go see if Will's back yet,' he commanded, voice hollow with shock. 'My God–'

'William's still doing good?'

'He's great.' Ishael's handsome features appeared to have taken on a red sheen. 'I didn't, um, recognise you, Steve.'

Switch smirked. 'Well, I'm not ten years old anymore, and you know, the eye. You can't plan for these things, eh. I remember you too. I used to take the piss out of your stupid name, but I guess that's what you get when you grow up in a gypo commune. I see you've jumped up the chain of command. Cleaning pots last time I saw you, wasn't it?'

'Someone had to do it.'

'Well, you're looking pretty dapper these days too, I notice. So did Marta.' Switch jabbed an elbow in her side.

Marta felt her cheeks bloom. 'Shut *up*, Switch,' she said, suddenly feeling no older than Owen.

Ishael too, looked a little uncomfortable, but before he could reply Paul rescued both of them by changing the subject. 'Do you mind explaining what's going on here, Switch? You said you had an uncle in Bristol. You forgot to mention he was part of an underground resistance group!'

Switch shrugged. 'I didn't want to get your hopes up. People die young in this country.'

'Where the hell is he?' came a loud voice from the corridor outside, and Marta jumped as the door burst open. A muscular Afro-Caribbean man stepped into the room, a beaming grin on his face. His curled hair was slightly greying, but his face lacked any meaningful age lines. The only real age was in his eyes.

'Stevie! Is that really you?'

'Hey, Unc! Long time no fucking see!'

Switch jumped up from the sofa and was swallowed up in a huge bear hug. William's face looked like it would crack if he smiled any wider, and Marta thought she saw the glimmer of tears in his eyes, the light of answered prayers. She found herself smiling too. She listened to William's laughter, great heaving gasps, and realised he was sobbing, tears streaming down his face. She thought about her brother, and her own eyes filled with tears.

William pushed Switch out at arm's length and looked him up and down. Switch was no more than a toy in his huge hands.

'Oh, my boy! My *boy!* I never thought … Goddamn, you're so different!' William pulled a hand across his face to wipe away tears. He frowned. 'What the hell happened to your eye?'

Switch grinned. 'I jumped off a train and hit a wall,' he said, causing William to bellow with laughter.

'As good a reason as any,' he said, and Marta was not sure if he believed Switch or thought it was a joke. Switch was grinning but Marta remembered the day it had happened, the sickening thud he'd made as he slammed against the wall, the way he had seemed to slide down to the breakfall mats in slow motion. Her, Paul, Simon and a couple of others they'd been riding with had gone running over, expecting the worst. Switch had looked up at them through one bloody eye, and muttered, 'Fuck, that *hurt.*'

'Uncle, you haven't changed at all,' Switch said. 'I was expecting you to look older.'

'Ah, you're too kind,' William said. 'I always wondered what became of you, Stevie.' His eyes welled up again. 'I should never have let you go out that day…'

'It wasn't your fault,' Switch said. 'The damn government keeps fucking people in the ass, and it's about time we turned around and fucked them right back.' He turned to the others. 'Uncle, these are my friends, Marta, Paul, and, um, Paul's brother.'

'My name's Owen, you wanker,' Owen said.

William roared with laughter. 'Got spirit, this one. Like you had!'

The others were looking at Switch with questioning expressions. The physical resemblance was not exactly close. Switch explained, 'My natural parents were killed in the riots, I think. I'd been through one or two bad foster homes before Unc took me in.'

'I was taking a nap on a park bench,' William said. 'I felt this tugging on my shoe. I kicked out, and when I looked up I found Stevie here lying flat out on his back. He must have been five or six, and I'd just flattened his nose, blood everywhere. He'd been trying to steal my shoes. Six sizes too big for him, but hey.'

'I was going to sell them.'

'Man, that kid's spirit impressed me,' William told them. 'So I took him in. I raised him as my own, right here in this place. But, fuck, I turned my back. You can never turn your back, goddamn…'

'The government was rounding up street kids and transporting them up to the Manchester-Liverpool GUA to work in the steel factories,' Switch said. 'I was down at the homeless shelter scrounging a free meal, and the next thing I know I've got two guys dumping me in the back of a truck. I was ten years old, but one of those guys is half blind now.'

Marta smiled. She didn't doubt that for a moment.

'After a few months in some sweatshop in Manchester I was moved again, down to London where I was put to work cleaning the crap out of some abattoir.' He shook his head, grimacing at the memory. 'Those plastic mops, snap them and sharpen up the broken handle ends, that's the way I did it. Left the guard captain to bleed to death among the pig carcasses. Got out, took a bunch of other kids with me, and the streets looked after me from then on.'

William laughed. 'That's my boy.'

Owen was beaming at Switch. 'Man, if I ever get to be as cool as you …'

'You're doing okay as it is,' Paul said, putting an arm round his brother's shoulders, but shooting a look at Switch that clearly said, *don't encourage him.*

William couldn't keep the smile off his face, but he said, 'I'm glad you're back, Stevie, but I hear you have more problems.'

Switch gave him a brief account of the last day. 'We have to get out of Bristol,' he concluded.

'To France,' Marta added.

William turned to Ishael. He raised an eyebrow. 'If we can get these kids across to France, do you think they can raise us an army?'

Ishael shrugged. 'All the ports are closed except those transporting freight along the coast. Even if we could get a ship away, there are sea mines moored ten miles offshore. Not to mention the damn coastal guns, the patrols…'

'I had no idea it was so bad,' Marta said.

Ishael nodded. 'That son-of-a-bitch has got us roped off from the rest of the world. He gives our country a dumb new name, but there's nothing "Mega" about this failing place. It's falling apart under his nose and the rest of the world is laughing at us. It's apathy that's kept Europe from intervening, or worse, razing the whole country. I guess milk-face finally ran out of money for that dumb space program he's killing people for.'

'You know about that?' Paul said.

'Yeah, we know. We don't know why he's sending those overweight freighters up, just to watch them hit the lower atmosphere and disintegrate, but we can guess.'

'Europe, the States and China have fully active space programs,' William said. 'We think that the Governor wants a piece of the action, and a large slice at that.'

'Or more, he wants something that's up there, floating around.'

'What?'

Ishael shrugged. 'Your guess is as good as mine.'

Owen yawned, making William laugh. 'Looks like the youngster's had enough action for one day.' Despite Owen's loud protests, he continued, 'We'll find you a place to rest a little more. Meanwhile we will send some men over to the station to wait for the inevitable convoy. Maybe we can set them a trap to buy you some more time.'

'The Huntsmen?' Marta said.

William nodded. 'Rolling out those beasts takes time and effort. The DCA know they have to maintain some control. Let them off the leash in the GFAs and in a couple of days there'd be no cattle left alive between here and London, but what you can be sure of is that if they've gone to the trouble of releasing them in the first place, they're not going away until you're dead.'

With that grim prediction ringing in their ears, the Tube Riders were taken back to the old changing room they'd been allowed to sleep in earlier. Marta, who'd barely slept before, felt weary beyond words.

'Although this is our headquarters,' one of the guards told her, 'there are very few people who actually live here. Most of our recruits live in normal society, undercover. It's safer that way. Sometimes, though, we have training and we congregate here.'

'We're very thankful,' Marta said.

'What happens if the Huntsmen come in the night?' Owen asked.

The man smiled grimly. 'We'll post someone outside your room. You'll probably know from the screams.'

#

Back in the meeting room, alone now, Ishael turned to William.

'They didn't think this out too clearly, did they?'

'They're just kids. They're hurt and tired and on the run. I imagine they've seen a lot of death in the last few hours.'

Ishael grimaced. 'They might have Huntsmen on their trail yet Steve brought them straight here? Strikes me as stupid.'

'Stevie's not dumb. He knows how easily we can vanish, empty this place, leave no trace. The Huntsmen will come in and follow the scent until it leaves again. The DCA will write this place off as just somewhere they sheltered. Remember, the Huntsmen aren't looking for us.'

'Can we help them? Can we get them to France?'

William shrugged. 'It'll be easy enough to blow a set of gates and get them out of Bristol. Where they go from there is a little more tricky. I have an idea, but it's a long shot. You know what's in Cornwall, don't you?'

Ishael frowned. 'You know that's beyond risk.'

'It might be our best chance. There's no port we can get them out of.'

Ishael nodded. 'It's still risky.'

'First of all we need to buy them some time.'

Ishael looked grim. 'And in order to buy them time to get out we have to go to war. We have to go to war, William.'

The bigger man nodded. He frowned deeply, his lips tight. 'A lot of men are going to die if we go up against the Huntsmen. It takes a lot of firepower to stop one of those monsters.'

'A lot of men are going to die if we don't. The question is whether the information these kids have is worth it.'

Ishael looked grim. 'We might never know.'

'You're in charge. It's your call.'

Ishael took a deep breath and nodded. 'Okay. Send out the alert. Call the men together and get them armed. We need to have a watch on the station within the hour.'

Chapter Thirty
Darkness Rising

DREGGO STILL FELT groggy from the drugs, but she had been given little time to recover before guards had hauled her, still shackled, out into a large, dirty room where a group of Huntsmen and their handlers waited. At first she thought this would be her fate, to be set upon by a dozen or more of the things for the amusement of the scientists and government officials who waited in a group at one end. *By God*, she thought, *I'll take a few of them with me. The scientists, too.*

Her senses were slowly coming back. She felt changed, different, and not just physically. Something had happened to her face and a metal plate now covered half of it. With her right eye she could still see normally, but when she closed it her left was like a computer screen. She could call up information just by focusing her attention on menu buttons along the top edge, while the images she saw moved differently, pixilated. It was wired it up to her neuro-transmitters, because a simple decision would alter the vision in her left eye from infra-red to night-vision to heat sensitive.

Her sense of smell was stronger too. She could almost *see* the scent trails each man in the room had left. She could tell to within seconds how long they'd been standing in each particular position, which door they'd entered through, who they had talked to while waiting for her entrance.

And it also revealed to her something else that she suspected but had not known for sure until now.

The doctor, Karmski. His scent was all over her body, strongest in her most intimate areas.

While she had lain broken and unconscious, he had raped her. And she felt certain it wasn't the first time. His scent had a familiarity, one which she associated with all the darkest memories of her past. Those memories, she felt sure, had happened here, her transformed, unconscious body used as a plaything in dark chambers far underground, where, even if she could have made a sound, no one would have heard her cries.

'Dreggo.' Karmski stepped forward now, gesturing to the men around him.

'This is Mr. Clayton, and his associate, Mr. Vincent, from the Department of Civil Affairs. I think you might have met Mr. Vincent before.'

She didn't respond, but Karmski was right; Dreggo remembered the inept fool from St. Cannerwells Underground station, and she was disappointed to see he was still alive. Still, like the others, his time would come. They had let her live, and she fully intended to make that the worst mistake any of them could have made.

Clayton stepped forward. 'Dreggo,' he said, her name sounding awkward on his lips. 'I am Leland Clayton, Commander in Chief of the Department of Civil Affairs. I'm sure you're wondering what is going on here.'

'No,' she growled, and immediately realised her voice sounded different. Running her tongue over her teeth, it felt strangely synthetic. The Huntsman must have torn it out or bitten part of it off. They had repaired her well, but she felt less human than she had before; the memories of the girl she had once been were distant now, like faded photographs.

His voice sharpened. 'Well, we have decided that, rather than let you die from your wounds or simply killing you for interrupting a government investigation, you can be of some use to us.'

'Why would I help you?'

'Because we want the same thing. We both want the Tube Riders dead.'

'Who says I want them dead?'

Clayton smiled. 'Vincent told me about your grand entrance. He told me what you said. But neither he nor I believe you had any intention of aiding the Tube Riders. You just wanted to get close enough to kill them yourself.'

Dreggo actually smiled. The synthetic part of her face felt strange, alien. 'I guess we'll never know now, will we?'

'We don't care for your reasons,' Clayton said. 'But we're going to give you another chance, while at the same time doing a job for us. You will lead the Huntsmen in pursuit of the Tube Riders.'

She glared at him. 'Now, why would I do that?'

'Because you want them dead, and we want them dead, but the Huntsmen are a law unto themselves.' He smiled. 'We want to try to keep the death toll down, if we can.'

'Why not just send me alone?'

'The Tube Riders managed to escape five Huntsmen, our own DCA agents, and, um,' – here he coughed a little – 'yourself. We want no more mistakes. We sent five Huntsmen before, one of which is now dead. This time we are sending twenty. You will act as their guide. Think of them as beetles inside a piece of drainpipe. We want them to get to the other end, we're just letting you hold the pencil that guides them.'

'I don't think you heard me,' she spat. 'Why would I ever help you?'

Karmski stepped forward. 'Because you have no choice.'

'I have every choice,' she said, eyes boring into his, wanting him to fall to the ground, wanting him to die.

Karmski laughed. 'Ah, my beautiful Dreggo. You have no choice at all, my dear. When we fixed you up, we left a little chip inside your head. One to make sure you do as you're told.'

Dreggo glared at him. 'So set it off. Do it! Kill me.'

Karmski looked surprised. '*Kill* you? Don't be ridiculous! What fear do you have of death after all that's happened to you? Something of a relief it would be, wouldn't it?'

Dreggo frowned.

'It won't kill you, my dear. But it's attached to the neuro-receptors in your spine. If we activate it, it'll just hurt like God himself has struck you. And we'll keep doing it until you start to obey. Of course, it'll kill you eventually, but all the nerve tissue in your body will have to fall apart first.'

'You wouldn't–'

Dreggo screamed as a surging white heat race up her spine. She arched her back, her legs collapsing under her as a sensation like a thousand scalding needles exploded across her body.

Then as quick as it had come it was gone. Dreggo found herself lying on the floor, the residue of pain fading away like water drying on her skin. Two guards stepped forward and hauled her up to her feet. Her back felt scrunched up like an old cloth, leaving her only able to stand hunched over as she gasped for air.

'Sorry about that,' Karmski said. 'But we felt it best you know exactly what we're talking about. It has higher settings. Oh, and I'm sorry, I forgot to tell you it kind of cramps up the muscles a little. I guess it feels like you've run a marathon now, right?'

Dreggo glared at him. 'I'll kill you one day,' she muttered, spit rolling down her chin, her mouth as numb as the rest of her body.

'I love cooperation,' Karmski said with a grin.

'What do I get from this?' Dreggo said, turning to Clayton.

'Aside from staying alive? You leave the Tube Riders dead, and you get to go free. That's it.'

'Where?'

'Anywhere you please. The GFAs, Scotland. Wales? We'll give you enough money to buy a small house in a remote area and an allowance to live on. What you don't seem to understand is that the government rewards those who work for it. It's a shame we had to persuade you to take the job.'

'Okay,' she said, relenting, accepting she had no choice. 'Tell me when I start.'

'Good,' Clayton said, smiling. 'You start right now.'

Dreggo looked towards the cluster of Huntsmen at the other end of the room. Most of them looked sedate, drugged. She wondered how she was supposed to control them when the modifications had left them little more than extremely dangerous and slightly rabid animals.

Whatever, she thought. Her priority wasn't with the Huntsmen, but with finding a way to free herself from the chip inside her, and then to find a way to take revenge on Karmski and his brethren. She didn't know how she would do it, only that somehow she would.

#

Clayton waited until they were out of the building before he pulled Vincent aside.

'Vincent, I need a quick word,' he said, walking away towards the rear of the building.

'Sure, what is it?'

'Just follow me a minute.'

Clayton waited until he had turned the corner and was out of sight of his driver. Then he took a deep breath. As Vincent followed him around the corner, Clayton stepped backwards, swung his elbow up and slammed it into Vincent's face. With a grunt of pain and surprise Vincent dropped to his knees, hands clutching at his face. Clayton swung round and kicked him hard in the stomach. Vincent grunted again and rolled on to his side.

'What – wait–'

Clayton pulled his gun and knelt beside Vincent. He pressed the barrel to Vincent's forehead, and the younger man's bloody face stared up at him in horror. Clayton flicked back the hammer.

'Leland, wait, don't–'

Clayton pulled the trigger. Vincent gasped as an empty click sounded. Clayton smiled.

'Go above me again and I'll kill you,' he said, voice barely above a whisper. His eyes narrowed, as hard as they'd ever been.

Vincent spat blood out of his mouth. The fear in his eyes told Clayton that Vincent understood.

'I thought–'

'I gave you a little rope and you hanged yourself. Every single order you give goes past me first from now on. I know you think getting the Governor's favours will get you my job. What your back-stabbing, sniveling ass doesn't realise is that when you fuck up I have to take the flack, and the Governor's disappointment is not something any man should have to face.'

Clayton stepped back, then reached down and hauled Vincent to his feet. Vincent pulled a cloth from his pocket and dabbed at his nose.

'A word of warning,' Clayton said, voice still low. 'Don't get too power-hungry. The Governor has all the power, and he doesn't want to give much of it up. Enjoy what you have and be happy with it. Now clean yourself up and I'll see you at Paddington at six, ready to move out. I trust you can find your own way back?'

Vincent, who had come with Clayton and wasn't sure where they were, nodded. Right now, he probably just wanted to be alone.

'Good.' Clayton stalked off around the building.

#

Vincent waited until Clayton was out of sight. He listened for the sound of a car door opening and closing, then a starting engine, and finally the sound of the vehicle moving off at speed.

As the sound of the car faded, Vincent sat down against the wall and dabbed at his nose again. During his training he'd been taught how to reset breaks and dislocations, and now he reached up and gripped his nose, feeling a little give where the bone had cracked. Counting down from three, he shoved it back into place, his eyes filling with tears.

He thought that the scream he let out might have been heard by the Huntsmen, ten levels or more underground.

Clayton, you're a bastard, he thought. *This isn't over.*

Chapter Thirty-One
Kind Strangers

'IT'S GOOD TO SEE YOU'RE AWAKE.'

Simon squinted, his eyes focusing on the boy who sat beside his bed. 'Where am I? Is this a hospital?'

The boy shook his head. About sixteen, he had unkempt mousy blonde hair, a soft, downy face, and a carefree smile. 'No,' he said. 'The nearest hospital must be fifty miles away. Father wanted to keep you here.'

'Where's "here"?'

'This is my house. My family owns most of the farmland around here.'

'Oh. Who are you?'

The boy leaned forward, an eager smile on his lips. 'I'm Carl,' he said. 'Carl Weston. Did you jump off the train?'

'Something like that,' he said, offering a weak smile in return. 'I'm Simon.'

Carl nodded as if he already knew. 'Well it's nice to meet you, Simon. Do you want something to eat? Something to drink?'

'Both would be good.' Simon tried to sit up in the bed, but as he shifted his body he felt a stab of pain in his side. He remembered the Huntsman's crossbow, how the bolt had felt in his side as he tried to hold on to the train. Like a red hot scalpel, cutting and scalding him with every movement, causing sweat to wash down over his face and tears to pour from his eyes. At the moment the train had bumped he had been close to unconsciousness anyway; he barely remembered hitting the ground, only how peaceful he had felt with the ride over.

'Thank you for saving my life,' he said. 'I don't remember quite what happened, but I know I should be dead now.'

Carl smiled. He reached out a hand and patted Simon's knee the way someone might pet a dog. 'Glad to be of service. The doctor said you should be okay in a few days. I think my father is a little suspicious of you, though. We don't get outsiders in these parts very often.'

'Where are we, exactly?'

Carl spread his hands, although all Simon could see was the inside of a rather quaintly decorated bedroom, a little wardrobe in one corner, and a green floral patterned curtain pulled across a small window to keep out the sunlight that pressed in around its edges. 'This is Reading Greater Forest Area,' he said. 'We're about ten miles from the London GUA perimeter wall. Did you come from in there?'

Simon didn't remember moving after he fell from the train, so quite possibly they'd found him right next to the tracks. 'Yes,' he said. 'Last night, I, um, took a train.' It was only half a lie.

'The trains don't stop out here. All the produce from our farm gets taken to a processing plant a few miles to the south and then a fleet of trucks deliver it to the GUA checkpoints at London or Bristol. Where were you going?'

'Bristol.'

'Why?'

Simon tried to shift his body again. For all the help this boy and his family had given him, they weren't great nurses. He had terrible pins and needles in his legs and lower back.

Carl flushed. 'I'm sorry, I shouldn't ask you so many questions. It's just that I don't meet a lot of strangers.'

Simon shook his head. 'No, it's okay. It's just that I'm not really sure why I was going to Bristol. It's difficult to explain.'

The boy craned forward. His eyes were as bright as a kindergarten kid being told fairy tales. Simon knew that if he if he started to tell Carl half of what he'd been through, Carl would wow and gasp and beg to hear the end of the story.

'Are you in trouble?' Carl asked, his voice barely more than conspiratorial whisper. 'If so, don't worry, I can protect you.'

Simon wanted to shout at him *this isn't a game,* but he forced himself to smile and shake his head. 'It's complicated. I don't know how much I can trust you.'

'I saved your life, Simon. And do you really have much choice?'

Simon nodded. 'That's true. Did you see any other people?' He remembered the Huntsmen, and wondered if they'd tracked him. Could they follow a scent moving as fast as a train? Were they out there, waiting for him? He said to Carl, 'Did you see anyone that looked, kind of, um, odd?'

Carl shook his head. 'No, just you. I was play – *walking* in the forest, when I found you by the tracks. It looked like you'd fallen off the train.' He shrugged. 'I suppose someone could have pushed you.'

'No one pushed me. I fell.' Glancing around the room, he saw no sign of his clawboard, and thought best not to mention it. There on the table beside him, though, set on a plate as if it were a biscuit to accompany a cup of coffee, was a long metal crossbow quarrel. Simon didn't have to guess where it had come from.

'I think my father wants to talk to the police, but mother won't let him. Knowing him, he'll want to know if there's a reward for you, but she says you're in no fit state to go anywhere and questioning you and all that stuff won't make you get better any quicker.'

'I didn't do anything wrong,' Simon said. *Or had he?* He was scared by his abrupt honesty. He was desperate for someone to believe him, someone to be on his side.

'My friends and I, we were in the wrong place at the wrong time,' he continued. Then, realizing he must sound like an actor in an old movie, he added, 'We witnessed something bad that we weren't supposed to. A crime. Now people are after us. I can't tell you any more, because it would put you in danger.' He strained to sit up. 'Please, Carl. It's very important that I get back on the train.'

Carl frowned. 'How? They don't stop.'

'That doesn't matter. I don't need it to stop.'

The boy looked confused. 'What do you mean? You just jump on or something?'

Simon grinned. 'Yeah, that's about it.'

This time Carl reacted as expected. 'Wow, that's cool. But Dr. Rhodes said you have a sprained ankle. He said it'll be difficult to walk.'

Simon frowned. The terrible pain in his shoulder had masked any others, but now that Carl said it, he could feel a dull throbbing in his ankle, with something tight like a bandage wrapped around it.

'Well, that might be problem. I can't fly or anything.'

'It would be cool if you could, though, wouldn't it?'

'Er, yeah,' Simon said, feeling a little like a spaceman fallen from the sky to land in the back garden of a bunch of simpletons. He watched as Carl's eyes glazed over, as though the boy were imagining himself in an old Flash Gordon movie. For a few seconds Simon said nothing. Then, starting to tire of the game, he cleared his throat. 'Uh, that drink would be really great just about now.'

#

Jess crept out from under the tarpaulin and rubbed her eyes. The barn had been a good place to shelter, in among the hay bales, and the tarpaulin had made a good makeshift sheet to keep out the draft. She actually felt quite rested, but at the same time as her body thanked her, her mind scolded her for letting too much time pass.

She didn't know how safe she was out here in the country, but she knew she had to find Simon quickly and get away. The Huntsmen could catch up with her at any moment. There was no way of telling how close they were.

The barn where she had spent the night stood at the edge of a field, completely isolated. There were no houses nearby that she could see, and no way of knowing who owned it.

The barn entrance looked out across a valley, a patchwork of green and yellow fields dipping away from her and then rising again a mile or so distant. The deepest part of the valley was forested, and she could see a church spire sticking up out of the trees. Jess breathed deeply as she stood by the road, her heart fluttering a little at the sight of such tranquility, wondering quite how Mega Britain had managed to separate into two such different ways of life. This sleepy country scene was as different from the dangerous, bloody streets of London as night was from day.

She stood still for a moment, listening for cars. Barring the trailer she'd seen in the field last night, she'd neither seen nor heard any form of transport at all. The road leading away from the barn was dirt and gravel, and during her flight from the men she'd not seen any real roads, only lanes and gravel tracks.

She headed west, back in the direction she thought she'd come from, but she couldn't be sure. The road angled slightly downhill into the valley, and she guessed there was more chance of finding a village in that direction. In a village she could at least get her bearings, find out where the train line was, look around for signs of a hospital or a doctor, someone who might have heard about or seen Simon. She had a terrible feeling that the most likely place she would find him, though, would be in a police cell.

She found herself smiling as she trotted along the lane, and wished she could have been here under better circumstances. Her parents' murders hadn't properly sunk in yet, nor had how much danger she and the other Tube Riders were in. The knife was wrapped in cloth and tucked into her sock, while the crossbow hung from her belt, covered by her shirt. Only her clawboard and Simon's were difficult to hide, but she had a small rucksack and had pushed them inside as best she could.

The hedgerows closed in around her as the road wound down, occasionally broken by a farm gate. The view vanished as she descended further into the valley, and the church spire was closer each time it peered between the trees up ahead.

Her ears pricked up as she caught the chugging sound of an approaching vehicle. She looked around, but there was nowhere to hide, no nearby gateways to slip through. She had no choice but to dip her head and try to look as inconspicuous as possible.

A small tractor appeared around a bend up ahead. She pressed herself against the hedge as it passed, but couldn't help glancing up at the driver inside. He was maybe sixty, weather-worn, almost bald. He nodded and smiled at her, then, perhaps realizing he didn't recognise her, frowned and started to say something. Jess dipped her head and walked on, putting distance between them. Behind her the tractor's engine cut out, and she glanced back just long enough to see the man stand up and twist around.

She turned a bend in the road and broke into a run, sprinting over the crunching gravel just in case the man decided to chase her. He might have just wanted to ask her where she was from, but it was too great a risk.

The church reared up in front of her and Jess dashed through the gate, dropping down behind a gravestone from where she still had a view of the road. The tractor hadn't started again and a moment later the farmer appeared around the bend, jogging lightly, head turning this way and that.

Outside the church he stopped, put his hands on his hips and shrugged. With what sounded like an expression of resignation he turned around and headed back to his tractor. Jess didn't move until the tractor had rumbled on almost out of earshot. Then she climbed to her feet, went out of the church gate and looked around her.

She was in the middle of a tiny village. Twin rows of quaint cottages lined the small street heading away from the church. A couple of roads led down between them, leading to more cottages. On the other side of a little square with a pond and a fountain in its centre, was a small village store.

Turning left, another lane led to a country pub.

It was the sort of place Jess would like to grow old in. Quiet, pretty, it was everything the city was not. She found herself walking over to the pond to peer down at the goldfish darting about under the water. Little silver discs gleamed down there too: money. It was a wishing well, and she found herself reaching into her pocket for some change. She didn't have much, but she figured a couple of coppers wouldn't make much difference.

'Safety for Simon, safety for all of us,' she whispered, and tossed a coin into the water. She sighed as it drifted down to the bottom and settled amongst the others.

'I hope it comes true,' someone said behind her.

Jess spun, one hand slipping beneath her coat to rest on the crossbow, but it was just a woman coming out of the shop, sixty or seventy years old, shuffling across the gravel towards her.

Jess smiled. She didn't think the woman had heard her, but she said, 'Me too.'

'Are you from over in Turnpike?' the old woman asked.

Jess started to nod, but the old woman cut her off. 'Old I might be, but not so slow as to miss hesitation. You're from a ways further than that, I'll bet.'

Jess just shrugged.

'No need to tell me, love. I've been here a while, I know how the world is. We're all either running from or towards something. The luckiest among us know what it is.'

Jess didn't know what to say.

'All I know,' the woman continued, is that regardless of where you're going, you look darn hungry.'

Finally Jess found her voice. 'Yes, I am.'

The old woman thrust a thumb back over her shoulder. 'I own the store. Why don't you come inside and I'll find you some breakfast.'

Jess smiled. 'Thank you,' she said. 'That would be wonderful.'

As the old woman led the way inside, Jess felt tears in her eyes and a lump in her throat. After what she'd experienced over the last twenty-four hours, for someone to show a kindness as simple as offering a stranger a meal, it was like a miracle in itself.

Chapter Thirty-Two
Fresh Scent

D REGGO SAT AT ONE END of the freight truck as the train rumbled along, watching the Huntsmen at the other end with suspicion, even though most of them appeared to be sleeping. Their heads were lowered, buried in their cloaks, and their knees were pulled up to their chins. All twenty of them sat pressed tightly together like a flock of birds at roost.

Emotions rose from them like steam, and she found it almost painful to sit and watch them as their combined hatred and sadness pressed at the wooden walls of the truck. She recognised one or two from her first days in the facility, remembering the human eyes behind the canine mouths and beneath the jumble of wires and electrodes. They looked more alien than human now, but once they had been men, innocents dragged off the streets into the hellish science labs and torture pits of the research facility.

Innocents just like her.

The freight truck bumped and Dreggo looked up at the door, wondering how much further they had to go. They had been traveling for about an hour, rumbling across the sleepers, the train bumping and jerking, depriving them of any chance of real sleep. She guessed they were somewhere out in Reading GFA, maybe halfway to Bristol. Belatedly, a call had come in from Bristol's branch of the DCA, informing Clayton of a disturbance this morning at the train station there. A group of kids had caused chaos, crashing a train and destroying a large volume of cargo in the process. Clayton had been furious that the call had taken so long to come in, but at least the Department of Civil Affairs had known the Tube Riders had gone where expected. Their predictability made them easier to track down, and Dreggo expected this mission to be over shortly. After which, of course, she had a little mission of her own to complete.

She looked at the Huntsmen again. Like flicking through files, she knew about all of them from the information Karmski's minions had uploaded into the computerised part of her mind. She knew which ones had been in active service, which ones contained blemished records, which ones were most likely to be uncontrollable once set loose. The scientists hoped that the data on each creature would help her control them, but it just scared her even more. From her own feelings she knew how much each Huntsman was hurting, and knew that madness and bloodthirsty insanity were just a simple order away.

One of the creatures stirred, its head lifting with a grunt, snout jerking towards the door. It shifted forward onto hands and knees, moving doglike towards the edge of the freight truck. As it reached the door, it lifted one hand and scratched at the wood.

Dreggo dropped into a crouch. She searched the data for information and found that this Huntsman, Craul, had tested highly in scent recognition tests. It had picked up something the others had missed.

'Craul, what is it?'

The Huntsman swung its head towards her. Drool hung from its jaws, and the skin moved back from the teeth in a snarl. 'Tube Riders.'

Dreggo raised an eyebrow. Could the disturbance in Bristol have been something else? Witnesses had spotted four people, but she knew the Tube Riders numbered six including the little kid. More likely was that they had split up.

Or perhaps one of them lay dead by the train tracks. It would take just minutes to stop the train and check.

Craul was growling and pulling at the door, locked from the outside. Dreggo knew the Huntsmen could break through if they really needed to, but it was worth Clayton thinking the DCA had control.

She tugged the radio from her belt, tapped in a number.

Clayton's voice fizzled on the other end. 'What?'

'We've got something,' she said. 'Stop the train. We need to check.'

A minute later the train began to slow, finally bumping to a stop. Dreggo waited while doors opened further down and the voices of men carried down towards them. She could hear a lot of them out there; no doubt they weren't taking any chances with a car full of Huntsmen.

Then keys rattled in the padlock. 'Stay back from the doors,' someone shouted.

'We're back,' she shouted back. She wanted to wait by the door and order the Huntsmen to attack them now, but the DCA agents would be heavily armed. Their time would come; she had sworn it to herself.

The door swung open. At least ten DCA agents stood there, weapons leveled at the Huntsmen. Dreggo felt sure the creatures could still overwhelm them if she gave the order. Many of them would be happy to die.

The Huntsman, Craul, snarled and took a couple of steps forward. 'Tube Riders,' he growled again.

'Craul, back!' Dreggo ordered, and to her surprise the creature responded, slinking back into the shadows where the others waited.

The men moved back to let her get down. 'Lower your weapons,' she said. 'The Huntsmen work on my orders. Unless I say, you're safe. *Unless I say.*' She glared at them, undermining the threat. On the heat sensors installed into her robotic eye, the faces of several men flushed red with fear.

Leland Clayton stood at the back, behind his line of defense, she noted. 'How was first class?' she called, pushing through the armed men towards him.

'What do you have?' he said, ignoring her sarcasm. She noticed he had one hand in his jacket's pocket, where no doubt his finger hovered over the button of the device that would stun her if she attacked him.

'One of my Huntsmen picked up a scent,' she said. 'I think the Tube Riders might have split up. Otherwise, we're looking for a body.'

Adam Vincent moved up alongside Clayton. His nose was bruised and blackened and one eye was swollen closed. He was limping from the nail gun wound and she smiled at his obvious discomfort.

'What happened to you?' Dreggo quipped. 'You fell asleep and the train rolled over you?'

Vincent glared at her. 'I cut myself shaving.'

'You shave with a sledgehammer?'

'Shut it, bitch.' Vincent turned to Clayton who, she noticed, had a little smirk in the corner of his mouth. 'One of them was hurt,' he said. 'One of the boys. The Huntsman shot him with a crossbow.'

'Let's do a sweep of the line,' Clayton said. 'See if we can find his body. The Huntsman smelled it when?'

'A couple of miles back.'

Clayton nodded. 'Can you pick up the scent yourself?'

Dreggo smiled. Clayton didn't want the Huntsmen released if he could avoid it. 'Not as well as they can,' she said.

Clayton looked grim. 'Okay, take two, have one track on either side of the line.' He lifted a finger to point at her. 'Keep them reined in though. I'll have guns trained on them at all times.'

She gave him a mock salute. 'Yes, *sir*.'

She took Craul and another Huntsman who had tested well, Jacul, and set one either side of the train line. Together they moved along the track, Craul and Jacul bent close to the ground, Dreggo walking along the tracks between them. Behind her four of Clayton's agents followed, their guns trained on the Huntsmen. Clayton himself walked at the back. Vincent had back by the train to conduct his men in a sweep of the nearby forest. The other Huntsmen had been locked back up in the freight truck. *Like cattle*, she thought bitterly. *Don't give up, my new friends. Your time will come.*

They had been walking for maybe twenty minutes when Craul let out a howl and darted towards the fence that kept people off the railway line.

'Stop!' one of the agents shouted.

Dreggo heard the click of a gun. 'Craul!' she shouted. 'Wait!' But the Huntsman had ducked down by a hole in the fence and pushed through.

'I'll shoot!' the agent shouted behind her, as the Huntsman emerged on the other side of the fence and dashed off into the forest.

'Craul!'

The agent fired. The *tak-tak-tak* of automatic rifle fire blasted through the trees, sending birds flocking into the air. Dreggo flinched back from the sound, shutting her eyes for a moment. Finally, as the agent stopped firing, she smelt cobalt in the air, her enhanced sense of smell picking it up as thick as treacle. She looked through the forest towards Craul.

The Huntsman was lying face down about thirty feet away, not moving. Dreggo felt a sudden pang of regret; after all, Craul had simply been following his initial order to find the Tube Riders.

Dreggo searched her files. Craul had once been a man called David Wilson, abducted from outside his home in Green Park in October 2064. He was survived by a wife and two young children, who, if luck was with them, would be still alive and well, the children now close to finishing high school.

Dreggo hung her head. A bolt of guilt ripped through her, thicker than the Huntsman's crossbow quarrels in a pouch attached to her belt. It was government policy to send a certificate of death to any fallen Huntsman's family. She knew what it would say: David had died in service of his country; his death had been honourable.

That they had probably stopped mourning him ten years ago was no matter. That certain details would be omitted, about the cruel experiments that turned him into a monstrous killing machine, or that he would have eaten his own children without a moment's hesitation, didn't matter either.

Whatever he had become, all Dreggo could see now was a man lying dead in the grass, shot in the back while trying to follow orders. She tried to feel nothing, tried not to care, but somewhere inside her the part that was still human burned with rage and shame.

'What the hell happened here?' Clayton, who had dropped back, shouted, running up towards them. 'Keep the noise down, we're not in the city anymore! People take note of gunfire out here!'

'The fucker tried to run away,' the agent said, looking at his weapon with suspicion, as though it had fired itself.

Dreggo glowered. 'He was following the scent. Now one of my best trackers is dead.'

Clayton stopped a few feet away. He looked towards the fallen Huntsman and huffed. Dreggo watched him. Just behind his shoulder, Jacul waited by the edge of the tracks. A digital transmitter inserted into his brain meant she could speak to him with her mind; he could be on Clayton in a second. Another agent had his gun trained on Jacul, but at least Clayton would be dead before he had a chance to fire. Dreggo hesitated a moment, fighting the urge, but in the end she glanced back towards Craul's fallen body, and couldn't bring herself to sign Jacul's death warrant too.

Clayton said: 'You communicate with those things. They break loose out here and we have hell to pay. Remember that.'

'It was okay to have them roaming wild in the city.'

Clayton shrugged. 'There are lower standards there.' Dreggo glared at him. His broad generalization took in almost everyone she had ever known. 'Anyway,' he continued, 'one less of those monsters is one less to worry about.'

Something inside Dreggo snapped. She leapt at Clayton, barely aware that while in her vicinity he had slipped his hand back into his pocket.

She knocked him to the ground, one arm sweeping for his face, metallic fingernail inserts raking at his eyes.

Pain bloomed in her and everything seemed to vibrate, as though someone had stuffed her into a washing machine set on high power. She tried to scream but her breath caught in her throat; all her muscles felt bunched so tightly they might burst like blisters all over her skin.

Then it stopped. Dreggo opened her eyes, wiped away a sheen of sweat and tried to breathe as her heart raced. Clayton climbed to his feet. His free hand touched the scratch on his cheek that was a sign of just how close she had come. His other hand held the little box of pain Karmski had given him.

'Try that again...'

Dreggo bared her teeth. 'Always, *always* ... look over your shoulder, Clayton. One day...'

Clayton tried to match her stare but failed. He knew how close she had come. 'Just get on with finding those kids.' With his finger hovering over the button, his voice shook as he said, 'Or I'll have you put down like the dog you are.'

'You'd be doing me a favour.'

Clayton brushed himself down. 'Get another one out of the freight truck and get me those damn Tube Riders.' Without waiting for a reply he strode off in the direction of the train.

Dreggo glared at the other DCA agents in turn until they looked away. Then, commanding Jacul to follow, she went to investigate what Craul had found.

There was a hole in the fence, a disturbance in the undergrowth nearby. Dreggo bent close and found the fence had recently been cut open, perhaps no more than a day ago. Jacul growled as he smelled what she did: Tube Rider scent, mixed with blood.

So, the injured one had fallen after all. The question was, was he dead or not? Someone had found him and come back with wire cutters. She found several sets of footprints, three unfamiliar scents.

Jacul, a few feet away, growled.

'What is it?'

He pointed, saying nothing.

Dreggo nodded. She understood as she picked up the scent for herself.

The wet grass showed it had rained recently, and as a result the scents of the boy and the three who had carried him were a little dull, but a fifth scent was sharper, more recent. And Dreggo recognised it instantly as that of the boy's girlfriend, the one she had tried to follow.

How sweet, she thought. *He fell, and she came after him.*

She ordered one of the agents to call Clayton. A moment later he came jogging back down the track, Adam Vincent hobbling along behind him.

'We've got two of them out here,' she said. 'One is definitely mobile, the other could be dead. We can't tell. I'm pretty certain he's hurt at least. They shouldn't be difficult to track down.'

'Just two? So the others made it to Bristol?'

Dreggo nodded. 'I'll take three Huntsmen and track the two out here. You take the rest to Bristol and pick up the scent there. The handlers can control the Huntsmen for you.'

Clayton turned pale. One hand absently touched the mark on his cheek where she had slashed him. It was still bleeding slightly; he brushed the blood away with his finger and wiped it on his trousers.

'I can't leave you out here. How can I trust you?'

She pointed. 'That little thing in your pocket? You have a choice. We split up and follow both trails while they're still fresh, or we risk losing the Tube Riders. They escaped your pathetic attempts once. In Bristol they could disappear like rats down a drain.' She smiled. 'Of course, if you'd rather we stick together, I'm happy to take nineteen Huntsmen on a little outing in the country. I'm sure we could have lots of fun, out here, where the standards are ... higher.'

'She's right,' Vincent said. 'We've wasted enough time already.'

'Okay.' Clayton turned to Vincent. 'Order the handlers to secure the Huntsmen. When we get to Bristol we take only as many as we need, until she gets there. And you –' he pointed a finger at Dreggo, 'You stay in constant radio contact. As in every thirty minutes. I want to know exactly where you are. If you sight them, you call me. If you *think* you sight them, you call me. In fact–'

'Okay, I get you. If I just want a little love chat, I call you.'

Clayton glared at her for a moment. Then, with a grunt of annoyance he turned on his heel, and they all headed back towards the train, Jacul at the back with the agents' guns trained on him. The rest of the Department of Civil Affairs entourage waited near the train. Clayton told her a sweep of the area had found nothing but a ruined village. He offered to print her maps of the area from his laptop, but she refused.

'The only map I need is the one the Tube Riders left behind,' she said, tapping the side of her nose. 'Don't worry. I expect them to be dead by nightfall.'

'Good.'

The men opened up the Huntsman's freight truck again and Dreggo selected two more to accompany her in addition to Jacul. Several of the handlers who had also traveled with them as backup in case something happened to Dreggo, climbed up into the freight truck to secure the remaining Huntsmen.

Within fifteen minutes, the train had pulled away, rumbling on down the track, leaving Dreggo and her three Huntsmen behind. As the train rolled out of sight she turned to look at them.

Jacul was crouching by the hole in the fence. The other two, Meud and Lyen, were waiting for orders. She looked at them and nodded. Together they made their way through the hole in the fence, and away from the train tracks into the forest.

Chapter Thirty-Three
Government Policy

MARTA FOUND ISHAEL in an old dressing room not far from the room where they'd been allowed to sleep. He was standing by a wall that was covered in maps and charts, newspaper clippings, photographs and memos. He appeared to be studying a map of the city centre.

He smiled as she entered. 'Hi, Marta. Did you sleep okay?'

'Yes, thank you. Apart from the dreams.'

'I can imagine.' He looked uncertain for a moment, and his eyes flicked from her face to the floor and back. 'Sorry about the interrogation yesterday,' he said. 'Times are hard, and it's difficult to trust people.'

She raised an eyebrow and smiled. 'Especially those who walk in your back door unannounced.'

'I guess we'll have to lock it next time.'

She watched him as he turned back to the wall. He was maybe thirty, and while his face had the hardness of the streets his eyes still radiated kindness. She found herself wanting him to turn back, wanting him to look at her.

'I especially enjoyed the shower,' she said, breaking the silence. 'I haven't felt clean in a while.' Immediately she felt like an idiot. *What are you saying, Marta? You don't want him thinking about you being dirty.*

'No problem.' He turned back towards her, and Marta tingled with nervousness. *What the hell is wrong with me? I feel like I've met a film star.*

'This is our command room,' Ishael said. 'Really, you shouldn't be in here.'

'Sorry.'

'I forgive you.' He smiled at her again. 'From here we organise all the revolutionary activities that we don't do.'

She laughed, glad to be back in control of herself. 'Still waiting, huh?'

He nodded. 'The time will come. Probably a little sooner than we were expecting, with the sudden appearance of you and your friends.' She noticed how his smile dropped, as though he'd just been told the family he loved and cared for wouldn't be coming home again.

'How are the others?' he asked.

'Switch went off to spend time with his uncle. Paul and Owen are still sleeping. I think they're exhausted just from looking after each other, not to mention everything else.'

He took a step closer. 'And you?'

'I don't know.'

'You're their leader, aren't you?'

She shook her head, felt her cheeks redden. 'I don't know. I think they look to me because my brother was the first Tube Rider. They think that makes me leader by default.'

'It's hard being a leader, sometimes. Knowing that what you ask of others might put them in danger.'

She nodded. So, he understood.

'What happened to your brother?'

Marta looked down at the floor, seeing Leo's face there in the dirty tiles. 'I don't know,' she said quietly. 'He disappeared a couple of years ago.' She looked back at Ishael. 'There were rumours he'd been taken. That he ended up on one of those space ships.'

Ishael closed his eyes for a long moment. When he looked at her again she saw only regret. 'A lot of people have died because of what this country has become. Here, we've been building an underground army. We planned to start a rebellion, but I think we all knew it would never be enough. We might sting the bastard, but he'd still swat us away.' Ishael tapped his finger against a photograph fixed to the wall. It showed a strange-looking man taken over a distance. The man was facing the camera, his mouth slightly open in a look of anger, his eyes wide in shock. Marta saw they were dark red, like clotted blood.

'Is that him? The Governor?'

Marta knew very little about the Governor, only that he had been in power since before she was born. She had never seen him because he never appeared in public or on television. There were rumours, of course, but no one she knew had ever seen his face. He was like a dark lord in a tower, controlling Mega Britain through hundreds of lower ministers and officials while he hid away from public view. Most rumours said he was disfigured, scarred by fire, perhaps, or mutilated in an accident. The most common rumour she had heard was that his skin was abnormally pale, as though he lived underground, but there were other less believable ones. Some people thought he was nine feet tall.

Ishael nodded. 'The man who took this picture is dead. It's the only picture I've ever seen of the Governor's face. He was being transferred to a new government office, and the photo was taken at long range.'

'What's wrong with him?'

'We're not sure. We think his skin colour is due to albinism, but there are rumours that there are other strange things about him. Albinos have no fear of light, yet he is almost never seen outside. A former government worker who defected to us once reported that the Governor's quarters were kept at a higher humidity level compared to everywhere else in the building.'

'Why?'

'We guess it has something to do with his skin. Some other defect.' Ishael frowned. 'People say he's the result of a scientific experiment gone wrong. Or, perhaps, spectacularly right.'

'How do you mean?'

'The man had no proof, but he had heard rumours from the other staff that the Governor ... he could *do* things.'

'What things?'

'Move stuff around. Hurt people.' He shrugged. 'With his *mind*.'

Marta felt a shiver run across her back. 'Telekinesis?'

'I didn't like to use that word, but yeah, that's what the informant said. He also said there were rumours that the Governor was from a different place entirely.'

'He's not human?'

Ishael shrugged again. 'There were rumours that the space program is an effort to contact someone or something. That it has nothing to do with Europe or America at all.'

Marta cocked her head. 'People in London believe the Tube Riders are the ghosts of train suicides come back from the dead. But they aren't. It's just us. Me, Paul, Switch, and Simon. And, as of yesterday, Jess and Owen. Hardly legends, are we? The Governor is probably just a normal man with a couple of allergies.'

'Maybe. But looking at that photograph, do you really think so?'

Marta felt cold inside as she studied the picture, the red eyes seeming to know she was watching. Ishael moved nearer to her and put a hand on her arm. Normally, if a man she'd known only a day tried to touch her, she'd have knocked his arm away, but with Ishael it just felt right. She leaned against him, feeling more like a child than she had for years.

'We're going to help you,' he reassured her. 'We're going to find a way to get you over to France. And I'm sorry that we can't do more for your friends, the ones out in the GFA.'

Marta felt a sudden pang of regret. 'Did we abandon them?' she asked him. 'Should we have gone after them? The others call me their leader, but I don't know how, I can't lead…'

Ishael shook his head. 'You're doing fine. The others, this … Jess? You have to trust her. You have to trust that she'll find her boyfriend and find you.'

'He was hurt bad.'

'Put yourself in his situation. Would he want you to come after him?'

Marta thought for a moment. 'Simon … no. He'd tell us to go on. He'd tell us to see this through.'

'Then that's what you must do. You have to trust them to make it, and if they don't … you have to honour their memory by finishing this.' He smiled in a way she thought was supposed to reassure her. 'We'll help them any way we can,' he said. 'I'll post men to watch for them, and if they make it to Bristol, we'll find them. And if they still have that memory card, then we'll make sure they get it to you.'

Marta closed her eyes. Jess's desperate shout as she leapt off the train into the dark echoed inside her head. She opened her eyes again, the memory too painful. 'How can it end?' she whispered in a quiet voice. 'How can we end all this?'

'I don't know.' He forced a grin. 'Everything pans out in the end,' he said. 'One way or another, it'll work out.'

'But which way? The right or the wrong?'

Ishael said nothing. Marta knew there was only so far he could reassure her without it sounding false. They'd grown up in the same country. They both knew the way things were.

Ishael pulled away from her. 'I'm sorry,' he said. 'I have to go.'

'Where?' *Don't leave me.*

'I have to go the station and oversee our defenses. I can't ask my men to do what I won't do myself. If you can wake your friends, one of my men will come and drill you on how we're getting you out of the city. We have a plan in place.'

Marta bit her lip as she realised this man was putting his life and that of others on the line for theirs. When the Huntsmen came through the station there was no guarantee anything could stop them. And Ishael would be standing in the front line. *Don't beg him to stay*, her mind screamed at her. *You barely know this man. Don't show such weakness.*

Something in his eyes made her feel he could read her mind. He reached up and ran a finger down the side of her face, his touch as gentle as a breeze.

'It'll be okay,' he said. 'It'll work out.'

Marta's lip trembled. She didn't trust herself to say anything. Ishael flashed a smile, turned, and was gone.

CHAPTER THIRTY-FOUR
FRIENDS, ENEMIES

'THANK YOU VERY MUCH, but I really should get going.' Jess started to stand up, but the old woman shook her head.

'Good heavens, girl, after what you've been through, you ought to have a shower at least.'

'Well, I guess. If that's all right?'

'Of course it is.'

The old woman led Jess up the stairs at the back of the living room and showed her into a pretty bathroom, all frilly drapes and flowery patterned towels and mats.

After the old woman had left, Jess stripped off and climbed into the bath tub. She switched on the shower and squeezed her eyes shut as the hot water doused over her, wishing she could cleanse more than just her body. The horrors of the last day were still so fresh in her mind that she couldn't imagine ever being without them.

She hadn't meant to talk to the old woman, but sitting across from that kindly face she'd been unable to help herself. The woman reminded her of her own grandmother, dead some ten years now, with soft, caring eyes, and an easy smile.

She hadn't told the woman everything, but she'd still said too much, maybe. She was looking for her boyfriend, she had said, fallen from the train, but carried away before Jess could get to him. They had been heading for Bristol, looking to start a new life away from the troubles in London, but some men had started a scuffle in their carriage, and Simon had been pushed through an emergency door. How much the woman knew about the trains, she hadn't said, but she had nodded carefully while Jess spoke.

After ten minutes Jess switched off the shower and climbed out of the tub. She dried herself and dressed in spare clothes she had brought from London. Her other clothes were so ripped and soiled that she stuffed them into a waste basket, hoping the old woman wouldn't mind.

She was feeling a lot better as she picked up the rucksack containing her weapons, the clawboards, and the last of her leftover food, and went back down to the living room.

She was humming to herself as she pushed through the door into the living room and found a bulky middle-aged man standing next to the old woman.

'Ah, Jessica dear. I hope you feel better now.'

Jess took a step back. The man, too, looked alarmed.

'This is my son, Roy, the one I was telling you about. Roy Weston.'

The man stared at Jessica with barely disguised hatred. 'You–'

'Roy was telling me they found a boy. It sounds like your Simon–'

'Mother!'

Jessica took a step forward, one hand going to her forehead as though she might faint at any moment. *They had Simon!*

'He's alive? Where is he?'

Roy Weston didn't answer. His eyes moved to her rucksack. Jess watched as he stepped across in front of the old woman and glanced behind him, looking for something hard to hold on to. He settled on a large quartz bowl and lifted it in front of him.

'Roy, what are you doing?'

'Be quiet, Mother! Girl, I don't know who you are, but I want you out of here right now, or Heaven help me…'

Jess followed his gaze. The crossbow she had stolen from the Huntsman was half exposed at the top of her rucksack.

'The boy was seriously hurt, Mother,' Roy said. 'Someone had tried to kill him, and my guess is it was this little bitch here.'

'Roy!'

'No, I didn't – it's not mine!'

'You get a two minute start, girl, and then I'm coming after you with a shotgun.'

Jess knew he didn't actually *have* a gun, otherwise it would be trained on her now, but she didn't wait for a second warning. Grabbing her bag, she turned and bolted back through the door into the hall, looking for another way out. Behind her she heard the old woman shouting over her son's angry demands for a telephone.

He's going to get a gang after me, Jess thought. *Whatever serves for law enforcement out here in the damn woods is now officially alerted to my presence.*

She went through into a small kitchen, past a little terrier dog that watched her with confusion from its basket. A door led out into a quaint garden which Jess sprinted across, vaulting over a wall at the end into an adjacent field. A few moments later she heard shouting from the garden behind her, but she was already climbing over another hedge into the next field along.

As she ran alongside the hedgerow towards a distant gate, her mind was a confusion of bitterness and sadness. The old woman had shown her genuine kindness, only for her buffoon son to charge in and throw his accusations around.

Still, Weston's entrance had solved one problem for her: she now knew where to find Simon. Before her shower, the old woman had talked with pride about how her son was the biggest landowner in the village. All Jess had to do to find the biggest landowner was to find the biggest house, and that was easy.

From where she stood, the field dipped away into a valley, and there, at the top of the far rise, overlooking the whole village, stood a large manor house, glinting white in the sun.

And somewhere inside it, if she could get there before Roy Weston and his lynch mob, she was sure she would find Simon.

Chapter Thirty-Five
Ambush

DREGGO AND THE THREE HUNTSMEN were crouched behind a low wall that bordered the back lawn of the manor house. Dreggo was still, concentrating, but the Huntsmen fidgeted, their lips curled back, their eyes darting around them. They were hungry, but there was no time to eat now. They had found the Tube Riders.

Well, one of them at least. Following the trail had been easy. Not expecting pursuit, the men who had taken the injured Tube Rider had battered their way back through the forest, leaving a path of broken vegetation she could have followed in the dark, even if the scent trail had gone.

They had circled the house earlier, and found no scent leading away. The boy was still inside, hopefully laid up with his injuries. And if he was, Dreggo doubted he would be guarded.

Easy pickings.

But that was just one. Leading away from the same spot by the railway line, the trail of the Tube Rider's girlfriend had been fresher but less clear, because she had been alone and moving fast. However, her trail had become erratic, doubling back on itself, even swinging round to cross over the same path again.

She had got lost trying to follow her boyfriend. Dreggo and the Huntsmen had followed her trail until it finally emerged from the woods in the corner of a field, but at this point, Dreggo had turned the Huntsmen back around and they had backtracked to the other trail, following it to the house. The girl would come, Dreggo knew. She was after the boy, too, and the best way to trap her was to use the boy as bait.

Behind her the Huntsmen stirred. A whine escaped from Jacul's lips, while Meud and Lyen bobbed their heads like hyenas, tongues lolling.

'Be quiet,' she muttered.

'Eat...'

Dreggo grimaced, as she always did when she heard one of them speak. Their canine muzzles and tongues weren't designed for speech, but they still had human larynxes. What came out was a low, cheese-grater voice that sounded like a metal file scraping away human skin, and each time they spoke it reminded her of how close she'd come to ending up as one of them.

Dreggo would have problems soon. She was overriding their orders by keeping them here; their natural instincts were to break into the house and kill the boy. Then, with the Tube Rider dead, their reward would be his flesh.

She didn't need their mind-link to sense their uneasiness. She had to keep them happy or she would lose control.

'Come on,' she hissed, and led them away from the house and through a cluster of farm outbuildings until they reached a barn. Dreggo heard the shuffling of cattle inside.

'Just one,' she ordered them. 'And keep it quiet.'

Meud's eyes widened and his jowls pulled back over his teeth. He looked crazed, rabid. 'Eat...'

The other two had already moved towards the barn. 'Listen to your transmitters,' Dreggo told them. 'Be ready when I call.'

They nodded, but she knew they weren't paying attention. She hoped their hunger would outweigh their thirst for mindless slaughter.

She headed back towards the house as the sound of something heavy dropping to the ground came from behind her. To their credit, it sounded as though they'd chosen an isolated target, for the rest of the cows continued their slow shuffling, their occasional moo. The Huntsmen knew stealth as well as any assassin; they just rarely chose to use it.

She resumed her vigil at the same place as before. Dreggo felt sure the girl would come from this way; she would be thinking like a fugitive, and would take what she believed to be the safer way in, around the back.

Unsure how long she would have to wait, Dreggo let herself drift for a while, thinking back on her childhood, back when Mega Britain was young and the perimeter walls weren't yet finished, when people could go out into the countryside and sit by rivers and under trees, eating sandwiches and drinking juice in the sun. She remembered the journey out of London into the tranquil fields and the rolling hills, but she also remembered the streams of people heading in the opposite direction, in towards the city, the suitcases and the weary faces, the armed guards lining the roads, the cranes rising up above the trees and the groan of heavy machinery.

It had left conflicting impressions on her, and she realised that through it all she hated the countryside and the people who had been allowed to remain here, hated its illusion of safety. Her parents had never again taken her outside the perimeter walls, and her life had spiraled downhill until her eventual capture and abuse at the hands of Karmski and his government toads. Now, coming back here, she felt the urge to shatter the apparent tranquility that these people lived under. She had to live in Hell, so why shouldn't they?

She was still lost in reminiscence when a girl slipped out of the bushes not fifty feet from her and darted towards the back of the house.

Dreggo ducked down behind the wall as the girl reached the back of the house, turned and looked around her. Dreggo had no doubt that this was the Tube Rider; although the girl was wearing different clothes Dreggo could see the girl's hanging board poking out of her rucksack, and in her hands she held a Huntsman's crossbow.

Dreggo smiled. She would enjoy turning the stolen weapon on the thief.

The girl climbed a set of steps to a porch and peered in through a dirty window. Dreggo could only assume that around the back of such a large house were the servants' quarters. After a moment the girl cracked open the door and slipped inside.

Dreggo waited just a few seconds and then hurried across to the door. She too glanced inside and saw what looked like a kitchen pantry: shelves packed with cans and jars, hanging sides of meat, great sacks labeled as corn and flour. She gave a brief wistful smile at the storybook air of the house, and then slipped inside. Through an arch in the far wall wooden stairs led up.

Dreggo had taken just a few steps when she heard the girl above her on a higher landing. She was trying to be quiet but Dreggo's advanced hearing had no trouble picking up the creaks and shifts of her footfalls as she crept up along the wooden floor and up the next flight of stairs. Dreggo was tempted to kill her immediately because she knew the other Tube Rider was inside, but a sadistic part of her wanted them to die in each other's presence. Let them think everything was going to be all right, and then take it away. Wasn't that what life had done to her? Wasn't that the way it always was?

Someone opened a door below her. Above her, she heard the girl freeze, then tip-toe quickly away, open a door and slip inside. Glancing around a corner behind her, Dreggo saw a woman dressed in a white apron start up the stairs. Dreggo hurried on and slipped into an alcove in the wall a few feet from the top of the stairs. The woman came up behind her, quietly whistling to herself. At the top of the stairs the woman had a choice of right or left.

If she chose right, she would see Dreggo and would die.

She chose left.

Still whistling to herself, she walked along the corridor, past one of the doors behind which the girl was hiding, and disappeared out of sight.

Dreggo waited a few moments and then, as she'd expected, a door opened and the girl stepped out on to the corridor, looked both ways and then hurried on up the stairs towards the next level of the house. Dreggo gave her a few moments and then followed.

Just as she reached the landing halfway up, where the stairs turned back on themselves, she heard another door opening below her. She froze again, listening for the creak of the stairs.

Nothing.

The girl had reached the corridor above. Dreggo climbed to the top of the stairs and peered around the corner of the wall. The girl was about halfway along the corridor, peeking through a keyhole.

'Simon?' Dreggo heard the girl whisper. 'Where are you?'

Dreggo felt a brief pang of guilt for what she was about to do, but she brushed the feeling away. Why should they live? Why did they deserve it more than her?

The girl had reached a door near the end of the corridor when Dreggo saw her expression change. Relief crossed her face as she opened the door a crack and leaned in. A moment later she slipped inside and closed it behind her.

Dreggo trotted down the corridor and leaned close to the door. Inside, she heard their voices.

From her belt she pulled a long, serrated knife.

#

Simon was lying on his back in the bed, his eyes half closed. Jess felt her heart race at the sight of him. He was a little beaten up, his face crisscrossed with band-aids, but he was breathing. That was enough.

A blanket covered his body but one arm was exposed, a tube attached to a drip bag feeding into his arm. He also had bandages wrapped around the ankle. Her heart sunk; if he couldn't walk they would have a problem.

'Is that you, Jess?'

Jess started. He had been watching her the whole time she had been staring at him.

'Simon, oh thank God...'

He smiled weakly. 'I'm *so* happy to see you.'

She smiled. 'Yeah, me too.'

'Come closer.'

She moved around to the side of the bed and he lifted up his hand to take hers. 'I didn't know if I'd ever find you,' she said.

'You came after me? Where are the others?'

'In Bristol now, I hope. Simon, we've got to go—'

Even as she spoke his eyes widened, but before he could speak Jess felt something cold at her neck, and a strong arm wrapping across her chest.

'Isn't this sweet?' Dreggo sneered, her mutilated face close to Jess's. 'A lover's reunion.'

Simon tried to rise, but his body was weak from the medication and his injuries. 'Let her go—'

'Don't worry. You'll be joining her soon.' Dreggo jerked Jess's head back. The girl struggled, one arm trying to reach Dreggo's belt, but Dreggo hauled her backwards across the room.

'I gave you a choice, and you chose wrong. You'll pay for what happened to me. All of you will.'

Jess squirmed again. She tried to twist away, heedless of the knife at her throat. She figured that Dreggo was going to kill her anyway, so she had nothing to lose. Twisting back towards Simon, she tried to reach for Dreggo's belt again. As she looked down, she saw the bottom of the door shift forward an inch.

'Stop struggling, bitch,' Dreggo spat. 'I wanted your boyfriend to enjoy this, but I guess I'll have to make it quick —'

Dreggo screamed and jerked backwards. Her arm dropped away and Jess fell forward towards Simon's bed. She twisted round, reaching for her crossbow, and saw a boy, maybe no more than sixteen, jabbing a long metal pole into Dreggo's back.

'Get Simon and run!' the boy shouted.

'Who...?'

'Carl,' Simon muttered. There was something wry in his voice, as though Carl's sudden appearance hadn't surprised him at all.

Jess looked towards him. 'Can you walk?'

'I don't know.'

'*Try!*' Carl screamed, jabbing Dreggo again with the metal pole, this time in the neck. Jess heard a crackle of electricity, and Dreggo screamed as she tried to roll out of range. She groaned, twitched, and was still.

'Come on!' Jess pulled the tube out of Simon's arm and pulled him upright. 'We have to go, Simon. We have to go *now*.'

She hauled him up out of the bed and pulled one arm over his shoulder. He was wearing his own spare clothes, but there was a mound of padding around his shoulder where someone had patched up his crossbow wound.

The boy, Carl, took Simon's other arm. 'He's drowsy from the medication,' Carl said. 'We weren't expecting anyone to come and pick him up so soon.'

Jess glanced at him. The boy appeared to be smiling. 'Um, thanks.'

'Are you Jess?'

'Yes, but how did you—'

'He talked about you. *A lot.*'

Jess found herself smiling back. 'We have to hurry,' she said as they reached the stairs and started down.

'What on earth is that thing back there?' Carl jerked a thumb back over his free shoulder. 'I saw it – *her*, whatever – outside. Obviously she wasn't after me or I'd be dead now.'

'Her name's Dreggo,' Jess said. She didn't say that they'd left Dreggo for dead. 'I don't know what she's doing here, but–'

They stopped as a howl that sounded like metal scraping on metal echoed through the house. Jess's blood seemed to run cold. Her heart hammered in her chest and she wondered just how they were going to get out of this. One nightmare kept being replaced by another.

'What's *that?*' Carl gasped.

Jess started to walk again, forcing her legs to move before they turned to jelly and failed all of them. 'I don't think you want to know, but I've got a terrible feeling that it came with her.'

'That cyborg woman?'

Jess had noticed the metal on Dreggo's face. Someone had taken her away and fixed her up like the Huntsmen, and it was obvious who. That they should be here together could hardly be coincidence.

'Carl, we have to get away, otherwise many people could die, including you. We need transport of some kind.'

'We have a car, but Father took it out this morning. There aren't any buses or anything, only the trains, but they don't stop.'

'Did Simon tell you how we were on the train?'

'Yes, you hung.' He pointed at the clawboards poking out of her bag. 'With those things. He said they're called clawboards.'

'What's wrong with Simon's ankle?' Jess asked. 'Is it broken?'

'No, Rhodes – that's our doctor – said it's just a sprain. He might be able to walk but he won't be able to run.'

'Shit.' They had reached the back door. 'He has to be able to run,' Jess said. 'He has to. He can't get back on the train otherwise. It's the only way!'

'With that ankle, there's no wa – wait! I know! I have just the thing!'

'What?'

'Get down into the woods. Go straight through the back garden, and keep going straight. There's half a path, but if you lose it keep heading in the same direction. When you get to the ruined village, follow the remains of the road past the old post office. It leads to an old station.'

'Thanks, but what about you?'

'Wait for me there.'

Jess nodded. Carl's eyes were bright, exhilarated, as though this were some wild storybook adventure. She wanted to tell him that this wasn't a game, that people had and would soon die, when another terrible scream came from an outbuilding not far from them.

'Bugger,' Carl said. 'That's the cattle barn. Sounds like something's in there with the cows. Best get going before it comes out.'

'Huntsmen,' Jess whispered, before she realised what she was saying.

'You have Huntsmen after you? Are they even real?' When Jess nodded he said, 'Holy crap. What did you *do*?'

'No time to explain. Thanks, Carl, for everything you've done.'

The sound of a car engine joined the commotion coming from the barn. Jess glanced up to see the vehicle swing around a gravel driveway at the side of the house and slide to a halt not far from them.

'That's my father,' Carl said. 'Perhaps he can help.'

Four doors opened, and a group of men climbed out. Two other cars pulled up behind the first and they heard another stopping around at the front of the house.

'Hey! There they are! They've got my son!'

'No, Father–'

One of the men cocked a shotgun. The first man shouted, 'The girl's got the boy! Take her first, we'll question him later.'

'Run!' Carl hissed, pushing Jess towards a gap between the outbuildings and the house that opened out into a manicured garden. 'Don't stop until you get to that station!'

'Simon, you're going to have to forget about me carrying you,' Jess said, slipping out from under his shoulder. 'I'll find us a place to rest, I promise.'

'Stop, or we'll shoot you dead like the city dogs you are!'

'Father, no!'

The men started across the open driveway. To their left stood the house, to their right was the clutch of outbuildings. They'd taken no more than a couple of steps when the back door of the house broke open and Dreggo stumbled out, one hand on her forehead, the other clutching a crossbow.

#

Carl was quickly descending into a nightmare. He saw the woman's weapon, and remembered the bolt Rhodes had taken out of Simon's side. He pointed. 'Shoot *her*, Father! Shoot the robot woman!'

One of the men raised his gun without hesitation. He fired at Dreggo, the bullet narrowly missing her as she swayed sideways and dropped to her knees. The bullet hit the stone wall near to the door.

'Weston, we need the police!' another man shouted.

Behind Carl, Jess and Simon were halfway across to the trees. He no longer had the cattle prod he'd used to stun Dreggo, and he felt naked without any kind of weapon. Dreggo was less than twenty feet away. If he didn't move and no one shot her, she'd be on him in a few seconds. He stared, shocked, as Dreggo bared her teeth like some kind of animal. With her half metal face and the crossbow in her hand, she was like a cyborg she-devil out of a comic book. He couldn't move.

Dreggo suddenly looked away. She glanced back towards the group of men, most of whom had taken cover behind their cars. Carl counted at least ten. He knew most of them; they were his father's hunting companions, poker friends and a couple of farm hands. Most were good with a gun.

'Huntsmen! To me!' Dreggo screamed. A growl came in response, and something leapt up and over the barn gate and dashed towards them. Two others followed behind it. At first Carl thought they were very tall priests, in their brown robes with the hoods that covered their faces, and then he saw the twisted claws that should have been hands, heard the slavering growl of what sounded like dogs, saw the silver crossbows that hung at their waists.

'Weston! We've got to get out of here!'

'Shoot the devils!'

Carl loved his father, in a way. He'd suffered badly in the name of discipline over the years: regular split lips, the occasional black eye, and one particularly bad time he had lost a tooth. Yet, still, Roy was the only father Carl had ever known, and abusive monster though he sometimes was, Carl didn't want him to see him die.

Tears filled Carl's eyes as the Huntsmen leapt to the attack. The men lifted their guns and fired practically into the Huntsmen's faces. One fell back, its face a mess of broken bone, blood and metal, but the other two kept on, charging into the midst of Carl's father's friends, their crossbows firing, their claws and their teeth ripping and tearing. Carl heard the screams of his father and the other men, saw their blood, watched them fall, watched them die.

He was transfixed for what felt like hours, but it was little more than a few seconds in real time. In that time, though, watching the one-sided slaughter, he knew that he had to run, or he too would die. He also knew that if he just headed for the woods after Jess and Simon, they would all die. He had something that could help them, something which could get Simon back on the train.

While Dreggo's attention was fixed on her murdering Huntsmen, Carl slipped around behind her, ran around the side of the house, and pulled open the door to the basement.

Chapter Thirty-Six
Repression, Production

'MAN, STEVIE, YOU DON'T KNOW how it makes me feel to see you again. It's like there was this bulb inside just burning low, you know. Now it's just flared up again, and I feel damn fine.'

'You too, Unc.' Switch sipped from the can of beer William had given him. It was a little old and tasted slightly sour, but it was still beer, a rarity. 'I never thought I'd see you again.'

'I never forgave myself, you know, for letting them take you.'

'It wasn't your fault, Unc. Shit happens, we both know it. But it all comes back around and this time it's us ready with the shafting rod.'

William laughed. He brushed away tears and they clinked glasses. 'I always thought I might see you again, Stevie,' he said. 'You just had too much to just give in. The system just couldn't break you.'

'And I ain't about to give up yet.'

'I'm amazed you still remembered where we hid out,' William said. 'You've been gone almost ten years.'

'I'm amazed you were still here.'

'We thought about moving, but the UMF didn't have anywhere better to be. The DCA don't have the same power here, and unless we made a move they wouldn't spare the resources to search for us. We've mostly been stockpiling arms and extending our network. It's only recently that we've engaged in any live action.'

'What's that you're calling yourselves now?'

'The UMF. The Underground Movement for Freedom. We felt we needed to put a name to it.'

'The *umph*.' Switch grinned. 'I guess it has a ring.'

William grinned even wider than Switch had done. 'Boy, you're a hoot. We prefer the U-M-F, but whatever gets people going, I guess. You tell your friends about us?'

'I only tell the others what they need to know. It's safer that way. They get caught, there's nothing they can say. Interrogators are paid to know when someone's lying ... and when someone's not.'

'Kid, you get more like me every day.'

They were sitting in the front row of the old theatre, a dark and dusty stage in front of them, lit only by a couple of bare bulbs hung against the back wall. The whole setting had an expectant feel to it, as though a troupe of dancers might suddenly burst out of the wings at any moment, though the layer of dust around Switch's feet said that no one had used this theatre for entertainment in many years.

'You scared, Stevie?' William asked. 'About the gate?'

Switch had been drilled on how the Tube Riders were getting out of Bristol. Ishael's men had made their preparations and plans had been put into action. Within the next few hours, if things panned out as Ishael and William hoped, the Tube Riders would be out of the city and heading down towards Cornwall.

'I'm fine, Unc. I'm more worried about you. If you attack the Huntsmen a lot of UMF men are going to die. And plus, I've only just found you again. You sure you can't come with us?'

'Stevie, man, my place is here. Just make sure you keep yourselves alive long enough for that information to get into the right hands, and I know we'll see each other again.'

'Why the fuck do you have to attack them? This isn't a bunch of DCA clowns you're going up against, this is the fucking Huntsmen. I love a good scrap, but Unc, I've seen what those motherfuckers can do.'

'We attack on our own terms or they attack on theirs. Don't worry about us. We have a few surprises up our sleeves, and even if they do break through, they'll never find us. There are safe houses, sink holes. Places we can hide. They're not looking for us, remember, they're looking for *you*. We just need to give you and your friends a head start, and I hope that one day, when this government is on its fucking knees, that me and you can have more than just a couple of beers together.'

Switch looked away, frowning. 'I don't want to see you get hurt, Uncle.'

William grinned, displaying pale yellow teeth. 'You won't see it. With luck you'll be long gone by the time the Huntsmen start feeding on me.'

'Don't fucking joke like that.'

William spread his hands. 'Listen, don't worry about me, kid. Stayed alive this long, haven't I?'

'I guess.'

They were silent for a while, sipping their beers, listening to the occasional creak and groan of the old wood of the theatre. Then, Switch said, 'Unc, what's behind that fence? When I was a kid it was completely off limits.'

William looked grim. 'I wondered when you'd ask. We have a bit of time, I think. Let's go take a walk, shall we?'

A few minutes later they emerged from a side door in a building a couple of hundred yards inside the fence. William ducked down behind a small wall and waved for Switch to join him.

Switch was amazed at the extent of the tunnel network William had led him through. Down through the rambling basement of the old theatre, Switch had seen where walls had been knocked though into sewage systems and then through again into other buildings. Some openings had been covered by hanging tarps or even doors, while others, especially those further away from the theatre, were barely disguised demolition jobs.

'Look,' William said, as they watched the two guards by the fence. 'They don't look particularly alert, but that's because all they're guarding is a little back road. The government has about forty percent of the city cordoned off, but without serious reconstruction work the best they could do was put up fences everywhere. They're electrified, of course, but that wouldn't stop anyone who really wanted to get in. Not that anyone wants to.'

William led them down a thin stairway beside the cathedral. They emerged on to the dockside.

'Shouldn't we be in disguise or something?'

William grinned, and Switch recognised the same adrenalin-fueled eyes that others saw in him. 'Not if we don't get seen.'

They walked along the dock beneath the shadow of an overhanging warehouse. The dusty, rusted and broken signs of clubs and bars long dead called to them from the shadows: Evolution, Club Crème, Lloyds, Walkabout, Café Underworld. Switch could only imagine the revelry that had taken place here in the years before the Governor and Mega Britain.

'Okay, it begins over there.' William pointed out across the water towards the far bank.

At first Switch couldn't see anything. All that was over there was a row of warehouses and factories, smoke rising from the chimneys of some, lights flickering in the windows of others.

Then he realised. This was what his uncle had brought him to see.

Industry.

'What do they make in there?'

'Processed food. At the far side of the city there's a gate where they bring in fresh produce from the GFAs. Vegetables and meat mostly, but they grow some amazing shit out there in greenhouses and the like. Strawberries, tomatoes, rice ...' William licked his lips. 'And they bring it in through the gate in trucks and in those factories they can everything up and make it taste like crap. Then it comes out for us to buy.'

Across the water a large garage door opened and a truck pulled out. It made a sharp turn near the water's edge and then headed off around the side of the factory.

'Where does all the metal come from to make the cans? Paul reckons they won't import anything anymore.'

William nodded. 'So they say. Up north they've opened up some of the old iron and steel mines, but I gather pickings are pretty thin. Most of it comes from decommissioned merchant ships.'

Switch nodded. He watched a group of people walking around the side of one of the factories, marching in an orderly fashion. He couldn't help but feel a little impressed. All his life he'd grown up in the squalor and decay of London, where nothing seemed to work and anarchy ruled. He had expected the situation to be the same in Bristol, but from where he stood the factories looked like a model of economic success.

'Looks good, don't it?'

'Yeah.'

'The economic situation in the country isn't nearly as bad as everyone says,' William told him. 'The government seized control of all the major companies. Those factories are government-owned, government-run. All the money from the food sales goes back in there. Or what that fucker doesn't spend on his ridiculous space program does, at any rate. The factories run on bio-fuel or electricity.'

Switch nodded thoughtfully. 'Why the hell does everyone hate what's going on, then?' he said. 'Looks all fine and dandy from here.'

William pulled something from his pocket. Switch had seen one before. He'd swapped a knife for one, once, but he'd dropped it running away from a fight a few months later.

He lifted the eyeglass to his good eye.

'Look at the people,' William said.

It took a moment for Switch to focus the lens and then to find the far bank of the river. Once he had, he panned along the riverbank until he came to the first group of people walking along the front of one of the factories.

'Shit, Unc, they're chained to each other.'

'This is what we fight against,' William said quietly.

Switch steadied his gaze. Dozens of men and women, even some children, walked with shackles on their hands and feet, the chains linked to each other so that if one tried to escape, the rest would have to go too. Armed guards watched them.

'Who are they?'

'Criminals, street kids, other people the government didn't like. Most, though, are surplus people from the GFAs. For the last forty years or so, since the Governor took power, the government has been making regular sweeps through the countryside, razing unwanted towns and putting the land into production under the ownership of landlords, usually the richest people from each area, those able to keep their families out of the factories with heavy bribes. A certain number of people were left behind to work the farms, and over time the communities started to build up again. But those that missed the initial cut, so to speak...'

William shook his head. 'They live in here, behind the fences. Many of them are old now, kept here their whole lives, but the younger ones were allowed to have children, keep the supply fresh. But all of them – every man, woman and child over the age of eight – work in alternate twelve-hour shifts. The factories work day and night.'

'Why don't they take the people from the cities?'

'Oh, I think they take some. But the city folk have more means, more fight. And they need people to buy the crap the factories churn out.'

'Why the hell isn't there an uprising?'

'There have been many. But the government has shit going on somewhere, developing weapons, creatures like the Huntsmen. There are three types of people in this country, Stevie. The pampered, out in the GFAs. Their lives are so goddamn easy they were quite happy to forget about their missing friends, get on with raising their crops, riding horses, playing bridge and drinking beer on Friday fucking nights. Then there are those in there, ruled by an iron hand. I've watched people die from here, Stevie, just for talking out of turn.'

'That's fucked up.'

'And then finally, there's us. What you might call the general population. Scrapping and batting against the government who keep us down with gangs of trigger-happy police and the threat of the Huntsmen. Discontentment rules, Stevie. We spend so much time fighting each other that our potency as a group is lost. What the UMF is trying to do is pull those people together. It's hard, boy, but it's not impossible. People are starting to come around. They figure if they're gonna die, they might as well do it for a decent reason.'

Switch took a couple of steps towards the river and squinted towards the far bank. As he turned away from the choppy waters, movement to his right caught his eye.

He dropped instinctively into a crouch and pushed back against the wall of the converted warehouse. William fell back beside him.

Switch glanced out. Two guards were moving slowly along the waterfront in their direction. They weren't moving with any urgency but there was no way Switch and William could get all the way back to the path by the cathedral before they were spotted.

He pointed them out to William.

His uncle grimaced. 'A patrol. We'd better get out of sight. This way.'

William led them back past the abandoned bars and clubs. He stopped by a door labeled Art Café and kicked it open. Switch followed him inside.

'Get down, we'll wait until they pass,' William said. 'They're just a patrol, they're not looking for us–'

The windows exploded in a deafening blaze of gunfire. Switch and William dived for cover.

'You're surrounded!' someone shouted as the dust settled. 'Give yourselves up and you will be returned to your stations with minimal penalty.'

'Minimal penalty,' William scoffed from the darkness behind a stack of old tables. 'Those bastards.'

'Wait here,' Switch answered. He lowered himself to the ground and crawled along towards the middle of the room where a metal pillar rose about four feet up out of the ground, ending in a wider table top. Switch leaned back against it and risked a glance around.

Two heads appeared outside the broken window. They were wearing blue police helmets and shouldering heavy guns. From the way they squinted nervously into the dark it was clear that they couldn't see anything inside.

'Uncle!' Switch hissed, a plan formulating in his mind. 'Move to your left and knock over that stack of chairs. Draw their line of sight.'

'Sure thing, kid, but I hope you know what you're doing.'

William crept through the shadows and stood up behind a table stacked on its end. He lifted a chair and tossed it twenty feet into a pile of others near the far wall.

There was a crash as the stack of chairs collapsed. The two guards rushed to the door and blindly opened fire in the direction of the sound. With their attention diverted, Switch pulled out a little metal star out of his coat, its edges honed sharp. Moving out of cover, he flung it in the direction of the guards.

His aim had the precision of long hours of solitary practice. The star hit the nearest guard in the eye, and the man went down screaming, blood spurting from the wound.

Switch was on his feet before the other guard could turn, a throwing knife in his right hand. He took a couple of steps closer as he gathered his aim, only to feel something shift under his foot, a broom handle or an old ashtray, maybe even a dead rat, stiff with rigor mortis. It took his balance, sending him sprawling to the floor, the knife landing tamely in the wooden wall beneath the window.

Switch looked up as the man raised his gun, only to see a flying chair slam into the man's face.

As the guard grunted and felt backwards, William leapt out of the shadows, a broken-off chair leg in his hands. One sharp thrust and the man lay still beside the other.

William helped Switch to his feet. 'I ain't a goddamn freedom fighter for nothing,' he said, a smile lighting up his face. 'But I'm glad to see my boy's growing up. Nice work with that shuriken there.'

Switch returned the smile. 'I learned everything from you, Uncle,' he said.

William's face fell grim again. 'Glad to hear it boy, but we'd better get out of here. Two ain't much to deal with, but in about ten minutes there'll be half an army outside.'

William led them through the mess of fallen furniture and out of a door at the back. A dark stairway led up, and from there they crossed an old floor where only rats and spiders danced now, pushed through another door and out on to a fire escape. They emerged on to a quiet lane behind the warehouse.

At the end of the lane they climbed up a grassy bank and over a wall into an overgrown garden around the side of the cathedral. They waded through it and jumped over a metal railing fence as shouts came from the waterfront behind them.

Running low behind a wall surrounding a fountain, they crossed the square and ducked into the doorway they had come out of before. Inside, William leaned back against the wall, breathing hard.

'Phew! Close one!'

Switch was about to reply, when he heard a muffled explosion followed by the distant sound of gunfire. It didn't come from the waterfront, though, but further away, back across the city, in the direction of the train station.

William gave him a grim smile. 'Ah, Stevie. I hate to lose you again so soon, but I think you'd better get back home and pack. Sounds like a train from Hell just pulled in over at Temple Meads.'

Stevie sighed and nodded. The Huntsmen had arrived in Bristol.

The chase was on again.

Chapter Thirty-Seven
Escape

THE JOLT FROM THE CATTLE PROD had messed with the electronic part of Dreggo's brain. She gradually began to regain control of herself, but as she tried to run down the stairs after the two Tube Riders and the country boy, while her mind felt clear, the receptors in her arms and legs were still misfiring, causing her to stumble and fall.

When she finally emerged from the house to find the group of men there, with their heavy, inaccurate shotguns trained on her, a red mist descended over her mind. All her life she'd been persecuted and abused. She didn't deserve any of her suffering, but it had happened anyway. Why should she suffer while these country fools lived in peace and prosperity?

Her heart was heavy as she ordered the Huntsmen on them, and somewhere inside her heart, another little piece of her lingering humanity died.

It was over in less than a minute. She walked over to the cars, their bodywork and windows now stained red. There had been eleven men in total, all of them now dead or dying, their bodies ripped up and torn open, their faces nearly unrecognizable. A couple of low moans came from those not yet expired. Of her Huntsmen, Meud was dead; a shotgun fired point-blank into his face had left him beyond any hope of repair. The others had picked up minor injuries, but nothing their enhanced tissue regenerative genes couldn't deal with over a few days. Now they waited, their bloody hoods lowered over their faces, for their next orders.

Instinct made Dreggo look up at the house, at the tall, vine-covered walls. A woman's face pressed against a window on the second floor, looking out, watching them. Her mouth was agape, and with her computerised eye Dreggo could see her lip trembling, her cheeks stained with tears.

A shock like an earthquake rocked through her heart, and she staggered beneath a sudden, overwhelming guilt for what she had done. This woman was now widowed, as no doubt were many others in the local area, their husbands, fathers, uncles, brothers, sons, slaughtered like the cattle her Huntsmen had fed on.

Just two days ago her friend Maul had been killed by that Tube Rider with the bad eye. Maul had loved her, and he'd been murdered without thought. Regardless of the situation they had been in, the Tube Rider with the bad eye had cut him down.

'Why should it be any different for you?' she muttered under her breath, still looking up towards the woman. 'No one spared mine. Why should I spare yours?'

The woman was openly crying now, her hands held up to her cheeks. Dreggo dragged her gaze away to the Huntsmen. 'Into the woods,' she ordered. 'Find them, and kill them.' Realizing she was about to cross another bridge that would subsequently fall behind her, she added: 'Kill the boy too.'

Lyen and Jacul raced off across the lawn. Dreggo followed at a walk, her head hung low. *I will not cry*, she told herself. *I will not*. But it was too late. From her one good eye tears flowed down her cheeks, and sobs jerked what was left of her heart.

#

Carl dashed through the woods after Jess and Simon. He hoped Jess had followed his instructions, because it was easy to take a wrong turn among all the poorly-planted trees.

He tried not to think about the slaughter he had just witnessed, the ripping, tearing claws of the terrible creatures. Mercifully he hadn't seen his own father die, because Roy Weston had fallen down behind one of the cars, but the claws had flashed over there too. There were no signs of pursuit, but it was surely underway by now. Running hard, he knew he would catch Jess and Simon soon, and he could only hope that their passage wasn't obvious enough that those creatures could follow.

Huntsmen, Jess had said. Carl had heard of them, but in the GFAs they were a myth, a legend. The kind of thing mothers told their children would eat them if they didn't go to sleep right away. They were monsters in the closet or under the bed, a child's nightmare.

He reached a small river and bounded over it in a single leap. The terrain started to rise again, and Carl followed a rough path up through the undergrowth of what had once been natural forest. The ruined town began a few hundred feet ahead.

Under one arm he carried something he'd found years ago in the ruined town, down in an old basement. It wasn't dissimilar to the boards that Jess and Simon had, except it was longer and had little wheels on one side. When his parents were out, he sometimes took it out and rode it up and down the hallways of the house, but there was nowhere outside he could use it because all the roads had been torn up and replaced with gravel.

The first ruined houses appeared to his left, and he veered in their direction to take him up through the old town. Why, he wondered, as he passed several old houses and the collapsed ruins of a corner shop, a rusty ice cream sign still outside, had the government felt it necessary to do this? To relocate so many people and then try to cover over any trace of them ever having been here?

He'd asked his grandmother about it, the only person prepared to say anything at all. She had told him that the government didn't think the countryside needed so many people, that it was easier to get things done with more empty space about. They'd chosen those best for the task, and left them behind.

Those best for the task? Like his *father*? Roy Weston had certainly been good at raising cattle and crops, but as a father he hadn't proved the best at anything. Carl swallowed a lump in his throat as he remembered that his father wouldn't get a chance to make that right now. He could only hope that Dreggo and the Huntsmen had spared his mother and Jeanette. He wanted to go back and check, but that was suicide.

'I can't go back,' he said aloud as he jogged up the half overgrown road that lead to the old station. 'Whoever you are, Jess and Simon, I'm with you now.'

He saw them then, up ahead, leaning against the overgrown steps that led up to the platform. Simon was doubled over, clutching his ankle and wincing in pain, while Jess was fiddling with a silver object. As he got closer he recognised it as a crossbow, the same kind that those beasts had carried. As he didn't think she was one of them, he guessed that meant that at sometime before he met them, one of the Huntsmen had ended up dead. The thought gave him some hope.

'Don't stop, Carl,' Jess said as he reached them. 'Get across the train line and up into the woods. Simon can't run anymore, so we make a stand here.'

Carl shook his head. 'You have no chance against four of them.'

'There's no way we can get Simon on the train. They trail us by scent, so running's no good. They're not after you. You might still get away.'

Carl held up the board. 'We can use this to push Simon along the platform when the train comes.'

Jess took it and turned it over in her hands. 'A skateboard? Where did you find it?'

'Skateboard.' Carl tested the name. 'I found it in one of the houses here. We don't have them out in the GFAs.'

'A tool of anarchy,' Jess mused. 'Who would have thought they'd ban skateboards?'

'Train,' Simon muttered.

Carl and Jess both looked up. From back in the woods came the low rumble of an approaching train.

'Quick!' Carl said. 'Up on to the platform.'

Jess turned to him. 'Carl, we can never thank you enough for this. After we've gone, please just run as far from here as you can. They won't follow you because we're too important to them, but just in case, make sure you get away. We're forever indebted to you.'

He forced a smile. He didn't have the heart to tell them what the Huntsmen had done to all the men back at the house. 'It was a pleasure to meet you,' he said. 'I just hope that wherever you're going, you manage to get there.'

Jess grabbed his arm and pulled him close, kissing him on the cheek. 'Be safe, Carl.'

'And you.'

'Huntsmen!'

Simon's single chilling word broke up their leave-taking. He was too weak to point but they could see anyway. No more than a few hundred feet away, two Huntsmen bounded through the trees towards them. One of them held up a crossbow, and they heard the fizzy ping as its quarrel loosed. Too late to move, they were lucky as it slammed into a wooden board not ten feet from where they sat.

'Up, quick!'

Together, Carl and Jess hauled Simon up the steps to the platform. Carl felt Simon's legs sag, and knew that however Jess had managed to get him to run, it had taken the last of his strength.

'Come on, Simon, I won't lose you again!' Jess screamed, practically dragging Simon along. Behind them, they heard the building roar of the oncoming train, and above that, the wail of the pursuing Huntsmen.

Up on the platform, Jess wrapped the straps of his clawboard around Simon's wrists, and then took hold of her own. Carl noticed how she avoided looking at him; her concern for his safety was there, but so was the knowledge that they were leaving him behind.

'Stand on this, Simon,' he said. 'I'll push you. Can you jump?'

'I don't know.'

'Just one more time, Simon!' Jess screamed into his face. 'Just *one more time!*'

Carl supported Simon on the skateboard. The Huntsmen had closed to less than two hundred feet.

'Leave me the crossbow,' Carl told Jess. 'I'll try to hold them off.'

Jess stared at him. The hardness in her face dissolved for just a second. He thought she would refuse, then she held out the weapon. 'Carl–'

'Save it. Get him moving!'

Together, they started to push Simon along on the skateboard, gradually picking up speed. The train had reached the edge of the station. It had slowed down as it passed between the platforms, but was still moving faster than Carl's father's car at full speed.

The train rose up on them like a giant metal snake, a piercing roar and the puffing of its oily breath filling the air around them.

'Faster – now ... jump, Simon!'

Simon cried out and jumped, pushing up off his good ankle. He lifted the clawboard, gritting his teeth as the stitches in his shoulder broke and blood began to soak through his shirt. Carl didn't think he'd make it, then the metal claw clunked down on the water drainage rail and he was jerked away from them, the train already passing them. Jess looked back at Carl.

'Go, Jess. It's a long one, you still have time.'

She stared at him again. Her eyes flickered between his and the crossbow in his hands, already wound and fitted with a quarrel. 'Carl ... thank you,' she said, her eyes glistening. Then in one motion she turned and sprinted down the platform. Carl watched her angle in towards the train, then leap up and catch on the rail, as graceful as a leaping deer.

He turned away. The train was still lumbering past. He had just seconds before the first of the Huntsmen was on him. He remembered three from the slaughter at his house, but there were only two now, and one, maybe injured, lagged behind. He thought perhaps he had a chance if he could disable the nearest one, but then he saw *her*, back in the woods, the half-metal leader who'd ordered the slaughter of his father and his father's friends. She wasn't even running, just walking calmly towards him. He only had time to loose one bolt, but he wished it could be for her. *Another time*, he promised himself.

He stood his ground. He had always been a dreamer, and he had a plan. But for it to work, he had to be quick. Once the train was gone he was finished, but what he hadn't said to Jess was that he had no intention of being left behind. He'd have to trust his luck just a little more, was all.

He'd practiced for this. He'd ducked and rolled and dived, firing his catapult or his air gun at targets both stationary and moving; old signs and shop windows, rabbits, birds, foxes. He'd hit with a good level of accuracy, and his target now was a lot bigger.

The Huntsman closed on him, its own crossbow coming up. At the last second, Carl dropped and rolled sideways towards the platform edge. The Huntsman's crossbow bolt fizzed through where he'd been standing and embedded itself in the wooden side of a freight truck. As Carl came up into a crouch just behind the Huntsman, he fired his own crossbow into the back of its head.

The Huntsman roared and tried to turn around. As it did so, Carl picked the skateboard off the floor and swung it at the monster's face. It hit the Huntsman just above the eye, and with another roar, it staggered backwards, right into the moving train.

Carl saw it lose its footing, saw it sucked into the gap between the train and the platform, saw it disappear into the dark shadows where the thundering wheels rolled.

The train was almost past him. Without thinking, he started to run alongside it, trying to time his spot. If he missed, he died, but if he stayed, he would die anyway. The woman and the other Huntsman would show him no mercy.

There were just three carriages left. As the next space between two rushed towards him, he counted down from three and jumped.

Metal hit him in the stomach and then he felt something hard slam into his back as the train's momentum rammed him against the front of the last truck. He cried out and hung on for his life, wrapping his arm over a dirty, sticky tube that stuck out of one truck and fed into the next. His back and ribs screamed at him, but he was on the train, he was safe.

As the last of the platform edge disappeared to be replaced by forest on either side, Carl let himself breathe, let himself close his eyes.

And there, for a few minutes at least, he let his face crumble up, let tears flow, and allowed himself to mourn.

Chapter Thirty-Eight
Battlefield

CLAYTON WATCHED WITH UNEASE as the Huntsmen were unloaded inside Bristol Temple Meads train station, deserted now on his orders. The handlers urged the leashed beasts forward, occasionally dishing out a sharp stun which resulted in growls of pain that echoed across the cavernous space above them.

Clayton wondered what a casual bystander might think of all this. Behind him, his men were unloading what looked like a train straight out of a nightmare. The Huntsmen moved slowly across the platform, hooded faces lowered, their rough breathing and the occasional growl the only sounds.

The handler, Jakob, waved to him. 'What?' Clayton asked.

'We've got a scent,' the man told him. 'We're a few hours behind but if we set the dogs off now we can run them down. These Tube Riders have to sleep at some point.'

Clayton nodded. 'Get the Huntsmen over there. Make sure the new ones are familiar with the scent.'

'Yes, sir,' Jakob replied.

Clayton grimaced. The last thing he wanted was for the malfunctioning monsters to dash off after the wrong people. He'd seen a lot of bloodshed in the last twenty-four hours and was growing weary of it.

I want this finished, he thought. *I want this over with.*

He knew, though, that the only way to end it was to see those kids dead, and a part of him suffered at the thought of it. He'd done many bad things in his life, and he was about to do another. He knew, as no doubt the Governor did, that the Tube Riders had done nothing wrong. They were just another group of misfits trying to make something out of the mess Mega Britain had become. If there was anyone who ought to die...

Clayton squeezed his eyes shut, trying to keep out the thought. Treason was a strong word even in peace times, and to utter those thoughts out loud could see him dead. But there was something not right about everything, and part of Clayton wished he'd been born in a different time and place.

Instead he let himself think of Dreggo, the girl under his control whom the DCA were forcing to lead the Huntsmen. The bulge of the remote in his pocket pressed against his side, and he felt a sudden flush of regret for what he'd done to her. She'd attacked him, but his words had provoked her. What had he been thinking?

There are lower standards there, he had told her. But those were the Governor's words, not his. Clayton rubbed his eyes. Were the Governor's threats turning him into a similar monster? Dreggo was no different to the Tube Riders. The wrong place at the wrong time. Yet something about her just made him hate her. Maybe it was that without the remote in his pocket, she would kill him in an instant, perhaps as he deserved.

'Got to give them credit,' someone said beside him, and Clayton jerked back to the present to see Vincent standing there, looking in the direction of the damaged train that had derailed just beyond the platform edge, having collided with a stationary train. The debris was yet to be cleared.

'What?' Clayton said.

'They're putting up a hell of a fight over this.'

Clayton smiled. 'They've got spirit,' he said.

'Kind of a shame we've got to see it ripped out of them,' Vincent said. 'But I guess that's just how it goes.'

Clayton looked at Vincent. The agent's face was a mess of bruises but that same cold stare was there. Clayton could read the younger man well. There was no conflict behind those eyes, simply a desire to see the job done as efficiently as possible, ideally in a way that would allow personal gain. Vincent had allowed the Tube Riders to escape once, and suffered for it. He wasn't about to do it again.

'Sir!'

Clayton turned, noticing how Vincent turned also; that same desire for command still there, despite everything.

A DCA agent stood behind them. 'They went down the stairs,' the man said. 'Into the parking garage. The trail's clean down there because the area is disused. Want us to roll them out?'

Clayton considered. The chances were high indeed that they were still in the city, hiding out somewhere. Maybe they thought their trail would go cold, the scent would fade.

'Okay, let's do this,' he told the agent, looking back over his shoulder towards the train. He frowned. 'What's going on with those?'

Several of the handlers had shackled a group of Huntsmen together using a chain with individual manacles.

'They're the reserve, I think,' Vincent said.

'The what?'

'They're using the first group to track. These others are the heavy artillery, so to speak.'

'Jesus Christ. This whole operation is just waiting to fuck up.'

Already Clayton was regretting letting Dreggo go after the other Tube Riders. She had called him just once in the hour and a half since she left them, with nothing to report. He was fuming. What was she doing, having a goddamn picnic?

'At least they've cleared out the station,' Vincent said with a smirk. 'If there were people around it would be like letting a group of rabid foxes loose in a chicken coop.'

Clayton rolled his eyes. 'Just keep an eye on the ones to the left.'

One of the handlers called to him. 'All four went into the parking garage together. I'd guess they were running by that point.'

'Well, in after them we go, then,' Clayton muttered, following the man down the steps. Behind them, three handlers were directing the chained Huntsmen down.

'We should have stuck with five,' Vincent said. 'This is turning into one ugly fucking dog show.'

Clayton said nothing.

The door to the parking garage was ajar. Inside, the darkness was almost impenetrable, except for a small glow on the far side, several hundred feet distant.

'Let's get on it,' Clayton said and stepped inside, his gun drawn as a precaution. He moved wide around the side wall as the handlers pushed the Huntsmen down the centre.

'Looks like they just bolted straight across, sir–'

An explosion rocked the entrance just behind him, sending Clayton sprawling to the ground amid a shower of sparks and debris as the back of the parking garage roof collapsed.

'Find cover!' he screamed, just as huge spotlights came on at the far end of the parking garage, blinding him.

The air filled with gunfire, bullets pinging off the concrete around him. Clayton glanced back at the door and saw a couple of his men half buried under the rubble. A couple of Huntsmen lay still beside them, but there was no way to know how many were dead.

The gunfire came again, automatic weapons, and he rolled behind a chunk of fallen masonry that moments before had just missed landing on his head. To his right he heard a growl and then a scream as a Huntsman took a bullet, a thud as it slumped to the ground.

'Return fire!' he shouted.

'What about the Huntsmen?' Jakob shouted from nearby. 'Chained up they're just waiting to die! Release them and we'll win this fight!'

Clayton frowned. Even now, ambushed, bullets flying around his head, he didn't want to. But the way in was blocked, and their attackers, whoever they were, were heavily armed and covering the only way out. One or two more explosive devices and the battle would be lost.

'Do it!' he shouted. 'Set them loose! And God help us if they don't know who they're fighting against.'

He heard a click, the wrist locks binding the monsters opening by automatic control. Even as heavier gunfire cracked against the concrete around him, he heard a roar go up in union from the Huntsmen. Risking a glance up out of his hiding place, he saw them running into battle.

Like the devil's own cavalry, the Huntsmen raced across the parking garage towards the attackers hiding behind their blinding spotlights. As gunfire turned on them, several Huntsmen dived forward and rolled across the floor like whirling, spinning ninjas, while others leapt up and clambered across the beams and lintels of the parking garage roof. Others dropped to their knees, crossbows and other weapons in their hands, loosing their arsenal at the enemy, covering those who moved in towards close combat.

There were only perhaps ten or twelve involved in the charge, but the enemy's organised position fell into sudden disarray, guns firing wildly, bullets spraying in desperation as the Huntsmen advanced. He watched as one Huntsman was shot and felled, only to leap to its feet again, claws stretching to tear and maim.

One of the spotlights took a bullet, sparked and went out, quickly followed by the others. Men began to scream.

Clayton didn't want to think about how he would round up the Huntsmen once the carnage was over. With the spotlights no longer trained on him, he waved his remaining DCA agents forward. 'After them!' he shouted. 'We need prisoners. We need to know who the hell these people are!'

Clayton let his agents get a decent start and then he followed after them. Leading his troops from the front was hardly the plan; that's why the Huntsmen were here.

#

In fact, Clayton was last bar one. As Clayton jogged after his men, Adam Vincent got up from his own hiding place, behind a support pillar left at an angle after the explosion, and moved after Clayton. His gun was in his hand, and he was wondering when would be the best time to put a bullet in Clayton's back.

#

From behind the row of abandoned cars his men were using for cover, Ishael had detected the Department of Civil Affairs agents coming through the door from the station on an old, hand-held heat detecting radar scanner. He knew immediately how important the Tube Riders were by the sheer number of agents – at least thirty, maybe more. He could see their steady blips on the radar, but worse were the pulsing blips that appeared to be Huntsmen, the body heat they gave off far higher but unstable, as though they were flushing hot and cold at two-second intervals. He felt his own blood chill at the thought of them, especially when he realised how many the Department of Civil Affairs had brought. He knew instantly that his own group, twenty-four armed and capable men, wasn't nearly enough.

With the DCA agents and the Huntsmen crowding through the doorway, Ishael's men had detonated the bomb. Looking at the scanner, he'd seen five or six DCA agents killed or hurt by the rubble, but not nearly as many as he'd hoped. One or two Huntsmen were down, their blips flickering wildly, but it was difficult to tell if they were dead or even disabled. He prayed at least a few were. Most of the survivors had ducked down for cover, and he had felt confident his men could pick them off or at least keep them down using the scanner and the spotlights they had brought.

Only when he saw a group detach from the main contingent, all of their blips pulsing like little heartbeats, had he realised just how hopeless their situation was.

Now, looking up, as the Huntsmen raced across the open space of the parking garage, heedless of the bullets flying around them, he felt he was looking into the face of Death himself.

A man standing beside him grunted and slumped back, a crossbow bolt in his neck. As his blood pumped out on to the oily concrete, Ishael barely had time to reflect on how many good, loyal men he was about to lose.

'Back!' he screamed, waving towards the parking garage exit. 'Out on to the street!'

He turned, just as a snarling Huntsman launched itself across the top of the car towards him.

Ishael gasped like a frightened child as the snarling jaws broke from beneath the dark hood and darted for his neck. He pulled his rifle up at the last second, knocking the monster off course, the jaws missing him but one clawed hand raking his arm, pulling him around. As the Huntsman skidded and rolled past him, he clutched at his side, feeling blood flow from a deep gash. Someone shouted his name, but he didn't have time to move as the Huntsman wheeled and launched itself again. Ishael dodged sideways and the Huntsman struck the car, but it was already turning, its reactions far faster than his. He grabbed the car's loose rear door and slammed it into the Huntsman, but instead of being knocked back the creature gripped the door and tore it off its hinges, tossing it aside.

This is it, Ishael thought. *This is where it ends.*

'Die...'

But Ishael wasn't ready to die, not yet. For a second the image of Marta – the beautiful and brave Tube Rider – entered his mind, and he felt a surge of adrenaline. He scrambled backwards, dropped to the ground and rolled sideways, slipping underneath the adjacent car. As the smell of old oil and petrol filled his lungs, he saw the Huntsman's feet move as it came after him, and then it too dropped to the ground and tried to follow, its claws reaching under the car to rake at his legs.

Trying to make space, Ishael kicked at it, striking it once in the face. As he felt a jarring pain race up his leg, the lack of give and the strength of the beast's neck terrified him. It had felt like kicking concrete.

It caught hold of his leg and began to pull him out. He kicked again, aiming for its hood, where he hoped the eyes would be. He cried out as it shifted to the side, and then powerful jaws clamped down on his calf muscle, biting through the combat trousers he wore. Hot blood washed over his skin, and wondered if the creature would bite right through his leg.

Instead, its teeth released their grip and it jerked him backwards, pulling him out from under the car. For a moment he saw the Huntsman silhouetted above him in the light of one of his own men's spotlights, and then it dived at him, jaws snapping.

He closed his eyes.

'Pull it off!'

Ishael opened his eyes to see the Huntsman spasm in the air above him, a terrible wailing coming from its open maw. It scrabbled at its neck, claws pulling the hood free. Ishael saw what looked like a human head behind its dog-like snout, wires snaking across its scalp. Then it slumped away from him, landing on its stomach a few feet away. Two men rushed to clamp its arms.

'Well, well.'

Spotlights had come on again, pointed skyward now to leave the parking garage illuminated in a twilight glow, and Ishael could see the eyes of the man standing above him. Perhaps forty, his body was solid beneath the black suit, his jaw firm, unsmiling. His hair was flecked with spots of dust. Hard, dark eyes watched Ishael with contempt, but also, Ishael thought, with what looked like a hint of admiration.

The man waved his hand and two other DCA men came up behind him. 'Secure the prisoner,' he said. 'And find me a room. We need to have a talk with him.' As the agents moved forward, the first man glanced over his shoulder. 'Vincent! Move the men forward on to the streets. Follow them down and kill them if you can't take them alive. Find where they're hiding the Tube Riders.'

'What Tube Riders?' Ishael groaned, but the man just shook his head as if to say, *don't bother. We know.* Then he turned and was gone.

Ishael started to push himself up, but one of the agents stepped forward and kicked him hard in the face. Ishael was conscious just long enough to see the man lean down towards him, and then everything went black.

CHAPTER THIRTY-NINE
DEPARTURE

AS THE TRAIN RUSHED through the forest, picking up speed again, Jess inched her way along towards the front of the freight truck, her feet on a thin rail barely above the wheels, her clawboard sliding slowly along the water drainage rail above her. Occasionally it got caught on a piece of grit or caked mud, and Jess had to carefully remove one hand from the straps and pick out the obstruction with her fingers. Twice she had to hold on with her hand and lift the board over. Glancing down at the gravel and sleepers rushing past below, she was reminded just how close she hung to death; that a momentary slip would see her pitched off the train. She'd survived once; she didn't fancy her chances of surviving a second time.

Simon was five trucks ahead. At the end of her truck, she painstakingly climbed down into the working area that fixed the two freight trucks together before climbing back up on to the drainage rail of the next one. Just at that moment the train started around a wide bend. The trucks arced away to the right and she saw Simon again, what seemed like miles away, hanging from the side of the train, his head lolling back and forth as though every second was a fight against unconsciousness.

She'd pushed him hard through the forest, and she'd got him this far. If she could just get to him before his strength gave out again then she could save him, she could hold on to him until they reached Bristol. She had no idea how far it was, but it couldn't be more than an hour. She could do it; she could be the strength for both of them.

She glanced back down the train, and her heart almost stopped.

There, just three trucks back, a Huntsman was crawling along the top of the train.

Jess wanted to scream, but no sound would come out. As she watched it in horror, she felt all her last hopes fade away.

\#

Dreggo stood beside Lyen on the platform edge as the train rolled away into the forest. The two Tube Riders had escaped again; with the help of the country bumpkin boy even the wounded one had managed to get on to the train. Catching them would be easy; a simple radio call to Clayton would have twenty agents and Huntsmen waiting for them when the train arrived in Bristol, but still she couldn't shake the feeling of failure. Despite the tears, her hatred and anger were back, and being so close yet again only to have them escape made her feel weak and incapable.

The country boy, though, he impressed her. Not only had he killed Jacul, but he'd made a possibly suicidal jump on to the train. She would only know if he survived or not when she viewed his corpse in Bristol, but a leap like that had taken some faith, and lots of guts. Despite seeing her Huntsman cut down and pulled under the train, he had won her respect.

If Clayton could leave him alive, she'd enjoy killing him.

She pulled the radio from her pocket, intending to call Clayton and inform him of proceedings, and request he have the next through train stop for them. As she lifted it to her ear, though, she felt a crackle of static in her mind, the sign of a Huntsman's internal transmitter. Lyen shifted beside her; he'd felt it too.

The voice that came into her mind was broken and indistinct, but still it could come from nothing else.

'*...alive...*'

She glanced across at Lyen and he gave her a dark, feverish glare in return. Jacul wasn't dead. Through whatever twist of luck and fate, he had survived being pulled under the train.

She sent Lyen to check the tracks. There were no signs of a body, mutilated or otherwise, which meant, of course, that Jacul was still on the train.

She put the radio away. There might not be a need to inform Clayton after all.

\#

As Jacul felt his foot slip out from under him, he could only think of relief; that it was finally over, that he could rest. Then, as one arm reached out, his clawed fingers closing over something metal, he felt himself jerked away from the wheels of the train, and from the death that he would have so welcomed. The last vestiges of his human mind had prayed for the thundering salvation of the huge metal wheels, but the robotic part of his body, that which would obey orders until death, refused to let him go.

It was too late for his other arm. As he hung from the bottom of the train, he swung inwards, and struck the side of the nearest wheel. He reached out as a reflex to push himself away, and then it was gone, ripped off at the shoulder, his body filled with a thousand spasms of pain. He felt human blood, oil and fluids oozing down his side, mixed with those that bled from the crossbow wound. His mind was already drifting, and he estimated that he would be dead within half an hour. His human mind wanted to close his eyes and let him drift away, float back through the fragments of childhood memories that had survived his transformation into a Huntsman, but the machine part of him, the engineered part, knew there was a mission to complete, and that half an hour might be all he needed.

The Tube Riders, his prey, were on the train.

With his one good arm he hauled himself along the underside of the train, using his legs to support him while he searched for another hand-hold.

Inch by inch he made his way forward, the blurring wheels of the train never more than a couple of feet away. Then, finally, he came to the end of the freight truck, and saw daylight again above him.

Hauling himself up and over on to the mechanism that latched the two trucks together, he managed to stand, bracing his feet against the rocking of the train, hanging on with his one good arm.

There was a door in the back of the truck in front, but when he tore the lock free and pushed it open he found the truck packed full of crates, labeled with various food company labels. There was no way through, so he closed the door, and looked up at the top of the truck.

Fear wasn't something that the Huntsmen felt. Like a lot of emotions, it had been erased by the technology used to develop the minds of the killing machines, but every now and then Jacul would feel a certain sense of otherworldliness, as if what he was about to do was more dangerous than usual. He felt it now, but as he glanced down at the ground blurring below him, he shrugged what was left of his shoulders and began looking for a way up.

#

It was scant relief for Jess to realise that the Huntsman was missing an arm and appeared to have been through a serious battle. Blood streamed down its canine face and dripped on to the roof of the train as it closed on her. She was half a truck ahead of it still, but it was gaining. She was still one truck away from Simon, who appeared to be hanging on desperately. The back of his shirt was soaked in blood, his head lolled from side to side, and his feet kept slipping from the rail below him.

In the back of her mind Jess wished now that she'd not given her crossbow to Carl. After what he'd done to help them, she had owed him, and just hoped he'd managed to get away. Now, the best weapon she had was a knife, but even one handed, the Huntsman would make short work of that.

Just as she reached the end of the freight truck and began to climb around into the gap between it and the next, she glanced back at the Huntsman, saw it shift its head towards her. Protruding from its neck and glistening in the sunlight was the shaft of a crossbow bolt.

Jess's heart plunged. Carl had attacked this Huntsman, yet it still lived and was on the train. Did that mean Carl was dead?

She knew she might never find out. She squeezed her eyes shut against another wave of pain, and tried to concentrate on getting to Simon.

Then something slammed into her from behind.

She fell forward across the stubby metal joints between the trucks, felt them vibrating and shifting as they knocked the wind out of her. She gasped for breath, swinging her clawboard up instinctively. Something thudded into it, and she felt the inhuman strength in the Huntsman's remaining arm as it then tried to pull the knife free. Jess screamed, her resolve failing her as she looked into its muggy, bloodshot eyes, and wondered how it had closed the gap on her so fast.

It jerked the knife out of the wood and almost overbalanced, its knife hand clutching awkwardly at a maintenance handle beside the freight truck's door. Jess almost lost the clawboard, but managed to get it up between them again just as the Huntsman, using its legs for support, swung its knife at her again.

'Leave me alone!' she screamed.

As the clawboard deflected the slash, Jess struggled to hold on with one hand, the Huntsman's strength pushing her back. It would be a short fight, she knew; if she moved for her knife she would lose her shield or her handhold, and she couldn't survive without either.

The Huntsman's eyes followed her impassively, its mouth torn back in a snarl that revealed yellowed, gummy canine teeth. The breath was pungent, like that of a dog's, but the tongue was shorter, thicker than a dog's but not quite as squashed as a human's. Its nose, too, was thinner and paler than a dog's might be.

'Tube Rider!' the Huntsman growled, and Jess wanted to scream at the nightmarish sound of its voice.

The knife slashed again. Jess swayed away, the blade missing her by inches. She tried to swing the clawboard up towards its face, but it was heavy, and her strength was leaving her. As she looked back at the Huntsman, her eyes filled with tears.

Then something moved in her peripheral vision, and there was another figure in front of her, crashing down on the Huntsman's shoulders and knocking it briefly to its knees.

'Simon...?'

Sweat drenched his face, blood drenched his shirt and his eyes seemed about to roll back into his head as he swung an arm around the Huntsman's neck. 'Run!' he gasped, his voice slurred. 'I heard you scream—'

The Huntsman, with Simon wrapped around its shoulders, stood up and slammed him back against the door, knocking the wind out of him. Jess bared her own teeth and rammed her clawboard into the Huntsman's stomach, feeling an unnatural hardness there. *The thing's half metal*, her mind shouted. *There's no way we can kill it.*

Simon's clawboard was still strapped to his other hand, and he pulled it up and across the Huntsman's neck. The Huntsman growled and twisted its head, but it couldn't use its hand to pull the clawboard away or it would lose its grip. Jess tried to reach the knife on its belt, but it kicked her in the stomach, doubling her over. She looked up, wondering how much longer Simon could hold on.

#

'Jess, no!'

Simon smashed the clawboard into the Huntsman's face. Its nose burst, spraying him with blood. With his other hand he reached up and tore at the wires and metal plates that covered the creature's scalp, trying to disable it. It bucked at him but continued to hold on, so he stretched forwards, his fingers reaching for the creature's eyes.

He heard Jess gasp as the Huntsman's maw snapped at him, sharp teeth closing just out of reach. He grunted and thrust his fingers in through the soft tissue, squeezing as hard as he could, feeling the creature struggle as its eyeballs depressed and then popped like blisters, bathing his fingers in sticky fluid. Screaming now himself, he thrust his fingers deeper as the Huntsman thrashed, its free hand letting go of its hold, sending them both crashing back against the door. Simon hooked his clawboard behind the handrail to hold himself steady, even as his fingers pressed deeper towards the Huntsman's brain. He felt it buck again, felt its arm slip behind it, pushing against his belly.

'Die, you evil fucking *bastard!*' he hollered, at the same time becoming aware of a new, acute pain somewhere in his midriff, a twisting coldness, and the sudden warmth of blood down over his stomach and thighs.

The Huntsman gave a final, shrieking roar and sagged against him, an expulsion of dead air exiting its lungs for the last time. Simon let go and pushed it away. Its eyes closed, almost in relief, and it slipped down between the joint mechanisms and under the train.

There was a bump, and then it was gone.

Simon sagged back against the truck door, one hand still attached to the clawboard stuck behind the handrail, the other going to his stomach, feeling the warmth there, the handle of the knife that stuck out, so, so little of it. Somewhere he was aware of Jess screaming, but the sound was hazy, unclear. His vision blurred just as someone else dropped into view, someone he recognised from his bedside. A young boy. What was his name?

What ... what was his name?

Simon's head lolled back.

#

Jess watched as the Huntsman pressed its knife into Simon with its last dying move, and then fell away under the train. She saw Simon slump back, the front of his shirt slick with blood, both his own and that of the Huntsman. His eyes rolled, his breathing coming in small gasps.

A figure appeared above her, squatting on the top of the freight truck. She cried out, pulling her clawboard up, before realizing with some surprise that it was Carl. Somehow he'd made it on to the train. He looked none the worse for his battles with the Huntsmen, but his eyes widened as he saw the blood that covered Simon.

'We have to stop the train,' Jess said to him. 'Go to the front, threaten the driver, something, I don't know. Anything! We *have to stop the train.*'

'Break the door open. You might be able to rest inside,' Carl said.

Jess nodded. Turning behind her, she rammed her clawboard against the truck door. It had a padlock, but didn't look strong. Sure enough, after a couple more desperate slugs, the door popped open, swinging inward.

There were some crates secured near the far side of the truck, but there was a little space left between them, and with Carl's help Jess was able to haul

Simon inside. He was barely conscious, and they propped him up with his back to a wooden crate. With the door shut, the peace inside the truck was harmony compared to the grinding, thudding cacophony that had surrounded them outside.

Carl looked at Simon, then at Jess, his face grim. 'I'll go up to the cab,' he said. 'I'll see if I can stop the train.'

Jess nodded. 'Be careful,' she said, trying not to let her voice break up.

Carl gave her a quick smile and went out, shutting the door behind him.

In the relative calm of the freight truck, Jess mopped Simon's forehead with a rag. His face was ashen, his lips white from blood loss.

'You know, don't you?' he said suddenly, his voice almost as she remembered from their first meeting, soft, peaceful, like a cool park in the middle of a busy city. She remembered his smile too, and he gave her one now, warm, easy. She felt her heart jump as it had done that first time, back in the street near Charing Cross where he'd stopped her and asked her for the time.

'I know what?'

'That I love you. That I love you more than anything.'

'Yeah, I know.'

'And that ... it's time for me to go now.'

Jess's breath caught in her throat and she almost choked. She hadn't tried to stop the bleeding; she knew how bad his wound was, but still, hearing it in words made it suddenly so real. She wanted to cry but no tears would come. She just felt empty, hollow.

'There are a million things I want to say to you, Jessica,' Simon told her. 'But there isn't the time. Perhaps in another life, another time, we could have been together longer.'

'Simon, shut up! Just shut fucking *up!*' She wanted to shake him, make him take back what he was saying.

'I just want you to know that I love you. You are my ... my ... light.'

'*Simon!*' Jess was hysterical. She'd found him, she'd brought him back. She'd saved him once, and he'd returned the favour, but at an incalculable cost. 'I didn't come so far just to lose you again!'

'You'll never lose me. I'll always be in...' He reached up a hand, his face scrunched up with pain, and touched her chest, just between her breasts. '... in ... here.'

'Simon, no...'

One of his hands dropped into hers. His fingers squeezed momentarily tight, and she felt something hard there. 'Don't give up ... on us...'

For a moment she didn't understand. Then she looked down and saw what he had pressed into her hand – the little camera memory card. For a second she hated the thing, wanted to throw it away, but she realised that if she did, his life, like those of her parents, would have been wasted. He was right. As much as it tore her up inside, he was right.

Simon began to cough, doubling over. She patted his back, lifting him up straight, felt the weakness in his shoulders, the sagging of his body.

'I love you, Simon!' she gasped, as his eyes locked on to hers, narrowing slightly, then going suddenly wide, desperate, his shoulders and neck tensing, a whining sound escaping his mouth as his last breath left him.

'Jessica–' he gasped, and then went soft in her arms.

'*No!*'

Jess's howl filled the small space between the cargo crates, seeming to make them rattle. Around her she felt the braking of the train, the slow bumping as it ground towards a halt, but she didn't notice anything at all, not even when, a few minutes later, the side door opened and Carl looked in to see her leaning back against the crates, Simon's body held in her arms, his blood drenching her clothes.

#

Carl looked at her face, saw the pain there, the utter, complete grief in her beautiful face, and he wanted to cry too, not just for the young man whom he had known so briefly, but for the girl who had lost him. Carl saw in the dead hollows of her eyes that Jess's life had moved a step closer to darkness, and sensed the sadness torturing her heart. As she closed her eyes and leaned closer to Simon's body, part of Carl wished she would never open them again.

Let life spare her too, he thought, tears springing to his own eyes.

Chapter Forty
Prison Break

MARTA COULDN'T SEE ANYTHING. Below her she could feel the rumbling wheels of the bus, but hidden away in a thin compartment below the floor she had little way of knowing in which direction they were heading. Beside her, Paul and Owen were talking quietly in the dark. Owen had that familiar excitement about him, which Paul was trying to hush. Marta smiled. It was probably better for the kid to keep his spirits up. She had lost hers long ago.

Switch was on the other side of her. Feeling a need for conversation, she nudged him softly. 'Tell me again what's going to happen.'

'Uncle and his men will create a diversion; draw the guards away from the perimeter gate. I'll slip out and attach a small explosive device to the gate. When it blows, the bus can just drive through.'

'I can't believe it'll work as easily as that.'

'Me neither. But I trust Unc. He's the best man I've ever known, and if I can't trust him I can't trust anyone.'

They both heard the bus's engine die and the rocking below them ceased. A moment later they heard a muffled explosion not far away.

'What was that?'

'I guess that's our diversion.'

Someone tapped on the floor. 'Your turn!' a muffled voice shouted.

Marta felt Switch's hand take hers and squeeze it lightly. 'See you soon,' he said.

She heard him slide away, and a second later daylight bathed them as Switch pulled away a loose panel in the side of the bus and jumped out. Marta squinted in the brightness. Switch gave her a weird spastic wink and replaced the panel, locking her in darkness again.

#

Outside, Switch looked around. The perimeter gate rose up in front of him, about thirty feet tall, built back into a concrete wall that stretched off in both directions, disappearing behind the roofs of the abandoned houses and buildings that rotted in the wall's shadow. William had told him that few people lived near the wall; it was too much of a reminder of times past. Now, the buildings were the haunts of drug addicts, whores and vagrants.

Behind him, the bus, an old government one, had stopped at a bent, rusty bus-stop sign just short of the gate. The driver, an undercover UMF man, was engaged in a heated exchange with another man, also of the UMF, masquerading as a fare-dodging customer. Switch had about a minute to take care of his job and get back to the bus before their ruse drew attention.

The gate itself looked unguarded. It was a small one; most of the major traffic came in though a much larger gate to the north of the city, William had said, but even so, Switch would have expected guards. Looking left, he saw the reason why; a burning car had drawn the attention of the gate's sentries, who now stood around it like tramps around a trash-can fire.

Switch didn't waste any time. He headed straight for the gate, leaning low, limping slightly. He wore a dirty brown shawl and a headscarf, while in his hand he carried a paper bag with the end of a glass bottle sticking out.

When he reached the gate, still unnoticed, he put the bottle down as close to the centre as he could. Then he began limping away.

'Oi, you!'

Switch glanced up. A green-uniformed guard jogged across towards him, waving an automatic rifle. 'Get the hell away from there, you fucking turd!'

Switch had one hand inside the robe, trying to pass off as an amputee. Out of sight, his fingers closed around a switch-blade. The other guards were over by the burning car, walking around it, trying to peer inside to see if there were casualties. With surprise on his side Switch felt quite sure he could take the guard out if the man caused him a problem.

'Sorry guv'nur,' Switch slurred. 'Got lost eh.' He cocked his face at the guard and gave a half-grin. William's men had caked his face with fake blood, and his own twitching eye only made him more pitiful.

The guard relaxed. 'Come on. Just get the hell away from the gate. You know the law.'

'Just tryin' t'get 'ome, guv.'

'Well, keep trying. Hey, wait!' The man pointed. 'You forgot your medicine, my friend.'

''E's empty,' Switch started to say, but it was too late. The man was already heading across towards the paper bag, nestled in between the two huge gates.

Switch started to jog for the nearest buildings. Beneath his robe he let go of the knife and felt for the small plastic box that would detonate the crude bomb.

He reached the nearest building and ducked into a doorway. Turning around, he saw the guard reach the bag and pick it up.

Switch closed his eyes. It was bad enough having to do it at all, but he didn't want to watch the man die as well.

He pressed the detonator button.

A roar filled the air behind him. The sound of ripping, tearing steel and splintering wood mixed with the screams of men. Switch opened his eyes to chaos; a wall of smoke and concrete dust bloomed up between him and the gate, so at first he was unable to see if they'd broken through. At the same time, gunshots began to ring out from the cover of the buildings to his right, where a group of William's men were staked out. Caught out in the open, several of the guards went down immediately, but a couple managed to take cover behind the burnt-out car, and from there they began to return fire.

Switch was behind them, though, so he slipped back through the dust alongside the perimeter wall towards the gate. Ahead of him, he heard the engine rumble as the bus began to move.

Gunfire came from above him, guards on top of the wall trying to pin down William's men. He grimaced. Their plan was moments from failure.

The dust began to clear. To his dismay he saw that the gate still stood.

'Shit, oh *shit*.'

As he got near he found that the bomb had badly damaged it, great dents and cracks in its steel surface, with its hinges buckled and misshapen, but still it remained closed.

He turned in the direction of the bus and began to run.

The driver almost didn't see him, and Switch heard the squeal of old brakes as the bus tried to stop. Jumping out of its way, he caught the rail to the side of the open front door and swung inside.

'Gun it, man!' he shouted at the driver, one of William's men. 'The gate's still up!'

'No way,' the man grunted. 'I'll see what I can do, but those damn gates were built to last.'

'It's our only chance!'

'Gonna tell the others?'

'No. If we don't make it there's a chance they won't be discovered.'

'Fat chance of that.'

Switch spun around. Marta stood behind him, while behind her Owen was helping Paul up out of a trapdoor in the bus floor.

'Get back out of sight!'

'We stand together,' Marta said.

The driver glanced over his shoulder. 'Well, damn well hang on to something, then.'

The bus lurched forward. Gunfire cracked all around them, shattering several of the windows. Switch ducked down behind the bus's dashboard, while behind him the others dived down between the seats.

'Here it comes!' the driver shouted. Switch glanced up just long enough to see the perimeter wall rising up around them, the gate no more than a few feet ahead.

'Yeah!'

The bus hit the gates square on. Switch slammed into the dashboard as the front window imploded, ducking his head to avoid shards of flying glass. There was a momentary thud and then a rush of forward movement, and to his relief Switch realised they were through. He heard the gunfire receding behind them as the bus bumped downhill, at first on a road, and then swerving off, bumping across an open area of grassland. The wind rushed past his face and he frowned, looking over his shoulder to see the road disappearing back to their right.

'Where the hell are you—'

Switch knew immediately that his words were wasted. The driver, bloodied and lifeless, was slumped back in the seat, a large shard of glass protruding from a neck injury that pumped blood down over his fake bus driver's uniform.

'Marta, Paul! We have another problem!'

Switch jumped up, trying to grab the wheel out of the driver's dead hands, but it was too late. The dead man lurched forward, pulling the wheel sharply over to the left. The bus, still moving downhill, bumped again and overbalanced.

Everything seemed to happen in slow motion. Switch was screaming at the others to hang on, even as he wrapped his arms around the wheel to brace himself. Behind him, he heard Marta screaming, Paul shouting at Owen, and Owen gasping as though this were yet another fairground ride.

The bus crashed over on to its side, cushioned slightly by a stand of bushes that smashed in through the windows. There was a grinding noise as the engine continued to revolve for a few seconds, then the internal workings of the old bus shuddered and went still.

Switch rubbed his head and pulled himself to his feet. He felt like he was standing horizontally, with the bus's seats hanging in the air to his left. 'Everyone all right?' he asked, feeling a little dazed but otherwise okay.

Three groggy voices came back affirmative.

'Is it going to blow up?' Marta asked, crawling across the broken bus windows towards him, a small cut on her cheek and some pieces of twig in her hair.

'No,' Paul said. 'Not unless there's a spark from somewhere. It's a common myth that vehicles blow up when they crash, and the bio-fuel buses use is less flammable than old petrol.'

'Thanks for the fucking infomercial, but we had better get moving,' Switch said. 'We've lost our wheels, but they've still got theirs.'

'Perhaps we should blow it up anyway,' Owen said, leaning against the sideways turned seats. 'Throw them off the trail.'

'He's got a point,' Marta said. 'How?'

Owen pointed at Switch. 'You've got something to light a fire with, haven't you?'

Switch grinned. 'Of course I have.'

'And the fuel's still flammable?'

Paul nodded. 'Yeah, less than petrol, but it'll still ignite, I think.'

'Good.' Owen nodded. 'Do it then.'

Switch cut a piece of his rope to use as a fuse. The driver's body yielded the keys to the petrol tank, but unfortunately the bus had rolled on that side. Instead, Paul and Switch had to break a hole in the bottom of the tank and feed the rope inside. Rust made it easier, but the three-quarters empty tank swallowed a lot of rope before they reached the fuel itself. The fuse wasn't long enough to be safe, and Switch insisted the others got clear before he set it alight.

He waited until they were twenty yards away, then he touched his lighter to the doused rope. 'Here it comes!' he shouted, watching a flame immediately strike up and rush towards the bus's undercarriage. Switch turned and dashed in the other direction, leaping over a stand of bracken into a small natural hollow, just as the flame reached the bus and an explosion boomed. Switch looked up to see the underside of the bus broken open, a pool of flame around the vehicle. He nodded with satisfaction as the flames raked at the side of the bus.

'Nice job, Switch!' Marta shouted.

'Thanks. Pocket fucking pyro, I am.' He grinned and turned to follow the others.

They were heading downhill, away from the bus, towards a stand of forest. They had no escape from the Huntsmen, of course, but the trees would give them cover against gunfire.

'What do we do now?' Owen said, running alongside Paul.

'We run,' Paul said. 'And we keep running.'

'Paul, that's a crap plan if ever I've heard one.'

Despite their fear, their exhaustion, and the bruises that littered their bodies, Marta and Switch both laughed.

'Well, you get working on a new one, and while you're at it, we'll keep running from the Huntsmen,' Marta said.

'Easy,' Owen said. 'The river.'

'What river?'

He pointed to the right. 'I saw it from the top deck of the bus before we crashed. At the very least we can get across it. Should make our trail more difficult for the Huntsmen to follow.'

'Paul, your brother's a genius,' Marta said.

'That's the benefit of a proper education,' Owen said. 'And lots of video games.'

'Well, you haven't solved what we're going to do once we cross that damn river,' Switch said. 'I can't fucking swim. And if we're walking I imagine even those DCA chumps will be able to find us.'

'I thought I saw some sort of boat. Maybe we can steal it, but we'd better hurry.' Without waiting for an answer he dashed ahead of the others, dancing between the trees like a deer running from fire. 'Come on!' they heard him shout back, before a sudden splash came from up ahead.

They jogged after him through the trees, emerging from a thicket on to a sharp riverbank. Owen was standing waist deep in the water.

'Dammit, didn't see it coming,' he muttered, looking down at his sopping clothes and then picking a piece of grime out of his hair.

The others looked down. The riverbank didn't so much slope away as drop vertically into the water, and a moment later they realised why.

'It's an old canal,' Paul said. 'I wonder what they used it for?'

'God knows. But it's here so we might as well make use of it. Where's that boat, Owen?'

'There.' He pointed. The others saw it, caught up under a tangle of trees on the canal's far bank, about fifty feet away. 'I didn't say it would definitely float, now, did I?'

To Marta it looked like an old barge, not dissimilar to ones she'd seen rotting along the sides of the Thames. Its hull was a rusty mottled brown, and hanging vegetation draped over the low cabin that stuck up at one end, clogging up its deck with ancient fallen leaves.

'Let's get across, see if we can set it adrift,' Paul said, climbing down into the water. 'Wow, it's cold!'

Together, they waded across the canal. It was no more than chest deep at its widest point, the flow of water steady but not dangerous as it tugged at their legs.

Switch got up on the boat first, and pushed his way through the foliage towards where the boat nestled against the bank.

'It's tied up!' he called back. 'I'll cut it free. Paul, Owen, help me push it away from the bank. Marta, go look inside. See if there's some kind of engine that still works.'

She nodded and pushed her way through the low branches towards the door down inside. She felt a brief pang of fear; there was no telling what horrors she might find inside this ancient, abandoned boat. She braced herself for decomposing corpses. She felt quite familiar with dead bodies now, but they had all been fresh.

Behind her, she heard Switch and Owen whooping with delight as the boat lurched under her feet and swung lethargically out towards the centre of the canal. Over them, she heard Paul demanding quiet. Turning back to the job in hand, she found the handle of the little door to be rather smooth, maybe sheltered from the weather. The door wasn't locked either, and opened without a sound.

It took Martha a moment or two for her eyes to adjust to the dim light inside. When they did, they widened in surprise.

The small cabin was well tended and ordered, like a miniature kitchen-dining room. There was a booth table at the back, complete with a vase holding dried flowers. In the middle was a small stove and beneath it a fridge, humming with power supplied by a generator somewhere. Near the front, set into an alcove in the barge's hull, was a small bed.

And on the bed, a man of about forty was lying on his side, watching her. He looked like a detective from a *film noir*, in plain but clean clothes, with his face clean shaven and his hair combed neatly over to the side. He had a thin, pencil moustache that curled at the ends. He raised one eyebrow and cocked his head as Marta gasped.

'Erm ... I don't believe I've made your acquaintance, young lady, but it appears that you and your friends have just hijacked my boat.'

Chapter Forty-One
Rescue

AT TIMES, CARL FELT he was supporting a dead weight as they headed down into the dark railway tunnel. Jess would walk a few steps and then suddenly slump against his shoulder, making him pause to get her moving again. She didn't speak much, but she didn't cry either, and Carl could only guess at what was going through her head. The darkness of the tunnel was a relief sometimes, because it hid the painful vacancy in her eyes. He had learned through her earlier hysteria that the Huntsmen had murdered her parents just two days before, and now with Simon dead Jess had no one left to live for. She had talked about turning her knife on herself, so now Carl was carrying all the weapons just to be safe. It was just talk, though, he knew. Death might free her from the pain, but he knew that somewhere behind those empty eyes, Jess wanted to live, if only to seek revenge.

The driver, upon Carl's sudden appearance, had stopped the train. As honest a man as Carl had ever met, he had helped Carl carry Simon's body back into the trees, accepting Carl's muted explanations, asking no more questions than necessary. By the time the grave was dug and Simon's body had been laid to rest, Jess had climbed down from the train. Carl had found her wandering in circles, her eyes blank.

At Carl's request, the driver had taken the train on, leaving them behind.

For a while Jess had lain down on the ground, her body shaking with fever and shock. Carl had kept her warm and tried to comfort her.

Part of him shared her pain, now his own father was certainly dead too, while part of him resented her for taking away his time to grieve. In a few short minutes he'd gone from being the kid with the murdered father to the shoulder that supported Jess's grief. The world, so bright and easy just a few hours ago now seemed so dark and unjust. Carl had frowned up at the blue sky, willing it to cloud over; willing it to give him some sign that the way things happened was preordained, that life wasn't just controlled by the stupidity of chance.

The clear blue had beamed back at him unflinching until he turned away.

He had needed to drag her to get her moving. He'd thought to let her say goodbye to Simon before they buried him in the forest, but for the first time Jess had shown a reaction, angrily pushing him away.

'Let him rot!' she had screamed, getting up and marching off down the tracks. Carl knew her words weren't a reflection of her true feelings, but a result of the frailty and loneliness she felt. She had lost him, found him again and saved him. And then, when everything should have been getting better, he had been taken away.

Carl had followed her until she started to slow down, watched her as her legs began to shake, and then caught her as she started to fall. Supporting each other they had walked along the tracks, their shoulders slumped under the combined weight of their collective grief.

He had to find her friends. That was the only way to help her, but by now they should be inside Bristol GUA. There was only one unguarded way in that he knew of, and that was the same way the trains went: through the tunnels. To Carl's relief, the train had left them only a couple of miles from the Bristol GUA perimeter wall, which began to rise above the trees as they got closer; not as tall as London's but still foreboding enough. Beyond it, plumes of smoke rose into the air from dozens of industrial holdings, one or two large enough to be visible above the wall. The clunking sounds of machinery grew louder as they approached.

Jess had said nothing as Carl led them down into the railway tunnel, the darkness closing in about them, clammy like cold sweat.

After thirty minutes of walking, they could see nothing but the faint glow of occasional emergency strip-lighting in either direction. Carl figured the tunnel would eventually come out somewhere, but he hoped it was sooner rather than later because back down the line, the rest of those creatures were following.

Then, up ahead, he saw lights.

'Come on,' he said to Jess, nestled into his shoulder. 'We're almost through.'

The girl said nothing.

They emerged into an old underground station. Carl didn't know much about trains or city stations, but it didn't look like somewhere passengers would get on or off, but for freight loading and unloading. There were no seats on the platform edge, no sign that there had once been shops, timetables, or trash cans.

He found some steps at one end of the platform, and helped Jess up. It was a relief to be off the tracks, because another train would be due soon.

They went up some more stairs, away from the platform. Emergency lighting bathed the passageway in a dull orange glow, enough for them to see the dust on the floor, the few footprints where it had been disturbed. None looked too recent, which also came as a relief to Carl.

The passage thinned, and the tiles beneath their feet changed from a sandy colour to a darker grey. There was little dust here, suggesting the tunnel was still in use. It headed off in two directions. Carl chose left.

The passage angled slightly uphill, reaching a sharp corner at the top of the rise. Just as they reached it, Jess moaned and leaned against him, causing Carl to stumble forward around the corner. He was looking at Jess, and he only knew he'd bumped into someone when the other man pushed him away.

'Hey, you!'

Carl looked up. A man wearing the black uniform of the Department of Civil Affairs stood right in front of him. He looked like he had been in a fight: bruises shadowed his face and one eye was swollen shut. Behind him were two more agents, supporting the limp weight of another man. This one looked far worse. Long hair crusted with dried blood hung down around a bloodied and badly beaten face.

Carl stepped back. 'Sorry,' he muttered, for lack of anything else to say.

'Who the hell are you?' the DCA agent said, and reached into his pocket for something.

'We got lost?' Carl ventured. 'It's pretty dark down here.' He looked down at Jess to tell her to run, but the girl's eyes were open, focused, and narrowed with hatred. 'You!' she screamed, as she snatched a knife from Carl's belt and launched herself forward.

The other man still had one hand in his pocket when Jess reached him. He didn't have time to scream as her knife raked his throat, spraying blood across the walls. He fell back into the other men, causing them to let go of their prisoner.

Carl reached for a knife of his own as Jess slashed at the nearest of the other agents, opening a wound on his face. As the shocked man reached up to feel for the damage, Jess rammed the knife into his stomach. The agent grunted and fell backwards, trying to pull the knife free.

'You little bitch!' the third man shouted, but as he lunged for Jess the battered man swung a fist up between his legs. The agent doubled over in pain and Jess pounded him on the back of his neck. He grunted and tried to punch her, but she kicked him in the groin and he fell to the ground, coughing.

Jess walked among the fallen agents, looking for a pulse. The leader was dead, as was the second man, but the third man was lying curled up and clutching his groin, otherwise unhurt. Jess sighed, pulled the knife out of the second man's stomach and slit the third agent's throat with the weary nonchalance of a mother tidying a child's room.

Carl felt a sick feeling in his stomach as he watched the clinical way Jess finished off the DCA men. Much as he hated to admit it, her actions reminded him a little of Dreggo: cold, merciless.

Jess wiped the knife clean on the shirt of one of the dead men and slipped it into her belt rather than returning it to Carl. The beaten man was sitting against the wall, watching them.

'Thank you for saving me,' he said. 'My name is Ishael. Who are you?'

Jess actually smiled, but it was wild, almost macabre. 'We're the Tube Riders,' she said.

The man's eyes went as wide as the bruises and swellings would allow. 'Jess and Simon?' he asked. 'I know your friends! I've heard so much about you.'

Jess looked at Carl, then back at the man. The strength drained out of her face, and she stumbled back against the wall, putting her hands out to stop herself falling. Carl heard a high-pitched moan, like a distant door creaking. Then, slowly at first and then faster like a sudden flood, Jessica began to cry.

CHAPTER FORTY-TWO
CRUISE

'They built it way back. Heaven knows why, but it goes all the way down as far as Exeter. We'll be there before nightfall, I should imagine.'

The Tube Riders watched the man who called himself John Reeder as he sat cross-legged on the bed, smoking a pipe. The aroma of tea leaves filled the air, and Marta for one wished he'd put the stuff in a pot and offer it around. The canal water dripping through a strainer on the top of the boat didn't look so appetizing.

'Thank you for not throwing us overboard,' Owen said.

Reeder cocked his head and grinned. A clump of hair detached itself from his neatly gelled scalp and he hastened to realign it. 'It's not often I get visitors. Even the government leaves me alone, and how many people can say that? I haven't moved the *Old Rose* in a few months, but there's still enough power in the tank to get you to Exeter.' He tugged on one curl of his moustache and shrugged. 'Not that I have a lot of choice really, is it? It's too far for you to walk. Where are you headed from there?'

Marta said, 'We're not sure,' at the same time that Switch said, 'Falmouth.'

The others looked at him. 'What?' Paul said.

Switch grinned. His twitchy eye flickered like a bird trapped against a window. 'I didn't really have time to tell you about the plan. I figured I would when things had calmed down a bit.'

Marta flicked a thumb over her shoulder. 'We're taking a canal cruise. Is it quiet enough for you now?'

'I guess, yeah.'

Paul started to stand, then shot a wry glance at the low ceiling and sat back down. Owen, sitting on the floor in front of the fridge, was the only one who seemed comfortable.

'Do you want me to leave the room?' Reeder said with a wry smile. 'Remembering of course, that it is, er, my room?'

'Isn't it called a cabin?' Owen said.

Reeder grinned at him. 'I also charge for conversation.'

Marta watched the man as he talked. From the moment she'd burst into the cabin and found him lying on the bed she'd found him captivating to look at, but not in a sexual, attractive sense. He was just so *odd*, so out of place that it was like looking at a time traveler, someone pulled forward a hundred years in time just to help them.

The barge's cabin was immaculately decked out in a 1950s style. Black and white prints of long dead actors and actresses hung from the walls. An old, brightly coloured tea set stood on a rack above the fridge, the ancient spider-webbed china cups rattling as they moved through the water. A gas hob balanced a wrought iron kettle. Tucked into one corner, behind the bed, was a jukebox, the like of which Marta had only seen once before, in a junkyard. She was desperate to ask him if it worked.

Rather than be alarmed at their presence, John Reeder had seemed reluctantly excited, like an old explorer pulled out of retirement for one last mission.

'Uncle told me to head to Falmouth,' Switch said. 'He said there was a way there we could get across to France. Didn't say how, but said we'd get further instructions later.'

'Where's Falmouth?' Owen said.

'Cornwall,' Paul told him. 'Don't they teach you anything in school?'

'Ah, you know it's all censored. Where's Cornwall?'

'Cornwall is the south-western tip of England,' Reeder said. 'It's famous for its beautiful beaches, a type of pie called a pasty and was once popular among tourists. Main industries were tin mining, china clay quarrying, fishing and farming. Main recreational pursuits were surfing, moorland walking, and a rather odd style of wrestling, in which the defeated party would be thrown square on his back. These days, of course, most of it is empty.'

'Empty?' Owen said.

Reeder pouted and frowned. 'How would you say? The government *closed* it.' He looked around at the others. They were all staring at him. 'About halfway across, after the moorland ends, they built a fence. Made everybody who lived behind it leave.'

'Why?'

Reeder spread his hands. 'Why do they do anything? They have their reasons. Luckily, if we're heading for Falmouth, we won't have to go that far.'

'We?' Owen said.

Reeder raised another eyebrow. 'What kind of a hostage would I be if I didn't accompany my captors to their final destination?'

While they were floundering for a reply, he climbed up from the bed and walked over to the miniature kitchen, ducking his head to avoid the low ceiling. With five people in the cabin it must seem a lot smaller than usual, Marta thought.

'Now, we've got a few hours before we arrive, and you all look a little hungry. Would you like anything to eat?'

'Hell, yeah.'

'Thanks.'

'What do you have?'

John Reeder looked at Marta. 'Fish, my dear, and a few pilfered vegetables from the GFA. My diet doesn't vary much. I'm a simple man as you can see.'

Later, sitting up on deck while the small boat whirred along the canal, tall trees rising up on either side of them, Reeder told Marta about his life on the canal.

Downstairs, Paul, Owen and Switch were playing a game of Monopoly on an old board Reeder had pulled out of a cupboard. It was a welcome respite from all the violence and death, but Marta couldn't concentrate and preferred to be up on the deck, watching the countryside pass by. She'd seen little enough of it in her life, and despite the threat of the Huntsmen out there somewhere, it helped to calm her.

'It's an uneasy world we live in,' Reeder said, sitting on a stool, one hand on the boat's wheel, occasionally shifting it slightly from side to side. 'The government tried to compartmentalise everything, but those of us that didn't fit into any particular vein just got skipped over. No one cared about a young man living on a riverboat. How old are you, Marta?'

'Twenty-one.'

Reeder nodded, not looking at her. 'You've seen a lot, I suppose.'

She shrugged. 'Until recently life was just usual, you know? I saw car crashes, riots, whatever. It was all just *life*. I did what I had to do to survive. It was hard, but I was used to it.'

They had told Reeder a shortened version of their story. They had no choice but to trust him, and he seemed genuinely willing to help.

'You know,' he said, 'your legend stretches far. Even I've heard mention of it.'

'Really?'

'Many people talk about the wraiths of the Underground.'

She raised an eyebrow. 'Is that what they say?'

'They say that the souls of the dead reside down there in the dark, screaming their pain at those who dare enter the tunnels.' He smiled. 'Stories get around you know. Even though most people can't travel anymore, stories still move. They blow from place to place, like the wind.'

'I'm surprised.'

'Why do you do it? Why do you "tube ride"?'

The way he said it, as if it was the strangest thing in the world, made her smile. She shrugged again. It was difficult to explain. 'Why do people do anything?' she said. 'Because it's fun.'

'But it's so dangerous.'

'Yes, it is.'

'Have people died?'

'That I know of, five. Maybe there were others, practicing alone. I don't know.'

'That's a lot of death to see. Why didn't you stop?'

Marta looked around them as the canal bank eased past. A willow tree hung over the water, its nearest branches scraping the side of the boat. *So peaceful*, she thought.

'Many did. At one point there were over twenty of us. Seeing someone die, though, it changes things. It sorts out who values life the most. Because the people who value life don't do it.'

'Don't you value your life?'

Suddenly Marta felt close to tears. Hearing someone say it reminded her how worthless she was, how worthless the country had made her. 'My parents are dead. My brother disappeared years ago. I had nothing else to do. I just ... carry on.'

'How did you get into it?'

'My brother, Leo, he was the first.'

'The first Tube Rider?'

'Yes.'

'How?'

Marta brushed the hair out of her face and fresh tears out of her eyes, and smiled. 'It's kind of dumb, really. He was drunk or stoned, or something. He wandered into the station by mistake. At least this is the story he tells – told.' Her bottom lip trembled. 'A train came just as he tripped and stumbled towards the track. Had it come a second earlier it would have crushed him. As it was, it should have killed him, but it didn't. His coat got caught on something, a hook, a loose piece of metal paneling, maybe. It literally picked him up and pulled him along. He managed to free himself a moment before the train went into the tunnel. He broke several ribs and one arm, but otherwise he was fine. And afterwards...'

'What?'

She shook her head. 'It was like he was a different person. He was enlightened or obsessed, one of the two. All he talked about was the trains. He even got himself a job working in a rail yard just so he could study the trains and find out if there was a way to replicate what had happened. He got a friend to help him design and build the first clawboard. Then he went down into the tunnels and learned. He started off on the slower freight trains, practicing until he'd perfected the technique. And then he started to invite people.'

'Sounds exciting.'

Marta smiled again. 'Yeah. I didn't get into it at first because I was the kid sister, you know? He wanted to protect me, so he kept it a secret. With his train obsession I just thought he was some anorak nerd. Then one day I saw him when I was riding the train home. It scared the shit out of me, and I thought it was a premonition of his death or something. I told him and he owned up. He took me along a few days later and I ended up as hooked on it as he was.'

She shook her head, wistful memories coming back to her. 'Tube riding, it's like nothing you can imagine. It hurts, you know, when you hook, and the train jerks you away. But it's a good pain, like when you have sore muscles after a workout, and you can't stop touching them. And then, when you're riding, for a few seconds your mind just empties as though the train's moving so fast you just leave it behind. Then after you brace with your legs you can see the people inside the train through the windows. Sometimes they look back at you, and it's like looking into a book. You feel like you know everything about them. It's just ... magical.'

Reeder patted her shoulder. 'Marta, dear. I would love to give it a try.'

'It's way too dangerous.'

'For an old man, you mean?'

'John, that's not what I—'

Reeder laughed. 'You're probably, right. I'm too old to be hanging off the side of trains. Barges are far more my pace.'

They were quiet for a few minutes. Marta watched as fish jumped out of the water, and birds called from the trees. For a while she leaned over the side of the boat and let one hand trail in the water. Finally, she said, 'Thank you for helping us.'

'Never underestimate the kindness of strangers,' Reeder said with a wide smile. 'Not everyone has become what the government drove them to. Most people, especially out in the GFAs, are just trying to get on with their lives the best way they can.'

'They're the lucky ones.'

'You could say that. There might not be the violence, but they miss out on certain things too. They can't travel outside of their particular area. The government pulled up most of the roads, just to make it a hassle to get around. If they are inclined to drive thirty miles on the gravel and dirt tracks for whatever reason, they eventually come up against concrete road blocks. There are no soldiers anywhere, but there doesn't need to be. It's such an inconvenience to go anywhere other than where the government wants them to go that they don't bother.'

'I'd still like to live out in the country,' Marta said. 'It's just so peaceful. The air's so fresh.'

'Yeah, it has that going for it. I don't miss the cities.'

'How do you survive out here? Where do you get your food from?'

Reeder shrugged. 'This way and that way. People know me in some of the villages. I do farm work, labouring sometimes. Odd jobs. In some villages I'm known for the baskets I weave from the canal reeds. Hence the name. *John the Reeder.*'

'Is that not your real name?'

Reeder smiled. 'I'm known by different names in different parts. It's safer that way. I forget just which name preceded the others.'

Marta could understand. 'You don't look the sort to do odd jobs,' she said.

Reeder grinned. 'Just because a man likes to look the part in his own castle, doesn't mean he won't get his hands dirty when necessary. Like you say, the world's changed.'

The door opened. They both turned to see Switch coming up out of the cabin onto the deck. He looked around at the trees, his bad eye flickering. When he saw them sitting in the little driving space at the back of the boat, he walked over, looking a little uncertain as the boat rocked along. Reeder was following a course close to the outer bank as the canal arced gradually right towards open farmland. Switch looked afraid that they would crash at any moment, and Marta found it comical after all the dangerous things she'd seen him do.

'We nearly there yet?' he said, ashen faced. Marta grinned.

'Boats don't move as quickly as trains,' Reeder said. 'We're going about fifteen miles an hour. We have several hours before we make it to Exeter.'

'Oh.'

'You look unwell.'

'Yeah, not feeling so great, eh. Must be all the excitement.'

'Seasick?'

Switch looked embarrassed. 'Nah, man. Of course not.'

Reeder smiled. 'It's a lot easier when you're driving. You want to try?' He pointed at the little wheel and the drive stick beside it.

'Ah, no,' he said. 'Looks way too difficult.' But even as he spoke, he climbed down beside Reeder and pulled up another stool. 'What does this do?' he said, pointing at a black button.

Marta patted him on the shoulder and stood up. 'Enjoy, boys,' she said. 'I'm going to use some of those hours to try and sleep, if that's okay with both of you. Call me if anything happens.'

Switch ignored her. 'So this button makes the fucker start?'

'That's the ignition, yes.'

Marta smiled as she climbed over the top of the protruding cabin towards the little door at the front of the boat. The canal was leaving woodland behind and weaving out across open farmland. She saw tractors and trailers standing idle in one or two fields, but no people. An image of the Huntsmen flashed into her mind, and her smile faded.

She felt safe for now, sooner or later she would see those horrifying half-human faces again, she was sure of it. How many times could they keep escaping?

As she climbed down into the cabin, where Owen was demanding an extortionate rent payment from Paul, she wondered how long they had left before the chase finally came to an end.

CHAPTER FORTY-THREE
FAMILY VALUES

CLAYTON LOOKED DOWN at Vincent's body as the men zipped it into a body bag, getting one last view of the slash wound across the younger man's neck. He was torn between the urge to smile at the death of a disliked colleague or to grimace at the loss of an important prisoner. Instead, he just cocked his head and pouted a little, waiting for the results from Jakob, who was hauling a Huntsman along on the end of a leash.

'Two scents,' Jakob said at last. 'A boy and a girl.'

Clayton nodded. That matched the footprints they had found, heading back down into the railway tunnels. 'The Tube Riders?'

'Definitely the girl. The dog is straining at the bit. The boy, I don't know. The dog doesn't seem concerned by it. It doesn't make any sense. Who else could it be?'

Clayton nodded again and pulled a radio out of his pocket. He had set the receiver to silent when they came across the dead agents, and now the display told him someone had been trying to reach him. He punched in a frequency.

'About time,' came a familiar voice. 'Where the fuck have you been?'

He sighed. 'Dreggo. I hope you have news for me, because I have some for you.'

'What?'

'I'll ask the questions. What happened out there?'

'We lost another Huntsman. Both Meud and Jacul are dead.'

'I don't care about the Huntsmen, they're expendable.'

There was a momentary silence on the other end.

'Dreggo?'

Her voice came back sharp and strained. 'One of the Tube Riders is dead.'

Clayton's heart jumped. Finally. 'Which one?'

'The boy. We found his body in a shallow grave not far from the perimeter wall. What do you want me to do with it?'

Clayton rubbed his chin. 'Leave it. You didn't see the girl?'

'She escaped. Some kid from the GFA helped her. He could still be with her.'

Clayton sighed again. Well, at least one was down. 'Did you find the memory card?'

'No.'

'Search the body again.'

'Why?'

'Just do as I say, Dreggo.'

There was another silence, followed by: 'You said you had news. What is it?'

'Never mind. Just get here now.'

Her reply practically made the radio burn in his hands: 'Fuck you and every one of the polished turds in your organisation.' The line went dead. Clayton felt a momentary clamminess on his hands, but as his fingers closed over the little device in his pocket the fear went away. He still had control. She wasn't about to get it back. But still...

He pushed the thought out of his head. With Dreggo back around at least they had someone who had better control of the Huntsmen. The damn things were constantly on the verge of causing chaos. Part of him wished the Department of Civil Affairs had done the work alone, but he knew the kids would have escaped. The cities were a mess; there were a million places they could hide, and a million people to hide them.

A scent, however, couldn't disappear so easily.

The phone in his other pocket buzzed.

'Yes?'

'Leland? I trust operations are going well?'

'Like clockwork, of course. You have information for me?' He recognised the other voice as a man named Robert Wade, one of his intelligence experts from the London branch of the DCA. Wade was a rare man who could be depended on.

'I have information for you,' Wade told him.

'Yes?'

'Of what help it might be I don't know, but we've followed up your leads and we've uncovered the identities of some of these Tube Riders.'

'Really. Do you have anything interesting?' Clayton was feeling thoroughly pissed off, and he found it difficult to keep the cynicism out of his tone. All he had to do was catch a group of street kids and he seemed to be starting a whole goddamn war. Already, far too many people had died.

'Maybe. One of the girls, Jessica Woods … her, um, now deceased father, Martin Woods, was a lower member of the government. Paul and Owen Morton live in a flat in central London which they actually own. The other two, the boy and the one whom you said had a bad eye, we can't find anything on them. Perhaps they were runaways. However, you might want to look at the details for one Marta Banks.'

Clayton rolled his eyes. 'Will I, really?'

'Yes, Leland, I think you will. Get to a computer and take a look at the documents I send you. Something rather unexpected has come up.'

#

Dreggo and Lyen reached the station an hour later. The Huntsman hadn't said much during the journey, but Dreggo was feeling more attached to the creatures the longer she spent with them. Looking into the still-human eyes, seeing the tortured intelligence that burned there, she could ignore the doglike snout and the raw scar tissue where the two parts of its face had been surgically fused together. They were human still, caught in a government net that offered only death as a way out.

Dreggo saw Clayton coming towards them. At his side were two handlers and behind him came a group of DCA agents. She felt an immediate warning signal go off in her head. Clayton usually came towards her tentatively or with a show of forced confidence. This time, though, he walked with genuine purpose. She put a hand on her hip and felt a knife hidden there. Maybe this time, if she was quick...

'Secure it quickly, I want to take a look at it.' Clayton pointed at Lyen, and the two handlers moved forward.

'Back off!' Dreggo shouted. 'What the hell are you doing?'

'Don't worry, we won't hurt him.'

'Who the fuck do you think you are?'

'Stand away, Dreggo. I won't warn you again.'

She saw the remote in his hand and the certainty in his eyes. With a growl she stepped back as the handlers closed in and secured Lyen's wrists. They pushed the Huntsman to his knees.

'What do you want with him?'

One of Clayton's men handed him an envelope. 'We just want to try a little experiment. A little recognition game.' Clayton pulled a sheet of paper out of the envelope. 'You sure he's secure?' he asked the handlers. They nodded.

'I hope he rips your face off,' Dreggo muttered.

Clayton flashed a look at her, and uncertainty appeared for just a moment before the purpose returned. 'Does this one have a name?'

'Lyen,' one of the handlers said.

'How appropriate. Lyen. *Lion*.' He looked right into the Huntsman's eyes. 'Tell me, *Lion*, do you recognise this girl?'

He held up the sheet of paper. Dreggo couldn't see, but Lyen's eyes stared for a moment then went wide. They flicked back and forth across the paper, and his eyes narrowed in a frown, the wires over his head pulling tight. His lips curled back in a snarl and then he began to shake from side to side. The word that came from his mouth was mostly a growl, but Dreggo's acute hearing picked it up.

'Marta...'

Lyen jumped to his feet, wrenching his hands apart, the shackles creaking as they barely held. The Huntsman snapped at Clayton, but one of the handlers activated the leash remote, and Lyen jerked as a shock tore through him. Another pulled a bag over Lyen's head and sprayed him with something that stank of chemicals. The creature sunk to his knees, his breathing slowing.

'Clayton, what are you doing to him?'

He passed the picture to her. It was a faxed copy of a family photograph, mother, father, brother, sister. At first she didn't recognise any of them. Then, as she looked closer, the girl became familiar.

'That's–'

'Marta Banks, leader of the Tube Riders.'

Dreggo looked closer at the other people. The photograph was old; the girl could only be fourteen or fifteen. The boy was older, maybe–

'Oh my God.'

Dreggo pointed at Lyen, trussed and bound, his face hidden. 'Take off that fucking bag.'

Before Clayton could protest, one of the handlers pulled the mask away from Lyen's face. Dreggo looked down on the creature, slumped forward on its knees, its eyes staring into space. Human eyes ...

'Lyen. Lion. *Leo*. Right here, Dreggo, we have Leo Banks,' Clayton said. 'Lost brother of Marta, and if our intelligence reports are correct, formerly a Tube Rider.'

Dreggo couldn't take her eyes off him. Now that she looked closely, the eyes were the same, as was the face shape. Only the rest, the terrible rest, was different.

Clayton snorted. 'Not that easy to see the family resemblance these days, is it?'

#

The Governor looked around his ruined room. The array of ornaments and precious artwork lay smashed and scattered across the floor. Tables and chairs were upturned, some of them in pieces. The cabinets along the wall had fallen forward, revealing old, stained wallpaper beneath. A door into an inner chamber had come loose of its hinges, and even the huge bay window had a small hairline crack.

The Governor took a deep breath, feeling the pull inside his body that the power had caused, feeling the urge to continue, to destroy more, to smash everything he could until the power grew so great that it destroyed him, too.

He let it go, regretting its onset but regretting more his inability to control it. Fearsome though it was, his power was unpredictable. He did not know how great its full potential could be, but it had been easy enough for him to seize power, to keep him in control of Mega Britain for more than forty years. It had enabled him to establish a state that barely remembered the past, and to control his subjects through a mixture of fear and misleading promises. And he wouldn't need it much longer; his spacecraft were almost ready. Just a few more years...

And now everything was threatened by a group of street kids. Power or not, he couldn't defeat an entire army. His own military was weakened by the transferring of material resources to the space program, and the Huntsmen, together with Dr. Karmski's other prototypes, while strong, were too few. His hopes had rested on keeping the European Confederation at bay with a series of charades, but if those kids managed to get across the Channel...

He pulled the internal phone off the wreckage of his desk and pressed the button for reception.

'Get my car,' he said, in chocolate-smooth tones. 'I'm going to Cornwall.'

He put the phone back down. He knew from Clayton's reports that the Tube Riders were heading that way. To what end he didn't know, but it was time to find out.

Chapter Forty-Four
Train

JESS WAS QUIET NOW as they headed down through the tunnels. Occasionally Carl glanced back at her, watching the way she absently stroked the dirty walls, her eyes following the trails in the grime left by her fingers. As they walked, Carl explained what had happened to his father and Simon to the man called Ishael, who turned out to be the leader of Bristol's Underground Movement for Freedom, an organization even Carl had heard of out in the GFA.

'I can only tell you how sorry I am for your loss and for hers,' Ishael said. His voice was muffled; the swelling around his jaw made speech difficult. 'Too many have died already, but I think this is just the start.' He in turn had recounted his knowledge of recent events: the arrival of the Tube Riders in Bristol, the attempt of his men to halt the charge of the Huntsmen and their overwhelming defeat, his capture and subsequent torture at the hands of the DCA agents.

'I don't know where they were taking me,' Ishael said, a haunted look in his eyes. 'But I expected to die.' Carl saw that the fingernails were missing on Ishael's middle, ring and little fingers of his right hand, and how Ishael grimaced with every step he took, as if someone had beaten his feet.

Carl had found a radio on the body of one of the dead men and now Ishael held it up. 'If there was a signal down here I could contact my men,' Ishael said. 'I know the frequency, but these walls ... they're just too thick and we're too far below ground.'

Carl didn't know where they were going, but both Ishael and Jess were slowing them down. Jess was unresponsive, but to Ishael he said, 'Can you please try to move a bit faster? The Huntsmen could be on us at any moment.'

The other man gave a pained half-grin, and Carl knew that once, not so long ago, he had been handsome. 'I'll do my best.'

Carl had also pulled three guns off the bodies of the DCA men. He had one, while Ishael had the others. Jess had made no response when he'd tried to give her one, looking right through him as though she were somewhere else entirely. Now, Carl held his own in front of him as he moved, even though he'd never fired a real gun before. He imagined it had a far stronger kickback than an air rifle.

They reached another fork in the tunnel. 'Head left,' Ishael said. 'Right goes back to the surface. We have to get out of the city, try to meet up with the others. The best way to do that is to steal a train.'

'You're joking, right?'

Ishael shook his head. 'The government has no heavy artillery. Mega Britain's army is mostly limited to foot soldiers, some old robots, and the Huntsmen. We don't know what missiles or other weapons they might be hiding, but there is practically no known air force or heavy ground artillery. So, what can possibly stop a train?'

#

A short distance further on they found a flight of stairs that led up to a loading bay. There they found a stationary train, its trucks standing empty. There were no guards in sight, and they were able to approach the cab unnoticed. Ishael, terrifying with his bruised and bleeding face and clearly at home with guns, hauled open the door, and with a wave of his stolen weapon instructed the surprised driver to start the engine and pull out of the station while Jess and Carl climbed into the cab. As the train groaned to life guards came running, but too late. The train, hijacked by a blond-haired, bright-eyed kid, a man with a battered face, and a red-eyed, mute girl was away.

Picking up speed, they roared out of Bristol Temple Meads station and away through the city, past old, crumbling city centre housing estates and large factories billowing smoke up into the air in great grey-white plumes. The side of the Avon Gorge rose in a wave up to their left, while the city swept away to their right, the apartment blocks and office high-rises poking up into the sky, with only the absence of any reflecting sunlight revealing their missing windows, their abandonment. Ishael sighed and muttered something about how it still looked the same as ever. Having never seen a city before, Carl couldn't comment.

'Where do you want to go?' the driver spat, showing more anger than fear. It had been a relief to Carl that the driver was not the kindly one who had helped him bury Simon.

'As far away as possible. Cornwall.'

'The line ends in Exeter but that doesn't matter. They're gonna catch you, you know.'

'We'll see.'

Carl listened to the exchange with nervous interest. He hoped the driver wouldn't try anything. For one thing he wasn't sure how to fire the gun in his pocket, and for another, while shooting a monstrous, murdering creature like a Huntsman was one thing, shooting an innocent person was quite something else. He wasn't convinced that Ishael knew quite what he was doing, but the longer they were in the train the further they got from the Huntsmen, and that was fine by him.

'You have a problem,' the driver said, pointing at a flashing light on the dashboard.

'What?'

'See that? It means they've switched the rails at the next junction. We're going to move over on to the other line about a mile further on.'

'The other line? Where does it go?'

'Same as this one.'

'So what's the problem?'

'The other line is for incoming. Anything coming along that track is going to hit us unless we stop and go back.' The man grinned, revealing gaps between blackened teeth. 'Huh. They must really hate you.'

'Is there any way we can override it?'

'No.'

What can stop a moving train? Carl remembered Ishael's question now, and thought he knew the answer.

Another train.

Ishael's eyes hardened and he jabbed the gun into the man's neck. 'Tell me. Believe me, I am desperate enough to kill you.'

'Okay, okay, but it's pretty useless. There's a manual lever half a mile from the junction. We hit that, the junction switches back.'

'Can we slow down, get out and do it?'

'We could, but there's another train behind us.' The man gestured towards a side mirror outside the train's window. 'We slow down and that one hits us. Good God, what have you people done?'

Ishael punched the dashboard with his free hand, immediately wincing. 'Shit, shit, *shit!*'

Carl reached into his bag. 'I can do it,' he said.

'What?'

Carl held up his catapult. 'I'm pretty good. I didn't have much to do outside of school, you know. I used to shoot at signs all the time. Sometimes birds and animals, although I used to feel a little guilty whenever I hit one.'

Ishael tried to laugh. 'You're joking, right?'

'Do we have a choice?' Carl replied. 'We have nothing to lose.' He glanced at Jess. The girl's empty stare followed the tracks as the train rushed forward, swallowing them up. She veered between frightening intensity and hollow emptiness as she battled with what haunted her. He wondered then if she would either notice or care if they smashed headlong into an oncoming train.

'Do you have a rock or something?' Carl asked.

Ishael looked around, but it was the driver who handed him something heavy from his pocket. It was a small hip flask. 'I couldn't give a fuck about you people but I don't particularly want to die either,' the driver said.

'It'll have to do,' Carl said. He wound down the window of the train and leaned out. A strong wind buffeted him in the face, making it nearly impossible to hold the catapult steady with its unlikely ammunition resting in the cradle.

'That's it up ahead,' the driver said. At first Carl couldn't see what he meant, and then he spotted it: a lever about three feet long, sticking out of a metal box with a flashing red light on the side. It was just like in the cartoons he had watched as a little kid, but damn was it thin, and it was coming so fast he barely had time to aim.

'Slow the train as much as you can!' Ishael shouted at the driver.

'You've got to hold my shoulders,' Carl said. 'I can't keep it steady.'

Ishael glanced at the driver, then at Jess. He put his gun in Jess's palm, folded her fingers over it and turned her hand so the gun pointed at the driver. Jess didn't react. 'She will shoot you,' Ishael told the man. 'If you make a move, she *will* shoot you.'

Ishael moved behind Carl and braced himself against the back of the cab. Carl smelt dried blood on Ishael's fingers as he put his hands on Carl's shoulders. Carl lifted the catapult, lining up the shot. He'd done this a thousand times in the forest, jumping and rolling, diving out of trees, over walls, aiming at rabbits, foxes, deer. He'd hit more often than not, but even when he missed he'd always get another shot, sooner or later. There would be no other shot this time.

Ishael's raw breathing tickled his ear as he tensed the catapult, the cradle held in his fingers, the metal hip flask pointed slightly up.

Ready, aim...

He let his fingers open and the little flask shot through the air, momentarily outrunning the train. Then, to Carl's amazement, it clanged against the lever and was gone, falling into the overgrown grass verge. In a moment the lever was behind him too as the train rushed past. Carl tried to look back to see if it had shifted or not, but it was already too far behind to tell.

'You got it!' Ishael shouted, just as a deafening gunshot rang through the cab. The driver gasped. Carl looked around and saw the man fall against the control panel and then slide to the floor, blood oozing from a head wound.

Carl stared at the dead man then looked up at Jess, her steady gaze on the body between them. He gripped the window edge and tried to force his breathing to slow. His heart was thundering faster than the wheels of the train over the sleepers below them.

'What happened?' Ishael asked Jess. 'Jess? What did he do?'

The girl didn't look at him. Her fingers opened and the gun dropped to the floor.

Ishael turned to Carl. He looked grim. 'Between you and me we have to figure out how to drive this thing,' he said.

'There's the junction,' Carl said, pointing through the front window. Half a mile ahead a second line branched off from the first. In the distance, they could see another train moving towards them, at this distance as thin and silent as a snake.

'I see it,' Ishael said.

'Are you sure it worked? I didn't see the lever move.'

They stared at the junction as they approached. It was impossible to tell which way the train would go, and Carl's eyes flicked from the rails to the other train and back. He felt Ishael's bloody fingers digging into his arm.

Ten seconds away, nine, eight, seven, six, five, four, *threetwoone* –

They screamed as the train jigged left, jerking them into the path of the oncoming train. Carl covered his face with his hands, resigned to the coming impact. Beside him, Ishael was shouting out for him to *open the door*, but his mind failed to recognise the command as the other train thundered towards them. He wanted to shut his eyes, but he couldn't, just *couldn't*, take them off the oncoming train–

—which suddenly jigged to their right, ducking away from them like a cobra vying for an opening in its prey's defenses, and then it was past them, roaring alongside their train and gone, disappearing in the mirrors behind them as it headed in towards Bristol. Another scream faded away on Carl's lips. He looked down to see that Ishael's blunt fingers had left bruises on his forearm.

'What just happened there?' Ishael asked, his voice shaking. He had bitten into his already swollen lip. Fresh blood dribbled down his chin.

'I don't know.'

'He lied,' a quiet voice said.

They turned to see Jess looking up at them, her face still devoid of emotion.

'What?'

'That wasn't a junction override,' she said. 'He just wanted you near the door, to give him a chance to push you out. He controlled the junction from the dashboard.' She pointed at a small computer display. Carl saw red lines on it and flashing symbols which must signify their train and oncoming rail junctions, but it was all gibberish to him. He didn't even know how to drive a car.

'I saw him press it,' Jess said. 'He knew that the other driver would want to avoid the crash and would open up an earlier junction, which is what he did.'

Carl didn't really understand. Ishael just shook his head and thanked Jess. The girl said nothing.

'We still have a train on our tail,' Carl said. 'What do we do about that?'

Ishael shrugged. 'I don't know.'

'Easy,' Jess said, in that same monotone. 'You release the trucks. Block the tracks.'

Carl smiled. 'I suppose you know how to do that, too?'

Jess pointed at another control screen. 'This one,' she said.

'You were watching him all along, weren't you?' Ishael asked her.

The tone of Jess's voice didn't change; neither did she look at him.

'Yes,' she said. 'I watched.'

Chapter Forty-Five
Bloodlust

Dreggo stood by the canal bank with a group of Huntsmen clustered behind her. The handlers stalked around them like lion tamers, their hands guarding the leash remotes. She was beginning to realise just how damaging the neuro-stunners could be: several of the Huntsmen twitched erratically or rolled on the ground, their faces shielded. One, back at the station, had failed to get up from a series of stuns. The others had watched the assault cautiously, their eyes flicking to Dreggo as though willing her to bid them attack the men who tortured them in the name of control. Despite their frayed, irrational minds, they were beginning to trust her.

She looked at the canal bank, at the scrapes in the earth where the Tube Riders had gone down into the water. Her Huntsmen had checked the other side, and found no evidence that they had ever got out over there. The canal, Clayton had told her, was part of a route built in the early years of Mega Britain as an alternative freight line between Exeter and London, to be used in the event of serious fuel shortages on the railways. Despite his assurances that it was no longer in active use, that there were no boats on it, she knew he was wrong. The Tube Riders had found something to take them away.

The scent had gone, of course. Even Huntsmen couldn't track through water, but Dreggo had no doubt it would be easy to cut the Tube Riders off. Two Huntsmen were already in pursuit, and unless the Tube Riders had found something with an engine, the Huntsmen would run down their quarry within an hour. There was no direct road that followed the course of the canal, and

Clayton's plan was to get in front of the Tube Riders and lie in wait.

'You can take them back now,' Dreggo said to the handlers. 'Take them to the train station and get your orders from Clayton there.'

'They went downriver?' one of the handlers asked.

'Unless they flew away.'

The man grunted. He barked orders at the other handlers and they started to move off, the Huntsmen clustered between them.

Dreggo sighed. She looked out at the water, and despite the conflict she felt inside she could appreciate how peaceful it was. There was another time, perhaps, another life, in which she would have sat down by the canal side and drifted off to sleep as the sun warmed her face, and the birds sung in the trees. Not now, though. There was too much blood on her hands, too much hate in her heart.

The radio fizzed in her pocket, startling her. She took a step backward as she dislodged a loose rock with her foot and sent it tumbling into the water.

The call was from Clayton.

'What do you want?'

'You've sent the Huntsmen back?'

'The others, yes. The two I sent to follow the canal have orders to report any sightings of the Tube Riders or wait in Exeter if they find nothing. I'll keep in contact with them.'

'Good. I hope you chose the Huntsmen wisely. I don't want them going haywire out in the countryside.'

Dreggo thought of the slaughter she herself had initiated in the Reading GFA. 'They won't,' she said. 'What have you done with Leo?' She found it impossible not to use the Huntsman's real name.

'Nothing. We're keeping him safe. I have a feeling he might come in useful.'

Dreggo said nothing. On the other end of the line she heard Clayton shouting at someone.

'Dreggo? You still there? Jesus fucking Christ. We've had another setback. Meet us by the gate the Tube Riders broke out of. We have to go by road because the others blocked the railway line.'

'How did they do that?'

'Don't ask. We'll meet you by the gate in twenty minutes. If you want to make yourself useful, get the Huntsmen to sort out the scrap by the gate. We have a bit of a situation there. A few civilians tried to get out while the gate was down. All the obvious rebels were killed or chased off, but a group of the general populace thought it would take the opportunity to have a goddamn picnic. I want the uprising quelled and the gate secured.'

Dreggo's heightened awareness sensed an extra tenseness in his voice. 'Clayton, what is it?'

She heard him sigh. 'It looks like we're going to have company. The Governor himself is coming down. He's going to meet us in Exeter.'

'Oh.'

'Yeah. So just get the job done.'

Before she could say anything else, Clayton cut the line. Dreggo frowned. If the Governor was coming, that was bad news for Clayton. She suppressed a little smile. Maybe, just maybe, she might have a chance to take them both out.

The faint sound of a gunshot broke the tranquility of the canal bank, reminding her of the world she lived in. A mile away, just inside the city gate, people were starting to die, and later, perhaps, their blood would be on her hands. With her face set in stone, she headed back through the trees, following the trail left by the Huntsmen and their handlers.

#

Outside the gate, Clayton grimaced. With Vincent's death, things had started looking up. Now that brief glimmer of hope had been quashed by the news that the Governor himself was coming to meet them.

'Get ready to roll out,' he shouted, as his men climbed up into the back of a battered old removal truck. They'd arrived by train and didn't have time to wait for reinforcements from London so Clayton had been forced to use what road transportation he could find. The underfunded Bristol branch of the DCA had come up with a serviceable land cruiser for himself, but his men had to make do with the hard wooden floor of a vehicle designed for carrying tables and sofas.

The Huntsmen, though, had fared even worse. The third of Clayton's commandeered vehicles was an old freezer truck with the coolant system turned off, and a hole broken through the back for ventilation. The creatures whined like cattle being sent off for slaughter as they were loaded up and sealed inside.

Not for the first time, Clayton cursed his country's lack of forethought. Tearing up the roads might have seemed like a good idea at the time, but he was faced with a tough, three-hour drive to Exeter.

'They're ready,' Dreggo said from behind him.

He turned to look at her. Back through the gate, a group of his men were setting fire to the piled bodies of the rioters. Her face was flecked with blood, her expression grim, and he knew she had unleashed the full horror of the Huntsmen. He wondered how she felt now. Most of the rioters had fled, but more than fifty were dead, their bodies torn apart.

'I guess you could call the gate secured,' he told her with a wry smile. 'Blocked with bodies.'

Her single human eye watched him impassively. 'He will kill you, you know,' she said.

Clayton felt a flash of anger at her bluntness and his fingers closed over the remote device in his pocket as he took a step closer.

'Not before I kill you first,' he said.

'Those people, and the others, and the ones yet to die,' Dreggo made a sweeping movement with her arm. 'It's all in your government's name.'

'You gave the order,' he said. 'You're more of a beast than they are, more of a beast than I'll ever be. After all, I stand for the principles of this country, such as they are. I live to protect it.'

'Good for you.' She turned and stalked away. Clayton watched her climb up into the back of the removal truck with his men.

'Animal,' he said bitterly, but as he turned to follow her he wondered whether he should be referring to her or to him.

#

As the truck bumped along the cracked and torn up tarmac of an old highway, Dreggo didn't look at the men who sat around her, their weapons resting on their knees. She sat right at the back, and as darkness fell outside she tried to let it drown out the pain in her head, the buzzing in her limbs, the low humming of fourteen hurting souls suffering inside the old freezer truck. Killing hurt the Huntsmen too, more than anyone knew, but like an addiction it just drove them on while their souls steadily died. The killing frenzy at the gate had sucked another layer away from the remnants of their sanity. It would not be long before they had nothing left to give.

Dreggo had given no order to attack.

She'd walked slowly back through the woods, her heart heavy, and had reached the gate just as the short battle was coming to a close. The handlers, anticipating her orders, had shocked the Huntsmen into a blind rage and then set them loose. She'd reached the gate to find her charges practically ankle deep in blood.

She tried to close her eyes, but all she could see were a thousand sickles swinging out of the darkness towards her.

Chapter Forty-Six
Crossed Paths

'WE'RE COMING UP TO EXETER,' Ishael said, glancing back at Jess and Carl. The girl was sitting in a corner, her chin on her knees. Carl was leaning out of the window, the wind blowing his hair back over his face. *Neither should be part of any of this*, Ishael thought. *They're both too young. They didn't need their lives ruined.*

'What happens there?' Carl asked.

'The line ends. We look for some other way to continue.'

'Where are we going?'

Ishael watched him. Carl looked more than tired, and despite the pain Ishael had suffered from the beatings, he knew that Carl was hurting worse. He was being braver than his years, and Ishael wondered how long it would be before cracks started to appear.

'We're going into Cornwall,' he said. 'We think there's a way to get across to France from there.'

'How?'

He wasn't keen to tell Carl what he knew until he'd managed to speak to William back in Bristol. So far, he'd had no luck with the radio, and he feared for his old friend's safety. 'I'll tell you as soon as I know,' he told Carl. 'In any case, Cornwall gives us a better chance because there are no people there.'

'None? Why not?'

'The government emptied it. Quite why, I'm not entirely sure, but the rumours cover everything from a military testing ground to a "play area" for government tourists. One person I spoke to years ago said that in Cornwall there were golf courses as far as the eye could see, and barely a soul using them.'

'Well, I'd prefer that to a military shooting range any day,' Carl said.

'Me too. I guess we'll find out soon.' Ishael dabbed at a deep gash on his cheek with a piece of gauze they had found in a medical kit in the train's cab. He'd told Carl earlier that he'd hit his face on the ground after his captors had pushed him. He didn't know why he'd lied; after all it appeared Carl had seen many terrible things himself, but something about the look in that DCA man's eyes as he'd dragged the piece of broken glass across Ishael's face like he was slicing butter, his dark eyes never once flickering with concern or guilt or regret, haunted Ishael enough to set that one aside, cover it over with fallacies and hope it stayed buried. Their pounding fists and kicking feet had been anger and resentment, but the glass, a piece from a broken window, had been pure callousness. Most of his wounds would heal and fade with time, but that one would stay forever.

'Can you do something for me?' he said, holding the radio out to Carl. 'The buttons hurt my fingers.'

'Sure. How does it work?'

Ishael showed him how to use it. 'We gave Jess's friends a radio. We need to try to arrange a rendezvous point. Your contact is called Switch. This frequency should work, but we're not getting through so see if you can pick up something else. Also, listen out for anyone trying to contact us from Bristol.'

'Okay, no problem.' Carl started to fiddle with the radio, but something else caught his attention. 'Wow! Look at that!'

The railway line made a gradual incline into a copse that stood at the bottom of a gentle valley. Evening was closing in, but the clouds had cleared just enough for them to make out the land around them, all disused farmland, the fields overgrown with shrubs, bracken and nettles.

Beyond the copse, the spires of a tall cathedral were lit up against the night.

'That's Exeter Cathedral,' Ishael said.

'Can we go take a look?'

Ishael gave him as sympathetic a look as his battered face would allow. The boy seemed to have momentarily forgotten the situation they were in. 'I'm afraid not,' he said. 'Exeter Urban Area is closed off like all the rest.'

Carl nodded to show he understood. Rising up beyond the copse a few miles distant he saw the grey barrier that kept people out of the city – Exeter UA's perimeter wall. 'That's a shame,' he said.

'We're not going inside. Our pursuers may have radioed ahead, depending on what back-up, if any, resides in the city.'

'What do they do in Exeter?' Carl asked.

'Textiles,' Ishael said. 'They make our clothes.'

'It's clever, really, to put all the same industries in the same place,' Carl said.

'I guess,' Ishael said, trying to keep the frustration out of his voice. Much as he liked Carl, he wondered what naivety was breeding out in the GFAs. 'I imagine that the idea was to focus people's efforts.'

Carl looked back at Jess. 'Are you okay?'

The girl took an age to look up at him, but when she did she nodded. 'Yes,' she said. 'When are we getting off?'

'In a couple of minutes,' Ishael said. 'Any luck with that signal, Carl?'

'Not yet.'

'Keep trying. Okay, I'm going to slow us down now.'

A few minutes later the train had slowed to a crawl. Carl and Jess picked up their things.

'Aren't you going to stop it?' Carl asked.

'No. I'll let it run right on into the station. If Exeter UA has been notified, then a runaway train will certainly focus their attention for a while. Not too fast, though. Enough people have died today as it is.'

Carl nodded. For such a young boy his face looked weary, haggard. 'Yeah, I noticed.'

'Okay, get ready to jump. I imagine this is going to be a lot easier for you two than it is for me.'

As he looked up, Jess actually smiled. 'We're barely moving,' she said, and stepped out on to the ground.

'Yeah, well,' Ishael muttered, thinking at the same time how good it was to see the girl smile.

Carl jumped down after her. Ishael tapped a new speed into the train's digital control and jumped down last, landing in a heap just as it began to speed up. He rolled over, feeling the press of a dozen welts and bruises. The train moved away from them towards Exeter UA, slowly picking up speed.

'Okay,' he said. Let's get clear of the tracks. Preferably to somewhere where we can see people coming in case we need to move quickly.'

Carl pointed. 'Top of the ridge?'

'That's good.'

#

The fizzing sound was coming from Switch's bag.

'What's that?' Marta said, looking around. 'Paul, can you grab his bag?'

The fizzing noise came again. Paul, still playing monopoly with Owen, pulled Switch's bag over. He unzipped it and rummaged around inside. 'God, he's got a lot of stuff in here! Knives, guns ... ah! What the hell? He's got a damn radio!'

He pulled out what looked like a large mobile phone but with less buttons.

'It's a walkie talkie,' Owen said. 'We had some of them in school. In science class we used to use them to call each other from different rooms.'

'Do you know how to answer it?' Marta asked.

'Press the red button,' Owen said.

'Hello?' Paul spoke into the mouth piece.

'Stevie? Is that you?'

Paul held up the phone to Marta and Owen. 'It's William,' he said, somewhat bemused.

Owen hit Paul with a pillow. 'Well, answer him then!'

#

'This way,' Ishael said, leading Carl upslope towards a thin stand of trees on the hilltop. Jess had gone on ahead, and was now sitting with her legs pulled up to her chin, facing away from them. Whether her eyes were scanning the surrounding countryside for the canal or just staring vacantly into space where the memories of Simon and her parents waited, Carl couldn't tell.

A few minutes earlier they had finally managed to pick up a signal, this one from Ishael's friend William, back in Bristol GUA. 'From what William told me, this supposed canal should pass by the southern side of Exeter,' Ishael said, sounding a little more positive now he knew his friend was safe. 'We should be able to see it from the top of the rise.'

'Jess doesn't seem to be getting too excited,' Carl said. 'Maybe William was wrong.'

'Let's hope not. We'll try to get back in contact when we reach the top.'

'You know,' Carl said, his voice wistful as he led Ishael up towards Jess, 'I used to dream of something like this happening. Going on an adventure and all that. Like in a storybook. Except now that I am, I'd so much rather be back at home. Doing homework, even.'

Ishael tried to smile. 'When you dream of adventure, you never see the blood so red,' he said.

They continued up the hill. Back to the right Carl could see over the perimeter wall of Exeter, see the rows of houses built on a hillside, the spire of the cathedral poking up from among them. He could see the railway line where it passed through the perimeter wall, could even see part of the track on the inside before it disappeared among the houses. He wondered what had happened to the driverless train engine.

They reached the ridge summit. Jess didn't look up at them as they put their bags down. 'See anything?' Ishael asked her.

'No water,' she replied.

Ishael cursed. 'Damn it, there should be a canal passing by somewhere along here. That's what William said. Carl, please try the radio again.'

Carl began to flick through the frequencies. Then he had a thought. He stood up, scanning the valley below them.

'What is it?' Ishael asked.

Carl turned to him. 'You said it's a canal, right?'

'Yes.'

'And it's no longer used?'

'That's right.'

'Canals aren't like rivers, you know. They take maintaining. A continuing water supply, dredging, that kind of thing. If no one uses them, they tend to go to seed.'

'You mean–'

'It could be silted up, overgrown. It could be right in front of us but we can't see it because there's no water at this end.'

'William said the canal went right to Exeter.'

'It probably does. But that doesn't mean it can be navigated that far by boat.'

Jess stood up. She pointed towards a line of trees. 'There.'

A thin line of trees arced through the middle of the valley and then swung around the rise below them, angling in the direction of Exeter. They hadn't noticed because of the rest of the forest in the valley, but now that Jess pointed it out, it was easy to see the slightly darker green of the fast-growing coniferous trees that had been planted along the canal side. Where they could see between them in places was just a belt of green, like an old forest trail.

'I thought it was an old railway line,' she said.

'Grab your things. We have to go,' Ishael said. 'We need to find where the others landed before it gets too dark to see.'

'The Huntsmen will be on our trail,' Carl said. 'Even if we find the others, how are we going to escape?'

Ishael patted him on the shoulder. 'One problem at a time, please. Come on, let's go.'

#

'I thought you said it went right to Exeter.'

Reeder glanced back at Paul as they climbed off the boat. 'It does. You just can't go that far by boat. It's a nice cycle ride, however. In the unlikely event that you happen to have a bicycle.'

For the last mile or so the canal had made a thin course through swampy green water, reeds and other water plants pressing in from either side, leaving only a thin navigable channel in the centre of the canal. Eventually Reeder had docked them at a section of bank he told them he had cleared himself. Beyond it the canal was completely closed off by vegetation.

'Don't worry,' Reeder said, leading them through the woods. 'You'll meet with your friends as planned.'

Owen, directly behind him, stopped. He put out a hand and Switch walked into it.

'Hey, kid, watch out!'

Owen turned to the others. 'I think we should stop trusting this guy,' he said. 'How do we know he's not been paid off to turn us in?'

Marta sighed. 'Owen, quit it. We'd either be dead or in a lot of pain by now if it wasn't for John.'

'He's nuts!'

Paul and Switch took one of Owen's shoulders each. 'Come on, kid,' Paul said. 'We'll get you some comic books as soon as we can.'

'Don't treat me like an idiot. Are we going to walk all the way to Falmouth, wherever the hell that is?'

Reeder turned around. He had a wide smile on his face. 'He's a bright one, your brother,' he said to Paul. 'Perhaps the rest of you should be less trusting of a kind hand. Something to consider as your journey continues. However, while I might live on a boat, from time to time I need to get around on land. Follow me.'

Marta raised an eyebrow at Switch who just shrugged as they followed John Reeder along a thin path cut through the woodland. Owen stood his ground a while, hands on hips, before giving up and following, cursing under his breath. As he dragged his feet along behind the others, Paul turned around. 'Don't get left behind,' he said with a smile.

'Yeah, yeah. I'm coming.'

'Don't worry, you'll have more chances to be a hero later.'

Owen just wrinkled his nose and shook his head.

#

They were halfway down the hillside when they saw the convoy. A land cruiser followed by two trucks, bumping quickly along a dirt road that swung down through the valley from the north. Full darkness was less than half an hour away, but still the vehicles had no lights on.

'We run, now!' Ishael shouted. 'The Huntsmen are in there!'

'Are you sure?'

'As sure as I need to be! Come on!'

Moving in an awkward, shambling gait that reminded Carl of some of the old men who sat outside the village pub on a Sunday afternoon, Ishael led them down towards the woodland and the dried up section of canal. The road ran parallel along the opposite side of the valley. As they reached the trees they heard the sound of the trucks as they passed by, less than three hundred feet away.

'Pray they're shut up tight,' Ishael said. 'They smell us now, we're dead.'

Carl glanced back towards Jess. The girl wore her rucksack on her back, the clawboard sticking out the top. In each hand she held a knife.

Through the trees they heard the sound of a vehicle slowing down.

'Faster!' Ishael hissed.

They dashed through the trees, trying to follow the course of the dry canal. Ishael went first, Carl behind him, trying to shepherd Jess. The girl seemed intent on being last, or perhaps the first to die should the Huntsmen capture them, Carl thought.

In front of him, Ishael tripped on a root and tumbled to the ground. Carl hauled him up again but Ishael's injuries were starting to slow him down. As they moved off again, Jess continued to bring up the rear, eyes scanning the forest behind them.

'Come on,' Carl heard her whisper.

Ishael looked around them. They had moved away from the dry canal because of a thicker area of trees. Now, in the falling darkness, he looked disorientated.

'Shit, which way were we going?'

Carl pointed. 'I think it's back that way.'

'Are you sure?'

'Wait.' Carl looked around for a rock. Testing its weight in his hands, he threw it hard up into a tree to their right.

With a collective cry a small flock of roosting birds rose and flew off to their left. Carl pointed in the opposite direction. 'That way is Exeter. Which means the canal is ... over there. Come on.'

As they moved Ishael cocked his head at Carl. 'Are you sure?'

'Birds never fly towards a settlement,' Carl said. 'Just one of the things you learn from spending the majority of your childhood in a forest.'

'Listen!' Jess shouted. 'Another truck.'

They squatted down low and listened. Through the trees they could hear the sound of another vehicle coming towards them.

'Do we go back?' Carl asked.

'No, we'll be surrounded. We have to try and get around it before it stops and unloads its men.'

They moved on through the trees, more cautiously now. The ground beneath their feet was getting soggy, so they had to be close to the canal again. Maybe here they would find Jess's friends.

Again they heard the grumble of a truck engine, behind them this time. They quickened their pace through the trees, swatting aside the low hanging branches and leafy foliage that clawed at their faces.

And then Carl bumped into Ishael, who had stopped in front of him. Jess almost ran into them both, looking up just in time to stop herself.

'What do we do now?' Carl said.

The woodland had ended. In front of them an open meadow stretched away alongside the clogged waters of the old canal. To their right the valley side rose, with barely a tree for cover. There was nowhere to hide.

'We have to hurry,' Ishael said. 'If they unload the trucks it won't take the Huntsmen long to find our scent. We have to stay close to the canal. If necessary, we can wade through the reeds to the other side and double back. Come on.'

They jogged down to the canal side and headed along the remains of what had once been a cycling path, the tarmac now cracked and barely visible through the rampant weeds.

'They still use this for pasture,' Carl said. 'Otherwise it would be overgrown.'

'A pity it isn't,' Ishael said. 'It would make tracking us just that little bit harder.'

Carl glanced back at Jess, but the girl had vanished. He looked around. 'Ishael! Where is she?'

Ishael pushed through the weeds into the meadow. He squinted into the gloom. 'Over there! Good God, what's she doing?'

Jess stood in the middle of the field, a knife in each hand, facing back towards the forest.

'Jess!' Carl shouted, but the girl didn't answer.

'It's suicide!' Ishael said. 'They'll kill her!'

'She thinks she has nothing left to live for,' Carl said. 'What do we do?'

'We can't just let her give her life away. Come on!'

They hurried through the grass towards her. Carl got there first, Ishael some way behind. Carl grabbed Jess's arm. 'No!' he shouted, trying to twist her around. 'They'll kill you if you stay! They don't want us alive!'

'They killed my mother ... my father ... Simon ... it's their turn to die.'

Carl glanced at Ishael. The other man nodded.

Taking one arm each, they began to drag Jess backwards towards the canal.

They had gone only a few feet when lights appeared through the trees back in the direction they had come from. A vehicle was making its way slowly through the undergrowth, the headlights on full beam now as the last light trickled away over the horizon. The sound of spinning wheels followed the groan of a powerful engine hauling it through the soggy earth, guiding it between the trees.

'Look, up there! It's the others!' Carl pointed. The land cruiser and the two other trucks were negotiating a dirt path down into the meadow. They too had their lights on now.

'Take out your guns,' Jess said. 'We stand and fight.'

'We'll be cut down!'

'There's nowhere left to run. Better to die with their blood on our hands.'

Carl glanced at Ishael, and saw the defeat in his face. The beating Ishael had taken had left scars more than skin deep. He had found out first hand just how ruthless the government could be. If the DCA took them alive, death might prove a mercy.

'We might take a couple of them with us,' Ishael said reluctantly, 'but if it comes to it turn the guns on yourselves. Don't let them capture you.'

Carl's gulped. Less than two days ago he'd been a happy-go-lucky country boy playing in the forest, shooting at signs and birds with his catapult—

'Wait!' he said. 'Lower your guns. Save the bullets.' He pulled the catapult out of his bag. 'With this I can take out their headlights, and they won't hear a thing. Now run at them! Angle right, back towards the canal!'

Ishael dragged Jess as Carl loaded the catapult with a rock he found in the grass at his feet. If he could take out the headlights, maybe the dark would give them enough cover to get back into the woods.

The closest vehicle – the land cruiser – closed to fifty, forty, thirty feet. Carl lifted the catapult and took aim.

Ishael put an arm on his shoulder. 'Not the light, you'll never break it. Aim for the windscreen. It will surprise them more.'

Carl nodded. The truck closed to twenty feet and began to slow down. He closed one eye, aimed, and fired.

The rock struck the windscreen and Carl heard a loud crack. The vehicle jerked to one side, the lights swinging away from them, momentarily leaving them in darkness.

'Now, the canal. Go!' Ishael shouted as the truck started to come back around. Its lights swept in a wide arc towards them. The cover of the reeds was just fifty feet ahead, but there was something there, something standing in front of the canal, waiting–

Jess slumped to her knees, just as the truck's lights came around to light up the field around them. Ishael turned to help her up, but she hadn't fallen. She'd seen the robed figure standing by the canal, waiting for them. Shock had felled her, the fight draining away.

Carl lifted the catapult, feeling utterly pathetic. It was useless against the Huntsman, but the gun was in his bag; he would never get to it in time.

They heard the audio click of a loudspeaker behind them. 'Stay where you are!' a man's voice boomed. 'Do not move!'

The two trucks came to a halt behind the land cruiser. Glancing up, Carl saw the Huntsman still standing by the canal. Little more than a shadow in the gloom, beneath the hood was a black pit of darkness. The creature started to walk towards them, robe wrapped around its body like some ancient druid. Carl felt his blood run cold.

Behind them, Carl heard the sound of the truck door slam.

'Well, well, it's a surprise to see you again,' a man's voice said.

Carl saw Ishael flinch slightly as he looked up. 'Take me, let the others go,' he shouted. 'I'll tell you anything you want to know.'

'Hmm. Bargaining. Well, considering that we have all three of you already, what makes you think I would consider your offer?' the man said. 'Don't worry. You won't die until we have your friends. You are meeting them here, aren't you?'

'I don't know–'

'Oh, *we* do. We intercepted your radio transmissions.'

'You bastard.'

The man gestured at the DCA agents pooling behind him. 'Secure them, get them into the truck. We'll take cover until the others get here. You, get away. Dreggo?'

The Huntsman by the canal had come closer, its hood hung low. Carl heard ragged breathing as though it were hurt or out of breath. Ishael had told him how these creatures were unstable, how they could tear you apart in a second regardless of their orders.

'Dreggo?' the man shouted back at the trucks. 'Get out here and call it off!'

Ishael put a protective arm around the shivering, trembling Jess, while Carl squatted down beside them. His heart thundered in his chest.

Then the Huntsman by the canal roared, and the cloak fell away. The earsplitting sound of machine gun fire filled the meadow, and for a second before the headlights were shot out of the DCA vehicles Carl saw two men where the Huntsman should have been, one standing tall, another squatted down. A third dashed out from behind them to where Jess, Carl and Ishael had ducked down.

But it wasn't a man at all. 'Hurry!' the girl hissed as the two men sprayed the trucks with bullets.

'Marta?' Jess stammered, surprised, the first real emotion Carl had heard in Jess's voice since Simon had died.

The girl called Marta led them down the slope towards the canal. Behind them the sound of breaking glass and tearing metal filled the air. Then the gunfire abruptly stopped, and Carl heard running feet, together with the confused shouts of the Department of Civil Affairs men trying to reorganise themselves. One shout hung above all others: 'Release the Huntsmen!'

Beyond the reeds more headlights flicked on, and an engine burst into life.

'Quickly!' Marta shouted. 'Get into the back!'

Carl saw a Land Rover, not unlike one his father's friend owned, but this one had clearly been tampered with to make it even better equipped to handle the rough terrain. The chassis had been jacked up, the wheels enlarged.

A young boy waiting in the open back helped to pull him up alongside the others. As the smaller of the two men vaulted over the side, Marta punched the metal back of the cab and shouted, 'Reeder, go!'

The Land Rover bumped off down a thin lane that ran along the top of the old canal, shielded from sight by a thin, reed-filled channel alongside the meadow which they had come from. A moment later it bumped up over the old edge of the canal and began to thread its way through the trees, following an old road or trail. Soon they were out of the wood and on the gravelly remains of a proper road, the Land Rover's headlights on dip but given additional shielding with metal flaps that hung over the lights, making them harder to spot from a distance.

Carl looked around the open back of the Land Rover as it bumped along. Two men in their early twenties and a young boy sat with their backs against the cab. Marta had got into the front.

One of the men was round-faced, prematurely balding and a little overweight. He wore spectacles and gave Carl a warm, fatherly smile. The other was wiry thin with a pinched, ratty face and short-cropped hair. This one appeared to be winking at Carl. The boy was thinner but clearly resembled the bigger of the two men, although he had a lot more hair. All of them, he noticed, were avoiding looking at Jess.

The girl lay by the edge, sheltered by the raised metal side of the Land Rover, one hand under her head, one hand over her stomach.

Her eyes were closed, but Carl was sure she wasn't sleeping.

CHAPTER FORTY-SEVEN
PAST LIVES

'I told you, I didn't know.'

Clayton glared at Dreggo. 'How the fuck could you not have known that wasn't one of yours?'

She shrugged. 'They didn't respond to me. I assumed they were too busy following the trail.'

'You lying bitch.'

'I guess you'll have to take my word for it.'

Clayton scowled and walked off. Dreggo gave an inward grin. The two Huntsmen she had sent to follow the trail had taken a detour into a field of sheep not far outside of Exeter. There was nothing she could do to reel them in now. She had to wait until they were done and hope they didn't find any human settlements to raid on the way.

Perhaps she should have mentioned it to Clayton. He had just seemed so busy...

'God damn it!' he shouted, turning back towards her. 'We have three dead and four more injured. How the hell did this happen?'

He was talking mostly to himself so she didn't answer. Instead, she said, 'I'll send two more Huntsmen to follow the trail. Get a map and find out the best way to cut them off. The radio transmissions said they were heading down into Cornwall.'

'Yes, yes.' Clayton looked flustered as he rubbed his head. His eyes were shadows in the dull glare of the convoy's one remaining headlight, but she could see the stress painted in dark lines across his face. 'Fuck, how could this happen?'

'To Falmouth,' Dreggo said. She'd been awake while a DCA radio operator had intercepted one of the conversations between the men back in Bristol and the Tube Riders on the boat. They'd probably known their open frequency would be easy to intercept, so they'd not given away many details. Falmouth, she thought, could have been a slip brought on by pressure, or a dud to deliberately throw them off, but it was the only lead they had. In any case the Huntsmen would lead them to the truth.

Despite Clayton's obvious panic at yet another near miss, Dreggo was quite enjoying the chase. The Tube Riders had proven wily, slippery prey, and it would make their eventual capture even sweeter. They were still running, of course, but heading into the open wilderness of Cornwall was probably a mistake. They were running out of land, and there were no active ports in Cornwall. If it was an airstrip they had their sights on, it would be easy to spot and dispose of with the rarity of flight these days. No, the chase was coming to an end, but it had certainly been an interesting one.

Cornwall. Clayton had said it was mostly empty. The bottom half was sealed off by a fence, what lay inside unknown to anyone outside the higher levels of the government. The northern part, from the River Camel up, was still used for grazing cattle and milk production. From the River Camel down, though, Clayton had just shrugged. *Empty*, he said. *Everyone moved to work elsewhere.*

She was certainly getting to see the country. The more she saw, however, the more she hated it. She hated the dumb violence of the cities, the blissful ignorance of the GFA people. She hated the way the government had torn up the roads, pulled down the signs. Everything stank of delusional, misguided leadership that was slowly tying the country into a knot. If you didn't clean or oil or check a car it would continue to run for a while, but soon its performance would begin to wane. Eventually, it would just stop dead. It was happening to Mega Britain, and a large part of her was pleased.

'He'll be angry,' Clayton said, brushing one hand through his thinning hair. 'We had them cornered, and they outsmarted us. They got away again.'

'They were lucky,' Dreggo said. 'That's all. One mistake and they might all be dead now.'

'But they're not.'

'Which is why we need to get moving.'

Clayton nodded. 'Okay. We roll out in five.' He gestured at one of his agents. 'You got me that map yet? We need to know how they're going into Cornwall. What's the quickest way? Which roads are still there, which aren't? Be quick about it.'

He pulled another hand through his hair. As the truck with the working headlight began to swing round, Dreggo caught a glimpse of his eyes.

They looked as bloodshot as the Huntsmen's.

He's suffering, she thought. *Finally, after everything, he's starting to hurt too.*

#

In the back of the frozen goods truck, sitting in the dark a little apart from the others, Lyen's mind toiled. He had smelled her; she was near.

'Marta.'

The photograph had sprung a leak in the sealed tank of his memory. Disconnected from his past, he was starting to remember small sequences, images, voices. The girl in the picture was Marta, but who was Marta? He knew her. How did he know her?

What had he been before this?

Lyen listened to the shouts and the gunfire outside. The sounds of violence, of war, and his tongue lolled from his jaws, the need to maim, to kill, rising up inside him.

The other Huntsmen shifted. Hoods fell back, some stood, others scratched at the walls of their prison. Lyen pulled the crossbow from his belt and fingered the mechanisms. How he knew to use it he no longer remembered, but the weapon was as much a part of him as his own hands. He had killed many men with it, and he hoped to kill many more. The blood in his veins wouldn't run warm without the blood of others on his hands.

Several of the Huntsmen had moved to the door and were pawing at the steel, whining like hungry dogs. Lyen stayed where he was, though, his eyes closed, trying to remember how he had known that the girl in the picture – the girl they were chasing – was called Marta.

#

The Governor's car, with its enhanced suspension, gave a surprisingly comfortable ride across the countryside, and he looked out of the tinted windows with interest at the towns and villages that they passed. Behind them, the small container truck that made up the second half of his convoy was having less luck, bumping heavily through the potholed remains of the roads, graveled over only on more common routes. It didn't matter; there was nothing important inside, not to him at any rate.

As always, when faced with the results of his policies, the Governor felt pangs of uncertainty. Had his GFA policies worked as they should? Was production up or down? Had pulling up the roads really helped focus people's attention on their work?

Until dark shut off the outside to everything but his own reflection, it heartened him to see the bales in the fields, the huge parked trailers laden with grain ready for transportation into the GUAs. He had seen farm workers laughing and joking as they went about their work. At least in the GFAs people looked happy.

Happiness, though, for the Governor, was of no importance other than to maintain productivity. He didn't care about their state of mind as long as the country still produced, still rolled on, with the end result being the finances for and the tools to build his spacecraft. As long as the country kept producing the spacecraft, and his spacecraft got gradually closer to their goal, the Governor, while not happy, was content. That was enough.

Turning away from the window, the Governor set his thoughts on the task in hand. These kids, these so-called Tube Riders, were running across the country with their proof of the ambassador's assassination, slipping between the fingers of the Department of Civil Affairs and the claws of the Huntsmen alike. On the one hand he admired them for their resilience, and thanked them for exposing some of the flaws of his system. How easy it was to get out of the cities through the railway tunnels! He had never considered it. And the Huntsmen, his pride, his success, had been shown up as unpredictable, unstable. Clayton had warned him, of course, but Clayton was a fool. Mega Britain ran so smoothly that Clayton had never had more to do than interrogate a few political prisoners. Faced with a real crisis the man was a fraud. It was a shame that Clayton's second was dead; Adam Vincent had shown ingenuity the older man lacked, but there were others in the lower ranks of the DCA who would welcome the chance to replace Leland Clayton as soon as this mission was over.

The Governor flicked down the sun shade above him and studied himself for a moment in the small mirror on its reverse side. His skin, milky-white, was in contrast to the dark sunglasses he wore. The texture of his skin was coarse and thick, but he was perfectly albino, just one of his many abnormalities but probably the most useless. An inverse effect was that it made direct sunlight intolerable. Vampiric, some might suggest, but it wouldn't kill him, not in short bursts at least. Merely irritate, at worst burn. It was more the fear of it that kept him out of sight these days, and the memories of the cruel experiments that had seen him exposed to measure its effects. He still had the scars.

All in all, he looked in good health. His face suggested a man in his late thirties or early forties, but Maxim Cale was a hundred and twenty-three years old. Extended life was just one of the many gifts bestowed on a shy, quiet little boy abducted from an innocuous Algerian village in the 1950s and locked away in the dark hell of a Soviet research facility in the wastes of Siberia for almost twenty years.

Night by night the screams had filled the dank, chilly corridors. Stern men in white coats marched back and forth, clipboards in their hands, sharp instruments in their pockets. That little boy was just one of dozens who saw their faces and bodies change with each passing day. As he grew into a man the changes to his body more apparent, until one day they gave him too much power, enough to escape from that icy hellhole just a couple of miles south of the Arctic Circle.

Many years later, his mind now as dark and as murderous as those who had abused him, he went back to that place to uncover the details of what had happened to him. He had found the place in ruins, all the records and artifacts and information taken away.

Where?

Someone somewhere knew, had noted down what had happened, knew where the technology had gone. It took him another ten years of searching, interrogating, and killing, to find out.

Afraid of the technology falling into the hands of the Americans or worse, the scientists had hidden it in the one place they thought no one else would ever be able to get at it.

Space.

The Governor wanted that technology back. He wanted to understand, wanted to know his origins, where his power had come from and why. And then he wanted to make use of it.

Maybe he should use these Tube Riders as his first test subjects. They were clever; their genetics were strong. He could give them power almost as great as his own, and then use them like he did the Huntsmen, turn them into killing machines to brush aside his enemies. All of Europe could fall, and after it, the former USSR. How he so wanted to make them pay for their crimes …

The Governor leaned back in the seat and closed his eyes, enjoying the soft reverie of world domination.

Part Three
Cornwall

Chapter Forty-Eight
Respite

MARTA STOOD ON THE HILLTOP looking east across Bodmin Moor in the direction of London, from where the sun would soon rise. Nothing moved out there, no people or cars, not even sheep or cattle. Reeder had told her they used to run wild, but had long ago been herded up by the people of the GFAs. Now, only rabbits lived up here, invisible among the grass that whipped back and forth like hair in the wind.

From her vantage point Marta could see almost to the edge of the moor, some ten miles east. The open grassland rolled away, punctuated only by a few rocky outcrops and some gnarly trees bent like old men by the incessant wind. It was pretty in a desolate kind of way, with the shadows stretched long across the hillsides, turning the valleys into lakes of dark water. She squinted, looking again for a house, but saw none.

She heard a sound and glanced back. Jess was coming up the hill towards her. Jess's shoulders were slumped, her eyes downcast. The change in her was as remarkable as it was tragic. Gone was the pretty innocence, the bright, sunny look. Gone, too, was the violent hatred that had replaced it. Now she just looked bleak, weary, her eyes struggling to focus on anything. Her cheeks were pale, and her mouth hung slightly open as though it took too much effort to close it.

'So little time,' Jess said, her voice barely audible over the wind. 'So little time, and they've all gone.'

Marta could say nothing to ease her pain. She continued to scan the moorland, half watching for pursuit, half waiting for the sun to show itself above the distant hills. She didn't want to think about Simon; it hurt too much.

'I thought I'd got him back ... I thought I'd got him.' Jess shook her head as she came to stand beside Marta.

Marta put an arm around her shoulders. She expected Jess to push it away, but instead Jess leaned in towards Marta like a child might to her mother. 'I might not have loved him in the same way that you did,' Marta said, picking her words carefully, 'but he was dear to me. He was dear to all of us.'

'I know.'

'I want this nightmare to end.'

'No, no,' Jess said in earnest, and at first Marta wondered what she meant. Then Jess shook her head again, the fervour briefly returning. 'It can't end. Ever. Too much has happened. We might win, or whatever, but my parents, Simon ... this nightmare will never be over for me.'

Marta looked down as Jess's voice rose. She felt guilty that Jess had to be a part of this. It wasn't her own fault; Simon had brought Jess to St. Cannerwells, but Marta knew he would never have made her come. But now Simon was gone, killed by the Huntsman; who was left to shoulder the blame? Her brother had started tube riding, and in the last few days she had graduated, reluctantly or not, to be their leader. The death of Jess's parents and now Simon should rest on her shoulders, surely?

'I'm sorry,' Marta said.

'It's not your fault,' Jess replied, but Marta could feel the emotion behind the words, hear the unspoken second line: *but I want it to be. I need someone to hate.*

Behind them, Reeder was cooking up some fish and potatoes for breakfast, the smell drifting upslope towards them. Marta welcomed it like an old friend, her stomach growling in anticipation.

John Reeder, for all his eccentricities, was proving a valuable ally. His old Land Rover, adapted for the harsh terrain, and his experience of living on the fringes of GFA society, had been invaluable. Without their chance discovery of his boat, they might all be dead. Certainly Jess, Ishael and the boy, Carl, would be prisoners, maybe all of them. They'd managed to outwit the Huntsmen and the Department of Civil Affairs again, but she wondered just how long they could stay half a step ahead.

It had been Owen's idea to disguise themselves as a Huntsman in order to trick their pursuers, an idea so simple only a child could think of it. They had gambled that Huntsmen had been loosed on their trail, and that the DCA would be fooled into thinking one had kept with them long enough to appear at the right moment to trap them. Using guns that William had given Switch, again without their knowledge ('If you get caught, what you don't know you can't tell,' had been his familiar response), it was a case of shoot before being shot while dragging the others to safety. Paul had insisted they just aim for the lights, use the confusion and the surprise to get away, but despite his agreement, Marta knew Switch had aimed straight for the truck windows. Switch didn't have the same qualms about killing people that Paul did.

Jess moved away from her, wandered a few feet down the slope and sat down on a rock, her eyes drifting across the valley below. There was nothing that could be said to make her feel better, so Marta turned and headed back towards the group.

Reeder had begun to dish out the food and most of them were eating. Paul sat together with Switch on a flat rock, while Owen and Carl were sitting on a tarpaulin spread out by the side of the Land Rover. Reeder smiled and handed her a plastic dish, then set about preparing his own. She looked around and saw Ishael standing alone, looking out towards the west. As she went over to join him, she realised how happy seeing him again had made her, even though at first she had barely recognised him behind the ruins of his face. Whatever horrors she'd seen, the thought of the DCA agents going to work on him like thugs made her sick inside. There was a case to excuse even the human-made Huntsmen, she reasoned, but any man who could commit such atrocities towards another with willingness and zeal was inhuman.

After they had stopped, Reeder, his field skills seemingly without end, had produced an old first aid kit, the plastic wrapping on the band-aids and bandages hardened and cracked with age. Using tweezers boiled sterile, he had reopened the half-scabbed gash on Ishael's cheek, cleaned it with antiseptic, and stitched it up. Then he had fixed up a gash in Ishael's scalp where his hair had literally been torn out, dressed his fingers where the fingernails had been torn away and applied an antiseptic lotion to terrible welts on the soles of Ishael's feet and to teeth marks on the back of one calf muscle. Ishael was at least recognizable now, and Reeder claimed he would eventually look 'better than new.'

Switch had been next, his knife wound re-stitched and dressed. Jess, Carl and Paul had been treated for minor cuts and scrapes. Only Owen and Marta had so far escaped unharmed.

'Hey,' Ishael said, as she came up beside him. He looked down at her food. 'Eat it while it's hot.'

'I intend to.' She prodded a potato with a plastic fork. 'I'm, um, glad you made it. We didn't know what happened back at the station. I thought maybe you...'

'Nearly.' He shrugged. 'It depends how lucky you call this,' he said, gesturing at his face. 'Whatever, I owe Jess and Carl my life.'

Marta nodded. She had heard a version of events from both Ishael and Carl, who had told her what he knew of their flight and Simon's death because Jess wasn't talking to anyone much. 'It's lucky they found you.'

'It's kind of hard to say, but if Simon were alive now, I'd probably be dead. I'm not sure how to describe how that makes me feel. On the one hand I feel happy, but on the other so desperately sad.'

Marta glanced at him. His bruises made it difficult to read his expression, but she could guess at the turmoil there.

'Do you think Jess resents me because of that?'

Marta shrugged. 'Jess is hurting. We've all lost friends and family over the years, but most of us have had time to grieve, to come to terms with it. Jess has lost everyone close to her in such a short time. We're all she has left.'

Ishael nodded. 'For years, all I wanted was for the UMF to come out from the underground, blow this whole thing wide open. You know, just get on with it. I never realised how much it would hurt to see so many people in pain. The dead, at least they have closure. It's the living who are suffering the most. Jess, Carl too. The Huntsmen killed his father, maybe his mother too.'

Marta nodded. She hadn't had much chance to speak to Carl herself, but Paul had taken him on as a second younger brother. Paul had told her about the attack on Carl's house. To Marta, not knowing was perhaps even worse. She felt terrible that Carl, like Ishael, had been dragged into this mess, and she knew how he felt; she had suffered with Leo's disappearance for years. Time could dull the pain, but it could never fully erase it.

Marta reached across and felt for Ishael's hand. He let her take it, and then squeezed hers in his. *Am I safe?* she wondered. *Can this battered man protect me? Can I protect him?*

She thought of Jess, of Simon's death, and of the pain Jess must be suffering. A sudden pang of guilt struck her. Ishael let go of her hand.

'What's wrong? I'm ... sorry. I shouldn't have–'

'It's okay. It's just...' She couldn't finish, but his small nod told her he understood. He squeezed her hand again, and she let her body relax.

'I hope that some good comes of all this,' he said.

'Me too.'

They sat on the ground for a while. Marta finished her breakfast. It was good, even though she had let it get cold after all.

Carl and Owen were talking quietly. Paul was eating. She caught Switch's gaze for a moment before he quickly looked away, not for the first time since they'd rescued Ishael and the others last night.

Surely not ... but she wondered. He had saved her life more than once over the last couple of days. In between she'd felt him edge closer to her, as though he had appointed himself her personal protector. He spoke to her in a kinder, less abrasive way than he spoke to the others.

It made sense. They had always been like siblings, but difficult circumstances had a way of pushing people closer. She had no feelings for him other than the same brotherly love she'd felt before, and now as she watched the back of his head as he dipped to eat, she felt nothing new. They were close, but there was nothing deeper there.

With Ishael though, just his presence made her feel good. She found him attractive, too, beneath his bruises. If anything, what he had suffered made her feelings stronger; that she'd come close to losing him before anything had ever happened. Could something happen between them?

Marta stifled a sigh. Maybe, if circumstances were different. On the run from the Huntsmen, homeless, maybe lost, was hardly the time to start building a relationship. In another time, another place, maybe. She swallowed down a lump in her throat.

'Come on,' Ishael said at last. 'We have to get moving.'

Just down the hillside from the camp, Paul, Carl and Owen were washing up the breakfast dishes. Switch had climbed to the top of the rise and was sharpening a knife in the shadow of a crooked tree. Jess stood nearby, gazing out at the view.

Reeder was tinkering under the hood of the Land Rover. He looked up as they approached.

'Any trouble?' Ishael asked. 'Maybe I can help. I know a little about engines.'

'No, she's fine. I'm just worried, as always. It's almost impossible to replace parts these days. I've not changed the oil in nearly a year, so the engine isn't working too great, but our biggest problem is fuel.'

'You don't have enough?'

'I think we can make it to Falmouth.'

Ishael forced a smile. Instead of heading south, Reeder had purposely taken them far further north-west than necessary in order to gain some time on the government men. The DCA's vehicles couldn't cover the ground so fast, and if they were using the Huntsmen to track them on foot, every mile opened up the gap further. Of course, they knew the DCA had intercepted their radio broadcasts, so there was a good chance the government would head straight for Falmouth to cut them off. However–

'We need to change course,' Ishael said. 'We're not going to Falmouth.'

Reeder raised an eyebrow. 'Are we not?'

'No. We knew they might listen to our radio transmissions. We had to throw them off. We need to go further south-west than that.'

'Where?'

'Lizard Point. It's a rocky outcrop into the English Channel. You know it?'

Reeder looked grim. 'Yes, I know where you mean.'

'Do we have enough fuel to make it?'

'What do you need there?'

Ishael took a deep breath. 'There's a tunnel there.'

'A tunnel?'

Ishael nodded. 'It was built back in the days before Mega Britain. It was originally planned as a second public tunnel to France, but the government changed its plans and downgraded it to trade and military uses only. Then, during the coup, the remnants of the old military sealed over the entrance. A few years ago, we broke into an old government bunker in Bristol. We stole some plans, hoping to find out more about the perimeter walls. Among them, we found details of the tunnel.'

Marta stared open-mouthed. 'You mean–'

Ishael nodded. 'That's how we're getting you to France.' He smiled. 'We're going underground.'

Marta started to speak, but John Reeder lifted a hand. 'Wait, don't get carried away, young revolutionary. I have a few more years on you, my friend. I remember hearing of that tunnel. The government never finished it. Got about halfway in, and then the coup came.'

Ishael shook his head. 'That's what everyone thought. The old government *didn't* finish it. The French did.'

'Now, how on earth did you figure that out? Where's your proof?'

'It was in the contract drawn up between the two countries. The British and the French were both to drill to the midpoint. The British finished their section before the coup, but sealed up the entrance to hide the tunnel's existence.'

'Are you sure they didn't destroy it entirely?'

'No. The plans we stole weren't the originals, they were plans updated by Mega Britain Officials. In a footnote it was stated that the tunnel had potential as a future invasion route to Europe, should the need arise.'

'They were going to finish it off and send an invasion force over to France?' Reeder scoffed. 'That's ridiculous.'

Ishael nodded. 'I don't think they ever planned to do it. They were just acknowledging the tunnel's potential.'

Marta touched his arm. 'How do you know the French finished it?'

Ishael looked at her, and then back at Reeder. Behind the bruises his eyes looked a little uncertain. 'We have strong reason to believe that the French would have kept their part of the bargain for the same reason.'

Reeder slapped a hand against his forehead with a resounding snap. He rolled his eyes. '"Strong reason to *believe*"? So, you don't know.'

Ishael cocked his head. 'We're about eighty percent sure.'

'That's just a number, my friend. Ninety-nine percent won't be enough if that tunnel proves to be a dead end. In the event we make it that far, it sounds like a coffin to me.'

'The ports are all sealed or closed. There's not an inch of water within three miles of the coast that's not covered by machine guns. It's our only chance.'

'But it's not much of one! You'd be better off setting up a couple of gun outposts and trying to pick them off as they surround us. It's crazy.'

'I think it's worth a try. If we get there with enough of a head start, we'll have time to turn around and get away if it doesn't work out.'

Reeder didn't look amused. 'Let's assume this tunnel is complete. That's the least of your problems. You do know it's behind the Fence, don't you?'

Ishael nodded. 'The sealed section of Cornwall. The area reserved for government officials to take a little holiday.'

Reeder laughed. 'Is that what you think? Is that really what you think?'

'What do you mean?'

'I take it you've never been as far as the Fence?'

Marta said, 'What's behind it?'

Reeder nodded towards the Land Rover. 'Get everyone on board. It's time to leave. As for that accursed fence, my friend, in a couple of hours you'll know exactly what's behind it, and I'm afraid you're not going to like it one bit.'

Chapter Forty-Nine
Menace

CLAYTON SCOWLED THROUGH the broken windscreen as the sun began to rise behind them, bathing the dirt track they were traveling along in pale sunlight. After more than three hours of laboured progress along the thin, overgrown lanes, the land cruiser's battered suspension and the cold early morning air were starting to get to him. Dreggo's Huntsmen were still tracking the Tube Riders' scent, while his men had been searching maps to try to find shortcuts to reduce back their quarry's time advantage. The Tube Riders' single vehicle could move much faster over the terrain, so only by second guessing them would Clayton's men haul them in. The problem was that half of the roads on the map were overgrown or otherwise impassable. They had been forced to backtrack several times, and all the while the Tube Riders got further and further ahead.

A small force had been dispatched to Falmouth to cut the Tube Riders off, but as Clayton had suspected, the scent trail was leading away from there, angling much further north. Falmouth was most likely a decoy, a town spat out at random in an attempt to buy them some time. Fortunately for Clayton's men, though, the Tube Riders were running out of places to go. Deep into Cornwall now, Clayton had ordered fresh reinforcements from London to move in and cut off the major routes out of the area, should the Tube Riders and their little band try to double back. They were heading for the sea. There were no active ports in Cornwall, neither were there any air strips. It occurred to Clayton that the resistance force they had battled in Bristol might have an ocean-equipped vessel hidden away somewhere in an abandoned fishing port, but it was unlikely. Even if they could get out to sea, the government's coastal defenses would easily pick them off.

Beside him, Dreggo twisted. He had brought her up to his vehicle in order to more quickly relay his instructions to the Huntsmen, but it made him nervous to have her so close. It was difficult to concentrate with one hand pressed into his pocket, fingering the little remote that would screw up her nervous system.

She looked at him and pouted. 'Are we there yet?'

'Shut up.'

Dreggo grinned and glanced out of the passenger window at an overgrown field they were passing. 'Where are all the people?'

'I don't know.'

'I'm sure you do but you can't be bothered to tell me.'

'That's right.'

Dreggo leaned her head against his shoulder, close enough that he could smell the distinctly metallic odor of the inserts in her face and head. He tensed, and saw her smile as a result. 'You know, Mr. Clayton,' she began in a childish, saccharine-soaked voice, 'if I didn't hate you with every inch of my body, and desire your death with every part of my will, I would probably find you attractive. In a grandfatherly kind of way.'

'I appreciate the compliment.'

'I would probably sleep with you, if I thought I could bring myself to touch you without wanting to tear you apart.'

'Give it a rest, would you?' Clayton tried to shift away, but the gearbox and the driver's seat blocked his escape.

'I haven't been with a man – willingly – in a long time, Mr. Clayton. Even though the pond scum you work with filled me up with bits of metal, underneath it all I'm still a woman. I'm a woman with needs.'

Clayton scowled at her. 'Just shut up, will you?'

Dreggo looked about to reply when a crackle of static burst from the car's internal radio.

Clayton leaned forward. 'What is it?' he barked.

'Mr. Clayton...'

Even Dreggo shivered at the sound of the Governor's voice. Clayton glanced at her before he answered. 'Sir? Yes, sir?'

'I trust you cannot yet confirm the capture of the Tube Riders?'

'Sir, I–'

'I thought not. Clayton, your incompetence is beginning to annoy me.' Beside him, Dreggo smiled.

'Sir–'

'It appears you have developed a stutter. I suggest you put your breath to better use by more accurately briefing your men. In the meanwhile, we will rendezvous at Fence Checkpoint Three in approximately two hours. I assume you have surmised that the Tube Riders plan to go inside?'

'They won't get far, sir.'

'You told me that back in London, and you told me that from Bristol, yet here we are taking a vacation in Cornwall with an unnecessary trail of bodies behind us.'

The radio clicked off. Clayton glared at it.

'Sounds like you're in trouble,' Dreggo said.

'Shut up.'

'You know,' she said, voice suddenly turning serious. 'We could start a revolution of our own.'

'What?'

'The Governor is coming to Cornwall. He'll be unguarded. We have your men, and the Huntsmen–'

Clayton lifted a hand. 'You talk of treason. I should kill you for those words.'

'Do it, I dare you. But with my last command to the Huntsmen I will order your death.'

Clayton's eyes narrowed. 'There's not time.'

With a slow smile Dreggo lifted a hand and touched her forehead. 'It's already done.'

'You bitch.'

Dreggo reached out and touched his knee. Her eyes narrowed. 'I control the Huntsmen, Clayton. Through a little kinship and a lot of cruelty on behalf of your men, they trust me. We have enough to practically sack London. We can fight him.'

Clayton shook his head with resignation. 'You have no idea what the Governor can do.'

Dreggo fingered a piece of metal that protruded from her upper arm and bent over her shoulder as a kind of armour. Where it passed through the skin was a stretchy plastic membrane that had been fused with her skin tissue and melded to the metal. She reached out and put her fingers on the truck's dashboard, pressing against the plastic. For a moment she appeared to strain and nothing happened. Then Clayton heard a creak and a fracture opened up in the plastic. His eyes widened. It would have taken a hammer to do the same amount of damage.

'I'm pretty sure I can imagine,' she said, wiping sweat from her hand off on to her shirt.

'You can't imagine it,' Clayton said, regaining his composure. 'Unless you've seen it.'

Dreggo closed her eyes. 'Well, pretty soon I'll have a chance to, won't I?'

Chapter Fifty
Breaking and Entering

REEDER STOPPED THE LAND ROVER on top of the rise. Ahead of them the dirt trail headed down into the valley, snaking through abandoned, overgrown farmland and into a thin thicket of woodland which spread across the valley floor. They could see it again as it broke out of the copse, angling up the hillside to where it ended at a small car park, a low brick building at its rear. A short distance beyond the building they could see a tall fence that stretched away for as far as they could see in either direction.

'Is there anything they haven't fucking enclosed in this country?' Switch said, climbing out and spitting on the ground. 'What the hell is behind *this* one?'

Reeder climbed out beside him and lifted a pair of binoculars to his eyes. He scanned back and forth. 'There. There's one.'

Ishael had climbed out beside Switch. Paul, Owen and Carl had jumped down from the back. In the front, Marta and Jess were both sleeping, their heads close together.

'What is it?'

Reeder handed the binoculars to Switch. He pointed towards a stand of trees on the slope just beyond the fence. 'Look there, just to the right of those trees.'

Switch put the binoculars to his eyes and scanned back and forth. 'I don't see anything...'

'Use the button here to focus it.' Reeder tapped the top of the binoculars.

'Ah, okay, got it. There! What the fuck is that?'

'What is it?' Ishael asked.

'It looks like a man. Sitting down, head slumped over. Is he dead?' He passed the binoculars to Ishael and glanced back at Reeder.

'He's not dead,' Reeder said. 'Just resting.'

'I thought there were no people in there,' Ishael said.

'It's not a man. It's a Mistake.'

'No,' Ishael said. 'He lifted his head. It's definitely a man.'

Reeder shook his head as Ishael passed the binoculars first to Paul then Owen and Carl in turn. 'You don't understand,' he said. 'That's what people call them. Mistakes.'

'Mistakes?'

'They used to bring them down here in truckloads. These days, so I'm told, they come in trickles rather than floods. Their experiments must be improving.'

Owen said, 'That's not a man. His face isn't right. It's furry, like a dog. Like one of those things. Are there more of them in there?'

John Reeder nodded. His face, smooth and youthful when they first met him, was now etched with worry lines. Even his neatly curled moustache had bent out of shape. He looked to have aged ten years overnight.

'Them, and worse, maybe,' he said. 'In varying states of repair. What you see before you, gentlemen, is Mega Britain's live experiment junkyard. In every failed experiment, if the test subject doesn't die, it ends up here.'

Switched cursed under his breath and looked around at the others. Paul took off his glasses and rubbed his eyes, while Carl sat down on a rock and ran a hand through his hair. Ishael's face was unreadable, while Owen lifted the binoculars and swung them back and forth across the far hillside.

'So to get to this tunnel we have to get through a whole country of fucking broken down Huntsmen?' Switch said. 'This just gets worse.'

Ishael pointed. 'I saw a sign on the gate saying Fence Checkpoint Three. Is it manned? I don't see anyone.'

Owen swung the binoculars round. 'Can't see any vehicles, but that building is quite big. There could be a garage or something round the back. There's another one. Leaning against the fence. They gonna cause us any problems?'

Reeder shrugged. 'They might do. I don't know.'

Can we get through that fence somewhere else?' Ishael asked. 'Cut through?'

'It's electrified.'

'It can't be,' Owen said. 'That bastard creature is leaning against it!'

'Maybe it's dead,' Paul said.

'It was moving!'

Reeder gave the others a wry smile. 'Quite possibly it's *feeding*. Let's not think about it too much. Hopefully it'll leave us alone.'

They went back to the Land Rover. Reeder turned them around and they backtracked down the hill before turning right and cutting through the fringes of the forest. Soon they were deep into the trees. Reeder slowed the Land Rover down and jagged the vehicle back and forth, following a route close to the road up to the checkpoint but just out of sight. A short way back from the edge of the copse, Reeder pulled the Land Rover to a stop and they climbed out.

'We have to go up there and see if the gate is guarded,' Reeder said. 'If it is, we then need a way to get through.'

'I'll go,' Switch said. He handed a gun to Paul. 'Paul can come as lookout.'

'I wanna come too!' Owen said.

'Stay here, kid,' Paul said, patting his brother on the shoulder. 'They'll be plenty of fights for you yet.'

Owen scowled, but didn't try to follow as Paul and Switch headed through the copse towards the building. As it appeared through the trees they could see it was bigger than they had first realised. At least the size of a small bungalow, the featureless concrete building hung low to the ground. There was an entrance in the front wall, and what looked like a window. There was no way from their angle to tell if there was a garage around the back or not.

At least fifty feet of open, grassy hillside separated the trees from the building. With the exception of some patches of longer grass there was almost no cover.

'This would be a whole lot easier at night,' Paul said.

'We don't have time. They'll have caught us by then.'

Paul looked at his watch. It was 6.40 a.m. It was only going to get lighter, and Paul felt like he'd been awake forever, despite catching a couple of hours sleep while they traveled. Their only hope was that the checkpoint hadn't been alerted to their approach.

Switch pointed left. That way the hillside dipped more, giving them more cover. 'We can get closer to the fence, come in from the side.'

Paul fingered the gun Switch had given him. He didn't want to use it; he hoped the checkpoint was deserted. Switch, though, in front of him, carried a knife in each hand, his whole body tensed, ready for immediate action. Paul wondered how much of this Switch thought was real, and how much was a game.

Switch went ahead, dropped in a crouch, inching up the slope towards the blank side wall of the building. There was no sign of any security cameras or lookout points. The whole place had an air of neglect and abandon.

'Cover me,' Switch hissed without looking back. Paul held the gun out in front of him as Switch rose up and ran low towards the side of the building. Paul, hands shaking, pointed the gun at the roof, at the corners, everywhere except at Switch.

Switch ducked down by the wall. He waved Paul forward. Paul steeled himself, then jumped up and dashed across the open space to join Switch at the wall. Breathing hard, heart pounding, he looked back at the trees. The others were out of sight.

'Round the back,' Switch whispered, the hint of a smile on his lips.

Without waiting for Paul, Switch dropped to a crouch again and moved quickly along the featureless side wall of the building. They had seen the door on the other side, but here there was nothing, no doors, windows, or vents. Paul just prayed it wasn't the entrance to an underground bunker, one housing a whole garrison of men.

'There's a way in,' Switch said, disappearing around the corner.

When Paul followed, he saw Switch standing at the entrance to a parking garage. Inside, an army-camouflaged jeep was parked at the back. The window was down. Switch leaned inside and pulled a set of keys out of the ignition. He held them up to Paul and grinned.

'Just got ourselves another ride.'

'Let's just get on with this.'

Switch nodded and slipped into the shadows at the back. Paul heard a door click open.

'Through here,' Switch said. 'Hardly big on their security, eh?'

'They probably don't get many guests.'

Paul followed Switch into a thin, grey corridor. Several doors branched off, all of them shut. At the end, a double door loomed. Above it, a sign announced: *Control Centre*.

Switch ducked down by the door. Paul stayed further back down the corridor, the gun covering Switch as the little man reached up and pulled down the handle. The door inched inwards.

Switch glanced back at Paul and waved him forward, one finger to his lips. Paul hesitated just a moment then crept up to the door. Switch pointed at the gun, then at his own back. Paul tried to glance inside, but the room was dark, and all he could see from this angle was the black metal edge of a table.

Switch gave the knives a little shake then slipped through the door.

\#

With Paul covering his back, Switch crept forward towards the low sofa at the front of the room. Ahead of it, he could see the top of a television set, switched off. On the sofa, judging from the neatness of their haircuts, were two men; the tops of their heads all he could see. He moved towards the centre of the room, arms out wide, knife blades glistening. He would take them both at once, before they even knew he was there.

One of them shifted, and for a second Switch saw the top of a book. From the posters on the walls and the small kitchen units to his left he knew this was a recreation room. Did that mean there was a guard on duty somewhere else? He knew silence was his best weapon. If one of them saw him, he and Paul would have a real fight on their hands.

He crept closer, just a couple of feet from the sofa's back now. He lifted his arms wider, the knives ready to arc in and slice the guards' throats. He prayed his feet didn't slip.

'Hey!'

Switch jerked forward at the sound of a voice behind him, knives slashing. The man on the left was too slow. Switch raked the knife across his throat and felt warm blood wash over his hand.

The other man, though, was quicker, the blade catching just strands of hair as he rolled forward on to the floor. Behind him, Switch heard a dull thud followed by a grunt from Paul.

He turned to see a man by the door, wearing loose grey clothes that could have been pajamas. His eyes looked sleepy but his hand was strong as he slammed a fist into Paul's face, sending Paul sprawling forward, his glasses spinning away across the floor. The man reached for a rifle standing near the door. Switch glanced back at the third man, saw him now at the back of the room, reaching for a gun holster hung on the wall. He tried to get around the sofa but the man was too fast. The handgun trained on him.

'Who the fuck are you?' the man by the door said, his rifle moving back and forth between Switch and Paul, who was crawling across the floor, blood dripping from his nose. 'Drop your knives, kid.'

'Jesus, Matt, he killed Ray,' the other man said, in a voice that revealed that *he* was a *she*, her hair cut short in a crewcut.

'Oh fuck, oh fuck,' the man said, rubbing his free hand through his hair, messy from sleep. 'I get up to this...'

Switch backed away against the wall, hands in the air.

'Drop the fucking knives you jippy-eyed little prick!' the woman shouted.

Switch did.

'What do we do now?' the one called Matt said, his rifle trained on Switch. Paul was crawling across the floor, patting the carpet as he looked for his glasses. Switch had never seen him left blinded before. He had no idea how well Paul could see.

'Ray's dead! I say we return the favor!'

'My glasses...'

'Shut up!' Matt stepped forward and stamped on Paul's glasses, crunching them underfoot. 'Kelly, you do it.'

'A pleasure. You're first, you squinty little bastard.'

As Kelly cocked her gun, Switch was sure he'd run out of luck this time. She was too close to miss.

But it was Paul who moved first. Crawling on the floor just a couple of feet from Matt, he lunged forward and grabbed the barrel of the gun, jerking the butt backwards into Matt's groin. The big man grunted and doubled over. Paul twisted the gun in the direction of Kelly and pulled the trigger.

The bullet hit Kelly in the chest and she staggered backwards into the wall, dropping to her knees. Her eyes went wide and her mouth fell open in an expression of shock and dismay. Then she tumbled forward, head striking the floor with a sickening crunch.

Paul looked back at Matt and rammed the butt of the gun into the man's dumbstruck face.

'That's for my glasses,' he said through gritted teeth, as Matt grunted and fell to the floor.

Switch jumped across the sofa and took the gun out of Paul's hands just before Paul dropped it, his arms going limp, the wall holding him up as he stumbled a few steps backwards.

The smell of blood filled the air, thick and pungent. One of the two dead guards, Kelly or Ray, had vacated their bowels on death, the stench of feces mixing with the smell of blood.

'You all right, Paul?' Switch said, touching his friend's shoulder. Your glasses, man.'

Paul, recovering his composure, shook his head. He gave a wry smile. 'I knew that ruse would come in handy someday. They're fakes. I've never needed them. Signs of vulnerability came in handy in my line of work.'

Switch grinned. 'Sly bastard. I'm impressed.'

'Yeah.' Paul was staring at Kelly's corpse.

'Get up,' Switch said, nudging Matt with his foot. 'Get back against the wall, hands in the air.'

The man did as he was told. 'Look,' he pleaded. 'Don't kill me, okay? I've got kids. Take whatever money you can find, take the guns, the jeep, whatever. Just don't hurt me.'

'We need you to open the gate,' Switch said. 'We need to get inside.'

Matt's eyes widened. 'What the hell do you want to do that for? You do know what kind of people live in there?'

Switch lifted the gun. 'That's our business.' He cocked the rifle with an efficient flick of his finger, like a veteran assassin lining up another kill. 'My friend here has a conscience; just look how he reacted to killing your friend. But I don't. I'll kill you like a pig without a second thought.' He took a step forward. 'Your choice,' he said.

'In the control room,' Matt said, one shaking arm lifting towards the door.

'Take us there. And remember, move too quick and you're fucking dead. We'll find it ourselves.'

Matt moved off down the corridor, hands still in the air. 'Get the others,' Switch told Paul. 'Bring them up here.' He turned back towards Matt, who had reached a door further down the corridor. The guard looked back. 'In here, all right?'

'Go inside. Slowly.'

#

Paul glanced back at the bodies on the floor behind him as Switch followed after Matt. Ray's body did little to him, but at the sight of Kelly his legs turned to jelly and he had to grip the edge of a table for support.

He had killed her.

He'd never killed anyone before. A bluffer not a fighter, he'd kept himself and Owen alive using whatever means he could to keep them fed and safe. Never before had he aimed a gun at someone with the intent to kill. Even if he'd missed, his heart would have hung heavy, but with Kelly dead, it was far worse. He felt like someone had driven a bore down through his spine and ripped out his soul. All he wanted to do was lie down and close his eyes, but he didn't have time. Switch needed help, and the demons in his head were nothing compared to those on their trail.

Outside, the cool air felt sticky against his face. Paul found himself gasping for breath, his hands on his knees. Looking up through eyes blurring with tears, he saw a group of people running towards him.

'Paul?' Marta said. 'Paul, are you all right?'

'Where are your specs, bro?'

Paul squeezed his eyes shut and wiped a hand across his face. He thought of all those who had died because of them, and all those who might die yet. *Their lives won't be wasted. They can't be.*

'We killed two guards,' he said. 'We took a third prisoner. Switch is getting him to open the gates.'

'Where?' Ishael asked.'

'Go around the back and in through the garage.'

Ishael hurried off, followed by Reeder. Paul forced a smile. 'I lost my glasses,' he said to the others. 'Never really needed them, so doesn't matter anyway.'

Marta gave him a strange look. *I've actually impressed her,* he thought.

He glanced at the building, just as a muffled gunshot came from inside. Reeder hadn't yet reached the building, but they stopped and looked at each other.

Marta started after them. 'Oh God, Switch–'

They heard a door slam. Paul felt at his waist for his gun, but somewhere he must have lost it. 'Get cover–'

'Hey.'

'Switch!'

The little man stood behind them all, around the front of the building. 'The main entrance is around this way. Quickly, we need to load up their food and weapons.'

'The gate?' Reeder said.

'I know the controls. It'll be open shortly.'

'Where's the guard?' Paul asked.

Switch's eyes were hard as he said, 'No loose ends.'

Paul gulped.

None of the others said anything as Switch went back inside. Paul exchanged a glance with Marta, whose bottom lip was trembling. Jess looked as cold as Switch. Carl and Owen just looked tired.

After a few moments they turned and headed back towards the Land Rover in the forest, leaving Switch alone to operate the gate. As Paul climbed up into the back with Owen and Carl they heard a low humming noise. The Land Rover's engine covered it for a few seconds until they were out of the woods and moving up the slope to the checkpoint.

The gate stood open. Switch was outside, the rifle in his hands. Reeder pulled up alongside him and leaned out. 'Jump in.'

Switch shook his head. 'I'll close the gate then bust up the lock mechanism. It'll buy us some time.'

'Switch, no!' Marta said. 'The fence is electric. There's no way through!'

He grinned at her, his eye twitching furiously. 'I'll find a way,' he said.

The jeep was already waiting on the other side of the gate. Switch had moved it. All he had to do was get over somehow.

'We'll wait for you,' Marta said.

'No.' Switch leaned into the Land Rover and put a hand on Ishael's arm. 'You lead them. Don't wait. There's no time.'

Ishael looked around at the others. 'There's no telling what state the tunnel might be in, even if we can find the entrance. We have to go.'

Switch looked at Marta. 'Don't worry. It'll be okay.'

Before she could reply, he stepped back and waved the vehicle forward. As they passed through the gates Paul turned to look back. Switch briefly raised a hand, then turned and jogged back towards the checkpoint building.

Switch, always the hero. Paul's stomach felt knotted. He wondered if perhaps this time his friend had taken on one feat too many. Simon was gone, a loss that Paul was still trying to comprehend. Jess was grieving, Marta too, but Paul hadn't had time to think about it properly. He thought if he lost Switch as well, his mind might just go into shutdown.

Turning away from the gate as though it were the grave of a long lost relative, Paul closed his eyes as the Land Rover bumped over the uneven surface of the field.

#

Switch watched from around a corner of the checkpoint building until the Land Rover was out of sight. Then he made his way back into the control room.

Matt, the last of the three guards, was tied to a chair, feet secured to the chair legs, hands tied tight behind him. Switch hadn't bothered with a gag.

Above them, a light fitting hung loose on its wire, having come unstuck when Switch fired a shot into the ceiling.

'We'll wait five minutes,' Switch said, undoing the cord that bound Matt's hands. 'We have that long. Then you will open the gate long enough for me to pass through. Once I'm through you will close it again. If it doesn't happen within one minute of it opening I will come back in here and I will find you and fucking kill you. Do not try to trick me. You are alive now only because I want you to be.'

The man looked up at him. 'Why pretend? They think I'm dead, don't they?'

Switch cocked his head. 'I find it difficult to trust,' he said, his voice never losing the icy, sharp tone that threatened to kill wantonly and at random. 'Sometimes, it's better for people to believe you are dead.'

'I won't tell a soul,' Matt said. 'I'll tell them someone operated the gate then went out. I don't know what happened.'

Switch ignored his pleas. 'I need to seal the gate from the other side. How do I do that?'

'There's a manual operation switch to the right of the gate once you're through. You need a pass card to open the control box.'

'I'll take the woman's.'

'Inside is a control panel. Bust that up and the gate is stuck. There's an override in the basement, but it'll take time to find. Who's chasing you, man?'

'If you stay alive you'll find out. I'm quite happy to kill you, though, if you're scared.' Switch cocked the rifle and held it up towards Matt's head.

'No, man, no! I'm sorry I asked, really sorry! I'm just an honest guy trying to earn a living.'

'Another reason you're still fucking breathing.' Switch put a hand on Matt's shoulder and leaned close, speaking quietly straight into Matt's ear. 'But cross me and I'll find you. My friends might be nice people, but deep down inside I'm an evil little shit and I'll quite happily cut your fucking face off.'

'I won't! I promise.'

'Good. Now, it's time.'

Switch pushed Matt's chair closer to the controls. 'When it's done, free yourself. The bonds are loose enough. I recommend you start running as soon as you can. Any direction is good. The people following me aren't as generous as I am.'

He grinned and went out of the control room, leaving Matt to operate the gate controls. On the way out he took the woman's wallet from her pocket and fingered through it for her ID card as he walked down the corridor. Just as he got outside he saw the gate swing slowly open. Good, Matt had kept his word. Switch walked through to the other side, and stood out of the way while he waited for the gate to close, swinging shut in a lazy arc.

Switch went to the door control box and used Kelly's card to open the outer panel. As soon as it opened, he lifted the rifle and fired one shot into the middle of the small keypad. He ducked his head away as it exploded with a crackle and a cloud of dust.

He glanced back at the building as he walked to the jeep. Matt didn't come outside, which was just as well, because Switch really was feeling in the mood for tying up loose ends. It was best that Matt stayed out of sight.

He slipped the key into the ignition and turned the jeep west, following the tracks left by the Land Rover in the soft, wet grass of the hillside.

Chapter Fifty-One
Vengeance

'MY GOD, CLAYTON, what the hell is that? What are they doing?'

Clayton's land cruiser bumped down the lane towards Fence Checkpoint Two in the valley below. The checkpoint itself was a low squat building nestled up against a tall fence that stretched out of sight in either direction. What had caught Dreggo's attention, however, was the raised monorail line that led along the valley floor and up to it, ran alongside it for a short way, then ducked back on itself and followed the same route back among the sparse trees of the valley floor.

At regular intervals of perhaps a few hundred feet, small ore-transporting trucks rode up to the fence, slowed as they came alongside, and then tipped sideways, emptying their contents over the fence on to the ground below.

The smell was astonishing. The pungent stench of rotting food hung like a veil over everything, as thick as foam.

'How the fuck do they stand it?' Dreggo said, glancing across at Clayton, who looked grim. She patted his knee, digging her nails into the cloth, feeling smug. 'Don't worry, I'm sure you get used to it.'

She knew her heightened sense of smell made it worse, but it was strong just the same. Clayton looked just moments away from vomiting. And over her neuro-sensors she could feel the Huntsmen growing into a frenzy.

Feeding time.

The fence and the huge trash pile had obscured their view, but as they climbed out of the truck a couple of hundred feet from the checkpoint, she was able to see the activity on the other side of the fence for the first time.

A horde of what she could only describe as human detritus crowded around the pyramid of waste, pulling the rubbish away, stuffing the rotten foodstuffs into their mouths, filling bags and primitive wooden carts with anything else they could carry. A steady stream of them trailed to and from the fence, half-human creatures staggering back and forth like zombies. And as Dreggo watched, every so often one would just stop, drop whatever it was carrying, and slump down into a crouch, head hung forward.

'Good God, so it's true after all. I never quite believed it,' Clayton said, coming to stand beside her. 'This is where they bring all Mega Britain's crap,' Clayton told her. 'Human and otherwise.'

Dreggo had never heard of this place. 'This is an utter abomination,' she muttered.

Clayton didn't appear to have heard her. 'The result of every failed government experiment, be it gene-splicing, mind-alteration, cryogenic, carbon fiber enhancement, *anything*, on human, animal or plant, gets brought here. And then we load up all our waste and bring it here to feed them.'

'You knew about this?'

'I'd heard of its existence, but I never quite realised the extent of it. I've never had reason to come here though. Few people do.'

Dreggo stared at the side of his face until he turned to face her. 'I can *hear* them,' she said. 'In my mind. Whatever your bastard scientists put inside me, it's in some of them too.'

'That doesn't surprise me. There are a lot of bad prototypes wandering around in there I imagine, many as deadly as the Huntsmen but with even less control.'

'I can feel their anger and hatred. If we go in there they'll kill us all.'

Clayton pointed. 'You see those over there? The ones sitting on the ground?'

'Yes?'

'The people in there are known as Mistakes. Most of them suffer from brain damage caused by whatever happened to them in the research labs. They can be dangerous, but studies made by researchers down here say that they won't usually attack without provocation. Most of the more dangerous burn themselves out within days of being put inside. They either fight until something stronger kills them, starve to death, or die of exposure. Those that survive are more docile. They only attack when disturbed. It's our bad luck that those fucking kids disabled the gate at Fence Checkpoint Three, but short of going another twenty miles north this is our only choice. With luck they'll be distracted by the dumping ground and we can slip past them.'

Earlier, Clayton had been fuming when they found the gate at Fence Checkpoint Three inoperable and two guards dead. Another guard was missing. Worse was that Clayton himself had been forced to call the Governor and rearrange the rendezvous, leaving yet another black mark on his record.

Dreggo had asked why the DCA didn't just cut a hole in the fence. Clayton had stared at her with disbelief and then asked how she'd like to have several thousand half-finished Huntsmen wandering through the GFAs.

Clayton shrugged. 'Don't worry, once we're over the hill we should be away from the worst of them. Then it's your job to keep us safe.'

'You'd know I'd never do that by choice,' Dreggo said with a thin smile.

'Then it's a good job you have none.'

They were interrupted by a nearby agent, who greeted Clayton with a salute and pointed back up the road down which they had come. They turned to look. A long black car moved slowly down the potholed track. Its windscreen and side windows were blacked out too, leaving the car so dark that it seemed to suck the light from the pale morning sun.

Judgment day, Dreggo wanted to quip, but her mouth had gone dry and no sound would come. She glanced at Clayton and saw his hands were shaking. A single bead of sweat made a trail down the side of his face.

The car pulled up in the shade of some trees behind their convoy and stopped. The engine cut out. There was a hum of a fan working somewhere, and then it too stopped. A few slow seconds passed, then the front doors opened and two suited men got out. One went to the back and opened a rear door, saying something they couldn't hear to the person inside.

Dreggo flinched as the Governor, the man on whose dreams and ambitions Mega Britain had been built, climbed out of the car and stood up straight in the shadows below the trees. He was far taller than any normal man, perhaps taller even than the Huntsmen, and beneath the black suit he wore his body was thick with muscle. He turned towards them, his movements slow and languid, his paper-white face expressionless.

'Clayton,' he said as his gaze found them, his chocolaty deep voice floating across the wet, dewy grass. Dreggo knew in that moment that everything Clayton had told her about this man was true, that he harbored a power beyond understanding, be it of the body or the mind. Beneath his blood-red gaze she had an overwhelming urge to drop her eyes and kneel. She knew, as Clayton did, that this was the man who controlled everything, that the so-called government ministers were just puppets to do his bidding, that the elections, held every few years, were merely for show. Even the mock parliamentary debates were merely a way of narrowing and refining policies which were then submitted to the Governor, the immovable Head of State. Whatever uncertainties existed about the set-up of Mega Britain's government, one thing was beyond any doubt: this man ruled.

The Governor glanced left and right as he trod carefully towards them across the grass, keeping to the shadows where possible. A low mist hung in the valley below them but the sun still shone overhead, and on one occasion where its light passed across his face, Dreggo saw his expression tighten, his eyes narrow, his mouth curl into a slight grimace. As he looked up towards it, he seemed to be issuing a challenge, that for whatever pain it caused his skin he would not back down, that he was a man prepared to fight even the sun itself.

The two guards who flanked him wore belts heavy with guns and stun weapons, but Dreggo knew they were as unnecessary as her thoughts of ambushing this man were foolish. Power emanated from him thicker than the mist, and Dreggo knew there was no one present who could touch him, not Clayton's men, nor the Huntsmen she commanded.

About five feet away the Governor stopped, standing in the last vestiges of shadow. His eyes flicked from one to the other, his face once again expressionless. His head tilted back, and his big nostrils flared, sucking in the stench around them.

'This place stinks like the gate into Hell itself,' the Governor said at last. His lips parted in a small smile which he aimed at Dreggo. Then, looking at Clayton, he said, 'I was wondering why you haven't had the gates opened yet.'

Clayton didn't bother to argue against what wasn't a question. Instead he nodded at the nearest agent and barked a quick command. The man rushed off.

'Sir, we're happy that you could be here,' Clayton said, 'to watch the capture and death of the fugitives in person.'

The Governor cocked his head a fraction. 'It's time to end this game of cat and mouse, Mr. Clayton. And it seems, in your incompetence, that I will have to do it myself.'

'Sir, I can assure you—'

'Few people see my anger twice, Mr. Clayton,' the Governor said, and

Clayton fell silent. 'Maybe one of these ... *children* ... would like your job, since they seem so much more capable than you.' Before Clayton could speak again, the Governor said, 'Perhaps you should check on the work of your men.' Then, almost as an afterthought, he added, 'While you still can.'

Clayton ducked his head and without another word he hurried off towards the checkpoint. Dreggo could almost smell his relief.

The Governor glanced at his guards. 'Help him,' he commanded them, and wordlessly they turned to follow Clayton.

Dreggo faced the Governor, her eyes trying to hold his gaze. She simultaneously loathed, feared and stood in awe of him. Part of her wanted to strike at him simply to see what he would do, see what extent of his power she could lure out.

'Dreggo,' he said, and his milky face softened, his lips parting slightly in a smile. 'I have anticipated meeting you with interest. Walk with me a while?'

She nodded and they fell into step, heading away from the Fence and the trucks. After only a few steps she realised that the Governor was deliberately leading her away, up through the trees towards the crest of the hill, until they were out of sight of Clayton's men, with only the cries and growls of the monsters crawling over the garbage clinging on to them. Even the smell began to wane.

At the same time she wondered how he knew her name, and where he was leading her, but the simple strength of his presence made every question seem trivial, as though *of course he would know*, and *who was she to question where he led her? She would know soon enough.*

'Are my thoughts entering yours?' he asked, breaking five minutes of silence.

'I think maybe,' she answered.

'Because yours enter mine,' he said. He took a couple more steps and then stopped, turning towards her. He lifted one hand and ran his fingers down her bare arm. Dreggo tensed for a moment then relaxed. His touch was not seductive in any way, it was more the way a proud father might caress a daughter. It was a feeling Dreggo could barely remember.

'Do not fear me,' he said. 'Clayton is right to fear for his life, but you should have no fear for yours.'

'I have failed you also,' she said, feeling guilt seep into her mind, aware it probably came from his. 'I was given command of the Huntsmen but only one Tube Rider is dead. The others are still free.'

The Governor shook his head. 'These ... Tube Riders ... possess more skill than they are credited with. No one running for their life should ever be underestimated. To learn how to capture is far easier if one knows how it feels to run, something Mr. Clayton knows nothing about.'

'Clayton is a fool.'

A thin smile touched the Governor's lips. 'Then we agree on something. Look at me, Dreggo.'

She turned her eyes upwards towards his, and though she stared hard, she could see no other colour there. His eyes were like two crimson marbles built into his face.

'Are we not one and the same?'

At first she didn't understand, because in her eyes they had no common ground. But in her mind—

'You were made like this too, weren't you? By scientists.'

'I prefer to call them God-mongers, or even devils, playing with a technology that was not theirs to use. But you are right, we both are, or were, experiments.' He cocked his head again. 'And depending on what way you look at it, we could both regard ourselves as failures ... or successes.'

Dreggo felt a frankness flood her, compelling her to speak. 'You're the cause of everything. All those people inside that fence are there because of what you did to our country. Everything is fucked, including me, because of you.'

The Governor began walking again. 'I know you went into Reading GFA,' he said. 'Did the people not seem happy there? The people you slaughtered as though they were nothing more than lame, useless dogs?'

Dreggo squeezed her eyes shut, the memory still fresh. 'I was angry—'

'And you don't think I am? Look at me. I am a monster. Every minute of every day I live in agony. I can't even stand out and watch a sunset without experiencing pain.' He wiped a hand across his huge forehead and sighed. 'It was my dream to have the country working as I knew it could. And from that everyone would be happy.' He shook his head. 'I've made mistakes, believe me. But I am trying to put things right. Do you trust me on that, Dreggo?'

She looked at him. Again came that urge to be frank. 'I don't know. Everywhere I look I see suffering, and in your name I cause more of it.'

'Everyone has to suffer in order to find peace. I'm still searching for mine, but let me try to help you find yours. I knew I would need to earn your trust to bring you on to my side. So I brought you a gift.'

Dreggo frowned. 'You brought me a...?'

The Governor pointed through the trees. There, back off the road, out of the sight of anyone further down the valley, was another parked truck. The front seats were empty.

Dreggo frowned. 'What's that? You brought me a truck?'

The Governor chuckled deep in his throat, a sound like wooden balls jostling together. 'Your present is inside,' he said. 'I left the vehicle there, out of sight, because the gift is rather a personal one for you. Go on, go inside.'

He waved her forward. Dreggo hesitated a moment before starting towards the truck. Was this a trick? A joke? The Governor didn't come across as a particularly humorous man, but what could there possibly be that she might want? All she'd ever wanted for as long as she could remember was to shed the blood of others, and now she'd had her fill of that.

The back door of the truck was open, a metal step folded down. The inside was dark.

Dreggo paused for a moment. She glanced back at the Governor, standing near the front of the truck. A shadow hung across his face. As she watched, he gave a slight nod.

Dreggo stepped up into the truck.

To her human eye it appeared empty, but the motion sensors on her robotic eye picked up something near the far wall, radiating heat, moving slightly. She switched off her robotic eye and let her human eye adjust to the dark, using her ears and nose to create a picture of the room. There was a stench inside, not of rotten food, but of feces. And the sound of sharp, short breathing, and sobbing. She stared into the dark as her eyes adjusted, and let herself see what the Governor had brought her.

There, no more than five feet in front of her, bound to a metal chair that was fixed to the floor, was a man she hated more than any man in the world.

Dr. Karmski.

He whimpered like a child, and she knew the smell came from his vacated bowels. His mouth was bound with duct tape, and the blood that dribbled over it showed how he had cut his mouth trying to wriggle it off.

Dreggo's knees sagged beneath her, and she looked away from him, eyes darting around the inside of the truck, unable to make eye contact. Beside him, on another chair, was a flat screen television.

She sucked in a breath. 'Oh God, no...'

She looked back at Karmski, and he was shaking his head, his eyes so wide she thought they might pop out of his head.

She still woke up sweating, the cold touch of clammy hands a lingering, faceless memory. The dark recesses of her mind knew what had happened, but just in case she couldn't remember, the Governor had brought it all here for her.

She reached out and switched the television on.

The first video was grainy, a shot of a laboratory from above, an empty operating theater. A young girl was brought in on a stretcher and lifted up on to the metal surface of the operating table. Her head lolled in unconsciousness. The camera zoomed in on the girl's face, and a lump caught in Dreggo's throat. A name came back to her, one she hadn't realised she still remembered.

'Deborah ... oh no...'

Karmski made a sound like a whistling kettle, and without thinking Dreggo reached out and clubbed his face with the back of her balled fist. Stunned, his head slumped forward.

The scene cut, but the same camera kept the view, only now it was dark, and the girl was sleeping. From the bottom right, a man came into view, and Dreggo recognised a much younger Karmski. He fussed around for a few seconds, before coming close to the girl and leaning over her face. Dreggo saw his tongue licking at her cheek, and she wanted to kill him there and then. Only a compulsion to see what happened kept her from tearing off his face.

A few moments passed and the girl didn't stir. As Dreggo watched, horrified, Karmski climbed up on to the operating table. His hands reached down to pull off the girl's hospital garb.

Dreggo had the best seat in the house, and the Governor hadn't spared her anything. Within seconds Karmski was fucking her unconscious younger self, his back heaving with the exertion.

Tears filled Dreggo's eyes, and she sobbed openly as the scene cut. Then it began again, a different room but a similar view, the same unconscious girl but with her hair cut short now, what looked like bandages around her wrists. Karmski appeared again, and again he mounted her. Dreggo cried openly, but this time the scene cut off early, moving to yet another a few months later.

Dreggo held her head in her hands as the scenes flicked past. Some were in colour, others in black and white, some from a distance, others close up. From the digital time displays in the corner of some of the videos, she watched a couple of years pass. Then there was a gap of several years, and the final, last video.

Dreggo, older now and with the memory of Deborah long gone, was carried by orderlies on to a similar operating table as before. Her body was bloodied and still, her face ripped open. She shivered, as though watching her own death on tape. Men came and went as the tape sped up, performing operations on her, repairing her body, inserting tubes into her arms and attaching metal plates to her skin. For one brief moment she thought she saw Clayton in the theater. Finally, the scene darkened as a light was switched off, and the video moved forward in quick time, stopping again as the doctor appeared in shot. As before, he approached her unconscious body, one hand running over the metal plate that covered half her face.

When she watched him pull off the surgical robe that covered her midriff, something inside her snapped. With a roar she punched through the television screen, the image exploding in a mess of colour and then vanishing. She stood up, breathing heavily, and looked around.

Karmski's rabbit-wide eyes watched her with terror.

'I hate you,' she growled. 'I want you to die.'

Karmski frantically shook his head, eyes wide. Dreggo felt a strange compulsion to hear what he had to say. She reached out and tore away the duct tape, amused to see it take some skin. Karmski screamed and spat a mouthful of blood on to the floor.

Dreggo backhanded him again, but not hard enough to knock him out. She wanted him to die knowing she had caused it.

'I'm sorry,' he cried. 'I loved you, Deborah.'

'Don't call me that. I was barely a kid when you started, you sick, sick man.'

'I made you beautiful,' he said.

'You made my soul black. Everyone I have killed was because of what you did to me.'

'That's not true. Please, I'm so sorry.'

Dreggo stared at him. The Governor said she could end her suffering. But how was that? By killing him? Or by *forgiving* him?

'*I love you–*'

She couldn't take any more. With a roar that was all her rage and resentment pouring out of her in a flood, she gripped Karmski's neck and began to squeeze. She couldn't look at his desperate face as his skin tore and his neck caved in with a sudden rush of warmth. She screamed again as his arteries emptied over her hands, and then heard a thunk as his head lolled over on to one side. She gritted her teeth and gripped tighter, wrenching until his spinal cord snapped and at last his head thumped to the floor, where it rolled and lay still.

Dreggo staggered backwards, turned and fell against the side of the truck before pushing herself up and lurching down the steps into the sunlight. The grass came up to meet her as she fell, and she put out her hands to stop herself hitting the ground. A moment later, a stream of vomit soaked the grass below her.

She choked, hot bile stinging her throat, gasping for air.

Chapter Fifty-Two
Mistakes

CARL SAT AT THE REAR EDGE of the Land Rover's open back, cradling a shotgun in his arms. He still felt a little strange around real guns – air-rifles had a lighter, less powerful feel. In the opposite corner, Owen sat, holding a handgun.

The hillside rolled away under them as the Land Rover joined up with an old road, the surface far better than anything Carl had ever seen inside Reading GFA. It was as though the government hadn't bothered to implement any movement restriction measures here once they'd moved the people out. The tarmac was almost complete, obstructed only by the overgrown hedgerows as they spread out and encroached on the road.

'Pretty quiet out here,' Carl said to Owen. 'We haven't seen any of those things in a while.'

'Yeah, keeping their heads down, eh. I imagine most of them die.'

Carl nodded. John Reeder had told them what he knew about the area, but Carl had wondered why the failed experiments weren't just killed. Reeder didn't know, but Ishael thought it was in case the government wanted the technology again in the future. The lab cells were full, and it was safer to keep the Mistakes out of the city. They also made a convenient guard for the tunnel, although so far none had bothered them.

'They don't even know we're here,' Owen said as they passed what might have been a woman sitting back in the hedge, head slumped forward against her knees. She didn't react as the Land Rover sped by, even as it splashed her with water pooled on the road.

'I wish the rain would stop,' Jess said behind them. Carl glanced back at her, but the girl was staring at the floor, as though her words had been for her alone. Carl grimaced, wishing there was something he could do for her.

Reeder's Land Rover didn't have an awning in the back. The light rain that had started shortly before they broke through the checkpoint was beginning to worsen. Paul was sitting beside Jess and holding a small piece of tarp over both of them, but Owen and Carl, who had both volunteered to sit at the back, had nothing. They were wet through.

'How far is this place we're going?' Carl asked.

'Ishael said about forty miles,' Paul told him. 'The problem is that the government pulled up all the road signs. He's guessing from old maps but he has no real idea where we are.'

'Typical,' Owen said. 'So much for revolution.'

Paul gave him a tired smile. 'Don't worry, kid. You're first in line to start the civil war.'

'Damn right.'

The Land Rover began to slow.

'What's going on?' Owen asked.

Carl and Owen stood up, looking forward over the top of the Land Rover's cab.

'Oh, shit, there's one in the road,' Carl said.

Owen cocked his gun. 'Let's blast it.'

Reeder leaned out of the cab and called back, 'Hold steady. We might be able to circle around it.'

'What *is* that?' Jess said.

As they came closer they realised it wasn't a human at all. It looked more like a bear, curled up in the road. Thick hair covered its body. Thin, human-sized legs were bunched up under it, and its face was buried in its arms.

'Perhaps it's dead,' Paul said.

Reeder closed to within twenty feet of it, and then started to turn the Land Rover to the right, trying to find a way around the creature without touching it.

'Ah,' they heard him exclaim. 'There's a ditch on this side. It's going to be a little tight. Hold on.'

'Keep your gun on it,' Owen said to Carl.

Carl pulled the heavy gun up to his shoulder, aiming the sight at the furry creature as it came up on their left. It still hadn't moved, but it was almost close enough to touch.

'We're going to hit it!' Paul said, leaning forward to look over the side of the Land Rover. The creature was directly below them, barely inches from the front wheel as the Land Rover moved forward in fits and starts, the wheels spinning in the mud to the right of the road.

The Land Rover inched further forward. The back wheel came level with the creature. A couple more feet and it would be behind them.

'Come on, Reeder,' Paul muttered, wincing.

The Land Rover jerked forward. Carl let out a deep breath as the back wheel moved past the creature. 'Just a little more,' he heard Owen whisper beside him.

Then everything went crazy. Reeder gunned the engine, only for the back wheels to spin, one in the mud, the other bumping into a pothole. Muddy water sprayed the creature, and the tire grazed against its side.

The monster leapt up with a grating roar, a scarred, scabby, blinded human face rushing up towards them. Thick, furry arms gripped the rear side of the Land Rover and the creature swung up into the back. Furry human hands raked at them and black, jagged teeth snapped at their necks as breath as thick as engine oil pulled vomit up into their throats.

'Oh, fuck!' Owen screamed, firing but missing.

Carl staggered backwards as the creature reached for him. Its claws were almost on his neck when it suddenly spun round, hands clenching into fists to knock a struggling Owen off its back and down into the road.

Paul leapt forward but the creature's arms came back up, knocking him down. He gasped as blood spurted from his nose.

Carl heard shouts and screams behind him as he swung the gun around and fired point blank into the creature's stomach, just as the Land Rover braked hard, throwing the creature forward into Jess, knocking them both down on top of Paul. Beneath blank eyes her knife slashed and hacked at the creature's back and neck.

Carl twisted himself, trying to get a clear shot. Just as he pulled the gun up the creature roared again, and this time the faint sound of replies echoed back from the trees and fields.

Carl fired into the creature's back and it jerked upwards, its monstrous face contorted with pain. Marta jumped into the back and smashed her clawboard into the creature's face, shattering its scarred nose to pulp.

Still it came on. The Mistake reached out for Carl, one eye hanging by a thread, broken teeth hanging from tendrils in its mouth. Jess stabbed it in the neck, and Ishael, behind her, almost severed a hand with a hack of his knife. The creature wailed and jerked backwards. Jess and Carl pushed it over the side and into the ditch.

'Where's Owen?' Paul shouted, pushing himself up, spitting blood out of his mouth.

Carl looked around. The Land Rover had bumped forward, and Owen was some way back down the road, lying motionless.

'Oh, sweet Jesus,' Ishael exclaimed.

The creature which now lay motionless in the ditch beside the road had awoken others with its screams. They came in a rush now, a dozen, perhaps more, some running, others on all fours, one even appearing to slide along the ground. Not all of them were obviously humanoid, and some bore closer resemblance to insects.

Owen lay in the road, thirty feet from the Land Rover, seemingly unconscious. The Mistakes were barely two hundred feet beyond him, closing fast.

'Owen!' Paul tried to shout, his voice barely more than a gurgle.

Carl didn't stop to think. He hurdled over the side of the Land Rover and sprinted down the road towards Owen. He grabbed the boy and hauled him into a sitting position, amazed how heavy even a kid was as a dead weight. Owen was breathing, but his eyes were closed.

'Come on, get up!' Carl shouted, slapping Owen across the face. He looked up to see the nightmarish host closing in amid a cacophony of calls and screams, just as a bloodied Paul reached his side and grabbed one of Owen's arms. Behind them, Carl caught a glimpse of Ishael standing in the road with a gun in his hands.

'Get him up!' Ishael shouted, and then stepped in front of them, between Owen and the approaching creatures. Machine gun fire rang out as he raked the Mistakes with bullets. Several screamed and fell away, but most still came on as Carl and Paul dragged Owen back towards the Land Rover. Ahead of them the Land Rover started to back up, Jess and Marta leaning down to help lift Owen over the side.

'Ishael!' Paul shouted as Carl jumped up to help the girls lift Owen. As they got him over the side the first of the creatures reached Ishael, who threw the empty gun aside and ducked sideways, ramming a knife into its side.

'Die, you fucker!' he screamed as the creature swung a huge hand at him. Ishael ducked again, trying to hold off a face that was doglike, all human shape gone. The creature's jaws snapped at him as Paul slammed his clawboard down on its back.

Carl grabbed Ishael's arms and pulled him up. The Land Rover started to move, just as something arced through the air and clanged against the metal floor just inches wide of Jess and Marta.

A metal pole, about the length of a man's arm, sharpened at one end into a point.

'They have weapons!' Carl shouted as the Land Rover pulled away, the nearest creature leaping after it. Its claws caught the back of the Land Rover and a screeching, ape-like face gnashed at them. Carl thrust his knife into its maw and ducked back, relieved as the creature fell away, taking the knife with it. For the first time in what felt like hours he let himself breathe.

His respite was momentary. 'There are others ahead!' Reeder shouted back. 'Hold on!'

Marta, Jess and Paul ducked low as the Land Rover smashed into something and bounced. Carl used one hand to steady himself as he reached for a rifle.

'We need to clear the road,' Ishael shouted.

Carl pulled himself to the front of the Land Rover and stood up behind the cab. Ishael climbed up beside him, holding Owen's handgun. Several Mistakes rushed towards them down the thin road. Hitting them was unavoidable, but the Land Rover wasn't built like a battering ram; eventually something would break, leaving them stranded.

Standing shoulder to shoulder, Ishael and Carl fired at the approaching creatures, trying to clear a path through. Blood sprayed from the Mistakes' bodies as their bullets found targets. Some collapsed into the road or fell into the verges, while some came on unaffected. One or two just stopped running for no reason, and slumped down into a crouch like the first creatures they had seen.

'We're clear!' Reeder shouted, as they swung round a bend in the road and sped down the remains of a slipway that joined on to a wide highway, the Land Rover bumping through potholes and bashing through tall weeds grown up through the cracks in the tarmac. There were no other Mistakes ahead of them, while behind them their last pursuers had lost interest and turned away.

Reeder drove hard for a few miles, then slowed the Land Rover down, picking his way more carefully through the potholes as before. In the back, the others crowded around Owen.

Paul, his face bloody, cradled his brother's head. Owen had a gash on his forehead which Marta wiped with a piece of rag.

'Is he all right?' Ishael asked.

Paul looked up at him, his eyes distraught, his face tight with worry. 'Come on, Owen,' he said.

Without opening his eyes, Owen smiled. 'I'm waiting for you to cry, big brother.'

There was a gasp of relief from the others. 'What the hell happened to you?' Owen said, looking up. 'You look like I just kicked your ass in a bitch fight.'

The others moved away to give them some space. Carl sat down at the back of the cab beside Ishael as Marta helped Jess into the front.

'We were pretty lucky there, weren't we?' Carl said.

Ishael nodded. 'We were. We're almost out of ammunition now. If we get attacked again we'll have problems.'

One glance told Carl how scared Ishael had been. The man's bruised and swollen face was pale, and his top lip trembled.

'They were human, too, weren't they? Just like the Huntsmen.'

Ishael pulled his knees up to his chest and rubbed at a tear in his trousers on his thigh. 'I keep telling myself that they have to die, that it's the only way to save the lives of others. If we get across to France—'

'They might do nothing. They might send us back.'

Ishael grimaced. 'With each additional bullet I feel less of a man and more like one of them. If we ever get there, who will we be?'

Carl had to think for a moment. He understood what Ishael meant, but he had no answer. 'I don't know,' he said. 'I guess we'll have to worry about it when we get there.'

'If.'

Carl looked at him. '*When.*'

Ishael stifled a laugh. 'The confidence of youth.'

'The pessimism of late middle-age.'

'I'm barely thirty!'

This time they both laughed. It was a welcome sound. Owen looked over, wondering what all the fuss was about. Even Paul smiled.

The soft thump of the plastic partition window sliding back broke up their party. 'Sorry,' Marta said. 'Reeder says we've got another problem.'

'What?' Paul said.

'It seems the battery of the Land Rover is running down. Reeder says we have to find a settlement and try to locate a recharging station or find another battery that works.'

'Aren't we close enough to walk yet?' Owen said. 'How far is it?'

'About fifty miles,' Marta told him.

Ishael shook his head. 'They'd run us down. Tell him to look for a small settlement, maybe the remains of a highway service station. We can maybe switch a battery from an abandoned car and bump start it.'

Marta nodded and turned around.

Carl looked around at the others. 'Not getting the rub of the green, really, are we?'

Owen stared at him. 'What the hell are you on about?'

Chapter Fifty-Three
New Order

'HERE. YOU MAY NEED THIS.'

Dreggo looked up. Hands as huge and pale as dinner plates held out a glass of water. She took it gratefully, finishing it in one swallow. She looked up into the Governor's expressionless face. 'I thought you might need these too,' he said, indicating behind him.

What she saw there was like something out of a mirage. A large plastic container filled with steaming water, beside it a small fold-out table holding a fresh set of clothes. She had no doubt they would be her size.

'Where did you...?'

The Governor smiled. 'I anticipated certain situations. Now, let me leave you a few minutes, and then we will talk more.'

The Governor disappeared around the side of the truck. Dreggo and slammed the rear door shut, cutting off the horrors of her past, maybe. Karmski was dead now; she had faced up to all the nightmares that had plagued her and dragged her through the bloodiest days of her life. She felt the murderous strength of revenge flooding through her, and her mind felt vital, clear and invigorated. She slipped off her bloodied clothes and let them fall to the floor.

She used a ladle to take the worst of Karmski's blood off her. It felt good to be clean, though it hurt her to see the extent of the damage to her body. Tears filled her eyes, but she washed them away with a handful of warm water.

The clothes the Governor had left for her were similar to those that Clayton wore, but sized for a woman and with a crest on the right chest that surprised her, a black circle with a pair of crosses in the centre.

It was a Mega Britain military rank. The crest on Clayton's uniform had a black circle with just one cross. Dreggo frowned. That little second cross meant Dreggo was officially Clayton's superior.

She looked around for the Governor. He was standing in the shade near the truck, his back to her, arms folded. She waited a moment, unsure what to say, but he seemed to sense her and turned. He smiled.

'Does it fit?'

'Yes, perfectly. But...' She wanted to say, *I'm a prisoner. I'm not here by choice.*

'Dreggo, I trust you,' the Governor said. 'I have delivered you a gift as a token of respect. Karmski was a great scientist, among Mega Britain's best. That he was in possession of a heart as black as coal was his undoing, as were the secret cameras that only higher government officials knew about. But still, due to his brilliance, his death weighs heavily on my heart. That, though, is a weight I am prepared to bear, if it brings me your trust, your respect.'

Dreggo had a million things to say. They clamored at her, refusing to form a queue. She blurted, 'I was taken in the first place because of you. I'm a ... a monster because of what your scientists did to me!'

The Governor lifted a hand. 'I admit we have research facilities. But the programs were supposed to be voluntary. I was never aware that anyone was being taken against their will, or of the atrocities. I can guarantee that a full investigation will be carried out once this terrible business is over with. I lead a large country, Dreggo. My eyes cannot see everywhere at once, and I trust few to see for me.'

She held his gaze a few seconds and then looked away. *Can I trust him?* His arguments made sense, but it was difficult to break the shackles of torture and abuse that had surrounded her all her life.

The Governor spoke. 'How did it feel, Dreggo? How did it feel with your hands around his neck?'

So he had watched her. She'd suspected he might. She held his gaze steadily. 'It felt necessary,' she said.

'The power of revenge,' he said, nodding, a small smile on his lips. 'I never did go for all that *turn the other cheek* business. Think about how you felt before, and how you feel now. Do you not feel free?'

'Freer than I've ever felt,' she admitted.

'And now imagine that you're still carrying that weight around your neck. Feel the years, the decades pass. How do you feel?'

She thought for a moment. 'Suffocated?'

The Governor nodded. 'I've helped you destroy some of the demons of your past. The demons of mine are a lot harder to find, but will you help me? Will you be on my side?'

Dreggo thought for a moment. She looked at the Governor, her eyes moving slowly down his face, past his neck, to his chest. She stared hard, concentrating, until she was sure she could hear the low thud of his heart. She stepped forward, lifted one hand, and touched him.

His own hands closed over hers and he pulled her closer, the strength she could feel in his hands and arms astonishing.

With her face just inches from his, she whispered, 'Yes.'

'Then Dreggo,' he replied, his voice a low rumble, 'Welcome. Now you lead this operation. Find me the Tube Riders, and let's bring this unpleasant matter to a close.'

#

Clayton knew something was amiss from the moment he saw the Governor and Dreggo emerge from the trees. Behind him, the cacophony from the dump and the scrounging Mistakes had begun to burrow into his skull, while the stench filled every pore of his body.

Opening the gate had been easy. The checkpoint guards, dulled over years of putting up with the smell, had not questioned his authority once they had seen his rank, and the gate was duly opened. Clayton's convoy now waited on the other side, the men and the Huntsmen all boarded and ready. It was just Dreggo and the Governor holding everything up.

Clayton looked around uncomfortably. A few hundred feet down slope, the grotesque carnival of rubbish clearing continued, the howls and groans of the Mistakes filling the air as they scrabbled for scraps of rotten food and anything that could be of use. It scared the hell out of him, watching the zombie parade, but he found the way they just switched off without warning at any time even worse. Dozens of them littered the slope, on their knees, heads slumped forward on their chests. The closest was not twenty feet away, its back turned to him, head hung forward. He had considered having his agents clear it, but the checkpoint guards had warned him that disturbing one Mistake might set off the rest of them. So, as he waited for the Governor and Dreggo, he couldn't help but glance over his shoulder every few seconds just to make sure the Mistake hadn't moved, that it hadn't come any closer. His fingers rested on his gun just in case.

They'd been gone more than two hours. Clayton had sent an agent off to find them, but the man had returned with terror in his eyes, babbling that the Governor did not want to be disturbed. Clayton hadn't asked for details; he didn't want to know. He now waited by the gate, alone besides the two checkpoint guards standing a few feet away, who were eager to get the gate closed and the electrification back on.

He noticed Dreggo's change of clothes immediately. The black DCA uniform was a stark difference to the bloodied trousers and ripped up shirt she'd been wearing before. Her hair, also, which had been a matted mess of blood, was now cleaned and tied back behind her head.

If it wasn't for the metal plate that covered half her face, he could almost have seen her as a woman.

As they walked towards him Dreggo chatted amiably with the Governor, smiles and even laughter passing between them. Above them, rising up from behind the trees that topped the rise, was a plume of smoke.

They stopped in front of him. 'Good work,' the Governor said. 'Are we ready to move?'

'Yes, sir.'

The Governor turned to Dreggo. 'Send two Huntsmen south along the Fence to pick up the trail. It seems fairly straightforward to me where they're heading though.'

'Land's End?' Clayton asked. 'If they can get out to the Scilly Isles they might be able to find a boat to take them down the coast of Brittany. There are rumours of pirates out there.'

The Governor shook his head. 'Again, Mr. Clayton, you underestimate them. They've led us this far. They could have turned south at any time, tried to find a port where they might have found someone willing to risk trying to smuggle them across the Channel. But they haven't because they know it's futile. They know there's no way out of Mega Britain by sea. They're going underground.'

'The tunnel at Lizard Point,' Dreggo said.

Clayton opened his mouth to say something to her. Then he noticed the rank crest on her uniform. So, he'd been relieved of power, replaced by this half human bitch. His anger boiled, but he said nothing. He felt the bulge of the remote in his pocket pressing against his arm. In her smugness she appeared to have forgotten about it, but he hadn't. And he'd use it before she ever got a chance to take it from him. They'd both go down together.

'Lizard Point is around three hours from here over uneven terrain,' the Governor said. 'We had best get moving.'

'I thought the tunnel was sealed,' Clayton said.

The Governor smiled. 'It is. But the Tube Riders don't know that.'

Clayton nodded. So, it was soon to end. Within a few hours they would all face their fates, his and Dreggo's undoubtedly among them.

He let his hand brush against the bulge in his pocket one more time.

Chapter Fifty-Four
Community

THE LAND WAS LEVELING out towards the coast when the engine began to choke. The Land Rover bumped a few times and then the engine cut out. Reeder frowned and dropped it into neutral to freewheel a few final feet before coming to a stop by the side of the road.

'That's it, I guess,' Ishael said. 'How far is it from here?'

'From the map I'd guess about ten miles,' Reeder said.

Marta sighed. 'We walk from here?'

'There should be the remains of a town just over that hill,' Reeder said, pointing at a rise ahead of them. The old weed-strewn highway angled up and over the crest of the rise, a stand of trees on either side. 'It might be worth a try to see if there are any old vehicles lying about. We might find a spare battery, or even another usable vehicle.'

'I'll go with Reeder,' Ishael said. 'The rest of you should stay here.'

'To hell with that,' Marta said. 'We stay together.'

'Live together, die together,' Jess muttered suddenly, and the others looked at her. 'That's what Simon would have said.'

Marta put a hand on Jess's shoulder. 'Jess—'

'He would also have wanted this seen through to the end.' She brushed a hand through her hair, matted and caked with dirt. 'His death *won't* be for nothing. We all go together, and if necessary we carry on to this tunnel place on foot.'

Marta looked at the others. 'Are we agreed?'

Ishael and Reeder both nodded.

'Okay.' Marta looked over at the back of the Land Rover. There, curled up in a huddle, Paul, Owen and Carl were sleeping soundly. 'I'd better wake them then.'

Five minutes later they were all standing on the road, the Land Rover emptied of its supplies. They all had bags slung over their shoulders. Marta, Paul, Owen and Jess still had their clawboards. Carl and Ishael carried the last of their guns, and Reeder held the map.

'If we see any Mistakes keep your voices down and give them a wide berth,' Reeder said. 'Chances are there'll be some in the town over there. What we don't want is to be attacked again, because we can't outrun them.'

The others nodded. With Reeder and Ishael in the lead they set off.

Owen walked close to Carl as they walked in a thin line down the side of the highway, staying as near to the hedge as possible. 'Do you reckon they still have baguettes in France?' Owen said. 'I'm bloody starving.'

'What's a baguette?'

'It's like a long stick of bread. They put ham and cheese inside. I saw them on a DVD about France we watched at school once.'

'You mean bread rolls? About this size?' He indicated with his hands. When Owen nodded, he smiled. 'We have those in the country,' he said. 'Mother used to give me one for lunch on schooldays. Cheddar and bacon was my favorite.'

Owen grimaced. 'Just shut up. You're making me hungry!'

'Yeah, I'm making myself hungry too.'

They were silent for a few minutes, and then Owen said, 'Do you think about your mother a lot?'

Carl nodded. 'Yeah, all the time. My father was a pretty tough man to live with, but somehow she managed it. Even when he was being a bully she was kind to me. She always loved me. Now, although I know my father's dead, I don't know what's happened to my mother. That cyborg woman might have killed her, or she might still be alive. I want to go back, but I know that right now I can't.'

Owen looked sad. 'I'm sure she's fine,' he said.

'Yeah, I hope so. I have to just keep believing it. It gives me something to hold on to. What about you? Is your mother back in London?'

Owen shook his head. He pouted his lips. 'My mother's been dead since I was a little kid, and my father's been gone as long as I can remember. I don't know what happened to him, but he took off somewhere and never came back. Even though I hate him for leaving us, I still hope that he found a decent life somewhere. Perhaps without the stress of dealing with Paul and me, life's a bit easier and he's happy.'

'I hope so.'

'A large part of me thinks he's dead, though,' Owen said. 'People don't get happy endings in this country anymore.'

'We might,' Carl said. 'If we escape from the Huntsmen, Dreggo and the DCA and get over to France, things might be different. We might get a bath, and we might even get a baguette.'

Owen smiled. 'Yeah, I hope so. But whatever happens, I don't think it'll be a happy ending for any of us. Simon's dead, your dad's dead, Jess's parents are dead. Tons of people have been killed. Even if we get to France, we're cut, Carl. How old are you? I'm twelve. *Twelve*. And I've killed men. Every time I close my eyes for the rest of my life, I'm going to see the faces of those men I killed. Nothing can ever gloss over that, not baths, not baguettes, nothing.' He shrugged. 'It's fucked. I just wanted to go to school, study about stuff then come home, play video games and be a pain in the ass for Paul.'

'I guess we just do our best, and see what happens,' Carl said.

'Yeah, that's about right.'

#

Paul, walking in front of Owen and Carl, felt a lump in his throat as he listened to his brother speak. He blamed himself for Owen being caught up in this mess, although he preferred Owen with him rather than back in London, alone. It especially hurt to hear Owen talk about his father, and the time was coming when Paul would have to tell his brother the truth. Owen had seen enough of life, he could handle the truth now, Paul thought.

In front of him Jess and Marta walked in silence, though Marta was holding Jess's hand tightly in hers. They looked like two very dirty primary school children on a class outing. Of all of them Jess was suffering the most, but he hoped the girl would find the strength in herself that Simon had loved so much and pull through her grief. Marta was being strong for her, Marta who was always strong for everyone. He hoped she wasn't about to crack under the pressure, because he felt that if Marta cracked, they would all fall apart. Switch's absence made it worse for her. Switch and Marta had always been close, Switch sharing a bond with her that he wouldn't allow with other people.

Paul always watched people carefully. He had learned over the years how to spot conflict in someone's eyes, and he had seen a lot of it in Marta's. He had noticed the way she looked at Ishael, and had recognised the pure delight she'd felt to see him alive. Paul also noticed the way she looked at Switch, almost with regret. But more than anything, he noticed the way she looked down, the sag in her jaw, the way her eyes hung at her feet when she thought no one was watching her. Here she was feeling a tentative love for someone, but in her heart she felt undeserving of it, felt that she had no right even thinking of it while people around her suffered and died.

He wanted to tell her it was all right, that she was allowed to feel something other than sorrow, that even amidst the ashes of their lives she was allowed to let a seed grow. He wanted to tell her, before something happened to him, before it was too late.

But again, as he walked along behind Marta and Jess, watching the way they leaned close like two long lost sisters finding each other for the first time, their hands and now arms intertwined, he could only keep his silence.

#

Ishael took the lead from Reeder as they reached the top of the hill. As the first rooftops of the town came into sight, he angled off the road on to the overgrown grass verge to give them a little more cover. Overhead, clouds had obscured the sun as it dipped towards the horizon, and a cold wind had risen. Darkness would come in an hour or so, and he was worried about what would happen then. Did these Mistakes become more active at night?

He jumped as his foot landed on something soft, and he looked down to see the decayed remains of a human lying in the grass at his feet. Hollow, bird-pecked eye holes stared up at him; a toothless black maw yawned wide. He took a few steps backwards in shock, but before he could say anything, one of the girls had seen it and let out a little cry of horror.

'Quiet!' Reeder hissed.

Up ahead of them, Ishael saw something detach itself from the hedgerow and take a few steps towards them.

'Down,' he said, waving a hand at the ground. 'Keep still and stay quiet!'

Marta inched up alongside him. 'Did it see us?' she asked, nodding towards the Mistake lurching across the road thirty feet ahead of them.

'Maybe.'

'This is unfortunate,' Reeder whispered. 'We haven't got time to get trapped here.'

The others had bunched up into a group. 'Want me to create a distraction?' Owen asked. 'I'll lead it up the road, then double back through the fields.'

'No you damn well won't,' Paul said.

'Just wait,' Ishael told them. 'Stay quiet, and ... wait.'

The seconds dragged past like a heavy chain. The Mistake took a few slow steps across the road, turned towards them once, turned away, and finally slumped down on to its knees. It grunted once and went still.

'Okay, move on,' Ishael said. 'Be careful not to disturb it.'

They moved on down towards the town. They passed the slumped Mistake, but it neither moved nor seemed to notice their presence.

Ishael glanced back as they passed, and saw the others do the same. His heart was hammering in his chest, the blood making his wounds throb. The thought of another mob of those monsters on their trail was enough to make his hands shake.

Then a light flicked on ahead of them.

'Well, would you take a look at that,' Reeder said, putting a hand on Ishael's shoulder and making the other man jump.

'John, where's it coming from?' Marta said.

'It's coming from one of the houses,' Reeder told her.

'But ... I thought this town was abandoned.'

'Yes,' Reeder replied. 'So did we. It looks like we were wrong.'

'And it looks like they have electricity too,' Ishael said. 'Those lights aren't flickering like flames or gas burners would.'

Ishael led them on towards the town. Evening was beginning to draw in, and as the shadows lengthened they had more cover than before. Even so, they kept to the side of the road just in case they came across any more wandering Mistakes.

The closest houses were just a few feet away. A row of bungalows lined a meandering road into the centre of the small town. Some of the gardens were overgrown; some of the windows were smashed. Other houses, though, looked well kept, lights pressing against curtains giving the impression that the town was just like any other, closed down for the night after a busy working day, its inhabitants safe behind their doors and in front of their televisions.

'Who the hell lives here?' Paul wondered.

A door opened just a few doors down.

'Back against that wall!' Ishael hissed, and they ducked down, just as two children danced out into the street.

'Tom! Brete! Come back inside!' someone shouted, a woman's voice, tinged with a hint of desperation. 'How many times have I told you?'

The children laughed and joked, pushing each other. As a shadow fell over them from the doorway, the boy disengaged from the tussle and dashed back into the house. The other, the girl, stood up and brushed herself down. She peered into the dark, eyes searching. Suddenly her arm lifted, a finger picking them out.

'Mother, there are some Wildmen over there, sitting in the dark. I count seven but there could be more. What are they doing?'

'Oh, fuck,' Ishael said.

'Get in the house now!' the woman hissed at the little girl.

Owen stood up. 'Wait! We're not Mistakes! We're just normal people! Help us!'

Paul grabbed his shoulder, but it was too late. A howl went up from somewhere in the forest behind them. A moment later a hideous shrieking sound rose in answer.

The woman had come out into the road. 'Who are you?' she shouted. 'If you're spies, then the Wildmen are coming now.'

'Let me go,' Marta said, standing up.

#

Marta stepped out into the dim glow emitted from the open door and faced the woman and the girl in the street.

'We need help,' she said. 'We have to get to Lizard Point, if you know where that is. Please, we're not Mistakes, and we're not spies. But bad people are following us.'

'Whoever you are, it's already too late,' the woman said. With a grin almost of resignation, she looked over her shoulder. Cupping hands around her mouth, she hollered, 'Redman!'

She was answered by a distant roar. The woman looked back at Marta. She was about thirty-five, and looked normal apart from something that was wrong with her arms. They were longer than they should be, stretching as far as her knees. Her fingers stretched even further, spindly like spiders' legs.

Marta stepped forward. 'Please help us!'

'Bring your people out into the light,' the woman said. Turning to the girl, she said, 'Brete, get inside. Fetch your father.'

A man already stood in the doorway. He looked normal, as far as Marta could tell. 'Who are these people?' he asked.

'They say they're not Wildmen, and they're not spies. Which begs the question, why are they here?'

'We have to get to Lizard Point,' Marta shouted.

The others had grouped up behind her. Carl and Ishael trained their guns on the darkness behind them. Jess had a knife in each hand. Paul and Reeder hovered at her shoulder.

'Please!' Marta shouted again. 'We're on the run from the government!'

'Forget these people,' Paul said, putting a hand on her shoulder. 'We need to get out of sight.'

Others had appeared further down the street. Doors opening, people stepping out to see what was happening. One or two started running towards them.

'Oh my God, what in Heaven's name is *that?*' Reeder said, and for the first time since they had met him Marta heard real fear in his voice. She looked up, and understood why.

Something huge and dark was loping down the street, head hung low, arms almost scrapping the ground. It looked like a human hunched over, but it was the biggest human Marta had ever seen. Even with its head slung forward it towered over the people that it passed.

'Who is after you?' the woman demanded.

Marta spread her arms, and for a moment the answer seemed hysterical enough to make her smile. 'Everyone!'

The man looked at the woman and nodded. He moved past them down the road, ducking into the hedge a few feet beyond them.

'What's he –' Paul began, just as a loud siren wailed and a chain of spotlights flicked on in a ring extending out into the darkness around the houses. The road out of the town lit up, and there, rushing towards them, they saw a motley group of Mistakes.

'Aim for the legs!' Ishael shouted.

'No!' the woman cried. 'Gunfire makes them worse! Take your people and follow Jin!'

Jin had to be the man. Appearing from the trees again, he waved at them to follow him back up the street, towards the approaching giant. Owen, Paul and Reeder didn't hesitate; Carl and Ishael looked around but seemed reluctant to move from their positions. Jess was standing stock still, eyes on their attackers, knives gripped tight.

Then something burst from the trees just a few feet away, leapt over a garden fence and dashed up the road towards them. Carl, closest to it, screamed in terror and spun towards it. His gun went off, and the top of the Mistake's head exploded, jerking it around. It gave a guttural, metallic howl, then tumbled backwards to the ground, where it twitched and writhed for a few seconds before falling still.

'No!' the woman screamed.

A huge cacophony rose from the forest.

'I told you about guns, you idiots!'

Carl's mouth fell open. He looked ashamed that his fear had overcome him, endangering them all. Marta felt awful for him, but understood. After the terrible things they had witnessed over the last couple of days, they were all starting to lose control.

'Go!' the woman screamed again.

Marta turned, just as the giant man reached them. He was massive, maybe twelve feet tall, his body a thick mass of muscle, his chest covered only by a thin waistcoat which revealed the enormous shoulders that hung on to overlong, muscular arms. His face was a mass of scars, his mouth lopsided, one eye lower than the other. He roared as he rushed at them, arms swinging like scythes.

'Redman, the Wildmen are coming!' the woman shouted.

The giant barely seemed to notice her, but his course veered slightly right and he passed by where the Tube Riders crouched, rushing headlong at the phalanx of monsters that came at them down the street. In his wake others came too, some recognizably human, others that resembled Huntsmen, still others who could be one or more different creatures combined, not all of them human.

Jin said, 'Hurry! We'll be swamped in minutes. There are far more of them than us.' He looked back at the woman. 'Lucy, I'll take the kids. Be safe.'

She reached up and touched his face. 'You too. I'll be there soon.'

He looked at her a moment, then turned and headed up the street, the Tube Riders following him, while around them others moved in the direction of the battle. More cries came from the wilderness beyond the ring of spotlights.

A screaming Mistake who looked mostly human leapt into view from between two houses, dashing into the road in front of them. Jin leapt straight at him, what looked like knives in his hands. The man turned on him, and Jin buried the knives into his chest. The Mistake screamed and collapsed to the ground. Jin barely pushed him off before he started running again. Where knives had been, his hands were human again.

'This way,' he shouted back, taking a street heading left. Marta glanced back once before she followed, and saw the Redman in the midst of the battle, huge arms flailing, Mistakes flying through the air like thrown toys. She shivered at the sight of it, but at least it was on their side.

'Come on,' Ishael shouted, tugging at her arm. She'd been lingering back; the others were all far ahead now.

They passed through a town square. People dashed back and forth, some involved in little skirmishes, others running away. In the midst of battle it was difficult to tell who were Wildmen and who were not.

'In there!' Jin shouted, pointing at a two-floored building ahead of them. Double doors were open, flanked by two men who were ushering others inside. The windows on the lower level were bricked over, while the higher level windows were barred. She saw from the faded sign that it was an old police station.

An explosion came from nearby, followed by a howl. Jin shouted something back that she didn't hear, just as a group of Mistakes raced into the square through an alleyway. Spears sailed through the air and three of them went down, only for them to climb back up off the floor and move on. One of the children pulled what looked like a pipe out of his clothing, turned and raised it to his mouth. Marta heard a whistling noise, then the nearest Mistake screamed and dropped to the floor, clutching at its eye. The child dashed after Jin.

Mistakes were all around them now. In front of Marta, Jess slashed the neck of one who reached for her, while Carl punched another in the face as Ishael grabbed it and hauled it back. They were just a few yards from the doorway. A hand fell on her shoulder and she swung her clawboard up and around, striking something birdlike in the face. It fell away, screeching.

Carl and Owen had reached the door, Ishael close behind. Paul pushed Jess away from a group of Mistakes grappling each other and dragged her towards the door. Marta was just behind them when she remembered Reeder.

She looked back.

John Reeder lay on the ground, something that looked half amphibian standing over him. His face was covered with blood.

'No–' She took a couple of steps towards him, but a strong arm closed around her waist and hauled her back.

'There's nothing you can do,' Jin said, dragging her towards the door.

'John!' she screamed, as the creature lifted a metal spear and thrust it down into Reeder's chest. The man's face twisted with pain as his head slumped back. His eyes fell on her for a second and his mouth shaped the word, *go*.

Marta gaped as the creature jerked the spear out of his body and flung it at her, just as Jin pulled her sideways through the door. The spear missed her by inches, hitting the wall behind where she had been standing, clanging to the ground.

Marta stared at the carnage outside. Reeder was just one of a number of bodies that lay scattered around the square. Small groups still fought, battling with sticks or bare hands. Then the door slammed closed, and a huge deadbolt slammed across. Marta closed her eyes and collapsed back into Jin's arms, tears of anger and frustration stinging her eyes.

Chapter Fifty-Five
Tunnel

AS THE CONVOY rolled past, heading upslope towards the top of the rise, Switch lifted his head. His neck ached from maintaining the position, keeping the guise up while Clayton, the Governor and Dreggo talked just a few feet away. It had been a risk to get so close, but he'd been right that the stench from the garbage would be too much even for the Huntsmen to differentiate him from it.

After separating from the others, he had hidden the jeep out of sight and then headed back to the gate to see what the Department of Civil Affairs would do when they reached the sabotaged checkpoint. As he'd suspected, they didn't cut through the fence for fear of letting out the Mistakes, but rather headed north towards the next one. Once he realised their plans, he moved ahead of them quickly as the road took them away from the fence, their trucks slower over the old roads. At the next checkpoint he'd found a place to hide the jeep and been in position near the gate long before they arrived.

He rubbed his neck as he moved off towards where he had hidden the jeep in a stand of trees. He'd been able to shift position a little, but they'd still taken far longer than he'd thought necessary just to get the gate open and their trucks underway. He'd sensed that a changing of the guard was in order when Dreggo had disappeared with the Governor and come back wearing a DCA uniform. The man identified as Clayton had obviously suffered some sort of demotion. It was all conflict that might prove useful later, as was the brief conversation he had been waiting so long to hear.

So, the Governor knew where they were going. That in itself erased all need for stealth because they were no longer being tracked, but that the Governor said the tunnel was sealed raised a bigger problem. Letting the Tube Riders run into a trap was the plan; let them head into the tunnel only to find it went nowhere except back, into the waiting teeth of the Huntsmen.

He frowned as he climbed up into the jeep and pulled off, heading due south-west, a map of Ishael's on the seat beside him, Lizard Point highlighted in red. Out of the field, he turned on to a small road that would take him around and ahead of the DCA, his jeep able to take routes their bigger trucks couldn't. He pushed the jeep up through the gears, picking up speed, not caring as the small vehicle lurched and jumped through the potholes of the old road. He took a certain delight in driving, something he hadn't done since he was about fifteen, in the days when there had been enough cars on the roads for it to be worth stealing them. It was no tube ride, but it was fun. Perhaps in another life he might have been a rally driver, he thought.

One of their radios had been lost during the fight in Exeter, and the rest of the Tube Riders had taken the other to stay in contact with William if necessary. The jeep was his only hope now, and he prayed it could handle one last journey. Getting to the tunnel and his friends before the DCA did was his only concern. He had to stop them going into that tunnel.

#

Dark was falling when he finally stopped the jeep at the top of a thin lane and climbed out. His body ached from the rough journey, and his stomach felt queasy. The knife wound in his side was sticky beneath the bandages, as though the rocking and jerking of the jeep had broken open some of the stitches Reeder had redone. He hoped it would hold just a little longer.

From here he could hear the roar of the sea and the grumble of the waves as they battered the cliffs. The damp air was thick with the smell of salt, and Switch breathed it deeply, tasting it back in his throat. He'd never been remotely near the sea before, and he found the smells and the sounds intoxicating. Perhaps, he wondered, he'd also been a sailor in another previous life.

Up ahead of him was a clearing. A wide avenue had been cut through the trees, and a large warehouse stood at the end of a long stretch of tarmac, wide enough for four vehicles shoulder to shoulder, in the lee of a steep hillside silhouetted against the evening sky. *Mickelson Packaged Goods* read the faded sign above the warehouse door.

This building, he was sure, disguised the entrance to the tunnel. Up the hill to the right another trail led away, and there, at the top of the cliff, were a cluster of huge windmills, their blades beating against the night sky. Below them, where he had just been, was a large shed housing several generators which still hummed with life.

The power was on.

A mile back down the road, he'd come to another fence, another gate. The padlock had been thick with rust, suggesting the place was abandoned. He'd had to break it open, and he'd left the gates wide, figuring that to put back the broken padlock would be a ruse gaining him a few seconds at most. In the entranceway, he'd left the bodies of a couple of Mistakes he'd killed, to try to give the DCA the impression that the gates had been broken in a long time ago.

There was no sign of the other Tube Riders. He had expected them to be here by now, so perhaps they'd encountered further problems. He had faith in them to make it, but their chances of getting here before the Governor and the Huntsmen were slight now. He had a couple of hours on them at most.

He looked up at the warehouse façade, the wide road in front of it, his curiosity rising. The Governor claimed it was sealed, while Ishael thought it went right through to France. Who was right? If the Governor was right, he had to head the Tube Riders off before they got here. But if Ishael was right ...

Curiosity got the better of him. He had to know for sure. He had to get inside, and find out for certain whether the tunnel was finished or not.

He approached the huge warehouse doors. They were maybe twenty feet high, tall enough to permit any kind of large cargo or military vehicle.

They were unlocked.

Switch slid them back on metal runners, the doors squealing as years of rust and dirt was scraped away. Sweat poured from his brow, and his throat was dry. He was hungry, thirsty and very, very tired, but he knew that whatever was going to happen was just hours away. First William, and then the streets, had raised him tough; he would last.

Inside, a cavernous darkness awaited him. He pulled a torch from his pocket and flashed it about. At least there were no Huntsmen or DCA agents that he could see. In fact, there didn't appear to be anything except a thirty foot wide stretch of tarmac, flanked on either side by bare earth.

The whole warehouse looked rather temporary, erected just to cover over something not yet finished but which was best kept secret. He shone his torch to either side, and located a set of switches. Flicking them brought high strip lights reluctantly into life, and the warehouse revealed itself.

At the back a rock wall faced him, broken only by a huge tunnel entrance at the end of the tarmac. A hundred feet high, it angled gently down into darkness. The tunnel looked finished, the roof rounded and polished smooth. Dim emergency lights reminded him of St. Cannerwells, and he could only reflect on how long ago those days seemed now.

Near the entrance was a single floored brick building. Inside, Switch found a dusty computer console and a bank of switches. He flicked a couple to see what would happen. One brought a gust of damp, musty air flowing out of the tunnel, and he knew he'd started up some sort of fan system. He flicked a few more. One, terrifyingly, caused scratchy piano music to boom out. He switched it off quickly, and tried another. This time he got lucky, and a flood of light burst out of the tunnel as huge overhead strip lights came on.

Switch went outside and looked down the slope of the tunnel. It was just an entrance ramp, because a hundred yards further on the tunnel opened out.

He jogged down to take a look. The tarmac stopped at the bottom of the ramp, yielding to bare hewn rock. Lights and fans hummed overhead but the floor of the tunnel wasn't quite finished, wooden boards and occasional piles of rock debris showing how work had abruptly ceased. To the right of the ramp were a series of huge storage garages built back into the rock, and Switch wondered what was inside. Cutting or clearing vehicles he imagined.

To the left though, was as impressive a sight as he'd ever seen. The entrance was nothing compared to this monster, the tunnel at least two hundred feet wide, and angling downwards below the ocean floor, stretching away as far as he could see. He expected it began to rise at some point, up towards the French side. There was no sign of an end from here, but it could be fifty miles long or more. Slight curves or angles would easily take it out of view.

So, it existed. Now he just needed to know how far it went. Who was right, the Governor or Ishael? Did it stop halfway across the Channel, or was it complete?

He hurried back to the Jeep.

Chapter Fifty-Six
Trap

Darkness had completely fallen by the time the Governor's car led the way up the dirt track to the old tunnel entrance. Dreggo confirmed one of the Tube Riders had been inside, but his scent trail was freshest leading back away down the track, the way they had come. Earlier they had caught the rest of the Tube Riders' scents heading into a small village a few miles back down the valley. Clayton had wanted to follow them and flush them out, but the Governor had decided it would be far more rational to lie in wait for them near the tunnel entrance. If they survived the Mistakes they would come eventually, he reasoned, and if the Tube Riders didn't survive, well, so be it.

'We set up camp back in the trees,' the Governor told Clayton by radio. 'Dreggo will have the Huntsmen patrol the area and await the Tube Riders' approach. My guess is they will come early in the morning, at first light. There is a good chance they will be on foot, so have your men set up sniper positions from the hill above the entrance and in the trees. Remember, no one is to shoot unless on my command. I want them inside the tunnel, where they can't get out. Get the doors open and see if the lights still work.'

He clicked the radio off and turned to Dreggo. 'Soon, very soon, things will be back on track and we can get back to running this country.'

Dreggo nodded. Part of her was sick of the countryside and wanted to return to London, while another part was aching to spill the blood of the Tube Riders. The feeling of her fingers breaking open Karmski's neck returned, and the deliciously euphoric sensation she remembered made her shudder. It would happen again with the Tube Riders, especially the bitch and the little fuck with the bad eye. Then they could go home.

'Give your commands to the Huntsmen, Dreggo,' the Governor said. 'I want the Tube Riders inside the tunnel. The Huntsmen are only to kill them if they come out. Anyone else, though, should be killed immediately. No errors this time.'

'Yes, sir. Consider it done.' She quickly established a mind link with the Huntsmen. She could feel their frustration at the long, bumpy journey, and their desire to kill and feast. Now was a time to be wary of them, she knew, because they were liable to disobey her commands if they didn't do either soon. She warned them, told them to keep themselves alert. One, though, was missing.

Lyen? she sent the link personally to his neuro-frequency. *Where are you?*
Yes...
Are you all right?
Yes...

She felt the Huntsmen being released from the truck under the supervision of their handlers. *Don't stray far,* she told him.

No ... stay close.
You are worried?
No...
You will see the girl soon enough.
Girl...
Be patient.
Patient...

She closed the link. He was all right. Showing him the photograph of his sister had been risky, but there was still a chance the knowledge could be useful. If the Tube Riders tried to escape, they might be able to force the girl to give up the memory card in return for her brother's life. The net was closing, this time for good.

#

Lyen looked around as the other Huntsmen were released from their bonds. One or two snapped at the handlers, but most were calm, aware of their orders and ready.

He slipped into the trees, planning to do a circuit of the clearing and then patrol the area up on the hill. The remaining human part of his mind really wanted to see the ocean. His eyes were good in the dark, and the moon was out, which would help. But, orders were orders.

Or were they? The image of his sister flashed in his mind, and he remembered the moment they had crossed her scent trail and then left it behind. He could go to her now, could see her again, couldn't he? After all, they were searching for her, because she had done something wrong.

She had to be killed.

Didn't she?

Lyen cocked his head. *Lyen,* Dreggo had called him just now. But his name was Leo. *Leo Banks.*

Lyen was a Huntsman, ordered to ensure the deaths of the Tube Riders. But he was also Leo Banks, brother of Marta, the Tube Rider. Leo Banks had been a Tube Rider too, he remembered now. He had been a Tube Rider and a brother. He was no longer a Tube Rider, but he was still a brother.

Were brothers supposed to kill their sisters?

Lyen was a Huntsman.

Leo Banks was Marta Banks's brother.

Which one was he? Which one was he supposed to be?

He realised he had walked further into the woods than he had planned. The fence was nearby; he could smell the metal on the wind. Beyond it was the dirt road which they had come up.

That road led back to Marta's scent. Marta, the Tube Rider and his sister. His target, and his kin. If he followed that road he could find her.

Lyen could kill her.

Leo could love her.

Who was he?

The fence was behind him now. The dirt trail was dark and silent, the night not even broken by the screams of the Mistakes they had been hearing for the last few hours. None of them came here, but there would be Mistakes where Marta was now. Mistakes would try to kill her.

Marta, his sister.

Lyen could kill Mistakes, he could protect her.

Leo could kill Mistakes, he could protect her.

Lyen.

Leo.

Which was he?

Lyen was a Huntsman. Leo was Marta's brother.

Lyen was Leo.

Leo was Lyen.

They were one and the same.

Marta was in danger.

Leo moved into a slow jog as he headed down the dirt track. Within a few hundred yards, he had broken into a full run.

CHAPTER FIFTY-SEVEN
GOODBYES

JOHN REEDER'S DEATH had hung heavily on all of them as they sat together in the basement of the old police station, now converted into a safe house of sorts. The last sounds of the battle above had died down some time ago, as the villagers found cover and the Mistakes lost interest and headed back into the forest. Owen and Carl had fallen into an uneasy sleep, the toil harder on the younger ones than the others, and Ishael knew Carl blamed himself for firing the gun. Ishael blamed himself for giving the order, but as Jin had told them, when the Mistakes came, they came, it was only ever a question of how many.

Jess, unwilling to speak to anyone, had gone off with Paul to help care for the wounded on an upper floor, leaving Marta and Ishael alone. After a while, Marta had fallen asleep, and Ishael had gone off to speak to Jin.

The man's face was blood-stained from the fight. Sitting on a metal chair, he was wiping himself down with a towel when Ishael approached.

'I'm sorry,' Ishael said, taking a seat beside him. 'I'm sorry we brought them down on your town.'

Jin shrugged. 'It happens often. Each time we lose a few more. It's the children we try to keep safe.'

Ishael looked at the man's arms, at the metal implants that bulged under his skin.

'Is Lucy all right?'

Jin smiled. 'I got word that she made it to another safe house. She can take care of herself better than I can.'

Ishael could resist no longer. 'Why do you fight each other? After all, you're all...'

'Mistakes?'

'Uh, yeah.'

'Why do white humans fight black humans?' Jin said. 'Or humans of one nation fight another? They're a lot more similar than we are to some of them out there.'

Ishael sighed. 'It's how the world is I guess.'

Jin nodded. 'We're all government rejects,' he said. 'But all of us are different. Back when that fence first went up and the first dumps were made, those of us that maintained a level of rationality banded together. We called ourselves the Free Folk. We made camps, joined with other groups, and eventually made settlements. We repaired houses, planted our own crops, even managed to find a few stray cows which we bred into small herds. We built generators, got the power back on. Together we rediscovered our humanity, but we can never forget what happened to each of us. We are reminded of that every day, when the Mistakes who are too far gone, those we call the Wildmen, wander into the village, or attack us like they did tonight. But we are free now, and we are the lucky ones, the ones able to rebuild. Not all of the people taken by the government were as lucky as us. Many of them are mindless and destructive, more animal than man. They attack us at random. Anything can set them off, a shout, a cry, a closing door.'

'How do you survive?'

'Any way we can.'

'And the children? Were they failed experiments too?'

'Some of the older ones. The younger ones, though, they're ours.'

Ishael was surprised. It obviously showed in his face, because Jin said, 'Not all of us can, but there are more than you might think who can still carry out normal human functions. Like childbirth.' He dipped the towel into a bucket of water at his feet. 'One of my children – Brete – was dumped here as a Mistake. The other, Tom, is ours by birth.'

'That's wonderful.'

'It's a life many of us never thought we'd have.'

Ishael was silent for a moment. He dipped a rag of his own into the bucket, and mopped his own face.

'I'm sorry about your friend,' Jin said.

'Reeder ... he was a good man. I didn't know him very well, but he gave up everything he had to help us.'

'Then that makes him as good a man as any.'

'You're right about that.' Ishael sighed. 'Thank you for what you did for us. We'd all be dead now if it wasn't for you.'

'We're wary of anyone we don't know,' Jin said. 'Wildmen come into our village in many guises. But we haven't lost our humanity.'

'I'm afraid we might bring worse down on you,' Ishael said, and briefly recounted what had happened. 'We have to get to Lizard Point,' he said. 'There's a tunnel there that we can take that will hopefully take us under the Channel to France. We have evidence that could bring war to Mega Britain, and with it, freedom.'

'While I don't envy the war, I think everyone wants freedom.' Jin was thoughtful for a moment. Then he said, 'We have vehicles. We can take you up to Lizard Point at first light. Before then it's dangerous to go outside. The Mistakes tend to calm down a little more during daylight.'

'What about the Huntsmen?'

Jin smiled. 'How many did you say there were? Ten? Fifteen? Don't worry about them. The Redman can deal with them.'

'The Redman ... you mean that giant?'

'He might look fearsome, but his mind is mostly human. In return for the care we give him, he protects us.' Jin smiled. 'There are some pretty dangerous Wildmen behind the Fence, but *nothing* is a match for a raging Redman. Not Huntsmen, not the Governor himself even.'

'That's a bold statement.'

'One you might agree with after seeing him in action.'

Ishael considered. 'He looked powerful, for sure. But against an organised assault, he'd be just another monster waiting to be tied down.'

Jin cocked his head, still smiling. 'The Redman is far more intelligent than you give him credit for. A group of Redmen could bring down the government.'

Ishael listened carefully. In his mind, plans began to form. 'It's a shame you don't have more of them.'

Jin looked regretful. 'There are others about. One of the problems with Redmen is that they're territorial. When the government filled those babies with growth hormones and animal genes and whatever else, they accidentally put in something that makes them fight each other. The government found that out the first time they tried to use them, which is why the survivors got dumped in here.'

'Unfortunate.'

'It is. But our scientists are working on it.'

'You have scientists?'

'When you spend the best years of your life as a damn lab rat, it's not surprising many people want to know what happened to them. Our technology is primitive, built up from nothing. There are other towns with bigger projects going on, but travel is pretty difficult because of the Wildmen. We have few working cars, and a rail line we tried to put down suffered from constant attacks.' He shrugged. 'But we're getting there.'

Ishael sat back in his chair. It was a like a microcosm of social evolution happening right under the government's nose. The government was throwing away its scientific detritus and that detritus was building itself up into a functioning society, one that was developing awareness and strength. One that could be a huge asset in the event of a war.

'Do you go beyond the Fence?' he asked.

'There are some tunnels. But like I say, it's difficult to travel safely. For every rationally functioning near-human that gets put inside, there are five Wildmen. Most of the good men don't make it as far as the towns, though we try to keep a watch on the main depositing points as much as we can.' He stared at Ishael for a few seconds. 'Life is hard here, don't get me wrong. But from what I remember, it's not that great on the other side of that fence, either.'

Ishael said, 'Back in Bristol I was the leader of the Underground Movement for Freedom. We have guns, and men. If your men can be organised into a fighting machine, then we can be ready to strike from inside if help comes from Europe.'

Jin laughed. 'You have grand ideas, my friend, and believe me, we'd like nothing more than to see that bastard cut down from his perch.'

Ishael said the words before he really understood what he was saying: 'I can help you. The UMF's network is far-reaching. We have small outposts in most of the major UAs.'

Jin smiled. 'You'd leave the girl for us?'

'Who...?' But Ishael knew he meant Marta. Staying would mean letting her go alone. He didn't know what might happen between them, but if he stayed behind he might never see her again.

Ishael stood up and walked away, going to a window and peering out into the night. A couple of dim streetlamps burned in the square, but it was otherwise empty.

Could he leave her?

He had grown up a revolutionary, living in tunnels and in basements, attics and sewers. Everyone he'd ever loved was dead, and for as long as he could remember his life had centred on ways to remove the oppression in Mega Britain. Ways to bring down the government. Here, among these people, these Free Folk, he'd found another link, another wedge that if sharpened could be driven into Mega Britain's charred and polluted heart. But if he stayed behind to help shape it, he would be giving up someone who had come to mean a lot to him over the last few days.

Leaving Jin to finish cleaning up, Ishael went out and back down to the basement room. He went inside and closed the door. Marta was awake, sitting back against the wall, staring at the floor.

'Hey,' he said, sitting down beside her and taking her hand.

'I'm so tired,' she said. 'I just can't sleep. Every time I close my eyes I just see death. Everywhere.'

'John Reeder was brave,' Ishael said. 'And so was Simon. This thing is almost over. A few more hours and you'll be through that tunnel into France.'

She was weary, but she caught his words immediately. 'You said 'you', Ishael. You're not coming, are you?'

She was astute. You had to be to survive in Mega Britain, but still she impressed him.

He took her chin in his hand and bent her head towards him. He pushed a dread of hair away from her eyes, and stroked the side of her face. 'Marta ...'

'Damn you, Ishael.'

'Marta, I...'

She squeezed her eyes shut and pushed him away. 'Why do you have to *stay?*'

'I can help them get organised. I can make them into an army. When you bring men from Europe we can strike from inside too.'

'Why can't they do that for themselves? Why do you have to *leave* me?'

'We'll see each other again,' he said, hoping his words sounded sure.

'No, we won't! It'll be just like when Simon fell from that fucking train! Over! You'll die, or I'll die or ...' Her voice trailed off as he pulled her close. She sobbed as he kissed her, his bruises smarting but his lips desperate, his tongue searching. She melted into him, crying as she pulled the blanket over them.

'Don't leave me,' she cried, tears streaming down her face as she pulled his hands around her body and slipped her own hands under his clothes.

#

Ishael was sleeping quietly beside her when Marta woke. She looked down at him, naked under the blanket, and she felt tears well up in her eyes again. Angrily, she brushed them away and climbed to her feet, pulling her own clothes back on, the dampness of old sweat unpleasant on her skin.

She needed some air, and she needed to be alone. Too much was going through her head.

She went outside, closing the door quietly behind her. She went up the stairs, past other rooms where people were sleeping or talking in hushed tones. She saw Owen and Carl sleeping inside an old cell, a couple of other people lying down beside them.

At the top of the stairs the main door was open. Two men stood guard, peering out into the night.

'Is it safe?' she asked. 'I need some air.'

'The Wildmen have gone,' one guard said. 'We've checked the perimeters and secured the town, but a lot of people like to stay inside the safe houses, just in case.'

'If you go outside just don't make any noise,' the other added. 'Don't stray too far from the safe house.'

'Sure, no problem.'

She stepped out into the square, immediately letting out a tiny gasp as she found the huge Redman sitting just outside, leaning back against an old monument. He watched her through big eyes, his chest rising and falling with slow breaths. He was even more impressive at rest, close to three times her height, his legs and arms as thick as tree trunks, his fingers alone almost the length of her arms.

They watched each other. Marta noticed blood on the Redman's waistcoat.

'Are you hurt?' she asked.

The Redman's table-sized head rocked slowly back and forth. 'A couple of scratches,' he said, in a deep voice that was surprisingly human. 'Always, just a couple of scratches. They can't hurt Redman.'

'I'm happy you're safe.'

'I'm hungry.'

Marta smiled. 'Me too.' She nodded to the left, towards a quiet street that was well lit, heading up towards what looked like a smaller square with a water fountain. 'I just need a little walk. It's been a long day.'

The Redman nodded. 'Keep eyes open. Be safe.'

'Thank you.'

Marta headed off, a thousand conflicting thoughts buzzing through her head like flies, and just for a moment she wished they would all clear off long enough for her to enjoy the moonlit night and the peace of what had once been a tranquil little country town.

Chapter Fifty-Eight
Reunion

LEO'S CHEST HEAVED as he came to a stop, several miles of running making his legs and feet throb. Up ahead of him the lights of the town rose out of the trees. He'd heard sounds of a commotion before, but the battle or whatever it was had died down now, and as he crept closer through the trees he heard nothing but the occasional hoot of an owl.

He froze, sensing something standing close to him in the darkness. It was one of the failed people, one who never made it to be a Huntsman. The figure was a few feet away, not moving, its back to him.

Leo took two quick steps forward and broke the man's neck, then lowered the body quietly to the ground.

Sleeping, resting or not, dangerous creatures became enemies on waking. It was best to have them eliminated.

He approached the first houses, dropping onto his belly to crawl through the last undergrowth before he reached a clearing illuminated by a large spotlight attached to a pole. Across the clearing the town started. He could see a thin alleyway ahead of him, blocked only by a barbed wire fence.

Leo assessed the situation. The creatures in the forest had attacked the creatures in the town, something that happened regularly he assumed, given the spotlights and the barbed wire that hung across the spaces between the houses. From what he'd seen though, the creatures attacked wildly with careless abandon. No one would expect someone to use stealth.

Huntsmen, too, had problems with stealth sometimes, especially during periods of hunger. But Leo was remembering a time before he used to be a Huntsman, when he'd had better control of himself. On his stomach, he crawled across the clearing and found a space beneath the wire to squeeze through.

He followed the alleyway to a junction, where he paused and sniffed the air, his ears pricked for sounds of approach. Marta's scent led off to the left, but as he turned his head back and forth he caught wind of a fresher scent coming from the right. He turned that way, walking slowly with his hood up, appearing to anyone who noticed like another of the townsfolk returning home.

He had expected to have to kill or break into buildings to get at her, but as he turned another corner, he was surprised to see her, standing a few hundred feet away next to a dry fountain, one hand trailing in the basin where water had once fallen.

Marta, his sister. He felt a lump in his chest pushing up into his throat, and a low growl escaped his lips.

To him, she was beautifully human, a living memory of his past that the government had failed to erase. But to her, he was still a Huntsman, and he knew it would be difficult to get close without her raising the alarm.

Leo moved towards the nearest buildings, stepping into the shadows where he was unlikely to be seen, and began his approach.

#

'He's gone, sir,' Dreggo said, jogging up to the Governor as he stood near the top of the ramp down into the tunnel. 'The Huntsman Lyen, the one who used to be Leo Banks.'

'What do you mean?'

'He's ignoring my instructions and he won't respond. I can hear him, but he's blocking his thoughts. He's distant though. I think he's gone after her.'

'His sister?'

'Yes.'

The Governor frowned. 'This is ... unexpected. We may have to change our plans.'

'Sir, I think he's heading into the village to warn her.'

The Governor's white face flushed with anger. 'We cannot have that. We may have to abort the trap and take them in the town. At worst they will come running here. There is nowhere else for them to go.'

Dreggo closed her eyes and concentrated. 'Sir, I can ... feel the Mistakes. The ones in the forest. I can sense something has happened.'

The Governor looked hard at her. 'Can you control them?'

'I don't know ... maybe.'

The Governor's eyes blazed. 'Do it. Call forth their rage, Dreggo. Bring them down on that town with fire in their eyes and hate in their hearts. And while chaos ensues, we will capture the Tube Riders and finish this.'

'Yes, sir.'

Dreggo moved off as the Governor called out for Clayton to assemble his men. She closed her eyes and sent her thoughts out to the Huntsmen and to the people who had almost been Huntsmen. She called forth their anger, sought out their rage. And distantly, through her mind, she heard them begin to respond.

'My Huntsmen ... I command you to go to war,' she whispered aloud. Around her she heard their minds spark into life and their bodies begin to move as they turned and sprinted through the trees, back in the direction of the dirt road and beyond it, five or six miles away, the town where the Tube Riders were hiding.

And among the nearby fields and the forests, she felt a buzz rise into the air as hundreds of shattered human minds began to boil with anger, brush away the pain of their wounds, and turn their thoughts to one last assault on the people who had hurt them.

#

Switch was having a good day. Lying in the grass feigning death not far from where the Huntsmen and the DCA agents patrolled, he watched with surprise as the men began to climb up into the trucks which then turned around and headed back down the road away from the tunnel entrance.

He was soaked in the blood of a Mistake he had killed, his clothes doused, his hair, his face, his hands sticky with it. It stank beyond belief, to the point where he had retched until his stomach was empty of the last of Reeder's breakfast and then some, but the ruse had worked. He'd overheard Clayton telling the Governor he thought there were Mistakes in the tunnel, and a Huntsman had patrolled just a few feet to the left of where he lay still without giving him more than a brief glance.

But now they were all leaving. There were two agents up on the hill, covering the entrance with sniper rifles, but he would easily kill them once the others were gone. Where were they going? What had happened to cause them to leave?

He sensed the others were in danger, but at the least their urgency and the leaving of the guards meant his friends were still alive. He had to help them, but first of all he had to secure the tunnel entrance.

Pulling a knife from his pocket, he began to shimmy through the long grass like a deadly snake, towards where the land began to rise.

#

Leo knew it was almost too late when the cacophony began behind him. He let his mind relax and the sounds flooded in, the Mistakes in the forest creating a backdrop to the roars of the Huntsmen, and above it all, the shrieking commands of Dreggo, their assumed leader. They were coming, all of them, and within minutes the village would be turned back into a battle zone.

Marta, just twenty feet ahead of where he crouched in a doorway, had heard it too. She looked around as though having just woken up, and the dim street lights reflected tears in her eyes.

She stood up. This was his chance, his only chance, before she was gone again.

He stepped out of the shadows.

'Marta…'

She turned. For a moment her face didn't change, then suddenly she seemed to recognise he was different to the other Mistakes in the town.

'Huntsman!' she gasped, backing off.

'No!' he growled, unable to think of anything else to say, and then, trying to prove he wasn't a threat, he slumped forward onto his knees, his hands spread wide on the ground in a praying gesture he hoped would look submissive and harmless.

Marta had been about to run, but now she paused. Perhaps she thought he was injured. Leo had only had seconds to make her understand before she called out for help.

For a moment his own name eluded him, so he used hers. 'Marta … *sister*.' He lifted up one hand and pulled the hood back so that she could see what was left of his face.

She stared at him for another long second. Then her mouth fell open, and she began to cry.

#

It was him. Leo. Her brother. She recognised his eyes, the deep blue that mirrored hers. The rest of his face was a mess, a doglike snout covering where his mouth had been, wires protruding from his temples and feeding in through holes in his neck. She was repulsed and joyous at the same time, washed away by a wave of emotions. Her brother wasn't dead after all. He was right here in front of her, but he had been subjected to a fate that might actually be worse than death.

She couldn't stop the tears that flooded down her face. 'Oh my ... what have they done to you...?'

'Huntsman...'

'*Why?*'

'Tunnel ... Governor ... Dreggo ... wait for you ... run, Marta...'

Her hands, tentative at first, cupped his face. She could feel metal under his skin. 'Leo, come with us, we can save you!'

'I ... save you.' He frowned, and a strange yelping noise came from his throat. She thought he might be crying. 'They come ... now. You ... must ... hide.'

Marta looked up, hearing the wail of the Mistakes. From somewhere not far away, she heard what sounded like an explosion. They were attacking again.

She climbed to her feet, pulling Leo up with her. 'Come on. We have to get back to the safe house.'

He stopped. 'No. They attack ... safe house.'

People were running past her now, people with spears and knives, running in the direction of the perimeter. The attack was imminent.

'This way,' she said, leading them into an alley. 'We can get back to the safe house, find the others, and then–'

A Huntsman stepped out in front of her.

Marta screamed and turned back. Another Huntsman appeared behind them.

'Lyen,' the first Huntsman growled. 'Lyen have ... *Tube Rider?*'

Leo put an arm around Marta. 'Prisoner,' he said.

'Kill her,' the second Huntsman ordered.

'Prisoner,' he repeated.

The first Huntsman sniffed at the air. 'Lyen ... Tube Rider ... smell same.'

The second Huntsman growled. 'Lyen ... is ... *traitor!*'

With a roar, the two Huntsmen leapt forward in attack.

#

Clayton's DCA convoy pulled up just outside the town. Ahead of them, the Governor and Dreggo climbed out of their car and headed straight into the fray, through the last trees and into the town, even as crazed Mistakes dashed past them and threw themselves headlong into the barbed wire. The Huntsmen were in there already, and now he was supposed to order his own men to join the carnage.

He couldn't decide who he hated most. The Governor and Dreggo, for their treatment of him, the Tube Riders for continuing to elude him, or himself for becoming a mere pawn in a war he didn't believe in.

He got out of the land cruiser. 'Get in there,' he said to the men as they climbed down from the trucks. 'Keep alert, wait for my command.'

As they headed into the battle, Clayton pulled his gun and followed, trying all the while to swallow down the realization that he might be walking to his death.

#

With a frenzy the Free Folk had never seen before, the Wildmen surged back into the village, flinging themselves at the doors of the safe houses while defenders fought to repel them. Ishael, watching from the second floor of the old police station with Jin at his side, knew that this time there would be no respite, that this time there were forces beyond simple insanity that were driving the Wildmen forward.

Down in the square, the Redman fought like a machine, flinging groups of Wildmen aside, a series of volcanic roars erupting from his throat. Across the square, Jin saw a group of shadowy figures standing back in the alleyways, and then a volley of bolts swept across the square and thudded into the Redman, knocking him back and away from the safe house door. The Wildmen surged forward, battering the windows and the door, trying to tear it down with their hands alone.

'We have to go out,' Ishael said beside him, his voice desperate. 'Marta's out there somewhere, and they'll break through eventually.'

'They've come for you,' Jin said grimly, but there was no accusation in his voice. 'We'll get a car for your people ready on the northern edge of the town. Get them together. When we counter-attack, you have to go.'

'What about Marta?'

'I can't help her. If she's out there, she's on her own.'

Jin's words stung. Ishael remembered waking and finding her gone, and knew that his words had driven her away. Now she was out there, in danger, and it was his fault. He cried out and punched the wall in frustration, sending slivers of agony from his missing fingernails up through his arm.

#

Jess listened to the commotion outside. The battle was on again, and this time it wouldn't end. She pulled two knives from her belt and headed for the entrance, where a group of Free Folk were gathering in preparation for a counter strike.

'I'm coming, Simon,' she whispered.

#

Paul, Carl and Owen were standing in the corridor when Ishael and Jin came down the stairs towards them.

'Where are Marta and Jess?' Paul said.

Before Paul could answer, there was a crash from the entrance lobby, and a roar from the Free Folk as they rushed out to join the fight. Among the screams they heard a familiar girl's voice.

'Outside,' Ishael said, and headed for the door. 'Come on!'

Chapter Fifty-Nine
Conflicts

LEO THREW THE FIRST HUNTSMAN OFF, reaching for the crossbow at his belt as he turned, using his other hand to push the second Huntsman away. Somewhere nearby, Marta screamed.

Leo kept his crossbow loaded at all times, unlike some other Huntsmen. He pulled it up as the first attacked again, and fired the bolt off into the Huntsman's face. The creature fell back, shrieking with pain and clutching at the bolt protruding from its cheek. Leo saw Marta rushing forward with a brick, just as the second leapt on him from behind, claws tearing at his face.

He twisted back, slamming the Huntsman into a wall, at the same moment that something hard and metal jabbed into his side.

The Huntsman fell away, and Leo pulled the knife free. The wound was bad, but not serious. He turned and threw the knife at the Huntsman, who was trying to load his crossbow. The Huntsman ducked, and the knife clanged off the wall behind it.

The first Huntsman was dead, its head a bloody pulp. Marta, her face hard, resilient, stood over it, covered in gore and breathing heavily. Leo leapt at the second Huntsman, knocking its crossbow away. It pulled another knife from its belt and slashed at him, but he punched its face and twisted its other arm behind it, bending until he felt the bones snap, the metal insertions breaking through the skin.

The Huntsman screamed. Leo reached for its neck but its teeth snapped at him, tearing open his shoulder. He roared in pain and raked its face, feeling an eye burst under his claws. The Huntsman gave him one last slash across the chest, and then Leo got his hands around its throat and pulled, hot blood and fluid washing over him as it died. He flung the body away.

'Marta...'

Marta was looking at him, a shell-shocked expression on her face.

'Safe now ... find others ... escape.'

'Leo, look out!'

He started to turn as she screamed, but even before he saw Dreggo's half-metal face at his shoulder he felt the spear she had thrust into his back. His body jerked upwards as the spear ripped through organs, and he tried to speak but no words would come. He saw Marta rush forward only for Dreggo to knock her away, and then he was on his knees with Dreggo standing over him.

'You betrayed me, and you betrayed us,' Dreggo said. 'It's a shame you won't get to watch your sister die.' She lifted the spear over her head and rammed it deep into Leo's chest.

Leo saw a million things flash before his eyes as the spear pierced his heart. He saw operating tables and needles, dark cells and strong chains. He saw death, pain, murder, hatred. And then he saw light, the smiles of Marta, his parents, his friends. He felt warmth and love, arms tight around him. He saw beauty and peace.

And then, as he closed his eyes, he saw light again.

#

Marta threw the brick at Dreggo as her brother slumped forward, the spear still protruding from his chest near the shoulder, but it bounced harmlessly off her shoulder. Dreggo turned to her and smiled as she wrenched the spear free.

'Now it's time to join your brother,' she said, moving forward.

#

The Governor stepped into the square. In front of him, the huge Redman was at the front of a counter-attack as a group of Free Folk forced the Wildmen back from the safe house. Several Huntsmen and DCA agents were down, while others fired shots or quarrels from the alleyways.

The Governor lifted his hands. A smile creased his lips.

Summoning all his power, he flung back the Free Folk and Wildmen alike, a wall of kinetic energy smashing into them like an invisible train. He felt his shoulders immediately sag, the power sapping his strength, and he gasped for air as he readied a second attack. Across the square, men, women and beasts lay stunned or dead. As the survivors began to climb wearily back to their feet, he unleashed a second blast, strong enough to break windows and send shards of glass raining down on the people back by the door of the safe house. Others were smashed against the walls, bones cracking, bodies slumping dead.

The Governor smiled. They were no match for him. He possessed a power no one in the world could fight against. A group of misfits and failed experiments had no chance against his strength.

As he felt the power begin to build again, he looked back towards the safe house and the depleted ranks of the defenders, just as the Redman's massive fist slammed into his smugly grinning face.

#

With a thunderous roar, the Redman lifted the Governor and flung him at the stone monument in the centre of the square. The Governor struck it head first and fell in a crumpled heap at its base. The Redman rushed forward and again lifted the Governor in its massive arms. As the Governor looked up, his eyes groggy, the Redman smote him against the ground, smashing the Governor how a child might beat a hated rag doll.

In his mind, the Redman remembered this milk-white monster, the man at the doorway of the cell where they held him chained, nodding with satisfaction as the scientists ran currents of electricity through the Redman's body and injected him with substances that made the Redman feel like his eyes were being pierced by needles.

The Redman associated nothing but pain with this man, and as he smote him over and over again, he could think only to destroy this monster, to break him like so many others had been broken.

Then suddenly, the Governor's arm snaked up, and the Redman felt bones in his wrist snapping as the Governor's impossibly strong fingers gripped him and twisted his arm away.

The Redman roared in pain.

The Governor, his face stained with a pinky-white blood, smiled.

'You dare to fight *me*? *You*? I *created* you!'

The Governor gripped the Redman's shoulders and flung the monster over his head. The Redman slammed down on his back. He looked up as the Governor came to stand over him, red eyes narrowed. As the Redman tried to rise, an invisible weight pressed down on him, pushing him down. The Redman writhed, trying to get up, but the Governor's power was too strong.

'You fought bravely, beast,' the Governor said. 'I only wish you could have been fighting for me.' The Governor closed his eyes. Redman heard a cracking, splintering sound, and roared one final time as the building above him began to collapse, a waterfall of masonry raining down on his head. The Governor jumped aside as bricks and lintels crashed down, burying the Redman under the rock.

#

As the dust settled, nothing remained visible of the Redman. The Governor let his breath come heavy, the exertion of the fight almost too much for him. He would never let be it known, but his power had grown weak through years of neglect, and the Redman, one of a group of mere foot soldiers created under his watchful eye, had come a lot closer to victory than he found it comfortable to admit. It was time to start awakening his power if he hoped to win this battle and make Mega Britain safe again.

He looked around the square, now deserted. Down side streets he could hear the sounds of a battle still raging. He let his mind drift, searching for Dreggo.

When he found her, he frowned. In danger? Surely there were no more surprises these people could conjure up?

He turned and headed off down the nearest side street, his mind searching for her.

#

Marta showed no intention of running away. She jumped at Dreggo even as the half-human former Cross Jumper came for her.

'I'll kill you, you evil fucking *bitch!*' Marta screamed, grappling with Dreggo, trying to get at her eyes.

At first Dreggo was a little taken aback by the ferocity of the assault, but her strength began to tell as she pushed Marta away and punched her in the face, knocking the Tube Rider to the ground. As Marta tried to twist out of range, Dreggo grabbed her from behind, planning to finish it quickly.

Then something happened.

The whole world turned white.

Dreggo screamed as pain surged through her like a phalange of firebrands. She squeezed her good eye shut until she thought it would burst, and she raked her own body with her hands as she rolled across the ground. She felt Marta slipping away from her, and through the agony that wanted to destroy her she screamed the only word that could possibly offer a solution:

'*Clayton!*'

#

He stepped out of the shadows to stand beside Dreggo's writhing form, his finger pressed so hard on the button of the stun control that the nail was white. With his other finger he turned a dial on the side up to the highest setting.

'Tell that bastard downstairs I'll see him soon,' Clayton shouted at her.

It was all he could do to stop himself kicking her as she lay at his feet. When finally he relaxed his finger, Dreggo was barely moving. A small groan dribbled from her throat and her body shook with spasms. Clayton looked up and saw Marta, one of the girl Tube Riders, standing a few feet away, staring at him, openmouthed. She was covered head to toe in blood and gore.

'Is she dead?' Marta asked.

'She will be when I'm done with her. Go now. Take your people and head for the tunnel on the coast.' He flicked a thumb over his shoulder. 'The Governor thinks it's a dead end. He planned to trap you there, but I've seen the plans. It's finished. It goes all the way through. Get across and you're safe, but you have to go now. The Governor is here, in this village. You do not have much time.'

Marta nodded. 'Thank you.' She seemed reluctant to move. She looked down at Leo's body and pointed. 'He was my brother,' she said.

'I know. And I'm sorry it had to be this way. I'm sorry that any of this had to happen. I'm sorry you had to live in this world, but if I can do just one good thing in my life ... just one thing that helps someone ... go *now!*'

Marta flashed him a quick smile of thanks then turned and ran. For a few seconds Clayton watched her go. Then he pulled a radio from his belt and switched it to his agents' common frequency.

'Agents of the DCA, this is your Commander, Leland Clayton,' he said. 'Something has gone wrong with the Huntsmen. The Governor has given the order to kill them all. Shoot on sight.'

He switched the radio off. He put it back on his belt and pulled his gun. Looking down at Dreggo, he said, 'It ends now, you fucking monster.'

He lifted his gun, but before he could pull the trigger, a voice from behind him said: 'Do you know the meaning of the word *treason*, Mr. Clayton?'

Clayton spun as fast as his training would allow. He brought up the gun with which he had dealt countless deaths, and his marksman's eye pulled the trigger on the man standing in the road behind him. He was quick, but the Governor was no mere human. Another man would have been dead, but the Governor moved just enough to take the bullet low in his shoulder instead of his heart. He grunted and staggered, but not before the gun had been torn from Clayton's hand by an invisible force Clayton would not have believed possible, leaving his fingers sore and aching.

The Governor took a step forward. He lifted his hands, but this time he didn't send Clayton tumbling away from him. Clayton jerked forward, and the Governor's hands closed around his neck.

'An eye for an eye, Mr. Clayton,' the Governor said.

Clayton looked up into the Governor's eyes as the iron grip tightened, and in the seconds before blackness claimed him forever, he stared deep into those crimson eyes, and was sure he could see the face of the devil himself there. The devil appeared to be smiling.

Clayton smiled back.

#

Marta had run down a couple of streets when she heard someone shouting her name. Turning, she saw Ishael running towards her. She fell into his arms, crying.

'Thank God,' he gasped. 'Quickly, you have to go. There's a car.'

Marta couldn't speak. Her throat felt dry and cracked, and no words would come. Ishael kissed her forehead and dragged her after him. A couple of minutes later they turned a corner and found a car waiting in front of them, its engine idling. In the back were Carl, Owen and Jess. Paul sat at the wheel. Jin stood beside the open front passenger door, with Lucy next to him.

Ishael didn't say a word as he pushed her inside and shut the door. The window had been broken, so Ishael leaned down and kissed her quickly on the lips. 'I love you, Marta Tube Rider,' he said.

'They took my brother, don't you leave me too!' she cried, finding her voice at last. She tried to hold on to his arm, but Paul pulled her back.

'Marta, we have to finish this!'

'You have to go now,' Jin said. 'The Huntsmen are all here. The tunnel entrance is clear.'

'Ishael!'

He pulled her hand off his arm. 'I'll see you very soon,' he said. 'In a better place.'

Marta felt Jess's arms around her shoulders as Paul steered the car away. From the back she could hear both Carl and Owen sobbing. Through the window, she saw Ishael standing beside Jin and Lucy, his arm raised. Then they turned out of sight.

She tried to stop herself from crying, but she couldn't. Tears rolled down her cheeks, cutting little channels in the grime and blood.

#

Dreggo opened her eyes to see the Governor's bloody face leaning over her. His shirt, too, was soaked with blood, and had a burn hole near the shoulder.

He reached out to pull her up.

For a moment she couldn't stand, but the Governor held her steady.

'My Dreggo,' he said, his rumbling voice containing a hint of sadness. 'What has he done to you?'

Dreggo looked down at herself. Parts of her clothing had been torn away, and the skin of her legs and chest bubbled with burn blisters. When she reached up to touch her face her skin was damp with blood and pus. Her whole body shook. She could still feel the shocks of pain coursing through her, and her vision seemed to flicker, as though her mind were switching on and off.

Clayton's bloodied body lay not far away. Beyond him was the body of a Huntsman, Lyen. Two others lay nearby.

Things started to come back to her in flashes.

'We have to go,' the Governor said. 'This finishes tonight.'

Chapter Sixty
Last Stand

SWITCH HEARD THE VEHICLE before he saw it and ducked out of sight, expecting it to signal the return of Clayton's men. Instead, an unfamiliar car bumped into the clearing and skidded to a halt just short of the warehouse doors. Switch recognised Paul at the wheel, and he hesitated only a second before dashing from cover, shouting the names of his friends as he ran.

Someone cried out in alarm and he saw a gun barrel appear at the rear window. He dived to the right as the gun went off, the muzzle flaring bright in the darkness. Rolling back to his feet, he remembered he was still caked head to toe in someone else's blood.

'It's me, you idiots! It's Switch!'

Someone else pushed the gun barrel aside as it roared again, but this time the bullet embedded itself harmlessly into the ground.

'Sorry!' Owen shouted. 'Can't be too careful what with all these monsters about!'

Switch unable to suppress a grin. The boy was like a twelve-year-old version of himself. Had *he* been behind the gun, faced with some screaming, blood-soaked man, he would have fired *three* times.

Paul climbed out of the car. 'God, it's good to see you again.'

'And you,' Switch replied. 'What happened down there?'

Paul shook his head. 'It's difficult to explain ... just *carnage*. Complete and utter carnage. Reeder is dead. Ishael stayed behind. One of the Huntsmen was

Marta's brother—'

'What?'

'It's complicated.'

'Sounds it. The Governor, Dreggo and the Huntsmen?'

'Still in the village when we got away.'

'Good, that gives us time.'

'Switch!' Marta shouted from of the car. 'Are you all right?'

'Never better, apart from the fucking smell. You need to hurry. You might have a head start now but it won't last long. The tunnel entrance is inside the warehouse. You need to take the car down into the tunnel and start driving.'

'What about you?'

'I'll be right behind you. I have work to do before they get here. To cover our backs, make sure they can't follow. Just trust me, I'll be fine.'

'Don't leave us!'

'I'll be following behind you. Unfortunately, so will the Huntsmen if I don't cover our asses.' He slapped Paul on the back. 'Get in the car. I'll get the doors open.'

As Switch reached the warehouse doors and flung them open, he heard the first howling from the woods. He shook his head. God, they were relentless.

After killing the guards, he had made sure the lights were still on, and then disabled the switches to make sure there was no way they could be turned off. He'd faced the Huntsmen in dark tunnels once before, and he had no intention of doing it again.

As Paul drove the car through the opening, Switch lifted a hand to wave. Once again, he thought, it might be the last time, but for their sakes he hoped it wasn't. If they didn't see him again, they would all be dead.

The car disappeared out of sight down the entrance ramp. Switch counted the seconds in his head. He had got up to around two hundred before he heard the sound of vehicles approaching. He ducked back into the nearest trees as a truck pulled into the clearing. Just one now, he observed. The battle had taken its toll on them, too, it seemed.

The truck paused just long enough for the driver to see that the warehouse doors were open. Switch thought the Governor was driving, but it was difficult to be sure. The truck moved on inside, cautiously, as though expecting a trap.

Good, he thought. *Give the others a little more time to get a head start. Every se-*

cond helps.

Switch waited a few seconds before stepping out of the trees. He was about to head for the tunnel entrance when he heard movement behind him. He turned to see several Huntsmen burst out of the trees, sprinting for the warehouse entrance, hoods pulled over their faces and crossbows ready in their hands.

Switch dived to the floor as death raced passed him, aware that any one of them might spot him and bring the whole wraithlike group his way. He would have no chance; you only got so many lives, after all. But they didn't, his bloody disguise still holding true as they raced after the truck and down into the tunnel, moving at speeds unnatural for any normal human. He counted ten, the last of their host.

He lay on the grass, holding his breath, until a couple of minutes had passed. No other Huntsmen came.

Hoping his luck would hold just a little longer, Switch climbed to his feet and followed them down into the tunnel.

#

Paul pushed the car hard as it bumped along the uneven tunnel floor. In the back seat, Owen and Carl had their guns pointing out through the broken glass of the rear windscreen. Jess sat on the left, directly behind Marta. Paul couldn't hear what Jess was saying as she leaned forward, but Marta had calmed down since the flight from the village. Paul had never seen her so upset before, as though the events of the past few days had finally broken her. Jess, on the other hand, seemed to have pulled through losing Simon and was growing in strength.

The immense tunnel stretched away ahead of them. Paul took a path along the left side, because the centre was covered with dusty tarps and wooden boards, as though the floor had never been finished. Even along the side he constantly had to steer round outcrops of rock both from the walls and the floor, as though the drilling equipment had failed to break through some harder seams.

For the first couple of miles the tunnel angled gradually downward before leveling out. The ceiling got lower and the walls closed in, but even after they had been driving for twenty minutes it was still fifty feet above their heads.

'Can you see France yet?' Owen shouted.

'Not yet! About another half an hour!'

'I'm hungry. Order me a baguette at the first café we get to!'

'Will do,' Paul said. His brother sounded slightly hysterical, and Paul knew Owen was making a conscious effort to keep up the humour. If Owen let the events of the last couple of days get to him it might simply fry his mind. While Paul didn't share his brother's forced enthusiasm, he did feel like a weight had come off his chest for the first time in years. Almost there ...

The tunnel meandered gently back and forth. Paul could always see a mile or so ahead. 'Any sign of pursuit?' he asked.

'Not yet. Whatever Switch did, it looks like he did a good job,' Owen said.

Paul nodded. Switch. He hoped his friend made it. He wouldn't mind sitting in a café in France with him, sharing a few stories. Talking about their adventures–

Paul's blood went cold. His mouth dropped open and he stared, disbelieving.

'Is that ... what I think it is?' Marta gasped from the passenger seat.

'I don't ... I don't know,' he said.

'It's blocked!' Jess shouted. 'They were wrong. They were all wrong. It's not finished at all!'

'That man lied to me,' Marta said. 'He told me it was finished!'

Paul slowed the car. Ahead of them they saw what they'd been dreading, the only thing that could possibly stand between them and safety.

An impassable wall of grey rock.

The tunnel ended abruptly. The construction work continued right up to the rock wall, the boards on the floor, and the piles of old scaffolding over on the far side. The rock face rose sheer out of the earth, stretching high over them to where it joined the ceiling above.

'Here they come!' Carl shouted, his voice breaking up. Paul thought he might be crying.

Paul stopped the car a short distance from the end of the tunnel. His heart felt as heavy as lead. His legs sagged as he climbed out and looked back, seeing a black car bouncing along the tunnel floor towards them. He had never faced his own death before, and the way it made him feel was stunning, the most hollow, empty, helpless feeling he'd ever experienced.

'Paul, get yourself together,' Owen said beside him. 'If this is it, we die like men, yeah? Not cowards.'

Paul looked at his brother, and his heart burned with love for him. He put an arm around Owen's shoulders and pulled him close. 'I –'

'Don't fucking say it,' Owen said, grinning. 'Jesus Christ, what kind of a pussy are you? We've got fighting to do.'

Paul started to laugh. A moment later Carl joined in. Within seconds they were all laughing, even Jess, united in their helplessness, but still, at the end, *together*.

Marta took a deep breath. From her face Paul could see she was swallowing down hysteria and trying to stand tall as their leader.

'Get behind the car,' she said. 'Here we make our last stand. The Tube Riders. Live together ... die together.'

'Maybe they'll write books about us,' Owen quipped.

'A stage play,' Carl said, his voice trembling.

'Whoever plays Paul will be a woman in drag,' Owen said.

'And whoever plays you will be a girl in a pink dress,' Paul said.

Owen raised an eyebrow. 'Man, you suck at retorts.' He grinned insanely. 'Come on, let's kill monsters!'

'Yeah!'

'Yeah!' A cheer went up from the others. Owen and Carl took up positions behind the car. Jess handed out knives to Paul and Marta, who pulled her pepper spray out of a pocket in her shirt, wondering if she would finally get a chance to use it.

About fifty yards away, the car stopped. The engine cut off, and the doors opened. The Governor climbed out of one side, Dreggo from the other. The human half of the girl's face was all burned up. Beside him, he felt Marta tense.

'I thought she was dead,' Marta said. She turned to him. 'Give me the gun, Paul. Give me the gun!'

'Wait, just wait a minute.'

'Now!'

'Grab her, Carl.'

Carl wrapped his arms around Marta as she tried to struggle free. Behind the car, Paul saw shadowy figures approaching down the tunnel. The last of the Huntsmen.

Carl had managed to calm Marta enough to keep her quiet. Paul glanced up over the bonnet of the car just long enough to see the Governor take a couple of steps forward. Paul had seen him briefly from a distance during the Governor's battle with the Redman, but now, seeing him up close, he felt overawed. This was the man who had built the perimeter walls, this was the man who had separated Britain up into sections and given the country a new name. This was the man in whose name the Department of Civil Affairs rounded up supposed dissidents and left them to rot in government cells. This was the man whose spacecraft crashed and burned into the streets of London, the man on whose hands was the blood of so many.

This was their leader.

Either the Governor didn't know they had guns, or he didn't care, because he had no cover. He spread his arms like a priest addressing a congregation.

'Give up, Tube Riders,' he shouted. 'It's over.' Behind him, the last Huntsmen assembled behind Dreggo. With her consortium of wraiths the girl looked like the Gatekeeper of Hell itself.

'We will spare your lives, if you give up without a fight,' the Governor continued. 'You have something that we want, that's all. Standing your ground now is futile. You cannot escape, but you can die. And you *will* die if you try to fight, I can assure you of that.'

Paul glanced at the others, but it was Jess who stood up, in plain view. 'One day, you'll get what you deserve!' she shouted. 'For everything you've done, for everyone you've killed and who has died in your name. You will see justice, you fucking ugly, milk-faced *freak*–'

The Governor started to open his mouth, but confusion suddenly spread over his face. He looked from side to side, frowning, as though searching for something. It took Paul a moment to realise what it was, for at first it was something so familiar to him that he hadn't even noticed it.

'Oh my God,' Marta said. 'Look!'

Behind them, back up the tunnel, two huge headlights appeared, accompanied by a roaring ocean of sound. It was a sound they all knew, one they had waited for a thousand times.

A train.

It rushed towards them down the centre of the tunnel, pushing a wave of splintering wood and flapping tarpaulin in front of it. Paul suddenly understood the mess in the centre of the tunnel: it had covered rails, rails that this monstrous, ancient freight train was now uncovering as it roared towards them, munching up the ground in front of it.

'It's going to crash!' Jess shouted, but Carl, a sudden realization dawning in his face, picked a chunk of broken masonry off the floor, turned, and hurled it at the rock face behind them. It hit with a small thud, releasing a puff of dust and leaving behind a small crater in what they had assumed was a wall of rock.

'Look! It's fake!' he shouted. 'It's not rock at all. It's *plaster!*'

Paul felt like someone had taken a foot off his chest. 'Switch is in the train, he has to be! He knew all along! Get ready!'

Back up the tunnel, Dreggo screamed, 'Kill them!' and the Huntsmen surged forward. Marta, Paul, Jess, and Owen grabbed their clawboards as the beasts closed the gap between them, still fearsome but looking so, so tiny as the train bore down on them all.

'Tube Riders, get ready to ride!' Marta shouted.

As the train reached them, Marta, Jess and Owen dashed forward towards the tracks. The Huntsmen turned in their attack to try to cut them off but it was too late; all three leapt forward and caught on to the wooden slats on the side of a cargo car.

Paul looked back. 'Carl!'

In their panic they had forgotten the boy had no clawboard, Paul realised. After all he had done for them Paul would not let him be left behind, but when his eyes searched for the boy he saw Carl had taken the last of their guns and had turned to face the oncoming host.

'This is for my father!' Carl shouted, raking them with bullets, the recoil causing his body to judder. Behind the Huntsmen, Dreggo and the Governor dived for cover. Several of the Huntsmen fell away, wounded. Others came on, crossbows rising. As the gun spat out its last bullets, Carl threw it aside and pulled a knife from his belt. 'Come on!' he screamed.

Paul had seen too many people die; he wasn't about to watch Carl join them. He grabbed the boy's arm and swung him around, pulled him towards the train. He held out his clawboard, offering one strap to Carl.

'With me!' he shouted, starting to run, pulling Carl after him. 'When I say, you jump for your life, Carl!'

Ahead, the front of the train smashed into the fake rock wall with a deafening crash, sending chunks of plaster raining down on the roof of the cab.

'One ... two ... three ... *jump!*' Paul shouted, and then together they leapt, the clawboard between them.

The metal hook caught on a wooden slat of the passing freight truck. Paul slammed against the side of the train. He was terrified the wood would break under their combined weight, and his feet scrabbled for a ledge somewhere. Beside him, Carl had found a hold with his free hand, and was struggling to find purchase for his feet. He glanced across at Paul and flashed a smile. As Paul smiled back, he could only think how he wished Switch could have seen them.

Madness. Complete madness. One moment he had been facing certain death, and now they were speeding on towards France, the Huntsmen and the Governor left in their wake. He looked for the others and saw they were all hanging on. He afforded himself a little smile of satisfaction.

#

Switch leaned out of the cab as the train raced on. Behind him, Marta and Jess were closest, with Owen on the same car behind them. Paul and Carl were several cars back.

'You have to move forward!' he shouted. 'I need to release the back trucks! It's our only fucking chance! Get into the cab!'

He watched, frustrated, as Marta and Jess inched towards him. Behind them, Owen was calling to Paul and Carl to get on to the roof and jump across the gaps between the trucks. He saw them make it across one, then dash forward, Carl far nimbler than Paul, who looked set to fall off at any moment. They made it across another, but they were still too slow …

Switch grimaced. They were on the first of the trucks he needed to release. With his right hand he steadied himself as he leaned out of the window, while in his left his fingers drummed against the casing of what looked like a radio transmitter.

'Come on…'

Marta and Jess had reached the cab. Switch helped them climb inside.

'Owen…?'

'Don't worry, he's fine.' Switch pointed, as he saw Paul reach across and get a hold on the first truck, Owen holding his hand steady. Carl stood behind him.

'Marta,' Switch said. 'Keep an eye on the controls. Keep the speed rising.'

'Why?'

He gave her a wide grin, his bad eye flickering wildly. 'Because I'm about to unleash arma-fucking-geddon,' he said, lifting up the radio.

'What do you mean?'

Switch stepped forward and pressed a button on a digital control screen. A computer image of the train appeared. Switch pressed a button that hung in the space between the first and second trucks. The word "release?" appeared, the words "yes" and "no" flashing below it.

He glanced out and saw that Paul had made it across. As he watched, Owen helped Carl get over the gap.

Switch looked up and grinned. 'Heads down,' he said. His finger jabbed out and hit the 'yes' button.

The train lurched forward as the rear trucks detached, leaving just one truck attached to the cab. Switch looked out of the window to see the detached trucks slowing behind them, falling away, coming to a gradual stop.

'One, two, three, four, five ... once I caught a fucking fish alive ... six, seven, eight, nine, ten ... then I let it fucking go again—'

Switch's finger depressed a red button on the radio control. A second passed. Then an explosion louder than he could have imagined rocked the tunnel behind them. The walls shook around them, and further back, increasingly large chunks of rock fell from the roof to smash into the tracks below. The train bucked, and for a moment he was worried it might derail itself. Then, as the tremors eased it shimmied back into line and sped on, carrying them away from the destruction.

Marta, pushed to her knees by the shock, stared at him. '*What* was in those trucks?'

'Our get-out clause,' Switch said. 'Guns, arms, explosives. Old ones, left behind. This whole train was armed as a supply for an invasion force. Everything was a little musty, a little old. I just wired up a simple charge. Looks like it worked.'

He glanced out one more time, to see what looked like a wall of water pursuing them down the tunnel.

'Ah ha ha, it worked!' he screamed. 'It fucking worked!'

'Switch, what the fuck have you done?' Paul yelled at him, climbing into the cab.

'Just made sure no one could follow us,' he said, grinning.

'You're fucking *insane!*'

'Too late,' Marta said. She pointed. 'Look!'

#

The Governor watched as the train plowed past them, the coverings over the rails breaking up in front of it like a wooden wave. His heart was heavy with disappointment, with the shame of being outsmarted once again. These kids, the Tube Riders, had displayed a level of ingenuity that he would have to try to follow, or his carefully sculpted Mega Britain would disappear in the same way that they had.

He turned and started walking back toward the truck. The Huntsmen still followed the Tube Riders, but it was too late now. The Tube Riders were gone, escaped, and all that was left for the Governor was to begin preparations for war. The European Confederation would undoubtedly come now, and when it did he had to be ready. He felt quietly confident, though; Mega Britain had a few surprises that their military leaders would not be anticipating.

'Dreggo,' he shouted. 'Order a retreat. We leave for London, now.'

It took him a few moments to realise she was no longer there. When he looked back, the train was speeding away, its last trucks just passing him, but his eyes were still good. He could see her, up near the front, hanging on to the side.

He sighed, saddened. She would have made a perfect second. She was a rare person, one who might understand him, but she possessed demons of her own, and despite his best efforts, she still had to chase them down.

'Good luck,' he whispered, climbing into the front of the car and starting the engine. 'One day I hope you come back to me.'

He started to pull away, but he had gone no more than a few hundred feet when a massive explosion rocked the tunnel.

Behind him, he saw a row of freight trucks explode. The roof of the tunnel above the explosion seemed to shimmer, to vibrate, and then the whole thing collapsed with a deafening roar. The Governor slipped the car into gear and it lurched away, just as a wall of grey-green water burst down through the rock above.

As the huge wave rushed towards him, the tunnel roof collapsing above it, the Governor slammed his foot on the accelerator and drove for his life.

#

Dreggo pulled herself up over the back of the cab and pulled a knife from her belt. Her face, her arms her legs, her entire body ached from the jump. But she had made it.

It ended now.

She watched as the youngest Tube Rider helped the teenager from the GFA into the cab. The one with the bad eye was climbing out onto the roof, while the cowardly one was hiding back inside with the two girls. No matter. They would die together, or one by one. It was their choice. She braced herself against the rocking train, while behind her the water roared.

#

'Switch, no!' Paul shouted, as he tried to haul Marta back. Marta struggled against him, wanting to get out of the window after Switch, who was closing on Dreggo as she climbed up on to the roof of the train.

'Let go of me, this is my fight–'

'Stop him!' Paul shouted at Carl and Owen, but it was too late, the boys were already climbing out after him. Was he the only one with sense? They had no chance against Dreggo; their best chance was to get into the cab and attempt to knock her off when she tried to climb in. Going out to fight her on the roof of the rocking train was suicide. She would cut them down one by one.

'Let me go!' Marta shouted. 'She killed Leo! She killed my brother!'

'So you want her to kill you too?'

'Let me *go*, Paul!'

He looked towards Jess for support, but all he saw was the other girl's ankles as she climbed out of the window.

#

Owen put one hand on the roof of the train to steady himself as he tried to follow Switch and Carl. Carl looked as uncertain as he felt, but Switch looked as at home on the moving train as he did on the ground.

'Come on!' Switch roared, and leapt forward at Dreggo, knife flashing. She easily parried, and knocked him sideways with a back-handed slap. Carl leapt at her feet but she kicked him in the head. As he slid over the edge, Owen jumped after him and caught his hand. With his other hand Owen held on to a drainage rail as Carl tried to find a foothold, his legs dangling out over the rushing rock below. A little further along, Switch was climbing back up as Dreggo turned on him.

'The water's getting closer!' Owen shouted. 'Knock her off! You have to knock her off the train!'

Switch swung himself up, knife hand flashing through the air. Dreggo stepped deftly to one side, one lightning-fast hand catching hold of his wrist. Switch cried out in pain and dropped the knife as Dreggo held him out in front of her. He tried to reach her with his other hand but she was too strong. His eyes rolled in his head as Dreggo's iron grip crushed his wrist.

'You can run and you can hide, but can you swim, Tube Rider?' she shouted at him. '*Can you swim?*'

She turned towards the side of the train, ready to fling him off into the roiling mass of water that was just a couple of hundred feet behind them now.

'Switch!' Owen shouted, but he knew it was too late. Holding on to Carl he had no chance to stop her, and he knew they would be next.

From the corner of his eye he saw movement, someone running along the top of the train. He twisted his head and saw Jess, two knives held high over her head as she sprinted towards Dreggo. The girl's face was set, her lips tight, her eyes hard.

'Jess, no!' Owen shouted. The girl ignored him, leaping at Dreggo and plunging her knives into either side of the girl's neck. She rammed them in to the handles as Dreggo let go of Switch and staggered backwards.

Switch slid sideways over the edge of the train, head lolling, the pain of his shattered wrist sending him close to unconsciousness. 'Grab him, Carl!' Owen shouted, and Carl reached out with his spare hand and caught Switch's shirt. Owen watched Carl brace himself with his feet and pull Switch close.

Owen looked back towards Jess. Jess was screaming incomprehensibly into Dreggo's face, as the leader of the Huntsmen staggered backwards, her arms tight around the girl.

Owen tried to scramble forward but it was too late. Dreggo took one more step backwards and then vanished, falling over the end of the train.

Owen caught one last word, hollered over the cacophony of sound: '*Simon!*'

For a second they looked impossibly small as they struggled together in front of the looming wall of water. Then it engulfed them, and they were gone.

#

Paul looked out of the front of the cab. In a rear view mirror he could see parts of the battle going on behind them, but his focus was on the front. Up ahead of them, the tunnel started to angle upwards as it approached the French side. How much longer they could stay ahead of the water as it brought the tunnel roof crashing down, he didn't know.

Marta was crying somewhere behind him. He pushed forward on the accelerator control, and the engine's scream filled the cab. It would be close.

'Paul, Jess is gone,' Marta cried, and he glanced back once to see Marta holding something tiny up in her hands. It looked like a computer chip.

'She never intended to come back,' Marta sobbed. 'She went out there to her death.'

Paul turned away, his heart heavy. There was nothing left he could do now except keep the train moving forward.

The tunnel began to rise more steeply.

'Come on, just a little more...'

In the mirror, Paul could see the water splashing the back of the train.

Ahead of them, the rails disappeared beneath what looked like two huge doors.

'Hang on!' Paul shouted.

He closed his eyes as the train struck the doors and burst out into the cool light of dawn. Behind them he heard a huge *whoosh* as the water erupted out of the tunnel entrance. It rose high in the air and then battered down around them like a lake falling from the sky. Water showered the train's windscreen hard enough to crack it.

'We have to jump!' Paul shouted, feeling the sudden lurch of the train as the certainty of rails beneath it disappeared. They'd run out of track. Not everything was finished on this side, either.

Paul swung one of the doors open as the train meandered towards a stand of trees. He looked back to see his brother, Carl, and Switch leap off the side of the train. Beside him, Marta was still sobbing. He grabbed her and hauled her to the door.

'Marta,' he gasped. 'In case we don't survive this, I just wanted to say...'
'What?'

He shook his head. 'I have no fucking idea. But whatever it was, it was going to be profound.'

She gave him a teary smile.

He took her hand.

They jumped.

Paul hit the ground and rolled, feeling the crunch of bones in his body. As water rained down on him he looked up and saw the train cab veer sideways into a stand of trees. It hit something and rose up into the air, for one second standing on its end. Then it crashed back down, broke apart, and exploded.

A wall of fire rose up into the air. Paul lay on his back and felt the heat even through the water that was still pouring down on him. As he closed his eyes he wondered why the water hadn't stopped yet.

A few minutes later, when he opened his eyes, he realised it was raining. Beside him, Marta was sitting up, watching the plumes of smoke rise from the wrecked train cab into the grey morning sky. He looked behind him, and saw Owen and Carl helping Switch to his feet. The little man was wincing with pain, one arm hanging limp.

Beyond them, Paul saw the remains of what had once been a building, a pair of train tracks stretching a short way out from the rubble to end in a grassy field where two freshly ploughed lines of earth now led up to the burning ruin of the locomotive.

Paul stood up. Something in his shoulder felt wrong, and he had a burning sensation in his chest. But, he was alive. He reached down with his good arm and pulled Marta up. The girl looked in better shape as she smiled up at him, her hair slicked against her face.

Wordlessly, they started walking back towards the ruined building, beyond which a pool of sea water now lapped calmly. As they reached the others, Owen, Carl and Switch stood up. Owen took Paul's other hand, making his brother wince a little, while Carl supported Switch with an arm over the little man's shoulder.

No one said anything.

They climbed up the slope, past the ruined building, past the pool of water and up to the brow of the hill. Rain battered down relentlessly, soaking them all to the skin. Behind them, the flames from the burning train still roared.

They stood in a line at the top of the hill, and looked down a gentle slope towards the sea. There, stretching back several hundred feet from the beach, they saw a gorge cut out of the rock, now filled with sea water that lapped gently against its bare rock sides. To a stranger, it might look like a canal, recently begun, cutting inland through the rising hillside, until the builders had just given up and gone home as the hill became too steep.

The tunnel to Mega Britain, closed off forever.

'I hope she's at peace now,' Marta said.

The others looked at her.

'Jess or Dreggo?' Switch asked.

Marta cocked her head. With her free hand she wiped her wet hair out of her eyes. 'Both, I guess.'

They were silent for a long while. Waves, building in the rising Atlantic storm, broke against the corners of the rock channel, sucking the water back, before surging forward to create curtains of splash rising up from the steep edges of the gorge. Out across the English Channel, dark clouds rolled and toiled, battering the water with driving sheets of rain.

'God, the sea smells good,' Switch said.

There were mumbles of agreement.

'You know, we have to go back,' Marta said. 'Sometime.' She sniffed. 'We left a lot behind.'

Carl said, 'Things will change when we go back. Things will be put right.'

Paul glanced at him. Carl's eyes, like Marta's, were elsewhere. His mother, maybe still alive, prayed for his return. One day, he promised himself, he'd see them reunited.

Owen was peering back over his shoulder. 'I don't know about you lot, but while I'm enjoying the view, the sentimentality and getting wet and everything, I'm pretty sure there's a town back there, and I'm not too keen to die of hypothermia when I could be sitting in a café watching TV and eating a baguette. Who's with me?'

No one laughed. But as he looked around, Paul saw the others were smiling too.

Epilogue

As the rain began to die down, the two children slipped out of the old air raid shelter and began to pick their way back across the beach towards home. They had one hand each on a bucket which was full of tiny conch shells. Mother had promised to help them make a mural for their bedroom if they could collect enough. Mother hadn't planned on the rain though, the temperamental Atlantic drift bringing in storms quicker than the gulls that invariably flew ahead of them.

The beach arced around to the left towards a headland where Father sometimes took them fishing in summer. Off the rocks there they'd caught baskets of cod and whiting which Mother would grill over the barbeque in the evening. Sometimes, they'd even caught a spider crab or two.

They were both obviously thinking of better weather and nicer days, because they almost tripped over the body lying in the sand not far from the water line. They were too surprised to scream, but they did drop the bucket, scattering conch shells across the wet sand.

'What is it?' the first child said in the dialect of French favoured in Northern Brittany.

'It looks like a girl,' the second replied.

'What's she doing here?'

'It looks like she's sleeping.'

They approached slowly. The girl was lying on her front, her hair spread out around her on the sand. Her clothes were ripped and torn.

The first child knelt down by the girl's face. 'Hello?'

'What's wrong with her?' the second child asked.

'What do you mean?'

The first child pointed.

The second child saw now. Something shiny seemed to be covering part of her face. 'I don't know. I think we'd better get Mother.'

'Look. She's awake.'

The two children watched as very slowly a hand reached out and scraped a line in the sand, the fingers leaving five trails which quickly pooled with water.

The two children scampered away across the beach, shouting for their mother.

Here Ends

The
Tube Riders

(The Tube Riders Trilogy #1)

by
Chris Ward

Are you ready?

The Tube Riders: Exile
(The Tube Riders Trilogy #2)

AVAILABLE NOW

Notes on the Text

First of all, to those readers familiar with the locations used in this novel, I'd like to offer an apology. Despite growing up in Cornwall, living in Bristol for six years, and spending long periods in London, I let my imagination run away with me. The landmarks and locations mentioned in the book are real but I have taken massive liberties with town layouts, street names, and virtually every other aspect that you might be familiar with. It is 2075, after all ...

To train enthusiasts, now fuming at me for the depiction of their beauties – while I tried my best to portray the trains used in this book as accurately as possible, I have molded them where necessary to make them fit my needs. But that drainage rail where the clawboards land really is there – I looked!

And to anyone from Cornwall looking for a quick way over to France, on a booze run perhaps, that second Channel Tunnel doesn't exist. That I know of ...

About the Author

A proud and noble Cornishman (and to a lesser extent British), Chris Ward ran off to live and work in Japan back in 2004. There he got married, got a decent job, and got a cat. He remains pure to his Cornish/British roots while enjoying the inspiration of living in a foreign country.

In addition to *The Tube Riders*, he is the author of the novels *The Man Who Built the World* and *Head of Words* as well as the *Beat Down!* action/comedy novella series under the name Michael S. Hunter.

Acknowledgments

The Tube Riders takes its origins from one drunken night way back in 2002 when I wondered what it would be like to hang off the side of a moving train. To whatever I had been drinking that night, I say thanks...

There are too many awesome people to mention who helped and inspired me to get this done. A big thanks goes out to my first beta readers, Isaac and Matt, and my proofreaders Lee, Fiona, Robin, Vasant and Rich. Your comments and suggestions helped make this a better book.

Thanks to Su Halfwerk at Novel Prevue for the new cover – you did a fantastic job as always, to Suzie for the wonderful formatting, and to Jenny Twist and John Daulton for your support and encouragement.

And thanks to my family, for your support in everything I choose to do with my life. Sorry for moving to Japan, but when the wind blows you have to go. Perhaps one day it'll blow me back to England.

Finally to my cat, Miffy, for getting me up so early each morning, and last but certainly not least, to my wonderful wife, Shoko, for keeping me focused and my feet on the ground. I am always yours.

C.W.

Printed in Great Britain
by Amazon.co.uk, Ltd.,
Marston Gate.